Maggie's Market

Dee Williams

__headline__

First published in 1997
by HEADLINE BOOK PUBLISHING

First published in paperback in 1997
by HEADLINE BOOK PUBLISHING

22

ISBN 978-0-7472-5536-9

Typeset by
Letterpart Limited, Reigate, Surrey

Printed in England by
Clays Ltd, St Ives plc

HEADLINE BOOK PUBLISHING
A division of Hodder Headline PLC
338 Euston Road
London NW1 3BH

This is for my dear Les who is always in my thoughts, and whose idea it was to write about a girl on a market.

I would like to thank all the staff at Portsmouth, Waterlooville and Horndean libraries for their help with my enquiries, and their interest in my work. Thank you.

Chapter 1

Maggie Ross wandered over to her window and looked down on to Kelvin Market. It was a warm May afternoon, and below her people were lazily wandering about, chatting and taking their time over their purchases, the morning's hustle and bustle long over.

She sighed contentedly. At twenty-seven she had everything she could wish for – a loving husband, two wonderful children and another on the way. So far 1935 had been another good year for them, and with the new baby, the best was yet to come.

'Will Daddy take me to the park tomorrow?' asked Jamie suddenly. He pushed his straight fair hair to one side and looked up at her. With his twinkling blue eyes and fair colouring there was no mistaking he was Maggie's son.

'Shouldn't think so. Saturday's his busiest day. What made you ask that?'

'I'm drawing a lot of boys playing football.'

Maggie smiled. Her husband, Tony, had a stall in Kelvin Market, inherited from his father. Tony told people he sold antiques, but in fact most of it was junk – small stuff, chipped china, brass animals, tools and rusty door knockers.

1

Tony was very proud of his dad and had been helping run the stall for years, long before he left school.

The licences and stalls were very special and always handed down; many had been fought over in the past. Tony's was at the top end that opened out on to Rotherhithe New Road, considered to be a very favourable position. The Dog and Duck pub was at the other end. Kelvin Market had stalls lining each side of the cobbled stone road. It wasn't huge, but it did open every weekday come rain or shine. Everyday things were sold there, and had been for as long as most people could remember. Along with Tony's other deals the market provided the Ross family with a good living.

Maggie first moved here when they got married in 1928, seven years ago. The sounds and smells from the market below had become part of her life from then on. Their rented flat was above Mr Goldman's bespoke tailor's shop, where Tony always had his suits made. Mr Goldman was a kind widower, a real gentleman who loved the children despite their stomping and shouting above him all day.

Maggie glanced at the clock. Almost time to collect Laura from school. As she moved away from the window she caught sight of her reflection in the long ornate mirror leaning against the wall, one of Tony's finds, now waiting for a new home. She smiled; she didn't need reminding that her once-trim figure was expanding, the baby bouncing around inside did that.

She looked at the top of Jamie's bent head as he concentrated on his drawing. Up here he was a quiet, sensitive and very loving four-year-old, but when he got downstairs the traders seemed to bring out the devil in him, and at times

Maggie had to reprimand him for being cheeky.

'Come on, Jamie, we've got to go and collect Laura,' she told him.

'D'you like my picture?'

'Very nice,' she said, as the paper was pushed under her nose. 'You are a clever boy.'

'Mummy, when can I go to school?'

'I've told you, after the holidays.' Jamie was two years younger than Laura and couldn't wait to be grown up like his sister. Although Maggie knew it would be lovely to have the new baby, which was due in September, to herself, she would miss having Jamie's chatter and mess around.

'Can I stay with Daddy?' Jamie's voice interrupted her daydreams.

'I'll see. He might be too busy to have you touching everything.'

Maggie loved Tony very much. He was a warm, affectionate Londoner, loud when he needed to be, but very loving to her and the children. It was ten years ago, when she was seventeen and he was nineteen that she really took an interest in him. She knew he was always after the girls and Maggie and her best friend, Eve, would hang around his stall hoping he would take one of them out. Although he did go out with Eve for a while, it was Maggie he married three years later. He was everything Maggie had ever wanted in a man, tall with unruly dark curly hair, and very handsome. His lovely brown eyes could send shivers up her spine when he gave her a sly wink.

He always made a fuss of the old dears that visited his stall. He'd put his arm round them, telling jokes and teasing them. He said it helped business. Somehow, but Maggie didn't know how, he did make a good living from the stall and they enjoyed a comfortable lifestyle. If he did manage to find a real antique, it was either passed on very quickly, or found a home in their cosy flat till the right price was offered.

She stood in front of the mirror, brushing her fair hair and gently pushing the soft waves into place. There were times when she did wonder about some of Tony's shady associates, but if she mentioned them he would only laugh her off saying, 'You have to play up to all sorts in this business.' He would then put his arms round her and, pulling her close, whisper, 'Just as long as nobody touches me and mine life's a piece of cake.'

Maggie tingled at the thought of his arms round her.

'Right, my boy, let's go and get Laura, and then we can all have an ice cream.'

Jamie was down the stairs before she'd finished the sentence.

Maggie pushed open her front door, and was immediately in the middle of the market.

'All right then, gel?' yelled Fred, who owned the fruit and veg stall. He heaved a heavy sack of potatoes on to his shoulder. As usual a thin unlit hand-rolled cigarette dangled from his lips. Maggie had never seen him without one.

'Yes thanks. Busy?'

'Not too bad. All right if young Jamie 'ere has an apple?' he asked, banging the sack down and causing the dust to rise. Despite his pale watery eyes and the worried expression he always wore, Fred, a thin wiry man in his fifties, was as strong as an ox.

She nodded. 'Course.'

'Tell Laura I've saved her a nice shiny one.'

'Thanks, Fred,' Maggie smiled, and moved on. She had known these people for years; they too were part of her life.

She loved the whole atmosphere of the market: the sound of trains rattling above the arches; the smell of roasting chestnuts in the winter – even the rotting veg on a warm summer night helped give the market its certain smell. The organ-grinder with his monkey dancing on top always raised a laugh, but when it jumped down and rattled his collecting tin woe betide anyone who teased it or didn't pay up. It was known to bite.

Jamie ran on ahead. The clip-clop of a dray horse's hooves on the cobbles made him stop. Jamie turned and smiled at Maggie. He loved horses almost as much as he loved football. The smell of beer filled her nostrils. The dray was on its way to the Dog and Duck. The singsongs they had in the pub were always great occasions, and the new baby's christening would be the next excuse for a knees-up.

Tony liked telling everyone that he wanted to get a nice house and shop somewhere in the country for Maggie and the kids, but she couldn't imagine being away from Rother-hithe. Her parents had been born not far from here, and her father had worked in the tea factory. They were dead now, killed in a train crash seven years ago when they were going on holiday. The loss still upset her, especially the fact they had never seen their grandchildren, not even her brother's daughter, Doreen, who was a few months older than Laura.

Maggie sighed as she slowly moved past the stalls, giving a nod here and a wave there. She shouldn't be thinking about the past, the future was far more exciting.

5

For some unknown reason Maggie's thoughts were still clinging to her lost family. If only her brother, Alan, was a little more friendly. He was four years older than her, and had passed his exam and gone on to high school. He had a good job in the city in an office. When he married Helen they moved to a posh part of London, Hither Green. Since their parents died he and Maggie didn't see a lot of each other, but Alan always invited them over sometime during the Christmas holiday. Tony said it was only to show off their house and garden. He always came home discontented after visiting them, announcing that one day they'd have such a house. Helen and Maggie didn't always see eye to eye either. Helen and Alan's only child, Doreen, always stayed clean and immaculate while Jamie would end up looking a wreck. Maggie could always sense Helen's disapproval.

Arriving at Winnie's stall of new and second-hand footwear, Maggie picked up one of the shoes for sale. 'These are nice. I rather like these.'

Winnie grinned. 'You'll have ter wait till your feet go down. You can't go running up and down your stairs in those heels, not in your condition.'

'I do miss me high heels,' Maggie sighed.

'Yes, well, that baby's welfare is more important than you dolling yerself up. If you fell down those stairs and did you or that baby a mischief Tony would never forgive you.'

'Yes, marm,' laughed Maggie. 'And I shan't be sorry when it's here. I'm sick to death of these shapeless things.' She pulled at her navy-blue smock.

Maggie thought the world of Winnie, a warm round

woman. She had been a tower of strength when Maggie had lost her parents and had been heavily pregnant with Laura.

'How you gonner get that apple in your mouth?' Winnie asked Jamie.

'I'm gonner nibble it,' he said grinning.

Winnie bent down and, grabbing his face between her rough red, weatherbeaten hands, planted a very loud kiss on each of his cheeks. 'When yer looks up at me with those big blue eyes and flutters those lovely long lashes, I just gotter kiss yer.'

'Yuck. You better not do that when I go to school,' Jamie said indignantly, wiping his face and then running the back of his hand down the side of his trousers.

'Why's that?' asked Winnie, giving Maggie a wink.

'Don't want the other kids ter think I'm a sissy and keep getting kissed.'

'Come on,' said Maggie, laughing. 'See you on the way back,' she said over her shoulder to Winnie.

'And don't you kiss me again,' shouted Jamie, looking behind and grabbing hold of his mother's hand.

Winnie blew him a kiss.

Maggie ruffled Jamie's blond hair.

'Oh Mum, don't.'

'We only do these things 'cos we loves yer,' she said.

Jamie smoothed down his hair and ran on ahead. Maggie watched him. She was so proud of her family.

Suddenly she saw Jamie stop and look round, puzzled.

'What is it, Jamie?' she asked, getting nearer.

'Daddy ain't here.'

Maggie was close to the stall. ''Allo, Bill,' she said to the young lad that helped Tony. Bill had been with him for the past two years, ever since he left school at fourteen. 'Tony had to go off somewhere?'

'Dunno. 'E ain't been 'ere all day.' Bill was a tall, gangly boy who blushed easily while talking to women. When Tony wasn't teasing him he spoke very highly of the lad.

'But he got the stall out, didn't he?' asked Maggie.

'Yer, but he went off just after that, and I ain't seen him since. What shall I do about the takings if 'e ain't back be then?'

'Don't worry, he'll be back long before then.' Maggie frowned. Although Tony was often off buying and selling, it wasn't like him to leave Bill on his own all day, or not to tell her if he was going to be late home. 'He'll be here in time to pack away. Look, I must go and collect Laura.'

'Yer, yer of course.'

Maggie and Jamie were turning the corner just as the children came racing out of the school playground.

It was the same school Tony had gone to when he was little, and it hadn't changed. The old red-brick building with its small windows was cheerless, depressed and in need of a lick of paint. Everything round this area, including most of the children, had the same sad run-down look about them. Maggie made sure Laura was always well dressed and well fed but some of her little friends looked undernourished and sickly, and they were always glad of any of Laura's cast-off clothes.

Jamie ran up to his big sister, who was clutching a piece of paper. 'What you got there?'

'Look what I done at school. Don't you touch it,' she yelled at Jamie.

'I only want to look.'

'Well you ain't, 'cos you might tear it.'

'No I won't.'

'Stop it, the two of you. Let me see it,' said Maggie, taking the colourful sheet of paper from her daughter's chalk-covered hands. 'It's lovely.'

'What is it?' asked Jamie.

'It's a tree in a field. Can't you see that?' Laura rubbed her nose.

Maggie twisted the paper. 'Yes, yes I can see, it's very good.'

Laura smiled and a slight dimple appeared on her chalk-smudged face. She tucked a strand of hair behind her ear. Every morning Maggie painstakingly plaited Laura's long dark unruly hair, hoping to keep it under control, but the ribbon would always slip off and she'd end up tucking it behind her ears. Her large brown eyes lit up. She was like her father, and had inherited his good looks. Tony's mother had always been very proud of her Italian ancestors, as was her only child. 'It's where me good looks comes from,' was something he would often boast about. Tony's mother would talk about Italy as if she'd been there, but the truth was she'd never set foot out of London till the council started the slum clearance and demolished the row of terraced houses where she lived. Bella Ross was moved out to Downham. She was an opinionated woman who didn't take to change easily and they did wonder if she would go, but when she saw her lovely new house, with a bathroom and indoor lav, she couldn't wait. Although Bella had always had the last word with everyone, including her late husband, Jim, Maggie was very fond of her.

'You can put it on the wall if yer like, Mummy,' said Laura proudly.

'That'll be nice.'

'Oh, I nearly forgot,' Laura suddenly burst out. 'I'm gonner be a maypole dancer again on Empire Day.'

'That's lovely.' Maggie smiled. It was only last week on 6 May, the day they had all celebrated King George and Queen Mary's Silver Jubilee, that Laura had been chosen to dance round the maypole. That morning Maggie and Tony had sat on the tiny seats in the playground and laughed at the state some of the little ones had got themselves into as they twisted and weaved in and out of each other while holding on to the long coloured ribbons.

The week before Jubilee Day had seen the dull streets transformed, with red, white and blue bunting draped everywhere, and flags hung from every lamppost and window. The shopkeepers and stallholders had done their bit to join in the festivities and the many pictures of the royal couple showed how much they were loved. Everybody had been in a happy mood, laughing and singing patriotic songs, and wearing silly paper hats.

That afternoon a party had been held in the school playground for the local kids, some of whom had stood wide-eyed at tables that groaned with sandwiches, jellies and ice cream, before they set about devouring the lot. The food had been donated by the local tradespeople, all trying to out-do one another. The weather had been kind and all in all it had been a wonderful day.

That evening had been the grown-ups' turn to celebrate. The Dog and Duck was almost leaping in the air with all the racket that came from within. All kinds of musical instruments arrived to form an impromptu band and the customers spilled out into the street dancing and singing.

'What's Empire Day, Mummy?' asked Jamie, tugging at Maggie's hand and interrupting her thoughts.

'It's the twenty-fourth of May, the day when we remember our Empire,' said Laura confidently.

'What's our Empire?' came the next question.

'When you go to school you'll see all the pink bits in the atlas of the world, and all those pink bits belong to England.' Laura was obviously pleased to repeat all that her teacher had told her.

Maggie smiled. Her daughter must be taking an interest, and enjoying her geography lessons.

When they returned to Tony's stall he still wasn't there.

'If 'e ain't here in time I'll put the stall away for yer, Maggs,' said Bill. 'And I'll bring the takings up to you.'

'Thanks, Bill. There ain't a race meeting on somewhere, is there?'

''Spect so, but he would have said.'

'I'm sure he'll be back before long.'

'I hope so.'

Although Tony liked Bill and had a lot of faith in him he didn't like to leave him on his own for too long, and for Tony not to tell Maggie he was going out was unusual.

When Jamie saw Winnie was busy with a customer he quickly ran past her stall. Showing her drawing to Fred, Laura collected her promised apple. As they trooped past Mr Goldman's window Maggie gave him a wave. She opened her front door and the children clattered along the linoed passage and up the stairs. There was a back door along the passage that led out to the small yard and lavatory.

After the children had finished their tea, it was time for the market to close. Maggie didn't have to look out of the window, she was familiar with the scene. Men would be tying covers over the wares on their barrows and pushing them into the lockups under the railway arches where they stored them overnight. Mrs Groom would be taking down all her second-hand goods that she had draped round her stall, and old Mother Saunders, who sold haberdashery, would be packing away all her bits and bobs and stacking them neatly into boxes to be brought out again tomorrow. Mrs Russell would be filling her buckets with water, hoping the weather wouldn't turn too warm and wilt her flowers.

There were many women running stalls on this market, most of them inherited from their fathers or husbands who had been killed in the war.

Tony would be home soon.

Maggie sat up when she heard the front door slam, but was a little surprised when Bill came in alone with the day's takings.

'Where's Tony?'

'He ain't back yet. I've put the barra away.'

'Thanks, Bill.'

'Tell Tony a bloke was looking for him.'

'Did he say who he was?'

'Na. Shifty-looking sod. Ain't seen him round 'ere before.' He grinned. 'By the way, tell him I sold that old lamp he's been trying ter get rid of fer weeks.'

Maggie smiled. 'Nice work, Bill. Fancy a cuppa?'

'No, ta all the same but I'm off out tonight.' He twisted his cloth cap round and round in his hands.

'Meeting a girl?'

12

'Na.' Bill blushed.

Maggie was teasing. She knew Bill was embarrassed about his spots, but he was only sixteen and would grow out of them, and with Tony as a teacher he too would soon have the gift of the gab.

'I best be off. See you tomorrow. Bye, kids,' he yelled out before clattering down the stairs and slamming the front door behind him.

Funny about Tony going off like that, thought Maggie, but I expect he'll be back soon for his tea.

Chapter 2

Later, when Maggie went into the bedroom to tuck the blankets round the children, Laura asked, 'Why ain't Daddy here?'

'I expect he's had to go out on business.'

'Will he be back soon?' asked Jamie from his bed on the other side of the room.

'I should think so, but you may be asleep.'

'Tell him to come and kiss me good night.' Laura snuggled down under the bedclothes, clutching her teddy bear.

'I will.' Maggie kissed her daughter's forehead.

'And don't forget me,' said Jamie, popping his tousled fair head over the covers.

'As if we could.' She bent down and kissed him. 'Now go to sleep, the pair of you. Sleep tight.' She closed the bedroom door.

In the sitting room Maggie picked up her knitting. She was beginning to worry. This wasn't like Tony. He always told her if he was going out. Besides, he would dress up if he was meeting someone important or going to a special auction. She smiled to herself – at least if he had to go out

15

with some of his cronies he would always bring her back flowers. When he went to play cards with Wally from the auction rooms, or to the dog track, he always brought her back a box of chocolates. He was so kind and thoughtful.

Maggie was restless and couldn't concentrate on the intricate pattern she was using for the new baby's matinée coat. She turned the wireless on and an orchestra's soft music drifted over her. She leant back in the armchair and closed her eyes.

As she drifted off she could see her mother and father smiling at her. She was dancing with Tony, the train of her long white frock draped over her arm. She looked into Tony's eyes, he bent his head and gently kissed her mouth. There were a lot of people shouting and laughing, but Maggie could only see Tony, her Tony – he was so handsome. She was so lucky that he loved her.

'Maggs, Maggs. Sorry, love, did I wake you?' A whispered voice brought her back from her dream.

Maggie quickly sat up. It was gloomy, the light hadn't been switched on, she was disorientated. 'Tony, is that you?'

'No, it's me.'

'Oh Eve,' said Maggie unable to keep the disappointment from her voice. Eve, like everybody else did, had used the front door key that hung behind the letter box to let herself into their flat.

'Well, don't sound so upset about it. You all right?'

'Yes. I was just dozing.'

'Kids in bed?' asked Eve, taking off her stylish beige straw hat.

Maggie nodded. 'Put the light on. What time is it?' She looked up at the wooden clock on the mantelpiece.

'It's nine o'clock.' Eve stood close to the mirror and ran her little finger over her bright red lips. She plumped up the back of her blonde hair.

'You on your own?' asked Maggie.

'Yer. Dan went in the Dog, so I thought I'd pop along to see if you was all right. Tony in the pub?'

'I don't know.'

'What d'you mean?'

Maggie sat forward. 'Eve, I'm getting a bit worried. Tony hasn't been seen all day.'

'What? Didn't he get the stall out?'

'Yes, but we haven't seen him since. Bill put the stall away. Eve, you don't think something could have happened to him, do you?'

'Don't talk daft, course not. He's probably met a mate and they finished up in a pub, and Tony's had a skinful and is sleeping it off somewhere. It ain't the first time, is it?'

'No, but he nearly always tells me if . . .' Maggie laughed. 'I'm beginning to sound like some nagging old wife.' Her laughter was false. Somehow, deep down, she knew something was wrong.

'I'll put the kettle on.' Eve stood in the doorway. 'You mark my words, he'll be back here with a big bunch of flowers and his tail between his legs.'

Maggie half smiled. 'I only hope you're right.'

Eve took the teapot from the kitchen cupboard. She knew this flat almost as well as her own, round the corner in Upper Road. As she clattered about with the cups and saucers her thoughts went to Tony. He was such a handsome devil. What was he up to? What if he was playing around? Maggie would go mad.

Eve smiled, remembering the time when they were silly young things and Maggie used to hang around his stall hoping he would take her out. It surprised them both when it was Eve he made the date with. Maggie got very upset over that and said she thought she'd lost him for ever. Eve managed to talk Tony into taking Maggie out. Eve's grin got wider; he hadn't got from Maggie what he'd got from her – well, not till he married her. He'd been a great lover. Not that she'd ever told Maggie. After all, it was Maggie he loved.

Eve stood watching the blue gas flame dance round the kettle. What had made her suddenly think about that? Was Tony starting to play around? He had never propositioned Eve since he'd married, but was that because she was too near to home? The whistle from the kettle brought her back to the present. She made the tea and walked into the sitting room with the tea tray. 'You feeling all right?' she asked Maggie.

'Bit tired. But no, I feel fine.'

'How many more you gonner have?' asked Eve, looking pointedly at Maggie's stomach.

'This will be the last. Only got room for one more bed in the kids' room.'

'What about in a few years' time? They won't wanner sleep together then, so will you move?'

'Dunno.'

'Tony still on about having that antique shop and the cosy cottage with roses round the door?'

Maggie grinned and nodded.

18

'Reckon he's been to too many films. I couldn't see either of you stuck somewhere down in the country.'

'Neither can I.'

When their conversation lapsed the usual sounds came drifting through the open window. Trains puffing and chugging above the arches, dogs barking and cats fighting, even the ticking of the clock seemed loud and invasive.

Although she knew the answer Maggie still asked, 'Will Dan come here for you?'

'I hope so. I ain't walking home on me own.'

'It ain't that far.'

'I know, but I still ain't walking home on me own.'

Later, when Dan came in, Maggie was again disappointed Tony wasn't with him.

Dan threw his trilby on to the chair and, bending slightly to peer in the mirror, smoothed down his dark hair. Dan was tall, broad and very good-looking, but then he had to be, Eve wouldn't settle for anything less. He had a steady job as a lorry driver, and with Eve working in the Council office, money wasn't a worry to them.

'Tony wasn't in the pub then?' asked Maggie.

'No. Didn't see him. Why?'

Maggie went through her story again.

'You sure he ain't been to the dog track?' Dan asked.

'He would have told me.'

'Yer, s'pose he would have. You ain't got a sandwich, have you? I'm starving.'

'What, after that bloody great dinner you had tonight?'

Dan grinned. 'Got to keep me strength up, gel, I'm a growing lad.' He put his arm round Eve and hugged her.

19

''Sides, you know I always perform better on a full stomach.'

'Not if you've had a skinful of beer you don't.'

'Ah yer, unfortunately that's when the mind's willing but the flesh is weak.'

Maggie laughed. She loved Eve and Dan like a sister and brother. Eve had met Dan at a dance and they'd got married very quickly, so quickly everyone had thought she was up the spout, but the truth was Eve didn't want children. Dan loved Eve, despite all the talk about her before they were married.

Dan sat down. 'Did he take his stall out this morning?'

'Yes, but Bill's been running it all day.'

Dan leant back. 'D'you know, I reckon he's met an old mate and they've gone out on a binge and he's sleeping it off somewhere.'

'That's exactly what I said,' said Eve.

'But it's not like Tony not to tell me.'

'Well, we all like to be let off the lead once in a while, gel.'

Maggie half smiled. Was she getting to be a nag? 'I suppose so,' she replied.

With no other suggestions, they all fell into a puzzled silence.

'Right, gel, on your feet,' Dan said briskly to his wife.

When Eve stood up Dan smacked her bottom. 'You ready then? Look, Maggs, sorry, but we've got to be off. I've got a long day tomorrow, got to take the lorry down to Dover to pick up a load.'

'What, on a Saturday?' asked Maggie.

Eve shrugged her shoulders. 'That's what 'e tells me. Reckon he's got a bit on the side.'

He looked at Eve. 'I told you, that's what the job's about. Go and see Tom if you don't believe me.' He winked at Maggie. 'Mind you, it's surprising what you can get up to in the cab, ain't it, gel?'

Eve looked away. 'I ain't saying.'

Dan laughed. 'Well, I wasn't the first to have your drawers off, now was I?'

'Yer. But in the end you was the lucky one that got me to the altar.' Eve put her hat on, and picked up her handbag. 'I'll call in tomorrow, Maggs.'

Dan bent down and kissed Maggie's cheek. 'And you give that old man of yours a right old ear-bashing when he gets home, making you worry like this. Bye, love.'

Eve checked her hat in the mirror, then kissed Maggie. 'I'll pop in tomorrow morning when I'm shopping, just to make sure you're all right.'

'You don't have to.'

Eve smiled. 'I'm so nosy. I've just got to find out where Tony's been and what he's been up to all day. After all, it might be somewhere exciting. Bye.'

Maggie stood at the window. The empty market looked eerie in the yellow glow from the gaslamps. She gave her friends' moving shadows a wave.

Although it was late she knew she wouldn't be able to sleep, so once more she picked up her knitting. The baby felt like it was doing a somersault. As Maggie gently touched her stomach, she smiled and let her thoughts drift to when Laura was born.

Tony had left early that morning, saying he had to meet someone, but would be home as soon as he could. Her pains had started almost as soon as he had closed the front door.

21

At first she didn't know what to do. If only her mother had still been alive. The doctor had told her labour could last for hours, plenty of time before Tony would be home. But what if the baby came before he got here? She'd been up in the flat alone. She'd had to get help.

Maggie had staggered down the stairs, and on opening the front door held on to it as a wave of pain made her legs buckle.

'You all right, gel?' Fred had yelled, coming over to her.

She'd shaken her head.

'Bloody hell. I'll get Tony.'

'He ain't here.'

'Where is he? Ain't he on his stall?'

'No. He left early, he had to go out.'

'What, 'e left yer like this?'

'I hadn't started then.'

Fred had begun flitting round her. 'Did he tell old Charlie where he was going?'

'I don't know.'

'Don't move,' he'd said in panic. 'I'll get Win.'

When Winnie had helped her back up the stairs she'd sat with her, holding her hand as the pains worsened.

'I gotter get you to the hospital,' Winnie had said, a worried look on her face.

'No, not yet. Not till Tony comes back.'

'Tony's old mate, Charlie, said he didn't know where he's gone.' Winnie had put a large warm comforting arm round Maggie. 'Come on now, love, think of the little 'en what's gonner pop out soon.' She'd looked concerned. 'I think the pains are coming a bit quick, don't you?'

'I'd rather wait for Tony to get home.'

Winnie had moved to the window and anxiously glanced out. 'Look, Mr Goldman will tell him you've gone.'

Maggie had gripped the arms of the chair as another pain took her breath away. 'P'raps you're right.'

'Good, I'll pop down and get Fred to get his van out, it'll be quicker in that.'

Winnie, red-faced and breathless, had been back almost at once. 'Right, got your bag packed?'

Maggie had nodded.

She had held on to Winnie's arm when they slowly made their way down the stairs. 'I must tell Mr Goldman,' she'd gasped.

'Don't worry, that's all taken care of.'

Everybody had shouted and wished her well as she'd staggered down the market. She'd even managed a smile as she climbed up into Fred's van. 'I suppose it's a bit different going to the hospital in a fruit and veg van.'

'Good job I ain't gotter call into Covent Garden first,' Fred had laughed anxiously. 'You might have ended up sitting on a sack of taters.'

'Or stinking of onions,' Winnie had said. 'Christ, that might make the little 'en go back in again.'

Laura had been born at six that evening. She had a mass of dark curly hair like her father.

When Tony had walked into the ward he'd been almost hidden behind the biggest bunch of flowers Maggie had ever seen. He'd thrown it on the bed and gently taken her in his arms. He'd kissed her mouth long and hard.

'Tony, don't,' Maggie had said, blushing and pushing him away. 'Everybody's looking.'

23

'I don't care. I want everybody to know what a clever girl my Maggie is. Is this ours?'

Maggie had nodded and smiled. She'd watched him lean over the cot at her side, and ease the blankets back.

'She's dark like me,' he'd beamed.

He had sat on the bed and held Maggie's hand. 'I love you so much.' He'd kissed her fingers. 'What we gonner call her?'

'I thought about Laura Margaret after me and me mum.'

'I like that. Welcome to the world, Laura Margaret Ross.'

Now tears began to run down Maggie's face at that happy memory. Tony had been with her when almost two years later, in September, her son had been born. James Anthony, a delicate-looking boy, took his father's and grandfather's names.

Maggie was told after that Tony had celebrated the first day of Jamie's life wandering round the stallholders with a bottle in his hand and they had all helped him wet the baby's head many times over. He was so proud to have a son and heir. Jamie worshipped his dad, who would take him to the park to teach him to play football. Some Sunday mornings he would take the children to Petticoat Lane while she prepared the dinner. Maggie was always terrified they would come home with a puppy or a cat, or even some baby chicks. Tony said he would like a stall there, but then he was always looking for new ways to make money, giving everyone the impression he was restless.

Maggie looked up at the clock. It was nearly midnight.

She suddenly felt alone and vulnerable, and very tired. Where was Tony? He should be home soon.

The ringing of the alarm clock woke her from a fitful sleep. It was early morning. The alarm continued its loud intrusive noise. Why didn't Tony turn it off? She put out her hand. His side of the bed was empty and smooth. It hadn't been slept in. Maggie sat up, cross. He had never stayed out all night before – well, not without telling her.

Maggie got out of bed and crept past the children's bedroom. It was Saturday so there was no need to wake them. She made herself a pot of tea and wondered about the stall. Today was the busiest day of the week. She was beginning to get very angry. If Tony had been out on the beer last night he should at least have thought about getting home.

She looked out of the window. Down below the market was beginning to come alive. She dressed herself. 'I'll be glad when you're born,' she said to the reflection of her bulge in the mirror.

She checked on the children, who were still fast asleep, then made her way downstairs and outside into the warm May sunshine. She knew if they woke up they would know where to find her.

''Allo Maggs,' said Fred. 'You're out and about early this morning. Keeping yer eye on yer old man?'

She gave Fred a smile. 'Something like that.' She didn't want to say too much at the moment.

''Allo, gel. Everyfink all right then?' asked Mrs Russell, standing back to admire the carefully arranged vases of colourful flowers she'd set out. The smell of the roses and carnations wafted on the early morning air. 'Hope it ain't gonner be too warm terday. This weather's a sod fer me blooms. Makes 'em all droopy in no time.'

'Could make yer bloomers all droopy an' all if yer ain't careful,' another stallholder called out.

'Don't want any of your old lip, Cooper.' She turned to Maggie. ''E can be a right saucy sod at times. Mind you, 'im and your old man always seem to hit it orf. Couple of saucy sods together, they are.'

Maggie liked Mrs Russell. She'd been on the market for as long as anybody could remember. Her trademark was the long black coat that she wore in all weathers. Tom Cooper reckoned she didn't wear anything under it in the summer. But come winter she sat with a piece of blanket wrapped tightly round her bent shoulders and secured with a large safety pin. Her hair was a nonde-script colour and always hidden under a man's flat tweed cap.

Winnie was busy putting out the shoes. ''Allo, Maggs. What you doing out this time o' morning, and where's that old man of yours? Ain't seen him round here yet. He all right?'

'Yes.'

'You look a bit knackered. You OK?'

'Not too bad. I'll talk to you later.'

At the end of the market Maggie could see Tony's stall had been set up. 'Hallo, Bill,' she said to his back.

He turned quickly. 'Where's Tony? He got a bloody hangover?'

'Bill, I don't know where he is.'

'What? Didn't 'e come home last night?'

26

Maggie shook her head. 'Do you think you can manage on your own?'

'Looks like I'll have to. Where the bloody hell is he? 'E should be here.'

'I know.'

'Well, he'd better be back soon. I can't even have a Jimmy without asking someone to watch the stuff.'

'When I've given the kids their breakfast I'll be along and give you a hand.'

Bill looked guilty. 'You don't 'ave to, Maggs. Sorry if I got a bit, well, carried away. It's just it ain't my stall and I'm not always sure what to charge the punters.'

'Tony's got a lot of faith in you, Bill. 'Sides, he often leaves you. Just do your best for now.'

Bill blushed. 'Yer, of course.'

Maggie walked back to Win's stall and sat on the chair she kept round the back.

'So. Where's that bloke of yours this morning? Ain't he well?'

Maggie looked round.

'Come on, tell me. What's the trouble, gel, you two had a row?' Winnie tucked her short grey hair, held close to her head with hairgrips, back behind her ears. A fringe cut straight across her forehead made a frame for her weather-beaten face. She had been working on this market all her life, starting as a child helping her drunken father, who knocked her and her mother about. Her mother took over when he died; now it was Winnie who looked after her invalid mother. She had never married as her fiancé, another market trader, was killed in the war. She hadn't had much education, but could add up faster than anyone Maggie

27

knew, and she had a heart of gold.

'No. Win, I'm worried. Tony ain't been seen since yesterday morning.'

'You sure?'

'Yes. Why?'

'I thought I saw him yesterday, about lunchtime I s'pose. Yer, it was about then. I was just going into the Dog for a quick half. He was talking to a couple of blokes, shifty-looking sods, they was. One was an old man and the younger one looked a right bruiser.'

Maggie stood up. 'Where did they go?'

'Dunno. They went up Rovverhive New Road way.'

'Was Tony with them?'

'Yer, I think so. Didn't really take much notice.'

'Bill said he wasn't at the stall all day.'

'Well, he wouldn't be, would he? Not if he was at the pub. I thought it funny, him walking away from the stall, but I guessed he'd just been in for a quick one as well as it's a bit warm.'

'I don't know what to think.'

'He could have gorn on to look for Ding Dong. Tony likes a bet now and again, don't he?'

'Yes.'

'Don't worry about 'im, he's old enough and ugly enough to look after himself. Yes, missis, half a crown a pair.' Winnie moved to the front of her stall. 'No you can't try 'em on. Look at the colour of yer feet – dirty cow.'

Maggie left her arguing with her customer and went upstairs. The sound of her two running about told her they were up and would be wanting their breakfast. Dad or no dad, food was the most important thing in their lives at the moment. Then she would go along to the Dog and Duck and ask Gus, the landlord, if he knew where the bookie's runner Dougie Bell – known as Ding Dong – might be, and if Tony went to look for him yesterday. And, she thought grimly, she'd ask about the two blokes Winnie'd seen him with as well.

Chapter 3

''Allo, Maggie. Don't often see you in here.' Rene, the Dog and Duck's barmaid, gave her a beaming smile. 'How yer keeping then?'

'I'm all right, thanks.'

'If yer looking for yer old man he ain't been in yet.'

Maggie smiled. 'No, I'm not looking for him. You don't happen to know where I can find Ding Dong, do you?'

Rene laughed. 'Ain't seen him either this morning. Why, you gonner have a bet?'

'No, well . . . Is Gus in?'

'Now *there*'s someone I can help yer with. He's in the cellar. Mind you, he is a bit busy. Anythink I can do for yer?'

Maggie felt ill at ease. She didn't want to tell Rene as before long it would be all around the market that she was chasing after Tony. 'No thanks, just want a quick word, that's all.'

'I'll give him a shout.'

'No don't worry, not if he's busy.'

Rene's smile parted her bright red lips. 'He don't mind. Gives him a good excuse to come up for a bit of fresh air and a drink.'

Maggie watched as Rene walked through the door behind the bar, her hips swaying very provocatively in a tight black skirt. Rene did really look the part with her white low-cut frilly blouse and blonde hair. She was very popular with the traders and punters alike.

''Allo, Maggs,' said Gus, coming through the door wiping his hands on a grey piece of rag, which he ran over his florid face and bald head. 'It's warm work down there shifting and lugging all the crates and barrels about. Anyway, you didn't come here to listen to me going on, so what can I do fer yer?'

Maggie looked anxiously at Rene, who appeared to be busy at the other end of the bar polishing her bright red nails.

'I'd like to ask you something.'

'Well, ask away, gel.'

'Could we sit over there?' Maggie pointed to the corner of the bar.

'Don't see why not. Fancy a drink?'

'No thanks.'

'Rene, give us a pint of best, there's a love. Bring it over, we'll be at the far table.'

'Sure, Gus.' She gave Maggie a puzzled look.

Maggie waited till Rene put the beer on the table and was out of earshot. 'Gus, I'm worried about Tony.'

'Why? What's he bin up to?'

'I don't know. You see he ain't been seen since yesterday morning.'

After taking a great gulp of beer Gus wiped the froth from his grey moustache with the back of his hand. 'What, 'e ain't bin home?'

Maggie shook her head.

'That ain't like him not to tell you, is it?'

'No. Winnie said she saw him come out of here yesterday lunchtime. He was with a couple of blokes.'

'Yer, that's right. They sat here talking together. Very quiet, they was. Shifty-looking buggers.'

'That's what Winnie said. He didn't say where he was going, I suppose?'

'Na, in fact he didn't seem to be saying much at all.' Gus wiped his face again with his piece of rag. 'D'yer know, now I come to think of it Tony did look a bit worried.'

'Worried?' repeated Maggie in alarm.

Gus finished his beer. 'Shouldn't think it's anyfink for you to fret about. You know Tony, could always put on the right face for the right people, and if he thinks there's a good deal going he don't like to be left out.'

Maggie nodded. 'That's true. Win thought he might have been looking for Ding Dong.'

Gus shook his head. 'Na, don't think so. 'Sides, if he wanted to put a bet on he'd leave it here with me. Look, excuse me, Maggs, but I must get on.'

'Course, Gus. Sorry to waste your time.'

'No trouble, gel, and don't forget me and the missis is always here if you want us.'

Maggie thanked him. Gus and Beatie were a nice couple and the Dog and Duck was a good meeting place, old and tatty and in need of a lick of paint though it now was. Over the years everybody made full use of it for weddings, funerals and any excuse for a party. Once the doors were shut Gus always told the police it was a private do, and the drinking went on for many hours. Mindful of her own need to be getting on, Maggie left the peace and quiet of the pub and stepped out into the bright sunshine, and the noise.

The sounds of kids shouting and screaming and the loud cockney voices of the market traders trying to sell their wares were trying to compete with the small group of Blackshirts on the corner who were telling the world how good Germany was.

Maggie needed someone to talk to, but everybody seemed to be busy. Although it was Saturday and Mr Goldman's shop had the closed sign in the window, Maggie knew he was in his back room. She pushed open the door, causing the tiny silver bell above to ring melodiously. The smell of new cloth tickled her nose. Tony always got his suits here, and they were always of the best quality.

Mr Goldman, in his black striped trousers and black jacket, shuffled from the rear of the shop where he had lived since his wife died. His shoulders were hunched through years of sitting sewing. He always wore his tape measure round his neck like a garland, even today on his Sabbath when he wasn't working. Maggie often wondered if he went to bed with it draped around him. His white hair was permanently stuck up, looking as if he'd had a fright.

'Maggie, Maggie, my dear. Come in and take a seat.' His lined face lit up and he pushed a chair towards her. 'You are looking very well. I trust the little 'ens are also well?'

'Yes thank you. Mr Goldman . . . this might sound silly, but . . . could I talk to you?'

'Of course, my dear.'

Maggie waited till he got another chair and set it down beside her.

'Right, my dear, now tell me what's worrying you?'

'It's Tony. He hasn't been home since he left yesterday morning.'

Mr Goldman took her hand and gently patted it. 'Now you mustn't worry about that young man. I've known him all his life. I dare say he's gone off to look for that cottage he's always on about. You know how he likes to give you nice surprises?'

Maggie nodded. 'I know. But surely he would have said somethink.'

Mr Goldman smiled.

'Has he told you somethink?'

Mr Goldman touched his lips. 'Don't worry, he'll be home soon. Mind you, I'll have to tell him not to keep too many secrets from you.'

Maggie felt anger rising up in her again. If Tony had gone to look at a cottage why the hell hadn't he told her? What was the reason for all this secrecy? 'Thank you, Mr Goldman. What else did he say?'

'Nothing really, just that he was in a hurry. It was when I was on my way home from fitting a client. I'm surprised he didn't get home last night, though. He must have missed the last train.'

'Train? Did he say where he was going?'

'No, not really. We only walked together for a short while and he said he had to catch a train. I just assumed it was about the cottage he is always talking of.'

'Thank you.' Maggie stood up.

'Maggie, I will be sorry to lose you as tenants.'

'Don't worry, Mr Goldman. I can't see me living in the country.'

'But what if he's put a deposit down?'

'He'll just have to get it back.'

Maggie's steps were a lot lighter as she left, but she was also very annoyed. Why hadn't Tony told her about his crazy idea? And what about the stall? He should have told Bill. Just you wait till you walk yourself in, she thought. You'll get a real mouthful, making me worry like this.

For the rest of the morning Maggie was backwards and forwards helping Bill and seeing to the children. She was impressed at how efficient Bill was, but as yet he lacked the skill and easy banter Tony had with his customers.

Eve came along just as Maggie was leaving the stall to get the children's dinner. 'What you doing down here?' Eve asked Maggie as she picked up a brass door knocker from among the knick-knacks, a large black china elephant, rusty spanners and chipped china.

'Tony ain't back yet.'

'What? Where's he gone now?'

'I don't know.' Maggie looked at Bill, who was busy with a customer. 'I'll be back in a while,' she called to him. 'Just going to get a cuppa.' Maggie took hold of Eve's arm. 'Come upstairs, I've got somethink to tell you.'

'Is it exciting or dirty?' asked Eve.

'It's about Tony.'

'That's what I mean,' said Eve grinning.

The children were happy to play round the market stalls and everybody kept an eye on them just in case they got into mischief. Upstairs in the kitchen Maggie put the kettle on the gas stove, then moved into the living room.

'So, where's this errant husband of yours then?' asked Eve, settling herself on the sofa.

'I don't know.'

'But I thought you said—'

'I popped in to see Mr Goldman this morning and he said yesterday Tony told him he had to catch a train. Mr Goldman reckons it was to see about this bloody country cottage he's always on about.'

'What, he went without you?'

'Exactly.'

'But what if you don't like it?'

'I don't like it.'

'But you ain't seen it.'

'I know, and that's why I don't like it.' Maggie sat next to Eve.

'Surely he would have told you?'

'Mr Goldman reckons he wants to give me a surprise.'

'Well, it'll certainly be a surprise,' laughed Eve.

'In more ways than one.' Maggie stood up when the kettle began whistling. She went into the kitchen and Eve followed her.

'Maggs, how far away d'you think he's gone?'

'Dunno.'

'Surely he should be back be now? He couldn't have thought he'd be staying overnight else he would have taken his shaving things.'

Maggie leant against the sink. Worry filled her face. 'I hadn't thought about that. We all know how fussy he is about looking smart.' She glanced at the shelf. They didn't have a bathroom in their flat, so all washing had to be done in the kitchen sink, and once a week the tin bath was brought up from the back yard for their bath. 'His shaving stuff's still here, and without fail he shaves every day.' Maggie's voice had a slight catch in it.

'Go and sit down, I'll make the tea,' said Eve.

'I've got to get the kids' dinner.'

'Don't worry about cooking, I'll send 'em up to the pie and eel shop, they'll like that. Would you fancy a pie and a bit of mash?'

Maggie shook her head.

'Go and sit down. And I tell you somethink,' yelled Eve from the kitchen, 'when he does turn up he's gonner get a right old nagging from me. I don't like to see you upset like this.'

They finished their tea and Eve went looking for Laura and Jamie to take them out whilst Maggie went along to the stall so that Bill could have a bit of lunch in the Dog and Duck.

All afternoon Eve sat with Maggie, hoping and waiting.

'What time will Dan be home?' asked Maggie.

'Dunno.'

'Will he know where to find you?'

Eve smiled. 'I should think so, don't you?'

The quiet moments that followed were unnerving and it seemed unnatural when their conversation went dead, so unlike their normal time together – they always found something to laugh and chat about. In the silence Maggie went through so many emotions, from anger to gnawing worry. Finally: 'I must get the kids in for tea. You don't have to stay with me if you want to go and get Dan's ready.'

Eve stood up. 'I will pop home, just to let him know what's happening. I can see him punching Tony on the nose after all this.' Eve put on her hat. 'See you later.'

Maggie sat in the chair. A tear slipped down her cheek. 'Why are you doing this to me, Tony?' she said out loud.

The sound of the children clattering up the stairs made her wipe her eyes as she rose to open the door.

'Ain't Daddy home yet?' asked Laura, rushing in past her.

'Mrs Russell said you ought ter give him a right pasting when he gets back.' Jamie eased himself on the chair at the table.

So everyone on the market was discussing it.

'Auntie Eve bought us some pie and mash,' said Laura. 'And he,' she pointed to Jamie, 'made me stand and watch all those eels the man keeps outside. They was all wriggling about in the tins.'

Jamie laughed. 'It was good when the man chopped their heads off. D'yer know, they still wriggled even when they didn't have any heads. Would we wriggle if we had our heads chopped off?'

'Come here and let me see,' laughed Maggie, cheered by their irrepressible chatter.

'No!' shouted Jamie, jumping off his chair and hiding under the table.

'Well, I think it's horrid, doing that to those poor things,' said Laura. 'They can't run away and hide.'

'I'm sure it was so quick they didn't feel it.'

'I hope so. What's for tea, Mummy?'

Maggie smiled. Laura soon forgot things when food was around. 'Just a bit of cheese on toast.'

'When's Daddy coming home?' asked Jamie.

'I don't know,' said Maggie.

'He will come home, won't he?' asked Laura, anxiously.

'Course. Now go and wash your hands, then I'll get your tea, and as a special treat I'll pop along to Tucker's shop and get a bottle of cream soda and some ice cream.'

'Wow,' said Jamie, opening his big blue eyes wide. 'Can we have lots and lots?'

Chapter 4

Maggie couldn't settle, and once the children were in bed she sat and gazed out of the window. She was pleased when she caught sight of Dan and Eve hurrying down the road.

Dan was first in the room. 'Ain't he home yet?' he asked, kissing Maggie's cheek.

She shook her head.

'You can see he ain't,' said Eve. 'Damn silly question to ask.'

'Thought he might be down in the bog.'

'Dan, I'm really worried. D'you think we should go to the police?'

'What could they do?'

'Dunno.'

Eve sat next to Maggie. 'Maggs, I don't like to ask, and I know it ain't none of my business, but . . .' she shifted her position, 'he ain't playing around, is he?'

Maggie sat bolt upright. 'You think he's left me for someone else, don't you?'

Dan shot Eve a filthy look. 'Course she don't.'

'Eve, d'you know somethink?'

Eve looked uncomfortable. 'No.'

'D'you think there might be someone else?' Tears slowly ran down Maggie's face.

'No, course not.'

'Then something must have happened to him.' Maggie stood up. 'I'm gonner go to the police.'

'Maggie, sit down.'

She did as Dan told her.

He sat next to her and took hold of her hand. 'I don't think you ought ter start involving the police . . . well, not just yet anyway.'

'Why?'

Dan lit up a cigarette. 'Look, me and Tony being good mates often talked about all sorts of things, and well . . .' He rubbed his hand over his chin. 'Some of his dealings wasn't always . . . kosher, yer see, and yer know he liked a bet.'

'I know he was always doing deals, but surely none of it was that bad that someone would . . .? Why do you think . . .?' Maggie was beginning to get upset at these implications.

'Quite a while back he told me he was worried.'

Maggie sat on the edge of her chair. 'Worried, worried, what d'you mean, Dan?'

'It was years ago. He told me he was involved with some right villains,' said Dan very quickly. 'But as I said, that was years ago. They might even be doing time.'

'You don't think they're back on the scene now, do you?' Eve asked.

Maggie frowned. 'If they are, why should they be interested in Tony? He ain't ever said anythink to me about being worried. And I think I would be the first to know.'

'You don't always see what's going on, even if it's right

42

under yer nose, not if you're that close to someone,' said Eve softly.

'Maggs, has Tony got anything, you know, real valuable?' asked Dan.

'Don't think so. If he has it ain't up here.'

'Could it be in the lockup?'

Maggie shrugged her shoulders. 'Dunno. But surely if it was that valuable he'd hide it away till he sold it.' She looked at Dan, her eyes full of tears. 'Wouldn't he?'

'Give me the key. I'll go down and have a look.'

'I'm coming with you.'

'No, you stay up here, I'll go.'

'No, I'm coming with you. If there's anythink that ain't right, I want to know.'

'Please yerself. You coming as well, Eve?'

'Course. I ain't missing nothink.'

All three went along to the lockup. Although it was late evening and the market deserted, for some unknown reason Maggie looked around feeling guilty.

Dan pushed open the large door and turned on the light. The smell of Mrs Russell's flowers filled the air. Tony's stall was just as Bill had left it. He shared this lockup with Winnie, Mrs Russell, and Tom Cooper. Tony always said he was glad they didn't have the smell of fish and rotting veg in with them.

'Can't see anythink worth leaving home for,' said Dan, picking up some of the objects on Tony's barrow.

'Well, if he had something that was worth a bob or two he wouldn't leave it on show, now would he?' said Eve, walking round and lifting with the toe of her shoe some of the rubbish and old sacks that were lying around.

'No, I reckon you're right, old girl. Let's look in all the corners.'

'Don't know if I want to go poking around in here. What if a rat jumps out,' said Maggie, standing well back.

Eve jumped. 'Don't say things like that, you'll frighten the daylights out of me.'

A train rattling overhead made Maggie start, and the intrusive noise forced them into silence.

'You two stand over by the door while I have a look around,' said Dan, when the train passed.

'My brave hero,' said Eve.

'I'll tell you somethink for nothink. When he does walk his arse in I'll give him what for,' said Maggie, her tears turning to anger. 'Making me worry like this.'

Eve put her arm round her friend's shoulders. 'You won't be the only one. Me and Dan will give him a right old mouthful as well.'

Maggie smiled. 'If he hears us, he'll never come back, he'll be too terrified.'

'Can't find anything that's worth more than a few bob,' said Dan, walking towards them.

'Perhaps this gang of villains made off with the spoils as well as Tony,' said Eve, laughing and trying to look sinister. 'Come on, let's pop in the Dog for a quick one.'

'I reckon that's a good idea,' said Dan.

'I'd rather not,' said Maggie. 'If you don't mind I'd rather get back to the kids, just in case Tony comes back and starts looking for me. Don't let me stop you two, though.'

'You go on, I'll stay with Maggie,' said Eve.

'OK.'

'Dan,' Maggie gently touched his arm, 'you won't say

44

anythink in there about Tony just yet, not till we find out more?'

'Course not, love. I'll only have a quick one, then I'll be back.'

'I've heard all that before,' said Eve.

Dan ignored that remark. 'But what if someone asks about him?'

'Tell them he ain't well, got a cold or somethink.'

'OK. See yer later, girls.'

'Come on, Maggs, let's go and have a cuppa tea.'

Dan was true to his word and didn't stay in the pub very long. He told Maggie nobody bothered to ask about Tony. After Eve and Dan left for home Maggie was on her own once again. She knew deep down something had happened to Tony. 'Please, Tony, come home,' she whispered. She was sure he hadn't just gone off of his own accord. Maggie knew if there was any way he could get in touch with her, he would.

Sunday seemed a very long day. Maggie was short-tempered with her children and she wished she had taken them over to see Tony's mother at Downham, but what could she say to her? Could Tony be over there? No, his mother would soon send him back.

Although Dan had told Maggie not to go to the police, if she hadn't heard anything by tomorrow morning, that's where she would be going as soon as she had taken Laura to school.

On Monday morning, a letter plopping on the doormat sent Maggie hurrying down the stairs as fast as her bulk would allow. She desperately hoped it was news of Tony, but was filled with despair when after opening it found it was an invitation to her brother, Alan's birthday party.

'He only has parties to show off,' mumbled Maggie to herself as she mounted the stairs again. She looked at the date, it was going to be the Saturday after next, plenty of time to make sure everybody got him a present.

She tossed the letter on to the sideboard. 'Now come on, you two,' she said to Jamie and Laura, who were sitting at the table. They had been asking questions about their dad ever since they got up. What could she tell them? 'You should have finished your breakfast by now.'

She noted Bill had got Tony's stall out, but she didn't stop to speak and deliberately hurried past all the other stallholders. At the school gates she kissed Laura goodbye, and made her way to the police station.

When they reached the door Jamie held back. 'What we going in here for?' he asked, holding Maggie's hand tightly. He looked very apprehensive. 'Has Daddy done something wrong?'

Maggie quickly glanced down at him. 'No, why? What made you ask that?'

'Well, he ain't come home, and when Mr Ding Dong went away, Daddy told me he'd done somethink wrong and was put in prison.' He looked at his feet and shuffled about. 'Daddy ain't in prison, is he?'

Maggie bent down and held him close. 'Don't be silly, of course not. I'm just going to ask the policeman if he's been hurt, and find out if he's in a hospital, and can't tell anybody where he lives.'

'Why can't he tell 'em where he lives?'

'He may have been in an accident and been knocked unconscious.'

'Oh,' said Jamie. 'Come on then, let's go and ask.'

'Can I help you?' asked the young policeman at the desk.

'Please, could I see someone in charge?'

'What's it in connection with?'

'Well, I don't know really. I'm just trying to find out about my husband.'

'Done a runner then, 'as he?'

'No,' said Maggie indignantly.

The policeman took up a large writing pad and licked the tip of his pencil. 'Name?'

'Tony Ross.'

'Address?'

'Twenty-seven Kelvin Market.'

'How long's he been missing?'

'Since Friday.'

The policeman looked up. 'I know Tony Ross. He's got a stall at the market.'

'Yes. I'm Mrs Ross.'

'You say he's been missing since Friday?'

Maggie nodded.

The policeman's face changed to one of concern. 'Wait here.' He disappeared through a door behind the counter.

Maggie sat on the bench seat that lined the dismal brown painted wall. But almost at once the policeman was at the counter again, a man in plain clothes with him.

'Mrs Ross,' said the man, 'I'm Inspector Matthews. I think I may have some news for you.'

Maggie's face beamed. 'You have?'

The Inspector looked uneasy, and Maggie became agitated.

'Look, I think you'd better come round. Go through that door.' He pointed the way.

'What about Jamie?' The sound of her pounding heart was filling her ears. She was suddenly aware that this could be bad news and she didn't want Jamie to hear it till she knew for certain.

'Bring him round. PC Brown will look after him.'

Maggie's hand was shaking as she pushed open the door. The Inspector was at her side almost at once. 'Follow me.'

Maggie was in a daze. She was led into a small room that had the words 'Detective Inspector Matthews' painted in black on the brown wooden door. The shelves that lined the walls were overflowing with papers tied together in bundles, and stacked high with box files. The desk was strewn with papers and the ashtray full of dog-ends. The only furniture was just two chairs and a desk.

'Please, Mrs Ross, sit down.' He waved his hand at the chair opposite him.

'What news have you got about Tony?'

The Inspector took a packet of cigarettes out of his pocket and offered her one.

Maggie shook her head.

He lit up and blew the smoke in the air. He gently tapped the end of the cigarette into the ashtray.

Maggie wanted to scream at him to get on with it.

'Mrs Ross,' he said slowly, 'did your husband have any distinguishing marks on his body?'

Maggie felt sick. Tony was dead. He was trying to tell her Tony was dead. She felt numb. She could hear the Inspector talking but his words weren't registering.

'Mrs Ross, Mrs Ross, are you all right?'

Tears ran down her face. She shook her head. 'Is he dead?'

'We don't know. You see, we fished a body out of the docks last night, he didn't have any identification on him, and until we find out who he is, we have to eliminate any missing persons.'

'No, not my Tony. It can't be.'

'Now if I could have a few details about your husband, that will help.'

Maggie could hear herself describing Tony.

'Would he have been wearing any jewellery?'

She nodded. 'He had quite a large diamond ring on his little finger, and a wedding ring on . . .' She had to stop.

'I'm sorry, but we have to ask these questions. Would you like a cup of tea?'

She nodded again.

The Inspector jumped up and quickly left the room, almost as if he were glad to get away.

He returned almost at once. 'PC Thurly will bring one in. Now, back to these questions. The body we found wasn't wearing any rings, though it could be that robbery was the motive for an attack. Now what about any distinguishing marks, like birthmarks, tattoos or moles – did Mr Ross have anything like that?'

'No,' said Maggie softly. She thought about Tony's perfect body, so strong and lovely. She wanted him here now, to run her hands over him. Tell him how much she loved him. Tell him she needed him to be with her.

The door opened and a cup of tea was silently put in front of her.

'When is your baby due?' asked the Inspector, out of the blue.

'September.'

'Do you just have the young man outside?'

'No, I have a little girl at school.'

'That's nice. Mrs Ross,' he hesitated. 'I'm afraid I'll have to ask you to come to the hospital with me to identify the body.'

'Do you think it could be Tony?'

'We don't know.'

'Tony had dark curly hair, and was wearing a navy coat . . .'

'Mrs Ross,' interrupted the Inspector, 'the body was naked when we found him.'

Maggie sat very still.

'Look, if you like we could arrange for someone to go with you. Do you have a friend or relation?'

'My mother-in-law lives out at Downham, and my friend's at work. I could perhaps get Winnie from the market to come with me.'

'I'll send one of my officers to go and get her. Which stall is she on?'

'The shoe stall.'

'Oh yes, I know it.' Once again he left the room.

When he returned he had Jamie in tow.

'Mummy, that policeman showed me his handcuffs,' said excitedly, 'and he let me see his truncheon. It ain't half heavy.'

Maggie struggled to smile. What would she do if the body was Tony? The children wouldn't have a father. How would she manage? Tears suddenly ran down her face.

'What yer crying for, Mummy?' Jamie's voice was full of fear and concern. 'They ain't gonner lock you up, are they?'

'No, course not.' She wiped her tears with the back of her hand and held out her arms. Jamie snuggled into her.

'Is Daddy in hospital like you said he might be?'

'I don't know yet. I've got to go and look at a man, just to see.'

'So he can't tell you if he's Daddy then?'

'No. I'm going with Auntie Win.' She looked up at the Inspector.

'It's all right, he can stay here. Would you like that, young fellow me lad?' He ruffled Jamie's hair.

Jamie gave him a dirty look. 'I don't like that, nor people kissing me.'

'I'm sorry, young man.' The Inspector bent down. 'And I promise not to kiss you.'

Maggie wanted to smile.

'Can I go back and wait with the policeman?'

'I should think so.' Inspector Matthews took hold of Jamie's hand and led him to the door. 'I'll be back. Did you want anything?'

'No thank you.' Maggie sat with her thoughts. What if it was Tony? She loved him so much, she couldn't bear life without him.

After a while the door burst open.

'What the bloody hell's going on round here? What you doing in a police station? I tell yer, girl, they'll be a riot down that market if they've got you in here and you ain't done nothink.'

The Inspector followed Winnie into the room.

'Win, I've got a favour to ask you.'

51

'Well ask away, girl. You know I'd do anythink for you, just as long as yer don't ask for money.' She laughed.

'Win, I think you'd better sit down.'

'Why? What's wrong?' Winnie looked puzzled as she glanced from Maggie to the Inspector.

Maggie began to tell her what had happened.

Winnie's eyes were growing larger and larger with every sentence. 'So what you're trying to say is that it could be your Tony what's laid out in the morgue?'

Maggie nodded and wiped her eyes.

'I'm afraid so,' said Inspector Matthews.

'Bloody hell, this is a bit of a shock.' Winnie fished around in her overall pocket for her handkerchief and blew her nose very loudly. 'What yer gonner do, gel?'

'I don't know,' whispered Maggie.

'Look, we mustn't jump to conclusions. Let's get down to the hospital and make sure first,' said the Inspector.

Winnie sprang up, 'Well, come on then, let's get it over and done with.'

'I'll take you in my car.'

'Thank you,' said Maggie.

'Come on, Maggs, hold on to me arm.'

Hanging on to Winnie Maggie walked out into the sunshine, but for her, everything had a black cloud hanging over it.

Chapter 5

The journey to the hospital had been made in silence. Now Maggie's mind was in turmoil as they hurried up the steps. What state would the body be in? She couldn't think of it as being Tony's body. Her stomach, like her mind, churned over. She didn't want to go in.

The Inspector noticed her distress and took her arm. 'Are you sure you're all right, Mrs Ross?'

'Yes thank you.'

Inside he said, 'Wait here,' and quickly made his way to the desk. He spoke intently to a young nurse, who nodded and glanced over at Maggie.

'This way,' said Inspector Matthews.

Maggie and Winnie followed him to the top of the stairs.

'It's down here.'

Maggie hesitated. Her legs felt like lead. She didn't want to go down.

'Come on, love,' said Winnie kindly. 'The sooner we get this over with, the better.' She took Maggie's arm and led her down.

They walked into the white tiled room. 'This is Mrs Ross,' said Inspector Matthews to a man in a white coat.

The cold clinical atmosphere with the smell of disinfectant and death made Maggie feel sick. She shivered. The man came towards them.

'Mrs Ross has come to look at the body we pulled out of the docks on Friday.' The Inspector hesitated before adding, 'It could be her husband.'

The man in the white coat nodded gravely. 'He's over here.' He moved across the tiled floor, his footsteps almost silent in contrast to the loud clomping sound the rest of them made as they followed him to a shape on a metal table. The shape was covered with a sheet.

'We were just going to start the post mortem on him.' He stood at the side and carefully lifted a corner of the cloth.

Maggie heaved, and the baby kicked. Her feet became rooted to the floor. They wouldn't move. She wanted to go and look, but couldn't.

Maggie swayed. Her head was spinning. Voices began to sound far away. Her legs buckled. In the distance she could hear Winnie shouting.

'Quick, get a chair.'

Then everything went black.

Slowly Maggie opened her eyes. The lights were bright and appeared to be moving round in circles. The man in the white coat was tapping her hand.

'It's all right, love. It ain't Tony,' said Winnie.

Maggie tried to stand up. 'Who . . .? What . . .?' she gasped.

'Just take your time,' said the man in the white coat, straightening up.

'It isn't your husband,' said the Inspector, 'and Mrs . . . here verified that. But I'm afraid you do have to tell me, just for the records, you understand.'

Maggie nodded.

'But only when you feel you are up to it.'

'I'm all right now.' She stood up and slowly moved towards the body.

Once again the corner of the sheet was lifted.

Maggie gazed down on a middle-aged man's face. It looked full of pain. 'No, this isn't my husband.'

'Have you any idea who it might be?'

Maggie shook her head and looked away. 'No, sorry.'

'Thank you. I'll take you back to the station. We'll have to ask you for a few more details about when you last saw your husband, and if you have any idea where he may have gone.'

In the car Maggie's feelings were confused. She was relieved the body wasn't Tony, but sad that she still didn't know where he was.

When at the station Maggie felt she had answered all the Inspector's questions, she asked, 'Is that it? Can we go?'

'Yes, thank you for now.'

She went to stand up.

'Mrs Ross.' He coughed, leant back in his chair and turned his pencil over and over in his clean, well-scrubbed hands. 'I'm sorry, but I do have to ask you this. Do you know if your husband was seeing another woman?'

'I can assure you he was not.' Maggie's answer was sharp.

'Thank you. But you do understand, we do have to ask.'

Maggie and Winnie, with Jamie between them, began to walk slowly back to the market.

'So how long's he been gone?' asked Winnie.

'I haven't seen him since Friday morning. Mr Goldman saw him at the station Friday afternoon.'

'What was he doing there?'

'If only I knew.'

Winnie stopped. ''Ere, you don't think he went to see his mum, do you?'

'No, he would have told me he was going. Besides, I normally do up a parcel for her. And it wouldn't take him all weekend to get there and back.'

'Yer, that's true. She lives out Downham way now, don't she?'

Maggie nodded. 'She was so upset when they pulled down all those old houses and moved the tenants away, but now she's got used to it she likes it. I think this is what Tony's got in mind for us.'

'Kent ain't that far away. Used to go down there hopping with me mum when I was a kid. She couldn't wait for August to get away from the old man.'

'Didn't he mind her going?'

'Na. Just as long as she was earning a few bob. 'Sides, with her out the way he didn't have ter bother to take the barra out, and he could get as drunk as he liked without her nagging.'

Maggie's thoughts went to her mother-in-law, who since tripping over in the garden and breaking her leg had been unable to get out as much as she used to. 'I'll have to go and tell her,' said Maggie out loud.

'Tell who?'

'Tony's mum.'

'Yer, but if I was you I'd wait till you've found out a bit

more. You know how she feels about him.'

Maggie smiled. 'Perhaps you're right. Tony's the apple of his mother's eye.'

They turned into the market and Jamie ran ahead. Winnie stopped for a moment and took hold of Maggie's arm. 'What yer gonner tell that lot?' She inclined her head towards the stalls.

'I don't know.'

'Well, you can guess we'll be having the coppers sniffing round here now, asking a lot of questions.'

'Yes.'

'And I don't reckon it'll go down that well with some of 'em. Most of 'em have got something to hide.'

'Even you?' Maggie gave her a faint smile.

Winnie laughed. 'Yer, I just see him asking, "And where did you get those boots from then, missis?" I could look up at him, flutter me eyelashes and say, "Off that bloke what you fished out the river."'

Maggie didn't laugh with her.

'Sorry, gel, that was a bit insensitive of me.'

When they reached Tony's stall Bill asked, 'Where's that old man of yours got to then, Maggs?'

'I don't know. Bill, he's not been around since Friday. I've just been to the police.'

'Bloody hell. The police? What for?'

'I want to find out where he is.' She lowered her head. 'And if he's still alive.'

Bill let out a long whistle. ''Ere, you don't think—'

'No, course not,' interrupted Winnie.

'Well look, you don't have to worry about the stall. I'll manage. I hope 'e don't stay away too long, though, otherwise we won't 'ave a lot of stock.'

'Don't worry about that for the time being, and Bill, if anybody, you know, who looks a bit suspicious, asks for him, send them up to me.'

'OK, Maggs. I hope this gets cleared up soon.'

'So do I.'

Winnie looked from one to the other. 'Bill, if anyone does ask for 'im, you'd better come and tell me first. Just in case.'

'OK, Win.'

Maggie and Winnie moved on.

'That's gonner be all round this 'ere market before you've had time to get the kettle on,' said Winnie.

'That might not be a bad thing. Someone might remember if he said anything to them. Then this mystery could be cleared up. Did you want to come up for a cuppa?'

'No thanks, I'd better get back to me stall. I never know if that Ada, what's supposed to keep an eye on it for me, helps herself to some of me profits.'

'She wouldn't dare.'

Winnie laughed. 'I've only gotter catch her once, then you wouldn't see her arse for dust.' She kissed Maggie's cheek. 'Now you go on in and put your feet up. I'll make sure Laura gets home all right.'

'Thanks, Win, I'll see you later. Come on, Jamie, up you go.'

For the rest of the day, Maggie's thoughts kept returning to that man laid out in the morgue. Somebody must be worrying about him. What if Tony was laid out in another place? Tears filled her eyes. How long must she wait for news?

At six o'clock Eve came hurrying up the stairs. 'Well, he back yet?'

Maggie shook her head and in a quiet voice told her about the trip to the morgue and the police station.

'Maggs, that must have been awful for you,' said Eve, putting her hand to her mouth and slumping down in the chair. 'What did the police say?'

'Not a lot really.'

'You don't think Tony's dead, do you?'

'I don't know what to think. Eve, what am I gonner do?'

Eve sat down and took a packet of cigarettes out of her handbag. She lit one and slowly blew the smoke into the air. 'You don't think he's gone off with another woman, do you?'

Maggie laughed. 'Course not. If there was any hanky-panky going on I'm sure I would have known.'

Eve nervously tapped the end of her cigarette into the ashtray. 'Yer, course you would have.'

'Eve, do you think Tony could be wandering around somewhere, you know, and lost his memory?'

'Dunno. I suppose that could happen, but then Mr Goldman saw him getting on a train.'

'I know.' Maggie sat on the end of her chair. 'But suppose after he'd been to see that cottage he hit his head. Those people wouldn't know who he was, would they?' Maggie was beginning to get excited about this theory.

'I don't know. But he must have something on him to tell them who he was, and an address for the cottage. They surely would know his name and where he came from.'

Maggie sat back deflated. 'I suppose so. It was just an idea.'

'I know.'

'Eve, I don't know where to turn.'

'I wish I could help. Now come on, let's try and be a bit practical. What about the stall?'

'Bill seems to be managing all right, but I don't know for how long . . .' Tears filled her eyes. 'Eve, what am I gonner do without him?'

Eve took her hand. 'We'll all rally round you.'

'Thanks.'

'What about your brother? You'll have to tell him.'

'That'll give Helen something to chew over. I'm not telling them just yet. By the way I've got an invitation to Alan's birthday party.'

'When's that?'

'Two weeks, I think – didn't really take a lot of notice.'

'You going?'

'Don't know. A lot can happen in two weeks.'

'You sure there's nothing around that might give you some idea where he is?'

'No. Mind you, I ain't been down his papers. They might give me a clue.'

Eve jumped up. 'Where are they? We can go through—'

'I'd rather not.'

'OK. Please yourself.' Eve looked a little put out. 'Did he keep a diary?'

'Shouldn't think so, never seen him with one.'

They sat talking and drinking tea for a while, then Eve said she had to go.

'I'll call in again tomorrow. You look after yourself.' She kissed Maggie's cheek and left.

After Eve left, Maggie thought about Tony's papers and

turned out his cupboard. Over the years she hadn't had a lot to do with his business, but hoped there might be a clue to his whereabouts amongst his documents.

For hours she sat poring over books and figures, surprised how detailed some of the transactions had been recorded. Most of the stuff came from the rag-and-bone man, Benny. Benny's name was in the book many times. Now and again the initial W was pencilled in, and some of the figures made her gasp. She didn't realise he had made that kind of money, but where was it? The book showed items he had bought at auctions. She remembered the times she went with him, and he'd mostly bought junk. But in this book were things she had never seen, or even knew about. Some had been bought and then sold on at great profit. So where was the money? The Post Office book didn't have a lot in, only thirty shillings, and she knew there wasn't any hidden in the flat. So how was he going to pay for this cottage? Was there money in a bank somewhere? If so, which bank? They didn't have a bank account. How could she find out? She straightened up, her back and head aching. She shoved the books into the cupboard. She would finish going through them tomorrow. She'd just about had all she could take for one day.

The following morning, as soon as Laura was at school, and Jamie went to play outside, Maggie opened Tony's wardrobe. At first she stood gently feeling his suits and holding them close to her cheek. Tears filled her eyes. They had his smell. 'Tony, where are you?' she whispered.

Quickly she went down all his pockets, fumbling, almost afraid he might come in and catch her. She found old train tickets, bus tickets, dog track tickets and cigarette packets. But there was nothing that gave her a clue or any hope.

Back in the living room she got down on her hands and knees and got his papers out again. Then she carefully ran her hand along the rear of the cupboard. She pulled out a child's exercise book that was wedged right at the back. She quickly ran her thumb over the pages. The book didn't have any figures in, but Maggie sensed it was very private. Guilt almost overtook her as she opened it. She had never poked her nose into his affairs before.

She sat at the table and began reading. There were names and addresses of most of the people they knew, also of some she didn't know. There was also a list of places with dates and times, with just an initial by the side. As she read on, the dates became more recent. They stopped before Friday, 17 May, the day he went missing.

If he was going to meet someone why didn't he write it down?

Jamie's yelling from the bottom of the stairs brought her back to reality.

'Mummy, Mummy, it's that policeman.'

Maggie stood up and quickly bundled all the books and papers back into the cupboard.

The door opened.

'Sorry, Mrs Ross. I hope it isn't inconvenient. Young Jamie here said it was all right to come up.'

'Yes, that's fine. Have you any news?' In her home he appeared tall, and he was quite nice-looking.

'I'm afraid not. But I thought I'd have a walk round the market and ask a few questions. You never know, someone may have heard something.'

'I bet that didn't go down too well.'

'You're right.' He smiled, and for the first time Maggie noticed he had a pleasant face and his smile crinkled his very blue eyes, quite unusual with such dark hair.

'I've been having a word with Mr Goldman, as he seems to be the last person who saw your husband, but he couldn't really throw any light on what we already know. What about Mr Ross's books?'

Maggie shrugged. 'Tony didn't really keep any.'

'You'll let me know if you find anything that could be useful, won't you?'

Maggie nodded. 'Would you like a cup of tea?'

'That would be very nice – if it's not too much trouble.'

'It's no trouble, in fact I was just going to make myself one.' Maggie suddenly felt very self-conscious at this man being in her home, and this silly bland conversation.

When she returned from the kitchen he was standing in front of the sideboard with her wedding photo in his hand. She noticed a small piece of paper with Tony's writing on poking out of the cupboard underneath. She quickly put the tea tray on the table, and wondered if the Inspector had seen the paper.

'You make a very handsome couple,' he said replacing the photo. 'Perhaps you have a photo of your husband we could have to place on file at the station?'

'Of course. There's one in this drawer. Do you take sugar?' It was the only thing she could think of to say. She felt desperate for him to leave so she might think about the list she had found in the book.

For the rest of the week Eve dropped in every evening, and

Inspector Matthews called in once again.

On Friday Maggie felt very low. Today was Empire Day.

Laura hadn't been sleeping well, and one night Maggie heard her shouting in her sleep. When she awoke she said she was worried about dancing round the maypole, but Maggie suspected it went deeper than that. Another night she was crying, and twice Jamie had wet the bed. A week had gone by since Tony left home, and it was having an effect on the children. Where was he? Was he still alive?

But today Laura looked very pretty in her pale blue frock that had frills from the waist down.

'This is Daddy's favourite,' she said, preening in front of the large ornate mirror. 'I wish Daddy was going to see me.'

'So do I, darling.' Maggie knelt on the floor to tie the pale blue ribbon round Laura's dark curly hair.

'Is he ever coming back to us?'

She had such a sad look on her face that Maggie just had to sweep her into her arms. 'I hope so,' she whispered.

'Well, I reckon it's rotten of him not to come home,' said Jamie.

'I'm sure he has a good reason,' said Maggie, standing up and regaining her composure. 'Now come on, we mustn't be late.'

The dancing around the maypole went well and the children who had had more rehearsals than at the Jubilee didn't get into such a tangle as the last time. Maggie decided to sit at the back of the playground. She didn't want to talk to Laura's teacher in case she asked about Tony. Her eyes misted over. Tony would have loved to have been here. He was very proud of everything Laura and Jamie did. Maggie was convinced he wouldn't stay away from them for long, not of his own free will.

That evening she was glad of Eve and Dan's company, and after a lot of persuading decided to go with them to the Dog and Duck. She felt very uneasy at the looks she received when they walked in.

'Still no news then, Maggs?' asked Gus.

'No.'

'Can't say I like the coppers hanging round here all the time.'

'Why's that then, Gus?' asked Eve. 'You got something to hide?'

'No I ain't.' He leant across the bar. 'I'll tell yer something else, old Ding Dong ain't none too pleased about it either.'

Maggie wanted to scream. How did they think *she* felt?

Gus's wife, Beatie, gave them a wave and came over. She was a short well-groomed woman, whose hair had been allowed to go grey naturally. Her pale face had just a hint of make-up, not like most of the landladies round here, who looked like they had just come off the stage. 'Have this one on the house, love.' She smiled at Maggie, then glared at her husband. 'Take no notice of him. Just remember if there's anythink I can do to help, let me know.'

'Thanks, Beatie. Do they think,' Maggie nodded towards the group of men at the bar who were deep in conversation, 'that I enjoy having the police keep coming round asking me questions?'

'Course they don't, love, but, well, you know most of 'em are into some dodgy dealings one way or another. Go and sit down and I'll bring the drinks over.' She returned with a flash of the lovely rings she always wore, with large stones that glinted when they caught the light.

'Thanks, Beatie.'

At the end of the week Maggie added up the takings from the stall. Now she had Tony's books to go by she noticed they were down considerably.

'OK, Maggs?' asked Bill, when he brought Saturday's takings up to her.

'You ain't took a lot this week,' she said, after counting out the day's money.

'Ain't got any new stock, 'ave I?'

'Sit down, Bill,' she said quietly. 'Nobody's been to ask about Tony?'

'Only that copper.'

Maggie bit the end of her pencil. 'I know some of the auction rooms Tony used to go to. I might nip along there, and I'll see Benny next week – he might have a few bits.'

'D'yer want me to come with you?'

'No, I don't think so. But if anybody's got something to sell, get word up here to me quick.'

'You gonner take over the stall then, Maggs?'

'Looks like I ain't got any choice.'

'Well, I reckon you're very brave.'

Tears filled Maggie's eyes. 'I've already got two mouths to feed, and in a few months there'll be another.'

Bill looked embarrassed. 'So you don't think Tony's coming back then?'

Maggie didn't know how to answer him.

Chapter 6

On Monday morning, after taking Laura to school, Winnie said she would keep her eye on Jamie. Maggie took the bus to one of the auction rooms she knew.

She'd forgotten the dank musty smell of this place. After studying the catalogue she wandered around, browsing through some of the junk on display. Chipped china, dented saucepans, rusting lawn mowers and garden tools – who would want garden tools and a lawn mower in Rotherhithe?

'It's Maggie, ain't it? Maggie Ross? I ain't seen you here for years.' The short tubby white-haired man came hurrying over towards her. He held her close and kissed her cheek. 'This is a nice surprise.' Wally looked around. 'Where's that old man of yours then?'

'Hallo, Wally,' said Maggie, ignoring the question.

'So how you keeping then? And what you doing round this way?'

Wally was an auctioneer. Could he be the W in Tony's book? Maggie hadn't thought about him as Tony had told her he'd retired. 'Thought you was at home putting your feet up.'

'Na. Couldn't stand it, and the missis couldn't stand me

67

under her feet all the time, so I thought I'd come back. I only do a couple of days. Still, it keeps me out of mischief and in the know.' He put his arm round her shoulders and laughed. 'See he's still getting his wicked way then.' Wally pointed to Maggie's stomach. 'How many's that make now?'

'Only three.'

'So where is the old bugger?'

'He's busy, so he asked me to have a look round,' lied Maggie. There was no way she was going to tell him the truth – well, not yet anyway.

'So he's sent you out buying?'

'Sort of.'

'What's he got his eye on then? Could always let you know if someone else is interested in it.'

'Don't really know. It has to be cheap. Perhaps a couple of vases, or cutlery. Just anything we could sell quick and make a profit.'

Wally looked uneasy. 'I'm surprised Tony sent you along. He always reckoned the little woman's place was in the home.'

Maggie smiled. 'I told him I needed a day out, so he said I'd have to work for it.'

Wally laughed. 'Yer, that sounds like Tony. 'Ere, come this way.' Wally took her arm and led her to a corner. 'So how much yer got to play with?'

'Not a lot.'

'Did he say if he's ready to shift some of the big stuff again?'

'Don't know. Why?'

Wally looked about him suspiciously. He lowered his

voice. 'See that sideboard over there.' He nodded towards a large ornate oak sideboard. 'Well, the drawer's locked and key's missing.' He looked around again and moved closer to Maggie. 'I happen to know there's a lot of silver cutlery in that drawer, it's the real McCoy, and if I could get a mate to buy the sideboard, then whatever's inside comes with it, and we could split the difference. Just so long as he keeps his mouth shut.'

'How do you know what's in that . . .'

Wally took her arm. 'Trust me,' he whispered.

'Don't anybody else know?'

'Only the bloke what cleared the house. Course, he wants a cut.'

'Why don't he get a key and sell it?'

'It's to do with an old girl's estate. That way the money would have to go to the next of kin.'

'Tony's done this sort of thing before then?'

'Yer. A few times. Didn't you know?' Wally looked concerned.

She laughed, she wanted this conversation to sound light-hearted. 'You should know Tony by now: he don't tell me everythink.'

'So why's he sent you down here now?' His tone had an edge of suspicion about it.

'He had to go away, and Bill said the stall was getting a bit low.' Maggie bit her lip anxiously.

'Sounds fishy to me. He bin away long?' Wally rubbed his chin.

'No,' said Maggie quickly. 'Just a few days.'

''Ere,' he looked round again before speaking, 'he ain't . . . you know, inside?'

Fear took hold of Maggie. Prison had crossed her mind, but surely the local police would know if he had been arrested elsewhere. She laughed again. 'No, course not, somethink to do with a auction in the country, and he fancied a few days away.' Although she had to carry on this easy-going banter, she felt she was getting in deeper and deeper with her explanations.

'That sounds like him.' Wally took her arm and held it tight. 'But you would tell me the truth now, wouldn't you?'

Maggie nodded smiling, but she could feel the undercurrent in his words.

'That's all right then. So, yer lookin' fer cheap stuff to sell on. D'you wanner wait for the auction?'

'No, I've got to get back.'

'Right then, gel, follow me.'

'Wally, do you want me to tell Tony what you said about that,' she moved her head towards the sideboard, 'when I get home?'

'Na, this lot'll go today. Some lucky sod's gonner make a few bob. But, Maggs, tell him ter come and see me real soon.'

'Anythink I should tell him about?'

'Na, just tell him I wanner see him, that's all.'

They wandered around and Maggie picked out to buy a hand mirror that had the silver peeling off the back, two small vases, a pair of miniature brass dogs, and a set of cut-glass bowls.

'You sure you can manage to get these bits home? If you fancy leaving them with me I could get the van round to you tonight.'

'No, thanks all the same, I'll be able to manage.' She

70

didn't want Wally anywhere near the market.

'Please yerself. Give that dirty old man of yours me best.'

'I will.'

'Say, why don't you and Tony come round home one of these evenings?'

'I'd like that.'

'Tell Tony to pop in and make the arrangements, and we could see about getting another game of cards going.'

'I will.' Maggie dutifully kissed his cheek and left.

As she sat on the bus all that Wally had told her about their scam went over and over in her mind. How often had they done that sort of thing? Her thoughts turned to that exercise book. Some of those initials were W. Could that have been dealings with Wally? Had something gone wrong? Could Tony be in prison somewhere? If so, would Inspector Matthews know? There were so many unanswered questions. She didn't really like Wally – he'd always seemed devious. She had seen this morning what sort of deals Wally was prepared to do, so maybe Tony had been keeping this kind of thing from her. She sighed. Perhaps she was trying to find some excuse for Tony leaving her.

As soon as she arrived home Maggie went straight to the cupboard and got out the exercise book. There were dates next to the initial W, but the entries still didn't make sense. She looked through the other book, the one that had all the money written down. If only this one had dates then she could see if they matched.

She went back to her purchases and carefully emptied her bag on to the table. She was pleased, she had picked out some nice bits, and with a cleanup they should bring in a few bob. Tomorrow she would go and see Benny the rag-and-bone man. She began to sing, then, remembering, suddenly stopped. Why was she happy? Nothing had changed. She sat down. She didn't want to be the one in charge, running the business, making the decisions. Please Tony, she begged silently, come back.

The following day Maggie went to Benny's yard. Though it had been a few years since she'd seen him, she knew Benny still lived here, as Tony often mentioned him, and laughed about his carrying a torch for his mum, Bella.

Maggie pushed open a small door set in the large corrugated door that fronted the yard and stepped through. Inside were piles of rusting junk: old mangles whose wooden rollers were almost worn away, tin baths with holes in, and a heap of broken furniture. Who would ever buy this rubbish? The smell of horse dung took her breath away – Benny lived over the building that housed his horse. Maggie carefully picked her way across the yard to the iron staircase that ran up the outside of the building.

She was only halfway up when the door at the top opened.

''Ere, what d'yer want?' Benny stood in the doorway looking down on her. He suddenly recognised her and a great smile lifted his thin but stern weather-beaten face. 'Well, if it ain't little Maggie Ross. What you doing round these parts, gel?'

'Hallo, Benny,' panted Maggie as she got to the top of the steep stairs.

'Come on in, gel. I've got the kettle on, just making meself a cuppa. Want one?'

Maggie wasn't all that sure she wanted anything to drink.

What state would his cups be in?

'Well, I'll be . . .' He pushed his greasy trilby back, scratching his forehead as he did so. You couldn't tell what colour his hat had once been – it was always a standing joke that Benny must have slept in it, since nobody ever saw him without it.

Benny was a thin wiry man who gave everybody the impression he was lazy and slow like his horse, but his pale blue eyes were always darting about, never missing a thing.

'Sit yerself down, gel. This is a nice surprise. What brings you round these parts?'

Maggie sat on the edge of the chair. Benny had one large room with the kitchen at one end and his bed at the other; it looked neat and tidy. He had lived alone all the years Maggie had known him; apparently his wife had died soon after they were married.

Maggie had made up her mind to tell Benny about Tony. He might know something, and had always been kinder than Wally.

As if reading her thoughts he suddenly sat next to her and asked, ''Ere, ain't nothing happened to yer old man, is there?' He sounded genuinely concerned.

Maggie looked at him. 'Benny,' she whispered, 'Tony's missing.'

'Sorry, gel, I don't get yer. What d'yer mean, missing? I only saw him, what, a week or so ago.'

The whistling kettle broke through the quiet. 'Just a tick, I'll make the tea.' He took a brown china teapot from the cupboard and after warming the pot he put two carefully measured spoonfuls of tea in and filled it with boiling water. He then took a bottle of milk from a galvanised bucket that stood on the floor, sniffed it and looking up, smiled. 'It's all right, it ain't gorn orf yet.' He brought the tray of tea things over to the table Maggie was sitting at. 'Ain't got any biscuits to give you. Nellie, that bloody horse of mine, eats 'em as fast as I buy 'em. Right, gel, now tell me what this is all about.'

Maggie went through the story. Benny didn't speak, but he listened very intently, his only movement to pour out the tea.

'So,' he said, when Maggie had finished, 'what d'yer think could have happened to him?'

'I don't know. Eve asked me if there was anybody else.' Maggie sniffed and fumbled in her handbag for a handkerchief.

'Did he take any of his clothes?'

Maggie shook her head.

Benny patted her hand. 'Well then, I don't think you've got any worries on that score. He was a bit of a ladies' man in his day, and he always liked to look good, but he did love yer, Maggs, you knows that, don't yer?'

She nodded. 'But I wish he'd kept me a bit more . . . I don't know.' She threw her arms up in the air. 'Told me more about what was going on.'

'Why's that, gel? Do you think he's mixed up in some funny business?' He coughed. 'We all like to dabble a bit, but what I mean is, real dodgy stuff, with right villains?'

'I don't know. I went to the auction room yesterday and Wally wanted Tony to buy a sideboard that he said had a lot of silver in.'

'That does happen now and again,' said Benny, leaning back in his chair and lighting his pipe. 'But you have to be

74

in the know, and trust the person you're dealing with.' He was lost in a cloud of smoke. 'Mind you, I've never got on with Wally. A bit of a double-dyed villain, if yer asks me. Sell his missis fer a shilling.' He laughed. 'Still I s'pose most blokes I know would sell their missis fer a shilling.'

'Benny,' said Maggie quietly, 'I've been to the police.'

He sat forward and waved his hand to clear the smoke. 'You 'ave? And what did they 'ave ter say?'

'Not a lot. I had to look at a body they took from the river. But I didn't know who it was.'

'That wasn't very nice for yer.'

'What do I do, Benny?'

'Now then, gel, dry yer eyes. You go on home and look after them two little 'ens of yours. I'll ask around when I'm out and about on me rounds. You'd be surprised what bits of information you can pick up when you're supposed to be busy. What about his muvver? What's Bella got to say about all this?'

'I don't know, I haven't told her yet.'

'Oh I see.' Benny sat back again and smiled. A dreamy look came over him. 'Always had a soft spot for Bella. I reckoned I would 'ave married her if she hadn't already been hitched to old Jim.'

Maggie smiled; she knew all about this one-sided romance. Tony often laughed to his mother about the fact that he could end up having Benny for a dad. That remark would bring Bella's mighty hand landing round Tony's ear, almost knocking him off balance.

'That was a good thing her getting that nice little house at Downham – mind you, I missed all that lot when they moved away.' He grinned. 'Made quite a few bob out of those places. Couldn't believe what some of 'em left in 'em.'

Maggie could see Benny was in a reminiscent mood. 'Benny, I've got to be the buyer now for the stall.' She tried to bring him back to business.

'Yer, I suppose you have till Tony gets back. Is that what you was doing at the auction room?'

'Yes, and I was wondering if you've got any bits I could buy, just to keep things ticking over, you understand. After all, I've still got to find the rent for the stall and the flat, pay Bill and feed the kids.'

'Course you have, gel. Come downstairs and we'll have a butchers through me stuff. There's a few bits you might be interested in. But promise me you'll look after yerself now.'

Maggie smiled. 'I promise.'

Once again Maggie made her way home, her bag full of various items that came from Benny's storeroom that was part of Nellie's stable. Maggie knew that, with a good cleanup, she could sell them at a nice fat profit. Everything she bought and sold would have the price on and would then be entered in a book. That way, when Tony came back he would be able to see what an asset she was to the business.

She picked up a china shaving mug and smiled. She was sure it had a silver rim. Benny must have known that. She turned it round, it was very nice. 'This will do for Alan's birthday on Saturday,' she said out loud. If she could find the right box it would look very expensive.

Chapter 7

It was six o'clock on Friday evening when Eve walked in. Maggie was doing her books.

'Just thought I'd pop in to see how you are. What're you doing there?' asked Eve.

'I'm writing down everything I buy and sell, so when Tony comes back he can see how well I've managed.'

'So you think he'll be back then?'

'I've got to hope, and keep the stall going.'

'Well, my girl, have you made a fortune yet?' asked Eve flippantly.

'No, but I'm not doing too bad.'

'Bill looked right miserable packing away when I came past. He was having a moan to that bloke Cooper.'

'What about? I've got his wages.'

'I don't think he likes the idea of working for a woman.'

'It is only temporary.'

'That Tom Cooper's a bit of a mean-looking sod.'

'He's all right. Him and Tony always seem to hit it off.'

'He was having a right go about the coppers hanging round asking questions.'

Maggie sat back. 'Eve, do you think Tony will ever come home?'

Eve took a packet of cigarettes from her handbag and lit one. 'I don't honestly know.'

'He's been gone two weeks now.' Maggie stood up. 'You would have thought I'd have heard something by now.'

'I would have thought so. Has that Inspector said any more?'

'No. Eve,' there was a catch in her voice, 'if Tony was alive surely he would let me know?' Tears began slowly to trickle down Maggie's cheeks.

'Yes, course.' She nervously tapped the end of the cigarette into the ashtray. 'Maggie, you mustn't give up hope.'

Maggie wiped her eyes. 'What am I supposed to think?'

'I honestly don't know. So,' said Eve, quickly changing the subject, 'have you made up your mind yet? Are you going to Alan's birthday party tomorrow?'

'Yes.'

'Will you tell them?'

'Think I'll have to. They're sure to ask where he is, and Laura or Jamie will tell them quick enough.'

'How are they taking it?'

'Well, Jamie has started wetting the bed, and that's something I can well do without. When the new baby arrives I'll have more than enough washing.'

'What about Laura?'

'She doesn't say a lot. She seems to have gone into a shell. A couple of times at night I've heard her crying and when I've gone in she stops and pretends to be asleep. When they break up for the summer holidays I'm gonner take 'em to Ramsgate for a few days. Here, you don't fancy coming with me, do you?'

'Dunno. Let's wait and see what happens by then, shall we? Have you told the kids?'

Maggie nodded. 'I thought they should have something to look forward to.'

'Yer, I suppose you're right. Maggs, what about Tony's mum?'

'I'll have to tell her soon, she'll be wondering what's happened to him.'

'He didn't go and see her that often since she was moved out Downham way, did he?'

'About every couple of weeks, so he would be more or less due to go there this Sunday morning. Just as long as Benny don't go over and tell her first.'

'What, old Benny the rag-and-bone man? He's not still struck on Bella, is he?'

'I think so.'

'He don't go over there, does he?'

'Dunno. Bella ain't said.'

'You don't think she would know anythink about Tony, do you?'

'Shouldn't think so. 'Sides, if he was there she'd soon send him packing.'

Eve smiled. 'I guess so. Bella Ross is a very formidable lady.'

When Eve left Maggie thought about Tony's mother. How would she take the news? And what would Alan have to say about it? She cleared the table. Well she'd know the answer to that one tomorrow.

Saturday, 1 June was warm and sunny all day. It was late afternoon when Maggie and her children, who were looking very smart, caught the bus to Alan and Helen's house at Hither Green.

As they walked down the road Maggie couldn't help but admire the lovely houses. Was she wrong not wanting a place with a garden for the children? It would be nice to hang out the washing on a proper line, and not in a tiny yard with the sheets flapping against the fence. And a bathroom indoors – that must be heaven in the winter. She sighed. Perhaps the time had come to talk to Tony about it, see if they could afford even to rent anything like this.

The door was opened by Helen, who was, as usual, looking very chic. The long powder-blue frock that clung to her slim figure made Maggie feel in her present condition fat, dumpy and inferior. Helen's make-up was perfect, and with her fair hair elegantly cut, she looked like she was worth a million dollars.

'Maggie dear,' she said, bending her head towards Maggie and planting a kiss on her cheek. 'How are you?' She lightly touched Maggie's stomach. 'Getting nice and plump, I see. Still, it don't last for ever. Only about three months to go, isn't it? Mind you, I'm so glad we only had one child. I don't know where you get the energy from to deal with two, let alone when you've got three to contend with.'

Maggie smiled a false smile.

'Come on in. Go and join Doreen and the other kids in the garden,' Helen said to the children, standing to one side to let them into the house. Turning to Maggie she added, 'Doreen takes up all of my time, what with dancing and piano lessons, and the hundred and one other things she gets involved in. By the way, where's that good-looking husband of yours? Is he coming over later?'

'Daddy's gone away,' said Jamie over his shoulder.

'Oh,' said Helen, raising her perfectly shaped eyebrows. 'And where's he gone to?'

'Dunno,' said Jamie.

Helen smiled. 'Shoo, out in the garden, children. So where is Tony then?' she asked Maggie as she ushered the children along the passage.

'I'd rather talk to Alan first, if you don't mind, Helen.'

Helen looked put out. 'Why, has he done a runner?' She laughed. 'Is it some dark secret you'd rather not tell me about?'

'No, but I would still rather like to talk to Alan first.'

'Please yourself. I'll tell him you're here. I must say you're making it sound very interesting, but don't keep him from our guests for too long, will you?'

Maggie waited for Alan in the kitchen. She looked round at the green and white cupboards, everything smart and crisp, just like Helen. She stood admiring the food neatly laid out on the small table for their friends – and felt very tempted to stick her finger in the red jelly. Helen had told her they didn't eat in the kitchen, they always ate in the dining room. Maggie smiled. They were bloody lucky to have a dining room.

'Maggs, Maggie. Helen said you were here.'

Her brother took her in his arms and kissed her cheek. He was taller than her and his fair hair that time had darkened was now slightly greying at the temples. But his blue eyes still twinkled. Today he looked relaxed and very handsome in his white open-neck shirt and grey flannels.

Maggie had always loved her brother, but over the years things had soured slightly; his wife, Helen, had come between them. She had too many airs and graces for Maggie's taste – for instance, she didn't like her friends knowing they had a stall in the market. She always told them that Tony had a shop. But Helen wasn't above fawning over Tony whenever she had the chance.

'So, Helen said something about Tony. He's not here then?'

'No. Alan, I know this is your birthday, and I don't want to spoil it, but I'm very worried. Is there somewhere we could talk?'

Alan frowned and looked concerned. He took Maggie's arm. 'We can go in the front room.'

'By the way, happy birthday.' She handed him a box that contained the shaving mug as they went along.

'Thanks.' Alan beckoned for her to sit on the fancy green brocade sofa, while he sat in the matching armchair facing her. 'Now what's the problem?'

'Tony's been missing for two weeks.'

Alan looked shocked. 'What do you mean, missing?'

'He hasn't been home.'

'Sorry, Maggs, but what are you saying? He's left you?'

Maggie was getting agitated. 'I mean he's gone missing, disappeared.'

'Disappeared?' repeated Alan. 'Have you been to the police?'

Maggie nodded and went into great detail about all that had happened.

'What can I say? Is there anything I can do to help?'

'No, not really.'

82

'How are you managing, moneywise, I mean?'

'The stall's not doing too bad.'

'But what about stock?'

'I've managed to get a few bits.'

'But what about when the new baby arrives?'

Maggie rolled her eyes. 'Christ, I hope Tony's back by then.'

Alan sat for a while in thought. He stood up and walked to the window. 'Maggs, I don't want to sound a Jonah, but has Tony got any kind of insurance?'

'Only the penny policy his mum took out when he was born, I think. Why?'

'Well, that's better than nothing, I suppose.'

'Alan, you don't think he could be . . .' She couldn't bring herself to say the word.

'We have to look at all possibilities, but of course until we've got a body you can't do that much.'

Maggie was stunned. He was talking as if Tony was dead, and it was all so matter-of-fact.

He came and sat next to her. 'Look, don't worry about it. I'm sure Tony will turn up soon with a very plausible excuse. You should know him by now.'

'But Tony wouldn't go off without telling—'

The door was suddenly pushed open. 'Come on, you two. You shouldn't monopolise him, you know, Maggie.' Helen looked from one to the other.

'Well, I don't see him very often,' said Maggie tersely.

'We are rather busy with this and that. Now come on, Alan, some people out here are dying of thirst.'

Alan stood up. 'We'll talk about this later.'

Helen smiled. 'This sounds most interesting. I hope your

dear Tony hasn't gone off and left you?'

The silence pounded in Maggie's ears.

'Helen,' said Alan, 'don't jump to conclusions.'

'Oh dear. Have I hit a raw nerve or something?'

'Alan will tell you later.'

Helen smiled. 'I can't wait. Now come on, the pair of you.'

Maggie and Alan made their way into the garden. The children were busy playing in Doreen's little playhouse at the end of it and their laughter and yells told everybody they were enjoying themselves. Alan put a drink in Maggie's hand. It was comforting to stand here with the warm early evening sun playing on her back. Yes, Tony was right, a garden would be nice for the children.

Different people, whom Maggie had met briefly before at Alan and Helen's dos came up and talked, but most of it was idle chitchat about what they had, and what they'd done. A few times when Maggie glanced across at Helen she seemed to be looking at her rather quizzically. When Helen realised Maggie was staring at her she quickly joined a group, throwing her head back and laughing very loudly. Maggie wondered if she really enjoyed this life, or if it was all a sham.

As the evening wore on Maggie caught sight of Jamie yawning. 'I think it's about time we went,' she said to Alan.

'Sorry we've not had time to have a proper chat. Look, I'll pop over next week, say Saturday, then you can tell me more about your troubles.'

'OK,' said Maggie. She was a bit put out that he would wait a whole week before coming to see her, even though he had a car.

'Tony might be back by then,' he said, cheerily, 'and I'm sure he'll have quite a tale to tell.'

'I hope so,' she said as she went to find the children.

Things were still the same when Alan called on Maggie the following Saturday.

'Alan, I don't know who to turn to next,' said Maggie. 'I wish Mum and Dad were alive.'

'You've got me and Helen,' he said softly.

Maggie looked at him. She wanted to say, 'Yes, but how often do I see you?' but she knew that wouldn't really be fair. 'Have you told Helen?'

'Course. She reckons he's just gone off on some wild-goose chase.'

She would, thought Maggie. 'Would you like a cup of tea?'

'Thought you'd never ask.'

Maggie went into the kitchen and made the tea. 'I forgot the biscuits,' she said, putting the tray on the table.

'Maggs,' called Alan after her. 'I know I shouldn't ask, but d'you think Tony . . .'

She quickly returned to the living room, her eyes blazing. 'No I don't think there was – is – another woman. Everybody asks me that. Did Helen say she thought there was?'

'Well, Tony was a bit of a lad.'

'He loves me, he always has. He wouldn't just go off and leave me. And he loves the children.' She sat on the sofa next to her brother. 'And what about the new baby? I know something's happened to Tony, I just know it.' Her tears fell, and Alan put his arm round her heaving shoulders.

'Try not to worry, Maggs. I'm sure someone will come up with the answer soon.'

'I hope so,' she sniffed.

'Have you been over to see his mother yet?'

'No.'

'I think you should, you know how she dotes on him.'

'Yes.'

'Look, I've not got anything on next Saturday, I'll come over and pick you up and we can go and see her together. Can you get someone to have the kids?'

'I'd take them with me, they like to see Granny Ross.'

'Well, please yourself.'

'Alan, do you have a bank account?'

'That's a funny thing to ask. No, why?'

'I just wondered how you would go about finding out about one, that's all.'

'Why?' he answered quickly. 'Have you found some money?'

'No.'

'Maggs, did Tony have much money?'

'No, we've got a few bob in the Post Office, but I wondered if he might have put some in a bank.'

'If he did there would be a bank book to tell him what he had. Have you looked for anything like that?'

She nodded.

'And did you find one?'

'No.'

'Then I think you can safely say that Tony hasn't got a bank account.' He stood up. 'Look, I'd better be going. Helen might start moaning if I'm late for dinner.' He kissed her cheek. 'Take care, see you next week.'

Maggie stared at the door, thinking Alan didn't really seem all that worried about her, but what did she expect him to do? And what about when the new baby arrived? How would she manage? She put her head in her hands and wept.

Chapter 8

The following morning Maggie decided she wouldn't wait till the next Saturday for Alan to go with her to Tony's mother, she'd go today. Who knew, Bella might even have some idea where to try next.

'After dinner,' she said to Laura and Jamie while they were finishing their breakfast, 'I think we should go and see Granny Ross.'

'Goody,' shouted Jamie. 'She's always got lots of sweets in her house.'

'I like Granny Ross. She told me that when we get a garden she was going to buy me a puppy.' Laura got down from the table and helped Maggie to take the dirty dishes into the kitchen.

Maggie shuddered. That was the trouble with Bella Ross – she was a very generous woman but sometimes her generosity could get out of hand. 'Well, we haven't got a garden, so we can't have a puppy,' said Maggie crossly.

'Will Daddy be there?' asked Jamie.

'I don't think so.'

'Mummy, has Daddy gone away for ever and ever?' asked Laura.

'Course not.' Maggie was busy at the sink washing up.

'Some of the kids at school said he's gone to prison.'

Maggie spun round, still holding the wet washing-up mop aloft. The water ran down her arm. 'Who said that?'

'Some of the bigger kids.'

'Well, you tell them it ain't true. And I'll be up that school giving them a bit of my mind if they keep spreading stories like that.' She continued washing up aggressively. That afternoon, dressed in their best clothes, they took the train to Downham.

For the second time in just over a week Maggie was walking down a tree-lined road though this time there were neat council houses either side. Laura and Jamie went skipping on ahead to Granny Ross's house. The thought kept invading Maggie's mind that it would be a lot better for them if they did have a garden and somewhere to play other than the market. Just because she and Tony had been brought up in Rotherhithe didn't mean their children shouldn't have the right to play on green fields. She wondered if she had been selfish over this. When Tony came back they would definitely start to make plans.

Bella Ross was standing at her front door when Maggie walked up the path.

'Maggie, Maggie love. What a lovely surprise! It's lovely to see you.' She threw her arms round Maggie and clutched her to her ample bosom. 'The kids went straight through to the garden. Anyway, how are you all?'

'We're all right. What about you? How's the leg?'

'See, I'm managing fine without me stick, but only for short distances.' She looked up the road. 'Tony not with you?'

Maggie was pleased the children had gone ahead, she didn't want them blurting it out. 'No, not today. Shall we go in?'

'Course. Let's go in the kitchen.'

Maggie followed her down the passage and into a bright modern kitchen.

'I'll put the kettle on. Look at those two out there,' said Bella, gazing out of the kitchen window and smiling. 'You'll have to let them come over for a week in the summer holidays; you'll need a break as you get nearer your time. Sit yourself down.' She pulled out a chair from under the table. 'How are you keeping then, love? And where's that son of mine got to?' Bella Ross spoke with such warmth Maggie was made speechless.

'I don't know quite how to tell you this . . . but . . .'

'What is it? You look worried.' Bella sat down, her face ashen. 'It's Tony, ain't it? It's me boy. What's he bin up to? He ain't in the nick, is he?'

Maggie shook her head. 'No.'

Bella put her hand to her mouth. 'Oh my God, it's worse? It's worse?' she repeated. Tears filled her eyes and ran down her cheeks. 'What's happened to him?' She clasped Maggie's hand. 'He's in hospital?' When Maggie didn't answer she whispered, 'He ain't dead, is he? Tell me he ain't dead.'

Maggie too had tears in her eyes. 'I don't know,' she whispered. 'I really don't know.'

Bella dabbed at her eyes. She sat up. 'What d'you mean, you don't know?'

Maggie swallowed hard. She gently patted Bella's rough work-worn hand. 'He's been missing for over three weeks, and nobody seems to know where he's gone.'

91

Bella pulled her hand away and jumped to her feet. 'Three weeks, and you've only just come over here to tell me!'

'But—'

Bella wasn't listening to Maggie. 'Three weeks, and what have you done to find him?'

Maggie wanted to shout at her to sit down and listen. To tell her her son wasn't a baby, that he should've let her know what was happening, that she was worried sick too – but instead she said quietly, 'I've been to the police . . .'

'The police!' screamed Bella. 'The police! Why?'

'I thought they could help me.'

'And what did they have to say?'

'Not a lot. I even had to go and look at a body they'd taken out of the docks.'

'Oh my God.' Bella quickly sat down again. 'Who was it?'

'I don't know.'

'That must have been awful for you.'

'Yes it was. Mum, do you know if Tony . . . well, has he been in trouble before?'

'Trouble? What d'yer mean, trouble?'

'I don't know. I went to see Wally at the auction rooms and he was telling me that him and Tony used to do deals, and I was wondering—'

'Don't talk daft, girl. All traders do deals.'

'I know. But what if he'd upset someone?'

'Christ, they wouldn't take him away just for doing a deal. Why, my old man was one of the biggest rogues under the sun, but he never put himself or me in any danger. Na, I think you're barking up the wrong tree there, love.'

'But where do I go from here?'

Bella poured out the tea. 'You wanner go and see Benny. He'll tell you if there's any funny business going on.'

'I went to see him last week.'

Bella slammed the teapot on the table. 'What? You went and saw him before coming to tell me?'

'I didn't know who to turn to. Besides, I wanted some stuff for the stall.'

'So, who else knows?'

'Well, all the market, and Eve and Dan.'

'Never trusted that Eve. She was always flaunting herself. Bit of a tart if you ask me. You know I thought that there was something going on between her and my Tony at one time.'

Maggie tossed her head in the air. 'That was a long while ago, before we got married.'

'You know about it?'

'Course, Tony told me. But I've never said anythink to anybody, didn't see the point.'

'Yer, s'pose you're right. I wonder what your brother will say?'

Maggie thought before she answered that. She didn't want Bella to know that she was the last to hear about Tony, so she said nonchalantly, 'I'm going to see him next Saturday.'

'Oh. I bet that stuck-up snotty-nosed wife of his will have a thing or two to say about it.'

'I expect she will,' said Maggie wistfully.

'Now about Tony. I can't believe he's just gone off and left you and the kids.'

'Neither can I. I was hoping he might have got in touch with you.'

'I would have clipped him round the ear and sent him packing if he had.'

'That's what I mean. I really do think something must have happened to him.'

Bella wiped her eyes. 'Course not. Look, we'll have to put our thinking caps on. Now what can we do next to find him?'

'I wish I knew.'

'So, who was the last to see him?'

'Mr Goldman. He saw him at the station, said he was catching a train.'

'Catching a train?' repeated Bella. 'Did he ask him where he was going?'

'You know Mr Goldman, he don't ask things like that.'

'Pity he ain't nosy like the rest of us and asked him where he was off to.'

Maggie played with the spoon. 'Mr Goldman thought he had gone to look at a cottage.'

'A cottage? Where?'

'You know, the one he's always on about in his mind.'

Bella laughed. 'Always had fancy ideas, that boy of mine. D'you think he went there, wherever it is?'

'It wouldn't take him three weeks.'

'No, love, you're right.'

'I'm worried that he might be lying in some hospital, you know, lost his memory or somethink.'

'I suppose that is a possibility, but surely he would have had some kind of identification on him.'

'That's what Eve and the Inspector said.'

Bella sat back. 'Three weeks you say? So how you managing?'

'Bill's been running the stall, and I'll have to do the buying till he comes back.'

'Yes, I suppose you will.' Bella looked thoughtful. 'Don't worry, Benny will help you on that score, he'll come up with some bits.' She gave a little smile. 'D'you know, he asked me to marry him after Jim died?'

'We always knew he was fond of you. So why didn't you?'

'He's nice bloke but he's been on his own for too long. 'Sides, I couldn't put up with his horse shitting in the garden.'

They both gave a little half-hearted laugh.

The back door was pushed open. 'Granny, can we have a drink?'

'Course you can, my boy. Tell Laura to come and get it.'

'OK,' and with that Jamie ran away.

Bella stood watching them. 'They're a couple of nice kids. You must be very proud of them.'

'Yes I am,' said Maggie. 'We both are, and that's why I don't think Tony has gone away of his own free will.'

'You could be right, love. I'm sorry to say it, but you could be right. But who would take him? 'Sides, what was he doing catching a train?'

'I only wish I knew.'

'He can't just disappear. Ain't you any idea who he could have gone to see?'

Maggie shook her head. 'I don't know where to turn without him. If he don't come back soon I'll have to find the rent and everythink else.'

Bella looked sad. 'You shouldn't be worrying like this, not in your condition. You shouldn't have to be the breadwinner. But you have got to think of what to do now. Taking care of yourself and the kids is a big responsibility for your young shoulders.'

For a while they were both silent with their own thoughts.

When it was time for them to leave Bella pushed two pounds into Maggie's hand.

'I can't take this,' she protested.

'Yes you can. I don't want you to worry about money as well, I've got a few bob tucked away.'

'Bella, have you ever had a bank account?'

She laughed. 'What the bloody hell would I want with a bank account? No, love, you always want ter get the cash in yer hand, then when you've spent it no one can take it away.' She kissed Maggie and the children. 'Now I don't expect you to come traipsing over here every couple of days, so drop me a line, and when that son of mine walks his arse in, you send him over to me to sort out, and I'll tell yer, he'll get more than a clip round the ear for making you, and me, worry like this.'

Maggie kissed her mother-in-law's cheek. 'Thanks. Take care.'

They waved back for as long as they could.

Well, thought Maggie, that was another hurdle over. In some ways she felt sorry for Tony, for when he did come back everybody would be having a go at him. She smiled. But he'd grin and with his winning ways he'd talk himself out of it. And in the meantime, financially, she'd have to manage, just like Bella said.

On Monday morning Maggie was surprised to see Inspector

Matthews walking round the market. She hadn't spoken to him for over a week and thought the police had lost interest in Tony by now.

'Is there any news?' she asked casually.

'I'm afraid not.'

Maggie could see some of the stallholders going into a huddle and looking at her suspiciously.

'Do any of Mr Ross's relations live round here?'

Maggie began walking back to her flat. 'No, his mother lives at Downham, but she don't know where he is.'

'You've told her then?' said the Inspector as he slowly walked along with her.

'Yes.' They reached her front door. 'Would you like to come up for a cup of tea?'

'That would be very nice. Thank you.'

They went up, Maggie pushed open the door and Inspector Matthews took off his grey trilby and placing it on the chair, smoothed down his dark straight hair with both hands.

Maggie went into the kitchen to put the kettle on. 'It's warm today,' she shouted out.

'Yes, it is,' he replied.

He pointed at the photo of the children when she walked in.

'They're a fine pair.'

'Thank you. Are you married?'

'No, not now. I lost my wife a few years ago.'

'I'm sorry,' said Maggie quickly.

'She caught TB.' For a fleeting moment he looked sad. 'We didn't have any children.'

'Would you have liked some?'

97

'Yes. They make a home, don't you think?'

Maggie laughed nervously. 'I don't know about make it, they're very good at wrecking it.'

'I'm sure that's not true. You have some nice pieces up here.'

Maggie felt like kicking herself. Had he only come up so that he could have another look round, just to make sure nothing had been pinched? 'My husband has a good eye for a bargain.'

'I can see that.'

As they sat drinking tea, Maggie was on her guard, very careful what she said to him.

He looked at his watch. 'I must be going.'

'Inspector Matthews, have you any idea what could have happened to Tony?'

'I'm afraid not.' He stood up and picked up his trilby, twirling it round in his hands.

'But he couldn't have just disappeared off the face of the earth. Someone must know where he is.' Tears welled up in her eyes. 'Have you tried the other police stations? Could he be in prison somewhere?'

'No, you'd have been told. His description has been circulated, and until someone comes up with something, I'm afraid there's not a lot we can do. Thank you for the tea.'

Maggie opened the door for him. 'Goodbye.'

When she heard the front door shut she waited a couple of minutes, then hurried down the stairs.

''Ere, Maggs, what's going on?' asked Fred, as soon as she stepped outside.

'Nothing, why?'

'What's he got to say about all this?' Fred inclined his

98

head the way she guessed the Inspector had taken.

'Not a lot. Nobody seems to have any idea what's happened to Tony.'

'Can't say I'm that pleased to have a copper nosing round here, keep asking questions.'

'Well, I ain't that pleased at having to be nice to one, but what else can I do?' Maggie tossed her head and walked on.

'All right, gel?' shouted Mrs Russell.

'Yes thanks.'

'I hope you're looking after yerself,' she said when Maggie got closer.

'Yes I am. I went over and saw Tony's mum yesterday.'

'Did you now. How's old Bella getting on? Heard she broke her leg.'

'Yes she did, but it's on the mend now.'

'That's good. She could always do a good knees-up, hate to think of her having to sit back and watch. She was a gel in her time. Always liked old Bella,' said Mrs Russell reflectively.

''Ere, Maggs,' Mr Cooper called out. Maggie walked over to his stall. 'Young Bill was telling me you've bin ter see Benny, the rag-and-bone man.'

'Yes, I had to get some more stock, why?'

'No reason. He couldn't shed any light on what's happened to Tony then?'

'No. You don't know if anybody ... well, I don't know ... had it in for him, I suppose?'

'No. It's a funny business, and I can't say I like the idea of these coppers keep popping up all the time.'

'Nobody does.' Maggie wanted to cry, to run away from all this.

''Ere, you all right, gel? You've gone a funny colour.'

'Yes, I'm all right. It's just that I don't know how this is all going to end.'

'Well one thing's certain, you've got to look after yerself and think about those kids of yours.'

'Yes I know.'

Maggie was very near to tears. But how could she look after the children and keep out of debt? She began to walk away. I suppose I could always borrow money from Alan if I was really desperate, but what would Helen have to say about that? she thought. Then there was Tony's mum — she'd said she had a few bob she could let them have. But how long would that last? She was so upset she had forgotten what she'd gone down for. She wanted to be left alone, and as she climbed back up her stairs she knew she must face the fact that she was in charge of her life until Tony came back — whenever that would be.

Chapter 9

On Saturday, when Alan arrived at Maggie's, he was very cross to learn that she hadn't waited for him to take her to Tony's mother.

'Why should I have waited? What good would it have done?' Maggie protested.

'Well, Helen thinks—'

'Alan, I don't care what Helen thinks.'

'Oh pardon me. We are only trying to give you some advice, you know.' Alan walked to the window.

'I'm sorry, it's just that I don't know which way to turn.'

'Well, what did Bella have to say about it?'

'Concerned, worried, like everyone else, but didn't have any answers.'

The babble from the market drifted up.

'And what do that lot down there think of all this?' He waved his hand at the market.

'Not a lot. They didn't like the coppers coming round asking questions, but that's dropped off a bit; we don't see them much now.'

The door was suddenly flung open and Eve came breezing

in. 'Hallo, Alan. Maggs said you might be over. Is Helen with you?'

'No, Doreen has a touch of the snuffles, and Helen didn't take her to her dancing classes.' He sat on the sofa.

Maggie felt guilty at not asking about his family. 'Is Doreen all right?' she enquired.

'Yes, but you know what a fusspot Helen is.'

Maggie smiled. 'Well, all mothers are a bit like that,' she said. But not as fussy as your wife, she thought.

'So, Alan, what's your opinion about this thing with Tony?' asked Eve, sitting next to him.

'Don't know what to think. But let's face it, he always liked to dabble in all sorts of things, didn't he?'

'So you think he might be in some sort of trouble then?' Eve crossed her long legs and blew the smoke from her cigarette high into the air.

Alan shrugged. 'Could be.' He looked at Maggie.

'D'you fancy a cup of tea?' she said quickly.

'Yes please,' said Alan and Eve together.

In the kitchen Maggie's knuckles turned white as she clenched her hands in temper. Why did everybody think Tony was up to no good? They didn't seem to care that he could have had an accident and lost his memory.

Soon after Alan finished his tea he said he had to go. As he kissed her cheek he said, 'Now don't forget, Maggs, if there's anything we can do to help, just let me know.'

'Thanks, Alan.'

'Bye, Eve.'

'Bye.'

When Alan shut the door, Eve stood up. 'Is that it? He didn't mention money.'

'I can't expect him to give me anythink. After all, he does have a lot of expenses.'

'Yer, I suppose he does.'

'Anyway, so far, thanks to Benny, I'm just about managing. Look, I must go down to Bill.'

'Course. Do you fancy coming out tonight?'

'Don't know.' She didn't feel happy at sitting in the pub without Tony and relying on everybody else to buy her drinks. Although Tony and Dan spent most of the time standing at the bar chatting and arguing with Gus over the Blackshirts and trying to put the world to rights, he always used to be there, and even after all these years when he gave her a wink and one of his smiles, her heart leapt.

'Well, think about it. Me and Dan will be over about eight.'

They walked down the stairs and out into the sunshine together.

'See you tonight,' said Eve as she went in the opposite direction to Maggie.

Maggie stood at the stall while Bill went for a pint. She watched the people coming and going, kids licking ice-cream cornets, and the mothers giving them a clout when they dropped it and started yelling. The young women who didn't have screaming kids hanging on to them were wearing pretty floral frocks. There was something about the summer that put a smile on most people's faces. She was miles away when Tom Cooper came over and stood beside her.

'Why don't you get yerself a chair? You shouldn't be standing around, not in your condition.'

She smiled. 'Thanks, Tom, but I'm all right.'

'Still no news then?'

'No.'

Tom was a real rough diamond: his thick dark bushy eyebrows that almost covered his eyes made him appear menacing. Tony always liked him, but a lot of the other stallholders didn't take to his ways, especially the fact that apart from selling material he did a few deals on the side, often undercutting them.

'Didn't like it when that copper was 'anging round.'

Maggie was getting very tired of hearing this. 'Nobody did,' she said quietly.

'I presume you've been ter see Bella?'

'Yes.'

'What's she got ter say about it?'

'Same as everybody else, but I think the novelty's wearing off round here a bit now.'

'Well, those bleeding Blackshirts shouting and yelling on the corner helps. Can't say I like what they're saying. Superrace indeed. Trouble is they keeps the punters up that end listening to 'em. If I had my way I'd run the lot of 'em out o' town.'

Maggie laughed. 'I shouldn't try if I was you. They're a lot younger and a lot fitter than you.'

'Yer, s'pose they are. But I'm a lot bigger. 'Ere, missis, keep that bloody kid of yours off me barra. Don't want bloody ice cream all over me stuff.'

A mouthful of abuse came from the mother and the child.

'And to you, ducky, as well.' He turned to Maggie. 'Don't know what the world's coming to. You wouldn't have caught me talking to an old man like that.'

Maggie laughed. 'Well, you wouldn't be hanging round a material stall for one thing.'

'Na, I'd be too busy tormenting that bloody monkey.' He pointed to the organ-grinder who was busy turning the handle on his machine, filling the market with tinny music. He was surrounded by scruffy children. 'It bites, you know?'

'Well, you shouldn't torment it. I've told Jamie and Laura to stay well away from it.'

Tom grinned. 'And I'd be pinching the apples, and making sure I didn't get another good hiding from me ma. 'Allo, Wally, what you doing round this way?'

Maggie quickly turned and was surprised to see Wally from the auction room walking towards them.

''Allo, Tom, Maggs. Just thought I'd 'ave a stroll round this way ter see how things were getting on. Tony about?'

'No,' said Tom. 'Ain't—'

Maggie quickly pulled Wally's arm. 'Look, when Bill gets back we'll go up and have a cuppa.'

'I'd rather have a pint. It's a bit warm today.'

'OK.'

'Tony in the pub?'

Maggie saw Tom open his mouth, about to speak, so she asked, 'Tom, will you keep your eye on the stall and the kids while me and Wally go up the Dog?' She wanted to tell Wally about Tony in private.

'Yer, course, Maggs.' He looked very puzzled.

They walked into the Dog and Duck, and Maggie went straight over to Bill, who was propping up the bar, making a pint last as long as possible.

'What yer having, gel?' called Wally after her as he moved towards the bar.

'Just a shandy. Bill, when you've finished could you get back to the stall? I want to have a quiet word with Wally here.'

'Was just going anyway,' said Bill quietly to Maggie. 'I've seen that bloke before. He's one of the blokes Tony's done deals with.'

'Yes I know.'

'One shandy, and a pint of the best,' said Wally, putting the drinks on the table. 'Oh, you going, son?'

'Yer, gotter get back. See yer later, Maggs.' Bill left the pub.

Maggie would rather have talked to Wally in her home but she didn't want to make a fuss.

'So,' said Wally, sitting next to her and taking the top off his beer, 'where's that old bugger got to now?'

'Wally.' Maggie looked around. Thankfully most of the other customers were deep in conversation. The sound of the Blackshirts shouting, and the traders' voices trying to sell their wares came drifting through the open door. 'Wally,' repeated Maggie, 'Tony's gone missing.'

'What?'

Wally's voice was loud, and a couple of the other customers looked over in their direction.

'What d'yer mean, missing?'

'Four weeks ago, he went out, and hasn't been seen since.'

Wally's face turned bright red. Maggie thought he was going to explode.

'But it was only, what – a couple of weeks ago – you come to the auction rooms and said—'

'Yes, I told you he was just away.'

Wally leant back in his chair. 'I thought he was in the nick.' He sat forward and his eyes narrowed menacingly. 'You sure he ain't in the nick?'

'I'm sure, all right.' Maggie wiped her brow with her handkerchief. 'It's very warm in here.'

Wally grabbed her hand. 'Now you listen to me, gel,' he hissed. 'I want the truth, d'yer hear?'

'Wally, you're hurting me.'

'And your Tony could hurt me.'

'Why? What d'yer mean?'

He sat forward and looked around. Maggie could see Gus was looking in their direction. Although she felt a little afraid, she knew she only had to shout and he would come running, but she had to find out more from Wally.

Wally lowered his voice. 'Me and him had quite a little deal going.'

'What, like you told me about?'

'Na, more than that.'

Maggie rubbed her wrist. 'What sort of deal?'

He laughed. 'I ain't saying, but did he keep any notes or books?'

'No,' she said a little too quickly.

'You sure?'

'Well, if he did I don't know where they are.'

'What about money?'

'What about it?'

'Where did he hide it?'

Maggie laughed; she didn't want him to see how worried she was. 'If he had hidden any away, I'd have soon found it.'

'You wouldn't keep anythink from me now, would you?'

'Why should I?'

'Look, why don't we go back to your flat and have a look?'

'What for? And why should I?' repeated Maggie.

''Cos I don't want anybody to find anythink that might incriminate me, savvy?'

'Why should it? Wally, have you any idea what might have happened to Tony?'

'Na. But I tell yer this: if he's tried to double-cross some of them big boys, well, it's curtains for him, that's for sure — they play very rough.'

Maggie stared at him. What had he and Tony been up to?

'And I don't wanner be mixed up in this.'

Maggie picked up her glass. 'Could somethink have happened to Tony?'

'How the bloody hell should I know? All I'm saying is, if he ain't in the nick, then where is he?'

'I wish I knew.'

'Have yer finished?'

Maggie nodded.

'Right, then let's get back to your place.'

'What for?'

'To satisfy my curiosity.'

'What about?'

'Don't argue, just do as I say.'

Maggie looked pleadingly over at Gus, but he was busy with a crowd of thirsty customers. She had no choice but to go.

Walking through the market she tried to attract some of the traders' eyes, but they were all too busy trying to outshout their rivals for punters.

Where were the children? Even they would help to dispel this situation.

As she mounted the stairs to her flat, a great feeling of doom began to settle over her. So Tony had been mixed up with some shady people. She closed the living-room door. How could she have been so blind, and where was this money?

'Right, where did he keep his papers?'

'I don't know.'

'Now come on, gel, don't play games with me.' He knelt on the floor, pulled open the door in the sideboard and rummaged through it, scattering newspapers and knitting over the floor. He stood up. 'What's this?' He held up an exercise book.

'It's the book I've been keeping. An account of what I've bought and sold, so when Tony gets back he can see what I've . . .' Her voice trailed off as he searched through the pages. She snatched it from his hand. 'Give it back, that's mine.'

'Now come on, Maggs, I don't want any trouble. Just give me Tony's books.'

Suddenly she was very afraid. They were alone together and this man was very angry. What would he do to her? 'I can't give you somethink I ain't got.'

'You better be telling me the truth.'

Should she tell him that she'd hidden them in Tony's lockup, just in case the police came looking for them? Tony, why have you put me through this hell? she asked silently.

Wally moved closer and Maggie backed away, afraid he

would hurt her. 'What's so important about them anyway?' she blurted out.

'I don't want 'em to fall in the wrong hands, so if—'

'Yoo-hoo. Maggs, it's me.' The door was pushed open and Winnie stood there, filling the doorway. 'Fred said you was back and I was wondering—'

'Hallo, Win,' Maggie said eagerly. 'This is a friend, acquaintance,' she quickly corrected herself, 'of Tony's. Wally.'

''Allo there, I've seen yer around,' Winnie said. 'You got any news of that little sod?'

'No,' Maggie answered for him.

'What's been going on? What yer been looking for?' Winnie bent down and began picking up the newspapers. 'This 'ere knitting ain't gonner stay white fer long if yer keeps chucking it on the floor.' She looked at the pattern. 'This is a pretty little jacket.'

'Yes, I've made it before, for Laura and Jamie when they were babies, remember?' said Maggie. She wanted to cry and throw her arms round Winnie's neck, she was so relieved to see a friendly face.

'I'd better be going,' said Wally. 'Now remember what I told yer?'

Maggie nodded.

When he kissed her cheek she wanted to slap his face.

'Bye, Maggs. Bye, missis. I'll let meself out.'

When they heard the front door close Maggie fell into the chair and cried.

'So,' said Winnie, 'what was all that about?'

'Oh Win, what would I do . . . I don't know . . .'

'Look, I'll put the kettle on and stay with yer fer a bit.'

'But it's Saturday – what about your stall?'

'Don't worry, they're all keeping an eye on it for me.'

Maggie blew her nose. 'But how did you know . . .?'

'First of all old Cooper said you'd gone for a drink with Wally. He said he was worried about you as Wally's a shifty sod. Then Gus come up and said he thought you'd looked uneasy in the pub. Then Fred said you'd come up here and you looked a bit peaky. So here I am large as life and twice as handsome.' She laughed.

Maggie's tears fell. The kettle began whistling and Winnie hurried into the kitchen. When she returned with the tray she sat at the table.

'Maggs, I know it ain't none of my business, but what did he want?'

Maggie too sat at the table. 'Win, he reckons Tony's mixed up with some villains.'

'So, what's it to do with him?'

'Don't really know. He wanted Tony's books in case he was in them.'

Winnie began pouring out the tea. 'And is he?'

Maggie hesitated. She wanted to confide in someone, but didn't want to put anyone else in danger. But Winnie was like a mother to her, and she could look after herself. Maggie decided to tell her everything that she knew. 'I don't know, they're in some kind of code, they don't make any sense.'

'Did you show them to him?'

'No, I've hid them in case the police want them.'

Winnie patted her hand. 'Clever gel.'

That kind gesture brought forth more floods of tears from Maggie. 'Win, I'm so frightened,' she sobbed. 'What am I gonner do?'

'First of all you're gonner drink this tea, and wipe yer eyes. Crying never solved anythink. Then you're gonner face up to this thing.'

Maggie looked up. 'What d'yer mean?'

'Well, I don't think Tony's coming back. Thought so for a bit now. Let's face it, he'd never go off and leave you and the kids, not of his own free will, now would he?'

Maggie shook her head.

'So,' continued Winnie, 'you've gotter be mother and father to your two, three when that one comes along. And you've gotter provide a roof and food. It's a pretty tall order, me gel, but you ain't the first, and you won't be the last. And if anybody offers you help, don't stand on yer high horse, you take it.'

Maggie remembered Bella had tried to tell her this, though she'd wanted to avoid facing up to it. 'Do you think he's dead?'

'Dunno what to think, but I do know if he could get in touch, he would. But remember, life's fer living, and you've gotter look after yerself.'

Maggie gave her a weak smile. She was so lucky to have someone like Winnie to lean on.

'Right, I'd better be going, and remember, gel, all that lot down there,' she waved her hand at the window, 'well most of 'em anyway, will always be around if yer want 'em.' She stood up and walked to the door. 'Oh, and by the way, if that cowson Wally ever comes round 'ere again worrying you, you send him down ter me.' She shut the door after her.

Maggie sat for a while thinking about Tony. He owed it to her and the children to come back, but till then she had to

112

do what Winnie had said. She was right. She had to get on with her life, for her children's sake as well as her own. Their future was up to her, and who knew, perhaps she could make a go of it. She could even try new things on the stall. A slight smile lifted her sad mouth. She would show Wally and the rest of them. She had to.

Chapter 10

Maggie waited until the children had finished their tea before she sat at the table. 'Now I want you both to listen very carefully. I've got something to tell you.'

'I bet I know what it is,' said Laura, her mouth turning down.

'Bet yer don't,' said Jamie.

'I bet I do. How much then?'

'Shh, the pair of you,' said Maggie.

'You're gonner tell us we ain't going to Ramsgate, ain't yer, Mum?' Laura was looking defiant.

Maggie was taken aback. With all her other problems she'd forgotten about her promise. 'No,' she smiled. 'Course we're still going. It's just that Daddy won't be coming with us.'

Jamie looked up at her, his pale blue eyes beginning to fill with tears. 'Is it 'cos Daddy's gone to prison?'

Maggie was shocked at that remark. 'No, course not. Who told you that? Was it those kids at Laura's school?'

'No, them down there.' He pointed to the window.

Maggie knew she had to try and brazen this out. 'You shouldn't be listening to the grown-ups' conversations, young man.'

'Well, where is he then?'

'I don't know.' Maggie was thinking that in some ways she wished Tony was in prison. At least then she would know his whereabouts, and that he was still alive. 'I don't know where Daddy is, he's gone away,' she said softly, holding back a sob.

'Why's he gone away then?' asked Laura.

'I don't know, but I'm sure he'll come back to us one day.'

'Don't he love us any more?'

'Of course he does.'

'Then why did he go away?' asked Jamie.

'I told you, I don't know,' Maggie's voice began to rise – she couldn't answer their questions.

'We ain't been that naughty,' said Jamie, wide-eyed.

'Well I reckon he's rotten,' said Laura. 'He didn't even bother to come and see me dance round the maypole.'

'I'm sure he would have done if he could.'

'Na,' said Jamie. 'It's too sissy fer Dad. I ain't doing it when I go ter school.'

Maggie tousled his hair.

'Don't, Mummy.'

'Come on, you can go out for a short while. Then after Bill's put the stall away and brought the money in, it's bed. I'm going up the pub with Eve and Dan for an hour or so.'

'What about us, can we come?' asked Laura.

'No you can't. I'll ask Mr Goldman to keep an ear out for you, so no running about, d'you hear?'

They both nodded vigorously.

'And then, if you're really good, perhaps tomorrow we can go and see Granny Ross.'

'Yippee!' yelled Jamie. 'I'll be good.'

'So will I,' said Laura, 'and, Mummy, can we still go to Ramsgate?'

'Course.'

Laura came and put her arms round Maggie's neck. 'You won't ever leave us, will you?'

'No, of course I wouldn't, but I will have to go away for a week or two to get this new baby, but don't worry, I'll be back.'

'Can we have a baby girl?'

'We'll have to take what they've got.'

'Can we have two?' asked Jamie, scrambling on to Maggie's lap. 'A boy and a girl? Then we've both got someone to play with.'

'I don't think they'll let me have two. Besides, it'll be very small for a long while.'

'Was we very small?' asked Jamie.

'Yes, and you were both very beautiful.'

They giggled.

'What happened to Jamie? He ain't very beautiful now.'

'Nor are you,' he said.

Maggie laughed. 'You are still very lovely, and I love you both very much.'

'How much?' asked Jamie. 'This much?' He held his arms out wide.

'Much more than that. Now, do you want to go out and play for a while before Auntie Eve gets here?'

They both scooted down the stairs. 'And don't get into any mischief,' Maggie called after them, adding to herself, 'All the love they have for us, Tony – how could you leave them?' She began clearing the tea things away before Bill brought in the takings.

★ ★ ★

Beatie gave them a wave as soon as Maggie, Eve and Don walked in the pub. It was very crowded, but Eve managed to find a seat as Dan pushed his way to the bar.

'You all right, gel?' Beatie asked, coming over to Maggie. 'Gus was dead worried about you when you came in lunchtime. He said you looked ever so upset.'

Eve glanced up. 'You was in here lunchtime?'

'I'll tell you about it in a minute,' said Maggie. 'It was good of him to tell Win.'

'Was it trouble then?' asked Beatie, worried.

'No, not really, just someone looking for Tony.'

'Did he say what he wanted?'

'No.'

'Didn't have any news then?'

'No.'

Beatie twisted a large diamond ring on her finger round and round. 'Remember, gel, we're all here to help if need be.'

'Thanks, Beatie.'

'Well, what was all that about?' asked Eve, as soon as Beatie had gone back to the bar.

Maggie told Eve everything about Wally.

'He sounds a right arsehole to me. Wait till Dan finds out about—'

'Don't say anythink to Dan,' said Maggie quickly. 'Well, not tonight anyway.'

'Why?'

'Ain't really nothing to tell.'

'OK. So where's these books then?'

'I've hid 'em.'

118

'Ain't yer gonner tell me where?' asked Eve petulantly.

'No.'

'Thanks. So after all these years—'

'Look, Eve, if you don't know, then no one can make you tell 'em.'

Eve laughed. 'Christ, Maggs, you're beginning to make it sound like somethink out of a cloak-and-dagger film.'

Maggie laughed. 'Well, you always was a nosy cow.'

'Thanks. I can just see me swearing not to tell the villains your secret.'

'Trust you to be swearing.'

They both burst out giggling.

Dan put their drinks on the table. 'What's tickling you two?'

'Not a lot,' said Eve. 'A bloke called Wally came over and brought Maggie in here lunchtime.'

'Eve, I told you—'

'Yer, so Gus was saying. He said he was worried about you.'

'Christ,' said Maggie, 'everybody's keeping their eye on me. I can see if I want to carry on with someone it'll have to be far away from me own doorstep.'

'You could try Ramsgate,' laughed Eve.

'Yer, but I'd wait till you've got rid of that lump first,' laughed Dan. 'It's a bit off-putting.'

A cheer went up when Ivy, who lived in the tenement buildings round the corner, walked in. Pints of beer were quickly put in front of her as she sat at the piano. Her large bottom hung over the piano stool, and when she played her thick arms wobbled. Her fingers, like fat sausages, pounded the keys and conversation almost ceased as everybody joined in the sing-song.

A smoky blue haze clung to the already yellowed ceiling. It hung round the dropped pendant lampshades that stuck out from the red plush walls. They hadn't been cleaned in years, so nobody knew if they were supposed to be plain or coloured glass.

Maggie felt relaxed for the first time that day. She glanced around the pub. Although it was old and in need of a coat of paint it had a warm atmosphere, and very happy memories. The large mirror behind the bar was one of Tony's finds, a typical pub mirror, very ornate with gold scrolls along the top and down the sides. Large bunches of coloured grapes were etched in every corner. She half smiled, remembering the trouble they'd had trying to fix it to the wall.

This was all such a contrast to Beatie and Gus's flat upstairs, which was well furnished and immaculate. Maggie had only been up there once, and that was when Gus used to have a poker school after hours. It had been she and Eve who, while walking home from the pictures, had overheard two policemen saying they were going to raid it. They'd run on ahead and banged on the back door. Why had she suddenly thought about that? That was years ago, long before Laura was born.

Maggie looked at her watch, it was almost ten o'clock. 'I'd better be going home,' she said to Eve.

'I'll come with you,' said Eve.

'You don't have to,' replied Maggie.

'I fancy a cuppa.'

'OK.'

'Be along in a while,' said Dan.

Maggie and Eve said their good nights to Gus and Beatie and wandered down Kelvin Market. The moon was full and the air warm.

'It's so peaceful down this end,' said Eve, as they strolled along arm in arm.

'So far. Just so long as those Blackshirts don't start any trouble.'

'Dan's been reading about all what's going on in Europe. He says things ain't that good over there. 'Ere, you don't reckon your Tony's run off and joined the army, do you?'

Maggie laughed. 'What? Can you honestly see him taking orders from anyone?'

'No,' said Eve, dismissing the idea.

'You can't believe this is the same place with all the racket that goes on in the day. It's so quiet now,' said Maggie.

'That is till chucking-out time.'

'And then with the trains up there, dogs barking and the cats fighting, and drunks singing . . .' Maggie laughed.

'Yer, well, it ain't exactly a peaceful street.'

Maggie pushed open the door to her flat and was taken aback to see Laura and Jamie sitting at the top of the stairs. 'Why ain't you in bed?'

They rushed down the stairs and, crying, flung themselves at their mother.

'What is it, what's wrong?' asked Eve, fussing round them.

'A man come and got us out of bed,' sobbed Laura.

'What?' screamed Maggie. 'Who was it? I'll kill 'im. My babies. What did he do to you? Why didn't you call Mr Goldman?'

'Mummy, Mummy,' Laura was trying to make her mother listen.

'Laura,' Eve took her to one side and sat on the stair next to her. 'Tell me what happened.'

'This man—'

'What did he look like?' yelled Maggie.

'Maggs, give her time. Let's go upstairs.'

Slowly they made their way up.

'Now sit on the sofa, both of you, and tell me and Mummy all what happened.'

'I'm gonner get the police.'

'Maggie, sit down. Let's hear what they've got to say first.'

Maggie, with tears streaming down her face, did as she was told.

The man they described must have been Wally.

'I'll kill him if he's hurt them,' said Maggie, jumping up.

'Maggie,' Eve's voice had a sharp edge to it, 'sit down and let them finish.'

'He didn't hurt us, Mummy. He said you told him he could come here, he said he was looking for Daddy's book.' Laura wiped her eyes on the bottom of her nightie.

'So why are you both crying?' asked Eve softly.

''Cos he told us our daddy was dead.' Jamie's face was ashen. With one hand he was clutching his teddy and the other was holding the front of his pyjama bottoms trying to hide the wet patch.

'The wicked bugger. The bloody wicked sod.' Maggie jumped up again.

'It ain't true, is it?' asked Laura.

'We don't know,' said Eve. 'I only wish we did.'

'We told him our daddy didn't have any books, he only reads the newspapers.'

Maggie knelt down and threw her arms round her daughter's neck. She wanted to laugh at the innocent words.

Jamie pushed his way into Maggie's arms.

'I'll make a cup of tea,' said Eve, going into the kitchen. While she stood waiting for the kettle to boil, she cried softly to herself. 'Please come back to them, Tony,' she wept, 'they desperately need you.'

When Dan came to collect Eve, the children were tucked up in bed. When she told him all that had happened he was outraged.

'You say he works at the auction rooms?' He began pacing the floor and balling his fist. 'I'll go over there Monday and have a word with him.'

'But, Dan,' said Maggie, 'we've got no proof it was him.'

'Why didn't Mr Goldman come up?' asked Dan, still pacing up and down.

'The children are told not to make any noise,' said Maggie.

'And it was that bloody bloke telling them Tony was dead that upset 'em,' said Eve.

'Look, I'm taking 'em to see Bella tomorrow and I'll tell her what happened. She'll know how to deal with him,' said Maggie.

'Hmm,' said Dan, 'I still reckon I ought to go and see him and knock his block off.'

'Well, he didn't take anything,' said Maggie. 'But I wish he hadn't said that to the kids.'

'You look tired,' said Eve. 'If you want me to stay the night, I will.'

'I'll be all right.'

'I'll pop over tomorrow night then,' said Eve.

'OK.' Maggie kissed Eve's cheek.

When they left Maggie sat on the sofa and let her mind drift to Tony. Could there have been some little thing in the past she had forgotten about? If only she had taken more interest in some of his dealings. But in many ways Tony played his cards close to his chest, said he didn't want to bother her with his business deals. Why was Wally so worried about those books? Tony had always been a wheeler-dealer like his father before him – it went with the job – but were some of these transactions so big as to warrant this behaviour from Wally? On Monday she would go and see Benny again. There had to be more to all this than anybody was letting on.

She looked in at the children. Jamie was tossing and turning. This had upset him. 'Please don't wet the bed again,' she whispered.

'Mummy.' Laura sat up.

Maggie went to sit on the end of her bed. 'Now come on, settle down.'

'If Daddy's dead why ain't we been to his funeral?'

Maggie gazed down at her daughter. She had been busy working this out for herself. 'We don't know if he is,' said Maggie, holding back her tears.

'But that man said—'

'Shh, you don't want to wake Jamie.'

'But, Mummy—'

'I know that's what that man said, but we don't know if it's true.' Slowly a tear trickled down Maggie's cheek. 'Now come on, you've got to be bright to see Granny Ross tomorrow.'

'I like Granny Ross. Mummy, what was our other Granny like?'

'Very kind. My mum and dad would have loved you two.'

'Her name was Laura, wasn't it?'

Maggie nodded. This conversation was so painful.

'Do I look like her?'

'No, you look like your dad. Now sleep. I'm going to bed, so don't disturb me till the morning.' Maggie kissed Laura's forehead. At the doorway she turned to blow her a kiss.

'Mummy, what if that man comes back again tonight?'

'He won't.'

Maggie closed the bedroom door. She went downstairs and wound the front door key, which hung on a piece of string behind the letter box, round and round the lock. Nobody was coming in without her knowing. As Winnie had said, Maggie had to be both father and mother to her children now, and nobody was going to harm them.

Chapter 11

Bella's dark eyes were blazing with anger. 'That Wally's a rotten sod, telling the kids Tony's dead. I'd like ter get my hands on him. I'd make him squirm, walking into your place, nosing about. My poor little darlings, fancy upsetting 'em like that.' Bella sniffed as she put a plate of biscuits and two glasses of lemonade on to a tray, then fished in her overall pocket for her handkerchief to blow her nose. 'And you say he wanted to see that book?'

'It seems like it.'

''Ere, take these out to the kids. Tell 'em they're having a picnic, that'll please 'em.'

'Thanks, Bella,' Maggie smiled, and quickly returned from the garden with the empty tray.

'Benny ain't come up with any ideas then?' asked Bella, who was sitting at the table looking very pensive.

'Not yet. I'm gonner go and see him in the morning,' Maggie sighed, and a tear ran down her face. 'What am I gonner do? I'm so miserable.'

Bella moved her chair closer. 'Well, I'm glad you brought this lot over to me.' She tapped her son's book and notes that were lying on the table. 'Nobody will get their hands on 'em over 'ere, only over my dead body.'

'Please, don't say that.'

'Sorry, Maggs, but I think we've gotter face up to it. I reckon Wally's right: Tony must 'ave been mixed up in some real dodgy business, and he's either laying very low till it all blows over, or,' she hesitated for a moment, 'he's dead.'

Maggie sniffed. 'Let's look through these together. Perhaps between us we can make some sense of 'em.'

They read through everything, trying to tie up figures, dates and names, and although some made sense, with most of them they just drew a blank.

Maggie sat back and threw the pencil on to the table. 'If only I could find a bank book, or something like that, then I would know how much money we're talking about.'

Bella rubbed her eyes. 'What sort of place has Wally got now?'

'Very nice, so Tony always reckoned when he went over there to play cards.'

'Did he go very often?'

'A couple of times a month, I s'pose – never took that much notice.'

'Could he have got a posh place on his wages?'

'Dunno. Unless his wife has money.'

'Never liked him, or her, stuck-up cow, always had plenty to say, tried to make out she was better than us market traders.'

Maggie laughed. 'Sounds a bit like Helen, my sister-in-law.'

'Yer, but your brother ain't bent! Wally's sort are for ever looking for a deal. Mind you it's always been like that on that market.' Bella sat back. 'My old man could be a right sod at times, but I always made sure I knew all what went on.'

'Did he ever get into trouble?'

'Always made sure he kept one step in front of the law.'

'Has the market changed much since his days?'

'Na, only the people. Had some right characters through that market, and a lot of poor buggers as well. Don't forget there's been a war and a depression. It was bloody hard in the twenties to make a living, not like today – you lot 'ave got it easy. I only wish I could get out and about more. I'd go and sort that Wally out. Bloody leg.'

'Well, wait till it's better. Then you can go and sort him and his missis out. I tell you what, in August, after Laura's broken up for the holidays, I'm taking 'em to Ramsgate for a few days. Why don't you come with us?'

'I'd like that, Maggs. That'll be real nice. I'll pay me way.'

'I hope so,' Maggie grinned and stood up. 'We best be going, it's school for madam tomorrow.'

'How you managing, gel?'

'Not too bad at all, thanks to Benny. He managed to let me have some stuff at a good price.'

Bella smiled. 'I'll always have a soft spot for him.'

'So why don't you marry him?'

Bella screwed up her nose. 'Could you honestly see me living over that stable?'

Maggie shook her head and laughed. 'No, definitely not.'

'That bloody horse of his should have been in the knacker's yard years ago.' Bella moved to her dresser drawer. 'Here, treat the kids.' She put a ten-shilling note in Maggie's hand.

Maggie gasped. 'I can't take this.'

'Course you can.'

'You gave me some money last week. I don't want you to think I only come over here—'

'Give it a rest. Christ, if I can't do something for you lot, well then Gawd help me.' Bella stopped. 'Remember, you're all I've got now.'

'But—'

Bella sniffed. 'Save it towards the kids' holiday.'

Maggie gathered the children from the garden and made her way to the front door. 'Thanks. I'll let you know if anythink happens.'

'Bye, kids. Bye, Maggs, take care.'

As Maggie walked to the station she felt a great love for Bella. She was right, Tony would never leave her or his mother, not of his own free will. So where was he?

When they turned the corner into Kelvin Market, Laura and Jamie ran on ahead laughing. But Maggie was filled with alarm when, after reaching their front door they came running back, their faces full of fear.

'The front door's open,' shouted Laura. 'I hope that man ain't inside again.'

Maggie hurried to her door and with the children hiding behind her, carefully pushed it open. She gasped. 'Mr Goldman, what are you doing here? What's happened?'

The children poked their heads round Maggie's skirt and cried out in fright.

The old man was sitting on the bottom of the stairs, blood running down the side of his face. 'I fell over,' he croaked. 'I was hoping to get back inside before you came home.' He began to struggle to his feet.

'What are you doing in here?' asked Maggie.

'I didn't know you was out, and when I heard a noise coming from your place . . .' He swayed and held on to the wall.

'Someone's been here?'

He nodded.

'Was it Eve?'

'No, it was a short stocky grey-haired man.'

'What?' screamed Maggie. 'That bloody bloke, I'll kill him.'

'You know him?' asked Mr Goldman, looking confused.

Maggie nodded. 'Did he say what he wanted?'

'I didn't get a chance to ask.'

'Mummy! Mummy!' screamed Laura. 'That's the man what come into us last night, ain't it? Mummy, I'm frightened,' she cried, clinging to Maggie.

'He's been here before?' asked Mr Goldman, clutching his handkerchief to his forehead.

'Yes, he came here last night.'

Jamie was squeezing Maggie's hand. 'I'm gonner go and find a copper, I'll have him put away for hitting you.'

'He didn't really hit me, he just pushed me, but it shook me up a little.'

'Well, if you're sure.' Maggie looked down at this poor fragile man sitting holding his head. She wanted to scream. How could anyone do this? What the hell had Tony been up to to bring this grief to so many? 'Do you mind if I just pop up to make sure everything's all right?' she suddenly asked. 'You kids stay down here and look after Mr Goldman.'

Maggie was breathless and uncomfortable as she mounted the stairs. She was also beginning to get very angry. How dare this man walk into her home? She should have removed the key, but nobody carried their door key with them in Kelvin. Should she tell the police?

She pushed open the living-room door. It was as she expected. Everything had been pulled out of the sideboard and scattered over the floor. She quickly pushed it all back. 'If I get my hands on him I'll wring his bloody neck,' she said, storming into the children's room. The contents of the drawers were scattered over the bed. She hurriedly put them back, too. There was no point in the children seeing this; it would only upset them. She closed her bedroom door on the mess in there that she would have to sort out later.

She put on a forced smile as she made her way down the stairs.

'Everything all right?' enquired Mr Goldman.

'Yes, there's nothing to worry about. Now let me get you back into your shop and see to that cut,' said Maggie, taking his arm.

'Thank you, that's very kind of you.'

Slowly they made their way into the tailor's.

'Laura, take that stuff off that chair,' said Maggie.

'Where shall I put it?'

'On the counter.' Maggie guided Mr Goldman to the chair. 'I'll get some hot water and a towel and bathe your head.'

'That's very kind of you. Everything is in the kitchen,' he smiled weakly. 'But really, I'm fine.'

Maggie very gently wiped the blood away; the cut didn't appear to be very deep. 'That's better. It don't look too bad. Now, are you sure you're all right?' she asked, straightening up.

'Yes thank you. Would you like a cup of tea?'

'I'll see to it in a minute. First of all just tell me what happened.'

'Well, I heard this noise, and when I saw your front door was ajar, I pushed it open wider and called out. You understand, I was just enquiring to make sure you were all right. I know you don't let the children bang about like that, and I was wondering if perhaps you might have been taken ill or something, and were trying to attract my attention.'

Maggie smiled. He was such a kind old man.

'When I looked up the stairs I saw this man, short and stocky, like I said. And he had bushy hair.'

Laura cried out, 'It is him, Mummy, it is him.' Her eyes were full of fear. 'Is he still upstairs?'

Jamie was at his mother's side, holding on to her hand.

'Course not,' said Maggie light-heartedly. 'Just been up there, ain't I?'

'He ran down the stairs when I called out. He pushed me to one side, and that's how I hurt my head. I'm sorry, I shouldn't have been so nosy.'

'You weren't nosy. I'm glad you was here.'

'He woke us up last night,' said Jamie, gripping Maggie's hand very tight.

'He did?' asked Mr Goldman.

'I was out and he came in the flat,' said Maggie.

'Did he steal anything?'

'No, he's looking for something of Tony's.'

'Is it very valuable?'

'No.'

'Just an old book, so he said,' piped up Laura.

'How did he know I was out today?'

133

Jamie gave a little sob. 'It was me. I told him we was going to see Granny Ross. I'm ever so sorry.'

Maggie put her arm round him and held him close. 'You mustn't be sorry, it wasn't your fault.'

'You'd better take your key off the string,' said Mr Goldman, 'just in case he comes back again.'

Maggie felt Jamie's body tighten. 'Yes, I suppose I should, but it's such a job getting up and down those stairs every time somebody calls.'

'I could have your key, and you can tell your friends to get it off of me.'

'Would you mind?'

He tapped her hand. 'Course not. Anything to help.'

'Thank you, I'll do that right away. I'll put your kettle on first, then we can have that cup of tea.'

'There's still no news of Tony then?' Mr Goldman called to Maggie, who'd gone to the kitchen.

'No,' she said walking back.

'I wish I'd have asked him where he was going that day.'

'You weren't to know you might have been the last to . . .'

'There, there, love, you mustn't think the worst. Now, what about this tea?'

Over tea Maggie told Mr Goldman that this afternoon she had been to see Bella.

'Ah Bella,' said Mr Goldman. 'A lovely woman. Everybody on this market loved Bella.' He leant forward. 'Do you know, when she was young she had wonderful long black hair. And those eyes. They would flash with temper, or sparkle with happiness.' He sighed. 'All of us young bloods were in love with her.'

Laura giggled. 'What, my granny?'

'Yes, my dear. We were all young once,' said Mr Goldman pensively. 'And your granny was a very beautiful woman. D'you know you could almost span her tiny waist with two hands.'

Maggie smiled. 'I know, I've seen photographs of her.'

'And are you keeping well, my dear?' he asked Maggie.

'Not too bad. This business with Wally has shaken me up a bit, and this warm weather don't help. I'll be glad when September's here.'

'Mummy's taking us to Ramsgate in the holidays,' said Laura.

'That'll be nice for you. Would you like me to come up and sit with you this evening?'

Maggie smiled. 'No, thanks all the same, but I'll be all right. Eve's coming round very soon. Come on, kids, bed. I'm very sorry, Mr Goldman, that this happened.'

'You ain't going out again and leaving us, are you?' asked Jamie in alarm.

'No, love, course not. Bye, Mr Goldman, and thank you for the tea.'

'You look after yourself, young lady, and remember, I'm always here.'

'Thanks,' she said as she ushered the children through the shop door, and she meant it.

'Yoo-hoo, Maggs. Come on, open the door.' Eve was rattling the letter box.

'Just coming,' said Maggie, as she plodded down the stairs.

'What's the game?' asked Eve, looking behind the door. 'Where's the key?'

'I'll tell you upstairs.'

'Well, if you ask me it's a bit daft you traipsing up and down these stairs every time somebody comes to your door.'

'I'll tell you why when I get me breath back.'

Eve threw her handbag on the table. 'Now what's all this about?'

'I'll put the kettle on.'

'You sit down, you look all in. You all right?'

Maggie sunk into a chair and, shaking her head, let a tear slowly trickle down her cheek.

'Maggs, Maggie, what is it?' Eve was on her knees in front of her friend.

Maggie went into detail of all what had happened that afternoon.

Eve jumped up. 'That sod again. I'm sorry, Maggs, but I reckon Dan'll be round there in the morning giving him what for.'

'I'd rather he didn't get mixed up in all this. I'm gonner see Benny first thing, then I'm going to the police.'

'D'you think that's wise?'

Maggie looked surprised. 'Why?'

'Dunno. It's such a mess. Did he find those books?'

'No, I took them over to Bella this afternoon.'

'So that's why you've taken the key away now? It's a bit late, though, ain't it?'

Maggie nodded. 'I didn't expect him back. Till I get another one cut, if at any time I ain't in, Mr Goldman's got a key.'

'Poor old devil, I bet that shook him up.'

'Yes it did, and it didn't do me a lot of good, I can tell yer.'

Eve took a deep breath and looked directly into her friend's eyes. 'Maggie, I think you've got to come to the conclusion Tony ain't coming back, and you've got to start looking after yourself, and those two.' She inclined her head towards the children's bedroom. 'And that new one as well.'

'At the moment I don't feel as if I've got the strength to go on.'

'You'd better find it then, me gel.' Eve threw her arms round Maggie's neck. 'Remember, I'm always here for you.'

Maggie couldn't answer.

Eve held her tight as deep heart-breaking sobs racked Maggie's body.

I'd take a deep breath and looked directly into Jframe's eyes, 'Maggie, I think you've got to come to the cockshop.' Kitty sat rocking back, and you've got to start looking after yourself, and those two.' She inclined her head towards the children's bedroom. 'And that, as well.'

'All the more reason I don't feel as if I've got the strength to go.'

'Nfar'd better find it then, me pet.' I've thrown her arms round Maggie's neck. 'Remember, I'm always here for you.'

Maggie couldn't answer.

I've held her tight as deep heart-breaking sobs racked Maggie's body.

Chapter 12

As the police station was en route to Benny's rag-and-bone yard, Maggie decided to go there first.

'Could I speak to Inspector Matthews, please?' she asked the fresh-faced policeman standing behind the desk reading through some papers.

He looked up. 'What's it in connection with?'

'My husband. Tony Ross.'

'Oh yer. Just a moment.' He disappeared through a door behind his counter.

Almost immediately another door was opened and Inspector Matthews came striding towards her. He held out his hand and shook hers warmly. 'Mrs Ross. How nice to see you. Any news?'

'No. Could we go somewhere and talk?'

'Course. Follow me.'

Once again Maggie was in his office.

'Please, take a seat.' He pushed a chair towards her. 'What's brought you here to see me? And where's your little chap?'

'Winnie's looking after him.'

'I see. Now, how can I help you?'

As Maggie started to tell him about Wally walking into her flat, she began to wish she hadn't been so hasty in coming here. She didn't mention his name as she was suddenly frightened of telling the Inspector too much.

He sat back in his chair, turning his pencil over and over in his hands.

Maggie noted his hands looked soft, so different from Tony's and most of his mates'.

'So what you're saying is that this man, who you say you don't know, came to your flat looking for something of your husband's, and accidentally pushed Mr Goldman to one side, causing him to cut his head?'

Maggie nodded. When he repeated her story it sounded very trite.

'How do you know he was only looking for something of your husband's?'

'That's what he told Mr Goldman.'

'So what was it that was so important?'

'I don't know. He didn't tell him.' Maggie began fiddling with her handbag. She could feel a flush creeping up her throat.

'Did he take anything?'

She shook her head.

'And what does Mr Goldman want to do about this assault?'

'Oh nothing, he doesn't know I'm here.'

'And you are quite sure this man didn't take any of your belongings?'

Maggie lowered her head, suddenly feeling very silly. 'No.'

'I'm sorry, Mrs Ross, but I don't understand why you're telling me this if nobody wants to do anything about it.' He leant forward. 'And you are certain you don't know who he was?'

Maggie shook her head. 'I'm sorry, I'm only wasting your time.' She wasn't going to tell him about Wally scaring the children the night before. She went to stand up.

He threw his pencil on his desk. 'Just a moment. So you think this could have some bearing on your husband's disappearance?'

'I don't know.'

'And you don't have any idea who broke into your flat? How long has your husband been gone now?'

'Over a month.'

'And you've heard nothing?'

Maggie shook her head. 'I'd better be going.' This time she rose to her feet quickly.

Inspector Matthews was also on his feet. 'I'll call in later and have a quick look round.'

'I'll be out for a while.'

He smiled. 'Anywhere interesting?'

'No, only to see Benny, the totter, to see if he has anything I can sell on the stall.'

'You wanner watch him, he's a bit of an old reprobate.'

'Benny's a kind man.'

'Yes I know, but I still wouldn't trust him. How are you managing?'

'Not too bad. Not used to being the breadwinner. I must go,' she said quickly. 'Bye.'

'Bye, Mrs Ross. I'll be round this afternoon, if that's all right with you?'

Maggie nodded, and closed the door. She wished she hadn't come to see him. It hadn't solved anything.

★ ★ ★

As the door closed David Matthews sat back down in his chair and lit a Park Drive cigarette. Maggie Ross was a lovely young woman. What had that husband of hers been up to? And where was he? Was there another woman? If not, why would he just go off and leave her and those smashing kids? And with another on the way. He tapped the end of his cigarette into the ashtray, his thoughts wandering. Maybe Tony Ross had been involved in something really dodgy. Perhaps he had welshed on a deal. There were plenty of villains in this area who would think nothing of doing away with anyone that upset them. Could he be lying in some warehouse with his skull bashed in, or in a sack at the bottom of the river? Was there anywhere else he could go to try and find out about what had happened to the man? Why, after bothering to come here, didn't Mrs Ross tell him who had come looking for something in her flat? He was certain she knew exactly who it was, but it couldn't have been one of the usual band of thugs – they would have taken everything.

He sat back and drew heavily on his cigarette. He had to admit he hadn't been too worried about this case. Foolishly he'd let his enquiries go cold as he had always assumed Tony Ross would turn up. But now, after all this time there had to be something more to all this, and he had to try to get a few answers. He stubbed out his cigarette aggressively and, taking his grey trilby from the hat stand, left his office. Maybe Benny the totter would provide a clue.

'You look done in,' said Benny, as Maggie slumped into a chair.

'I was a bit worried you might be out,' she said, pushing the damp strands of hair from her forehead.

'Would have been if Nellie had behaved herself. Don't think she wanted to go out today. Played about somethink rotten when I tried to put her harness on, so I thought: bugger it, let's have a day orf.'

Maggie smiled. 'I'm glad you did.'

'Now love, I expect you want a cuppa, don't you?'

Maggie nodded.

'Well, after that we'll go down and take a look at my stock. I've got a few nice little pieces I think you might be interested in.' Benny warmed the teapot and, after putting the carefully measured amount of tea in, added the boiling water.

'You ain't heard nothink more about Tony, I suppose?' asked Maggie.

'No, can't say I 'ave. I've asked around, but no joy so far.'

'Benny, Wally from the auction rooms paid me a visit on Saturday and again Sunday.'

Benny sat at the table next to Maggie. 'He did? What'd he want?'

'I didn't see him. I was out when he came. He woke the kids up and told 'em Tony was dead.'

Benny sat back and looked at her. 'He did what?' he said slowly, and his voice was full of anger. 'The wicked sod. What'd he do that for?'

'He said he was looking for Tony's books.'

'Did he find them?'

Maggie shook her head. 'He came back again on Sunday when I was over Bella's. He pushed poor old Mr Goldman over and cut his head.'

Benny tutted loudly and began pouring out the tea. 'Always said that Wally Marsh was a bad one. Is the old boy all right?'

'A bit shook up, but he's fine. I went to the police station before I came here.'

'And what did they have to say?'

'I felt a bit of a fool, really. I didn't tell the Inspector who it was, because, well, I was frightened to. I think I was wasting Inspector Matthews's time. But I was so angry with Wally, walking into my place like that.'

'He ain't got no right ter do that. I wish I was younger – I'd teach him a thing or two. You'll have to take yer key away from behind the door, love.'

'I've done that. Benny, what did Wally and Tony get up to? And why does he want those books?'

'Where are they now?'

'At Bella's.'

Benny smiled. 'D'yer know, I'd like to go over and see her sometime.'

'Why don't you? She'd be pleased to see you.'

'I might just do that one Sunday. Could always give her a hand with her garden.'

'Benny, about these books? They must be important. Did Tony ever tell you . . .?' Maggie began to toy with her spoon. 'Tony always liked you, you know.'

Benny pushed his greasy trilby back and scratched his forehead. 'Yer, I know. He loved a chat.' He stopped and looked up. 'Someone's coming up the stairs.' He rushed to the door and threw it open. 'Yer, what d'yer want?'

'Just a chat, Benny, just a chat.' Without being invited, David Matthews walked in.

'Mrs Ross,' he said politely, and removed his hat.

'Benny, you know Inspector Matthews?' said Maggie.

'Yer,' growled Benny. 'Well, what d'yer want this time?'

'As I said, just a chat.'

'Do you want me to go?' Maggie stood up.

'No, course not,' said David Matthews. 'Any tea left in that pot?' he asked Benny.

'You've got a bloody cheek. I'll just put a drop o' water on these leaves.'

'Thanks.'

'Well, what did yer want to chat about?' said Benny, banging the teapot on the table.

'About Tony Ross really.'

Benny sat down. 'Don't yer think if I knew anythink I'd tell this here little lass? Known her fer years, I have, and I wouldn't keep anythink from her.'

'I believe that. But what I would really like to know is who he did deals with.'

'How would I know?'

'Oh come on, Benny, everybody knows what you get up to. You must have heard something.'

Benny began to pour out the tea. 'All I know is that Tony, and Wally at the auction room, was mixed up in somethink. Don't think it was anythink big, mind, and that's *all* I know.'

David Matthews sat back. 'Was that who came poking his nose round your place?' he asked Maggie.

She nodded.

'Now listen,' said Benny. 'Don't you go telling him it was Maggie what put you up to this. You leave her out, d'yer hear?'

The Inspector lit up a cigarette. 'We've known all about

the rackets they get up to, but until somebody complains we can't lay a finger on them. I wouldn't have thought that it was bad enough for Tony Ross to scarper though.' He looked at Maggie. 'Would you?'

She shook her head. 'Look, I must go. I can't expect Win to look after Jamie for too long. Thanks for the tea, Benny.'

'I'll come down and help you pick out a few bits.'

David Matthews quickly drank his tea. 'I'll come with you.'

'Why's that?' asked Benny. 'Yer wanner have a quick poke round so you can see if all me stuff's kosher or not?'

'No, I'm not interested in your bits, unless you've got the crown jewels down there.'

'Why's that? Good Gawd, they ain't gorn missing as well, have they? Can't trust anybody these days,' Benny laughed. Although he didn't like coppers this one seemed fair, and unusually, he did have a sense of humour.

'No, it's just that I've got the car outside and if Mrs Ross wants any help with her purchases I can take her.'

'That's kind of you,' said Maggie. 'But I can manage.'

'Don't be daft, Maggs. If he's gonner give yer a lift make the most of it. 'Sides, that means you'll be able to take a bit more than usual.'

Maggie smiled. 'OK. I'll say that, Benny, you've always got an eye open for more business.'

'That's what it's all about, gel. Stick with me and you won't go far wrong.'

Maggie struggled into the passenger seat of David Matthews's car, her bulk beginning to make her movements difficult.

'Thank you for giving me a lift.'

'It's my pleasure, Mrs Ross. Looks like you've got a good eye for trinkets.'

'Yes, I seem to be buying different things to what my husband did.'

'But are they selling? That's the most important thing.'

'Yes. I'm keeping account of everything so that when he does come back he can see what an asset I am to the business.'

He stopped the car at the top of Kelvin Market. 'I'll give you a hand to get them up to your flat.'

'You don't have to. You can leave them with Bill and I'll collect them later.'

'It's no trouble. In fact, it's a good excuse to get out of the office for a few hours.' He helped Maggie from the car and collected her goods from the back seat.

'All right, Maggs?' shouted Tom Cooper.

'Yes thanks, Tom.'

Winnie gave her a wave.

'Jamie been all right?' asked Maggie.

'Yer, no trouble.' Winnie looked the Inspector up and down. 'Everythink all right with you?'

'Not bad.'

'Give us a shout if yer needs anythink?'

'Will do.'

'Seems the entire market's keeping their eye on you,' said the Inspector, noting everybody watching him walking with Maggie.

'Yes, they're a good bunch.'

'Do they know Wally Marsh came to your flat yesterday?'

'I don't know. Mr Goldman might have told them.'

'Why didn't you tell me you knew who it was when you came in this morning?'

Maggie blushed. 'I didn't want to.'

'Why?'

'I'll just open the door and then I'll take those.' Maggie went to take the box from him but he held on to it.

'It's heavy, I'll take it up for you.'

Upstairs she threw her handbag on to the table. 'You can put it down now,' she said anxiously. She wanted to get rid of him as soon as possible.

He put the box on the table and quickly took off his trilby. 'Mrs Ross, may I sit down?'

'Yes. What do you want?'

He twirled his hat round and round in his hands. 'I'm going to make a few more enquiries about your husband. You see, now I know he was an associate of Wally Marsh, I'm going to look into it a bit deeper.'

Maggie sat down. 'Do you think you will find out any more from Wally?'

'I don't know, but I'll be calling in again if I get any news. Will that be all right?'

Maggie nodded. 'Yes, of course.'

The Inspector stood up. 'I'll see myself out.' He closed the door quietly behind him.

Maggie sat at the table. She had to find out more about why Wally wanted those books. Tomorrow she would go and see him and perhaps do a deal with him: the books for information about their associates. It was the one way she could see she might be able to track Tony down.

Chapter 13

For a long while after Maggie and the copper had left, Benny sat and stared at the newspaper, his thoughts on what had been said earlier. He put the newspaper on the table. 'If only I could find out more about what's happened to Tony then I'd be in Bella's good books. In any case, I'll go and see her on Sunday,' he said out loud. 'Better make sure I've got a clean shirt on if I want to impress her.' He smiled. 'Might even have a bath. Wish I could persuade her to marry me. I could make her happy, and I need a good woman to look after me in me twilight years.'

He laughed and carefully folded the newspaper. His thoughts went back to the last time Tony came to see him, just a week before he disappeared. Benny hadn't told Maggie that he'd been, or how worried he'd seemed. Tony had casually mentioned he was in a bit of trouble, though that was nothing new for him, but he'd never said what about or that he was afraid of someone. Benny stood up. 'Silly sod,' he mumbled. 'If only he'd told me the full story I could have some idea where to start looking for him.'

He went down to the stable and put a nosebag on Nellie. He lovingly patted her head. 'We should 'ave gone out today, old girl. I don't want any of your nonsense tomorrow, d'yer hear? Did you see the way that copper was nosing round and casting his beady eyes all over the place? They don't miss a bloody trick. He knew Maggie was coming over here buying so it gave him a good excuse to look round. Must think I was born yesterday.' He stopped. 'I wonder if that copper knows more than he's letting on? I think I'll go and have a word with that Wally Marsh tomorrow, old girl, so I don't want any more of your tricks.' He smiled and gave Nellie another loving pat as she nuzzled close to him. As he closed the door his thoughts went to Maggie. He just hoped she didn't get too chatty with that copper.

Bella Ross was up and about very early for her on a Monday morning. She struggled on to the train, cursing her leg that was still giving her a little pain. The pent-up anger she was feeling towards Wally Marsh had given her the strength she needed to go out. She looked out of the window as they got nearer to her part of London. Downham was all right, but she came from the Smoke, and that would always be where her heart was.

She thought about Maggie. How dare Wally upset her and those lovely kids! She loved Maggie and Tony, but even he'd been a sod in his time. As a kid he was always in trouble, but always just managing to keep the right side of the law. It was different with the stallholders – if he'd been caught pinching he'd come home with a bright red ear where someone had given him a clout. Bella had often wished her and Jim had had more kids like all good Italian families did, but they hadn't been so lucky.

She smiled. Maggie could be a bit of an ostrich at times, preferring to bury her head about Tony's wheeling and dealing. Bella sighed. Maggie knew what had gone on between her friend Eve and Tony, but as she said, that was before they got married. Well, thought Bella, let's hope that was the end of it.

When Bella got off the train she caught the bus to the auction rooms.

She stood outside just looking at the windows. The whole place had been tarted up since she was last here, but that had been many, many years ago. Memories of her dear Jim came flooding back. Despite his faults, gambling and womanising, she had loved him with all the fiery passion that flowed in her Italian blood. She was never quite sure if her son had inherited any of his father's weaknesses, but if he had he never let on.

She pushed open the door and just managed to catch sight of the look of disbelief on Wally's face before his expression changed and he rose to greet an old friend.

The auction rooms' new young bloods looked on curiously as Bella was hailed as a long-lost soul. For years Jim had bought from this place, not all of it straight and above board, and they had made a good living.

Bella smiled at her welcome. 'Nice to see you again too, Wally. Me daughter-in-law – you know our Maggie – she said you was still here. Thought you would have retired years ago.'

'I did. How you keeping, then?'

'Not too bad.'

He took her arm and led her well away from the other men, to the far end of the showroom. 'Have a seat.' He pointed to a large, very old tapestry sofa.

Bella looked at it. 'Just as long as it ain't running alive.'

Wally laughed. 'Still the same old suspicious Bella. No, it came from a very respectable house.'

Bella sniffed. 'They can be some of the worse. Dirty cows, some of those toffs are. And not so much of the old. Anyway, mate, how are you?'

'Not too bad either. I did retire, but I got under me old girl's feet too much, so I come back again. Don't do a lot – not now – only a few days a week. So, what're you doing round this way? You live out Downham now, don't you?'

'Yer. I came back to see you. Heard you and my Tony had a good scam going.'

Wally's face fell. 'Shhh, keep yer voice down.'

Bella looked round, still smiling. She bent her head closer. 'Well, did yer?'

'Only the odd bit that come in, nothing big, mind.'

'So, where's my Tony now?'

'Don't ask me.' Wally too looked round in case his raised voice had attracted attention. 'Found himself a little floozie I shouldn't wonder. Always liked a bit a skirt did—' He took a sharp intake of breath as Bella's sharp elbow found his ribs.

'What d'yer do that for?'

'I'll give you take my Tony's name in vain. Now come on, tell me what this is all about.'

Wally's face flushed and he looked angry. 'How the bloody hell should I know?'

'Don't give me any of that. I know you went to Maggie's place looking for his books, and what was you doing frightening my dear little grandchildren? I tell yer,

Wally, you'll have to answer to me over that.' Bella moved closer. 'That was a bad move. Those kids mean the world to me.'

'How d'yer know that? Anyway, I didn't frighten 'em, I was just—'

Bella was smiling as she took hold of a large lump of flesh under his arm. She squeezed, then twisted it.

Wally screwed up his face in pain, but he didn't cry out.

'Cut the crap. So come on, what was you looking for? What gives?'

Wally turned grey.

Bella put her face close to his. 'And don't give me any old flannel. You ain't talking to young Maggie now, you know. And what about poor old Mr Goldman?'

Wally took his handkerchief from his pocket and patted his damp forehead. 'What about him?'

'You're lucky he ain't pressing charges.'

'It was an accident. I didn't mean to hurt him.'

Bella sat back and fiddled with her handbag. 'Try telling that to the beak.'

Wally was sweating.

'Now what was you after in Maggie's place?'

'Nothing.'

'Rubbish! I know all about you. Remember I was wheeling and dealing here years ago, so I know all the ropes.'

Wally's face was full of misery as he sat back.

Bella felt good. At last she knew she was about to get some answers to her questions, and they could lead to her finding her Tony.

David Matthews sat in his car outside Maggie Ross's flat,

his thoughts with her. Why would her husband go off and leave her and her kids? She was a fine-looking young woman with that pretty blonde hair and such blue eyes, so very different to Jean, his late wife.

He turned on the engine. What made him think like that? He had loved Jean and had been heartbroken when she and their new-born baby died.

He quickly lit a cigarette and slammed the car into gear. It was time to have a word with Mr Wally Marsh.

When he walked into the auction room it looked as if the place was empty. Then he spotted a group of people at the far end.

'Give him some air,' called out someone.

David Matthews moved closer. 'What seems to be the problem?'

'He's passed out,' said the woman, sitting next to Wally, slapping the back of his hand.

'How bad is he?'

'Dunno. Anyway, who are you?' asked Bella.

'Inspector Matthews. I've got my car outside if you think he should go to hospital. He don't look too good to me.'

Bella straightened up. 'You're the copper what's looking for my Tony, ain't yer?'

David Matthews looked surprised. 'Are you Mrs Ross?'

'Yes.'

'What are you doing here? I thought Maggie – Mrs Ross, your daughter-in-law said you lived at Downham.'

'That's right. But I had to come and see Wally here. Now the silly sod's gone an' passed out on me.'

David Matthews wanted to smile. Bella Ross was a woman he could get along with; she was like Maggie's friend Winnie, the salt of the earth who called a spade a spade.

Wally groaned.

'He don't look too good,' said one of his fellow workers. 'I reckon he ought ter go to the doctor's.'

'He'll be all right,' said Bella. 'Tough as old boots, is Wally.'

'He's gone blue round the mouth,' said the Inspector. 'I'll run him to the hospital. Would you like to come with me, Mrs Ross?'

'Yer, why not? I fancy a car ride. Then you can take me on to see Maggie.'

'Yes, ma'am,' David Matthews smiled. Bella Ross must have been quite a girl in her time.

Maggie sat down and kicked her shoes off. Her window was wide open but there was no fresh air. Her feet were swollen, making her shoes tight. She thought about what Winnie had said. She knew she was in charge of her life now. Tomorrow she would go and see Wally as she'd promised herself she would, and make him tell her what had been going on. If there were other blokes involved perhaps she could go and see them too, and find out the truth. And she'd have a go at Wally about him coming into her flat and frightening the kids. If she shouted loud enough he'd be sure to tell her what he knew just to shut her up.

Maggie looked at the clock. It was late afternoon and Laura would be coming out of school soon, so she made her way down the stairs.

Before she reached the hall, there was a loud banging on the front door and a hand poked through her letter box, fishing around for her key. Maggie stood on the stairs mesmerised.

A pair of eyes peered through the slit. 'Maggs. Maggie, you there?'

Maggie laughed and quickly pulled open the door. 'Bella, what a surprise!'

Bella was standing with Inspector Matthews right behind her. Maggie froze. The look on Bella's face told her something was wrong. 'What're you doing over here? What is it? What's happened? It's Tony,' the words rushed out.

Bella looked around. 'No, gel, it ain't Tony. Can we come in fer a bit?'

Maggie stood to one side. 'Course. I must ask Win to keep an eye out for Laura.' She left them slowly climbing the stairs.

'Was that Bella?' asked Winnie, when Maggs appeared at her stall.

Maggie nodded.

'She don't alter much, does she? Mind you, she don't look too happy. What's she doing with that copper?' Winnie suddenly stopped and put her hand to her mouth. 'Oh my Gawd, you ain't . . .?'

'I don't know what they want. Could you keep an eye out for Laura?'

'Course, love.' She took Maggie's hand. 'Don't worry about the kids.'

Maggie half smiled and turned. What were they going to tell her? Her legs felt heavy and trembled as she climbed the stairs. When would this nightmare end?

'Hope you don't mind, love, but I've put the kettle on.

Me and the copper here's parched.'

'What you doing over this way?'

'Been up the hospital.'

Maggie slumped into the armchair. 'The hospital?' she croaked. 'Why? What?'

The kettle's loud whistle sent Bella scurrying as fast as her leg would let her from the room.

Maggie looked at the Inspector. 'Is it Tony?'

He appeared surprised. 'No. We had to take Wally Marsh to the hospital.'

'Wally Marsh?' repeated Maggie. 'Why, what's happened? And what's Bella doing with you?'

Bella walked in carrying the tray of tea things. 'Here, Maggs, you ain't never gonner believe this but Wally Marsh – you know from the auction rooms – well, he's gone and had a heart attack.'

'No,' said Maggie. 'When?'

'This morning. We was just sitting talking when all of a sudden he went this funny colour.' She straightened herself in the chair. 'Mind you, after seeing my Jim, I knew what was wrong with him. Reckon he did it on purpose, crafty sod.'

'Who?' asked the Inspector, grinning. 'Your husband?'

Bella tutted loudly. 'No, silly sod. Wally.'

'What was you doing there?' asked Maggie.

'Went ter see Wally. I wanted a few answers as to why he keeps coming here.'

Maggie opened her mouth but no sound came out.

'That's why I happened to be there. I too wanted a few answers,' said David Matthews.

Maggie sat back.

'Here, love, get this down yer, you look all in.' Bella handed her a cup of tea.

'Is he . . .?'

'Not when we left the hospital,' said Bella, spooning sugar into her cup.

'Did Wally tell you what you wanted to know?'

'No, he was past talking by the time I walked in,' said the Inspector.

'What about you, Bella? Did he tell you?'

'Na. Didn't get a chance. We'd no sooner sat down when he said he had a pain. I thought he was buggering about at first. Even dug him in the ribs.'

David Matthews quickly looked up.

'It's all right,' grinned Bella. 'It wasn't the side of his heart.'

'What about his wife?' asked Maggie. 'Does she know?'

'One of the lads from the auction room went and told her. She arrived at the hospital just as we left. She's a stuck-up cow. Never did like her.'

Maggie looked at Inspector Matthews. 'So you haven't got any more answers?'

He shook his head. 'No, but I'll be making some more enquiries. By the way, Mrs Ross, you said "keeps coming here"? So Sunday wasn't the first time he'd been here?'

Maggie looked at Bella. 'No. I didn't tell you, but he came here Saturday night.'

'And d'you know, he told those lovely kids of hers that Tony was dead. That's why I went over – to sort him out. Bloody disgraceful . . .'

David Matthews smiled. 'Well, you certainly did that.'

'I didn't expect him to finish up in hospital. Serves him right.'

'Did he threaten you?' he asked Maggie.

'No, I was out.'

'Oh, I see.' The Inspector looked grave. He finished his tea and stood up. 'I must go. Thank you for the tea, Mrs Ross.'

'That's all right,' said Bella and Maggie together, which made them laugh.

'I'll see myself out.'

When he left Bella said, 'He seems a nice bloke for a copper.'

Maggie smiled but didn't answer. That too was exactly what she had been thinking.

Chapter 14

Six weeks had passed since Maggie had actually spoken to her brother Alan, the week after his birthday when he had come to take her to see Bella. They wrote now and again, and the last letter said he would be over Saturday, today.

Maggie was pleased to see he was alone, and as she made him a cup of tea, she told him what had happened over the past weeks.

Alan was very angry when he heard about Wally frightening the children, and pushing Mr Goldman over.

'He wants locking up. What's that policeman doing about all this?'

'Not a lot really.'

'Bloody incompetent, if you ask me. Where is he now?'

'Who?'

'This Wally bloke.'

'In hospital, he's had a heart attack.'

'Serves him right.' Alan was pacing the room.

'Alan, sit down, you're making me dizzy.'

He gave her a worried glance and sat at the table. 'Still no news then, Maggs?'

'No. I don't know what to think, and now this business with Wally.'

Alan fidgeted with his fingers nervously.

'Is there something on your mind?' asked Maggie.

'I didn't like to mention it before, especially now. But, Maggs, about that money I lent Tony – is there any chance—'

Maggie went pale. 'What money?'

He looked very uncomfortable. 'I wouldn't normally ask, well, certainly not under these circumstances, but Helen wants to go on holiday and—'

'Alan, I asked you what money.'

He looked up. 'Don't you know?'

'No I don't,' she replied angrily.

'Didn't Tony tell . . .?'

'No he didn't. How much was it?'

'Twenty quid,' he mumbled.

'What? Twenty pounds? What did he want twenty pounds for?'

'To get some stock, so he said.'

'Stock. He could buy a whole bloody warehouse full with that sorta money. Did he say what kind of stock?'

'No, and I didn't ask.'

'When was this?'

'About three months ago.'

'And you never told me.'

'Why should I? I thought you knew. 'Sides, after all this I didn't want to worry you.'

'So why you asking for it now?'

'As I said, Helen wants to go away, and she said you should—'

Maggie banged the table. 'I might have guessed it was bloody Helen.'

'Come on now, Maggs, it ain't the first time this has happened.'

Maggie looked up. 'What d'you mean?'

'He often borrowed money from me.'

'I didn't know that. Did he ever say what it was for?'

'Stock.'

'But we only sell rubbish.'

'He liked a game of cards, and the dogs, didn't he?'

Maggie nodded.

'Well, that's what I reckon it was for, but to be fair he always paid up, some times quicker than others.'

Maggie sat stunned. She knew Tony liked a flutter, but twenty pounds was a lot of money.

Alan was still talking. 'Me and Helen think he's got himself mixed up in something big and he's laying low till it all blows over.'

Maggie looked at her brother. 'I ain't got twenty pounds, Alan. We're just about keeping our heads above water. We did have thirty bob in the Post Office but I had to take that out.' Tears began to trickle down her cheeks. 'Where's this all going to end?'

'I'm sorry, Maggie.' He put an arm round her shoulder. 'Say, could you get it off of Bella?'

'No I couldn't,' she yelled, brushing him away. 'I'll just have to try and find it, won't I?'

'I'm really sorry about this. But I did promise Helen a holiday, and we've had quite a bit of expense, what with one thing and another, you understand.' Alan was clearly embarrassed at this conversation.

Maggie stood up and went over to the sideboard. 'I've got two pounds here that I was saving to take the kids to Ramsgate in the holidays. You'd better take that.'

Much to Maggie's surprise he took it eagerly.

After he left Maggie sat at the table and tried to work out her money. There were still nearly two weeks until August, so perhaps she could just about scrape enough together to go away. She mustn't break her promise to the children.

That evening Maggie told Eve about Alan's visit.

For a few moments Eve sat silent. She lit a cigarette, then said with venom, 'The bastard. He come over here just for his money? He ain't been near since that time he was going to take you over to see Bella.'

'But he has written a couple of times,' said Maggie defensively.

'And he took that two quid you was gonner take the kids away with?'

Maggie nodded. 'Eve, it was money Tony had borrowed.'

'Yes, so you said, but to ask you for it now . . . I can't understand Tony borrowing off him.'

'Why did Tony have to borrow off of anybody? Alan said it was for stock – if that's the case, where is this twenty pounds worth of stock?'

'Don't ask me. I still reckon your brother's got a bloody cheek. D'you know, I reckon that cow Helen's at the back of all this.'

'Doesn't matter who's at the back of it, Eve, where am I gonner get Alan's eighteen pounds from? I ain't got nothing to sell.'

'Dunno. Let him sweat for it.'

'I can't. After all, it is his money, and Tony shouldn't have borrowed it.'

'Suppose you're right. How are you managing? The truth now, Maggs.'

'Not too bad. But I don't know for how long when this baby comes. I'll have a job to get over to Benny's, for a start, and he don't always have anything worth buying. I wish I'd taken more interest in what Tony was doing, then perhaps I too could find other dealers.'

'And you might have known what else he got up to.'

'I suppose I have been a bit daft.'

Eve looked at her friend. 'I can let you have a few shillings to help out.'

'Thanks all the same, Eve, but I can't get into any more debt.'

'Call it a gift towards the holiday.'

'No, I couldn't.'

Eve didn't argue.

They sat for a while, both deep in their thoughts.

'Maggs, why don't you come up the Dog tonight? You could do with a bit of cheering up.'

'I don't like leaving the kids, not after what happened with Wally.'

'But he's in hospital now.'

'As far as we know.'

'Well, I think you ought to try and have a quiet word with Ding Dong Bell.'

'What, the bookie's runner? What good will that do? He ain't gonner give me any tips on what's gonner win the two thirty, now is he?'

'I know that, silly. But he might be able to tell you how

much Tony spent on betting, and who he associated with. Those blokes seem to know everything.'

'That's true. I could go in the morning.'

'Would Ding Dong be there then?'

'Dunno, but Gus will be able to tell me.'

'Sounds like a good idea. I must go, I'll call in later.'

'Thanks, Eve. But you don't have to.'

Eve smiled. 'Just like to make sure you're all right.'

Maggie tried all week to see Ding Dong but he wasn't around. Gus told her he reckoned the cops were after him and was lying low.

'As soon as he shows up I'll let you know,' said Gus. 'I could send him along to you if yer like?'

'That might be better. Then I could have a quiet word with him at home.'

It was Friday and the end of term. Laura and all her friends came out of school, laughing and giggling, loaded down with their end-of-year work.

'We going to Ramsgate tomorrow, Mum?' Laura asked eagerly.

'No, next week.' Maggie had just about managed to make enough for their trip. She took some of the many papers Laura was trying to balance.

'I'm ever so glad Granny Ross is coming with us.'

Maggie smiled. 'So am I.'

As his mother and sister were with him, Jamie got a little cheeky when they passed the stalls and tried to act grown up. He picked up an apple.

'Oi, put that back,' yelled Fred.

'How much?' he asked Fred.

'To you, my boy, ten bob,' laughed Fred.

He quickly replaced it in its neat paper nest. 'Mummy, did you hear that? He wants ten bob for that mouldy apple.'

'It ain't mouldy,' said Fred indignantly. 'I bet if I said you could have it for nothink yer'd soon take it, wouldn't yer?'

Jamie nodded.

'Well, go on, take it yer cheeky devil.'

Jamie ran away laughing.

'You shouldn't encourage him,' said Maggie. 'But thanks anyway.'

'I see Bill's keeping everything in order down there.' Fred nodded his head towards Tony's stall.

'Yes, but I don't know for how much longer I'll be able to get over to Benny's for stock.'

'I reckon Benny'll bring over a few bits if you asked him.'

'I expect he would, but I've got to try and be independent. I'd like to find other places to buy from, but till I have this baby I can't get about that much, and carry the goods home with me.'

'I can always pick up any bits with me van, you know.'

'Thanks, Fred. I don't know how I'd manage if it wasn't for all you lot to keep an eye on the kids when I have to go out.' Maggie opened her door and made her way slowly up the stairs.

That evening, when the children were in bed, Maggie got down to the list of clothes she was going to take to Ramsgate next week. Some needed buttons, and others wanted the odd stitch. She sat back and put her hands on her large stomach. Despite her problems with Alan, and her backache, she was feeling pretty good with herself. The market traders had had a whip round for some pocket money for the kids to take away with them. Of course, Bella was always willing to help. Maggie would often find a ten-bob note in her handbag when she got home from visiting her. She hadn't seen Bella for over a week. What would she have to say about Alan? She would be angry with Tony, especially as it looked as if the money had been used for gambling, and she would want to help, but eighteen pounds was a lot of money.

Maggie smiled. The romance between Benny and Bella hadn't progressed, and they'd had a good laugh after Bella had told her how he'd been over to see her wearing a brand-new shirt with the cardboard stiffener still wedged under the back of the collar. Maggie said he must have meant business.

Bella reckoned he'd even had a bath, and his sparse bit of grey hair had been plastered down with some sort of grease.

It would be nice for both of them if they could get together, thought Maggie, but she could never see Benny giving up his horse and stable to live with Bella, and Bella certainly wouldn't live with Benny, so it was stalemate.

Someone banging on the knocker roused Maggie from her thoughts. Thinking perhaps it was Ding Dong at last, she slowly made her way down the stairs. 'All right, all right, I'm coming. Keep it down, will you?' Maggie opened the door and two large men pushed her roughly to one side, walked in and quickly closed the door behind them. Maggie stood motionless.

'Well, where is he then?'

Maggie had never seen these men before and quickly took in their appearances. The older man was clean shaven with piercing blue eyes. He was wearing an expensive-looking grey suit and matching trilby, with his white hair just showing.

'Who?' croaked Maggie.

'You bloody well know who we mean: that old man of yours.'

'I don't know. What d'you want him for?'

'Our money,' said the younger, slightly slimmer man. He too was well dressed, in navy blue. He was dark and had a slight five-o'clock shadow. His dark eyes, almost hidden beneath bushy eyebrows, narrowed menacingly.

Maggie began to shake. 'Oh no, not somebody else,' she said softly, sinking down on to the stairs.

'Shall we go up? Then you can tell us where he keeps it hidden,' said the older man.

'There ain't any money here.'

'Don't give us that, darling.' The younger one roughly grabbed her arm and pulled her to her feet. 'We know all about Mr Tony Ross and the deals he does. So the boss here,' he jerked his thumb over his shoulder in the direction of the older man, 'wants his money.'

Maggie pulled her arm away and rubbed the red mark that was forming on her bare skin.

Slowly Maggie climbed the stairs, her heart beating furiously and her thoughts racing. What if they woke the children? She sat nervously on the edge of the sofa. 'Who are you?'

'Friends of your husband, so where is he?'

Maggie was taken aback. They didn't know Tony was missing. 'He's not here.'

The younger one, who was about twenty, began walking

round the room. 'We know he ain't in the pub, been there.' He went to open the children's bedroom door.

Maggie jumped up. 'Don't go in there. My children are in there asleep.'

'Sit down, Reg. We don't want to upset the little woman. You can see what a state she's in, and we don't want her dropping that lot while we're here, now do we?'

Reg sat in the armchair.

'Now, young lady. Are you going to tell us where your old man is?' The older man took a cigarette from a fancy engraved gold case and lit it with a posh lighter.

'I don't know.' Maggie was shaking with fear, and very slowly tears began to trickle down her cheek.

'For Christ's sake, gel, don't start crying. Mr Windsor here can't stand women crying.'

Maggie felt sick. What did these men want?

Mr Windsor picked up the heavy brass ashtray. He fondled it. 'Nice place you've got here. Mind you, I'm a bit surprised. Thought you would have lived somewhere a bit smarter.'

'What do you want?' sniffed Maggie.

'I told you – me money.' He smashed the ashtray down on to the table, making Maggie jump.

'I don't know nothing about my husband's affairs.'

'Well, in that case, missis, we'll just have to start looking for ourselves.'

Reg grinned and stood up. One by one he cracked his knuckles loudly.

Maggie's head swam, she thought she was going to pass out. 'There ain't no money here,' she said, trying to keep her voice down. 'You ain't the first to come looking. Wally

170

Marsh was here a few weeks ago and he . . .' She suddenly realised what she'd said: she'd told them Tony wasn't around.

'Well, well, well. So it's true then? Someone has done away with our dear Tony?' Mr Windsor waved at Reg to sit down. He put his face close to Maggie's. 'Or else he's done a runner.' He sat back. 'You say Wally Marsh was here? And pray what was he looking for? It couldn't have been money?'

Maggie was trying to think fast. 'I don't know. When I went to ask him he'd gone into hospital.'

'Yes, that was very unfortunate, poor Mr Marsh. I didn't know you were a friend of the family's, not having seen you at his funeral.'

'Wally's dead?' gasped Maggie.

'Yes, didn't you know? We began to get worried about our money when we didn't see Tony at the church yard. We all knew how fond of Wally he was.'

Maggie began to feel sick. 'Please, Mr Windsor, won't you tell me what this is all about?'

He slowly got to his feet and stood in front of Maggie. He took hold of her shoulders and gripped them hard. He was very close, and as he towered over her she could feel his hot breath on her face.

'It's about that bastard husband of yours. He owes us a great deal of money, and if he don't get it to us quick, we'll have to take it in kind.'

Maggie's head was pounding. She wanted to ask them so many questions, but was afraid. What had Tony been doing all these years? How much did he owe? And what had it been for? These men didn't know where he was, and Wally hadn't known – or had he? In any case, that was too late now.

Mr Windsor pushed her back in the chair and moved towards the door. 'We'll be back. Perhaps you'll have some answers or money for us next time.'

Reg came over and dragged Maggie to her feet. He put his face close to hers, and the smell from his bad breath made her feel sick. 'Now just you remember, Mr Windsor don't like to be messed about with. So when that husband of yours does turn up, tell him we're coming back to collect what he owes.' Grabbing both her arms he shoved her hard backwards, hitting her head against the wall.

He grinned, pulled at his shirt cuffs, then opened the door for his master.

As they went down the stairs, Maggie silently slumped to the floor.

Chapter 15

Eve was pleased Maggie had given her a front door key after that do with Wally. At least she didn't have to drag her down those stairs every time she came to see her. Over these past months she had felt increasingly sad as she walked down Kelvin Market. Eve worried about Maggie and this new baby. How would Maggie manage to pay the rent and run the stall when the weather turned?

It was late evening. All the stalls had long been put away, the rubbish had gone, and somehow after the hustle and bustle of the day there was an air of quiet loneliness about the place. The fact that Tony Ross wasn't around with his jokes and laughter didn't help. Eve smiled to herself; he was a bloke all the women could so easily fall for. A train rattling above broke the silence and her thoughts went back to the talk in the pub earlier.

Tony wasn't the most popular bloke in there at the moment. They had all been talking about poor old Ding Dong being picked up by the coppers. Most of them blamed Tony for buggering off like that and bringing the coppers snooping around. Dan had been up at the bar, while Eve had kept quiet and listened. Gradually people began to talk

173

about Tony. Gus reckoned he owed money to just about everybody. Was this the reason he'd done a runner?

Eve felt sorry for Maggie, she had always trusted Tony, and now it looked as though he had let her down. Eve knew that if she had played her cards right it might have been her having babies and sitting at home waiting for Tony, but that was something she had never wanted. Life was for living, and she would never be like her mother, who had had seven kids and countless miscarriages, and who had spent her life struggling from one pregnancy to another. The day Eve met Dan was the best day of her life. They both had the same attitude: to live for today. He was fun, and she loved him.

Eve looked up at Maggie's window. The light wasn't on, but perhaps she was having a quiet doze. Maggie was beginning to look very tired. Trying to run the stall, this business with that Wally bloke, and then on top of all that Alan asking for money, it was causing her a lot of extra grief.

'Where the bloody hell are you, Tony Ross?' Eve said to herself.

She didn't call out as she mounted the stairs, not wanting to startle Maggie or wake the children. She slowly pushed the door to the living room open and peered in. It took her a few moments for her eyes to adjust to the gloom, but then what she saw had her rushing to her friend's side.

Eve fell to her knees and cradled Maggie's head in her hands. 'Maggie, Maggie. What happened? Oh my God.' She sat back on her legs. 'Maggie, Maggie, can you hear me?'

Maggie groaned.

'Don't move.' Eve rushed into the kitchen and grabbed the towel that hung behind the door. She pushed it between her friend's legs. Maggie was lying in a pool of water.

Eve was bewildered. What if the kids came in and saw their mother in this state while she was getting help? But she had to do something. She gently pushed open the children's bedroom door. They were both sleeping peacefully. There was nothing for it, she would have to get help, and the nearest place had to be the Dog and Duck.

Eve ran all the way. She pushed the door open and breathlessly yelled out for Dan. Everybody looked round.

'My God, gel, whatever's the matter? You look like you've seen a ghost.' Gus was leaning on the bar.

'Where's Dan?'

'In the bog, I think.'

'Eve, you all right?' asked Beatie, frowning. ''Ere, you ain't just witnessed a murder, have you?'

The others near the bar laughed.

'No, I ain't. It's Maggie. She's lying on the floor in her flat. I think she's having the baby.'

'Oh my Gawd,' said Beatie. 'Gus, phone for an ambulance. I'll come back with you, Eve. What about the kids?'

'They're still asleep, or they was when I left 'em.'

'They on their own?'

'Yes.'

'You should have knocked up Mr Goldman.'

'Didn't think of that. Please hurry.'

'I didn't think the baby was due for a few weeks yet,' said Beatie.

'It ain't.' Eve was about to push open the door marked Gents when Dan came out.

'Hallo, love. You decided to come back for a quick one then?' said Dan, walking leisurely up to the bar.

'Dan, you've got to come back to Maggie's with me.'

'I'll just finish me beer first.'

'No you won't.' Eve grabbed his arm and pushed him out of the door.

As the three of them ran back Eve told Dan what had happened.

Eve fell to her knees beside Maggie once again as she lay groaning. She took her hand and gently squeezed it. 'I'm here, Maggs. You're gonner be all right.'

'It's OK, Maggs,' said Beatie. 'Gus has called an ambulance. Dan, go and wake the kids, dress 'em and take them up the pub.'

Dan nodded, his face went pale when he saw Maggie, and eagerly he did as he was told.

'Will she be all right?' asked Eve, looking anxiously at Beatie.

'Course. She ain't the first to have their baby on the floor, and I don't suppose she'll be the last.' Beatie gave a little laugh. 'And I reckon that's where a lot of the dirty deeds start out, don't you, on the kitchen floor?'

'The men, Reg . . .' whispered Maggie.

'Don't worry, there ain't no men here, love,' said Beatie.

Maggie drew her legs up and screamed out in pain.

They heard Laura cry out. 'Mummy, Mummy! What's wrong with my mummy?'

'Dan, hurry up and get those kids out,' shouted Eve.

'Auntie Eve, what you doing to my mummy?' said Jamie, coming into the room with his teddy under his arm, his hair tousled, and rubbing his eyes.

Eve stood up and with her arm round Jamie's shoulder gently ushered him away and out of sight of his mother. 'It's

176

all right. Mummy's just going to the hospital to get the new baby.'

'Why is she laying on the floor?'

'She's having a little lay down, she's very tired.'

'Oh.'

Eve was pleased he didn't want to pursue it any further.

'Will we take the new baby to Ramsgate?' asked Laura, coming into the room and trying to see what was happening.

'You'll have to wait and see,' said Dan, easing her towards the door. 'Come on, I'm taking you up the pub.'

Jamie's face lit up. 'Can we have an arrowroot biscuit? Daddy used to buy us those.'

'I think I could manage one of those,' said Dan. 'And what about some lemonade?'

'I want some as well. It's all dark out here . . .' Laura's little voice faded away as they disappeared down the stairs.

Tears slowly slipped down Eve's face. 'Those poor kids,' she said.

'They'll be fine,' said Beatie. 'I wonder what brought this on?'

'Could be all the worry about Tony. She's been under a lot of pressure lately.'

'H'mm,' mused Beatie. 'And if he don't turn up soon then it ain't gonner get any better for her.'

A few minutes later two well-built ambulance men walked in.

'Eve, you go with Maggie. I'll clear up here, then I'll see to the kids,' said Beatie.

'Thanks, Beatie.' Eve watched as the men carefully carried Maggie down the stairs. 'You'll have to tell—'

'Don't worry,' said Beatie. 'I'll let everybody know what's happened.'

Eve sat in the ambulance holding her friend's hand. She wanted to cry. Maggie was very distressed and she looked a terrible colour. A little prayer raced round Eve's mind: Please, Maggs, don't die.

'Benny Jones. What the bloody hell you doing here at this time of morning? And on a Saturday as well? You should be out earning a few bob.' Bella Ross was cross. She was in her old dressing gown and hadn't done her hair. 'You'd better come in. Don't want all the neighbours to see me like this.'

Benny removed his trilby, which wasn't the usual grotty old one he wore for work, and followed Bella down the passage. Suddenly Bella realised he looked both clean and very worried.

'What's up then, mate, that horse of yours died?'

Benny sat at the kitchen table. 'Dan New came to see me very early this morning.'

Bella glanced over her shoulder as she filled the kettle. 'What, Eve's Dan?'

Benny nodded.

'Didn't know he knew where you lived. What did he want?' Suddenly it hit Bella. She slammed the kettle on the gas stove. 'It's my Tony, ain't it? They've found his body. He's dead, ain't he?' Tears welled up in her big brown eyes.

Benny quickly hurried over to put his arms round Bella and hold her close. 'No, girl, it ain't Tony, it's Maggie.'

'Maggie!' she screamed, pushing herself away from him. 'Maggie? What's happened to her?'

'Calm down, love. Maggie's all right, but I'm afraid the baby was born dead.'

Bella stared at him for a moment. 'The baby . . . But it ain't due till . . . Poor Maggs.' She began to cry.

Benny held Bella round her wide shoulders. In all this sadness he wanted to smile. They must have looked a strange pair, a bit like Laurel and Hardy. He was thin and wiry, while Bella was round and cuddly.

Gradually her tears and sobs subsided and she drew away from him. 'Sorry about that,' she mumbled, fishing in her dressing-gown pocket for her handkerchief. She dabbed at her eyes. 'How do you know all this?'

'It seems Eve was with her at the hospital and when Beatie from the pub phoned to see how she was, they told her not too good. Eve didn't leave till the baby, another little girl by all accounts, was born. She phoned the pub, Dan was still there, and told him to come over and see me and ask me to tell you. He looked terrible – been up all night, so he said.'

'Why?'

'He promised Eve he'd look after the kids.'

'The kids.' Bella quickly put her hand to her mouth. 'Where are they?'

'They're in the pub. Beatie and Gus is looking after them till Eve can pick 'em up.'

'I've got to go and see Maggie, and I'll have to look after the kids. That bloody son of mine should be here. It's his fault she's lost that baby. I'll kill him when he walks his arse in here. I mean it, I'll bloody well kill him.'

'Do you want to go to the hospital first, or see the kids?'

'The hospital.' Bella half smiled. 'D'you know, we was going to Ramsgate next week. That would have been nice.'

'Perhaps you can still go when Maggie comes out. It might do her good.'

'Yes, you could be right – and, Benny, thanks.'

'What for?'

'For being a real mate and coming over and letting me know.'

He looked embarrassed. 'You know how I feel about you, Bella, and I'd like to be part of your family.'

'Now don't start on all that nonsense again. I'm going upstairs to get dressed otherwise I'll have me neighbours talk about me entertaining a man in me dressing gown. You can make another cup of tea if you like.'

Benny sighed as Bella left the room. Perhaps one day he might make her see that being together would be nice for both of them. For who knew how long they had left?

Maggie opened her eyes and tried to focus on a man who was walking down the ward carrying a bunch of flowers. 'Tony?' She desperately wanted it to be Tony.

He smiled. 'Maggie, sorry, Mrs Ross, I hope you don't mind me coming to see you. I was round the market this morning and I heard what had happened.'

David Matthews sat on the chair next to the bed and placed the flowers below her feet.

Maggie, who looked pale and drawn, gently eased herself up in the bed and pulled her bed jacket round her shoulders. She looked up the ward apprehensively. 'I thought only relatives were allowed in the maternity ward.'

'That's the one good thing about being a policeman – I

only have to say I want to ask you a few questions and that opens all kinds of doors.'

Maggie was suddenly wide awake. She shuddered at the memory of what had happened last night. Did he know about those men coming to her flat? 'Questions? What sort of questions?' she asked.

He smiled. 'That was just a ploy.'

She sunk back on the pillows. Tears filled her eyes. 'You know I lost my baby?'

He shuffled in the chair. 'Yes, yes, I do know. I'm very sorry about that. Everybody on the market's talking about it. They are all very upset.'

Maggie looked away.

He stood up. 'I'm sorry. I shouldn't have come.'

Maggie turned. She half smiled. 'It was very nice of you, and thank you for the flowers, they're lovely. I hope you got them off Mrs Russell?'

He didn't reply. At the door he turned and waved.

Maggie closed her eyes.

David Matthews stood outside the hospital and lit a cigarette. It was such a shame that Maggie Ross had lost her baby. She was a wonderful mother. If only he had some news, any news, about Tony Ross. He got into his car. The word was that the affable Mr Ross was in a lot of debt. Well, he certainly didn't spend much on his wife and kids. They weren't hard up, but they didn't live in the sort of luxury that the volume of his gambling money seemed to suggest.

His thoughts were rambling. How would she manage when winter came and the weather turned bad? She wouldn't be able to get the stall out every day then.

Matthews noticed the Blackshirts on the corner. The Nazis were a despicable bunch, and the papers were full of what was happening in Europe. What if there was another war? Who would look after Maggie Ross then? She was a lovely young woman who needed love and affection.

David Matthews sat for a long while wondering what his next move could be to try to find Tony Ross. The dog track knew all about him. They called him the big spender, and added that he'd been a big loser too. The bookie's runner, a Mr Bell, who was arrested a few days ago, said Tony owed him a lot of money. In fact, it appeared he owed money all round. The Inspector ground the end of his cigarette into the ashtray and started the car engine. He only hoped Ross hadn't been involved with Reg Todd and Mr Windsor. That could really be trouble for him now they were out.

Another thought struck him: it could also mean danger for Maggie. David Matthews banged the steering wheel in anger. 'Sod you, Tony Ross,' he said aloud. 'You don't deserve Maggie and those lovely kids.'

Chapter 16

Everybody waved as Maggie, with David Matthews at her side carrying her bag, turned into Kelvin Market.

'Good ter see you back,' said Winnie, wobbling up as soon as she caught sight of her. 'We're all really sorry about the baby.' She kissed her cheek and, smiling, gently patted Maggie's arm. They were old friends and didn't need to say comforting words.

'Everything all right?' Maggie asked Bill as she came up to the stall.

'Not too bad, Maggs. Could do with a bit more stuff. Benny brought a few bits over. I ain't paid him, though.'

'Don't worry, I'll get it sorted out. Bella been seeing to your wages?'

'Yer, ta.'

As Maggie moved on, her thoughts stayed with the stall and the pathetic display. How could they exist on what that must be taking?

'See yer still got that bloody copper in tow,' shouted Tom Cooper good-naturedly.

'Take no notice of him, love. You've been good for me business,' yelled Mrs Russell.

'Lovely ter see yer back, gel,' said Fred warmly.

Maggie couldn't believe her eyes when she pushed open the living-room door. The flat seemed to be full of flowers and fruit.

'Sit yerself down, Maggs. Kettle's on. You are gonner stay for a cuppa, Inspector?' Bella was beaming.

'If it's not too much trouble.'

The racket coming up the stairs told Maggie who was about to burst in.

'Mummy, Mummy!' The door was flung back and banged hard against the wall as Laura and Jamie came bounding into the room.

'We ain't half missed you,' said Jamie, burying his head in her lap.

'Hope you've been good while I've been away.'

Laura sat beside her. 'Granny Ross said they didn't have any babies left. Is that true?'

Maggie put her arm round her daughter's shoulder. 'I'm afraid Granny Ross is right.'

'Well, I reckon it was rotten of the hospital to tell us we was gonner have one, then take it away.'

'You can always ask again for another one,' said Jamie.

Maggie smiled. 'I don't know about that. You see, I have to ask Daddy first.'

'I don't see why. Daddy ain't here now.' Laura was pouting. 'Perhaps you could ask Uncle Dan. He might be able to help.'

David Matthews laughed. 'I don't think that would be such a good idea.'

'Auntie Eve might not like it,' said Maggie.

'Why? Don't she like babies, then?'

'Only mine.'

'Can we still go to Ramsgate?' asked Laura.

'I don't know.'

'Oh Mummy, you promised.'

'Give yer mum a chance to get her coat off,' said Bella.

'She's ain't got a coat on,' said Jamie.

'Well, can we go out and play then?' asked Laura.

'Yes, off you go, and don't get into any mischief.'

Laura smiled. 'Mummy's back,' she said, skipping out of arm's reach and adding defiantly, 'And don't you be like that hospital and break a promise.'

'Well, my being away didn't seem to bother them very much,' said Maggie to her mother-in-law.

'Don't you believe it. We had quite a few tears, and Jamie's been wetting the bed again, and Laura's been shouting in her sleep.'

'Oh Bella, I'm sorry. Have they been a lot of trouble?'

Bella smiled. 'No, it's been a real pleasure. It's taken years off me. Mind you, I don't know how you managed up and down those stairs all the time, and that bloody washing got caught on the fence more times than I care to remember. And as for dragging that tin bath up the stairs on Fridays . . . I dunno how you've been managing.'

'I'm sorry I've been a nuisance.'

Bella laughed. 'You ain't been a nuisance, love. I've enjoyed it. Fred brought the bath up for me, and put it away after. I wouldn't like having an outside bog again, though. Didn't like creeping out there in the dark.'

'You're getting soft,' said Maggie.

'Reckon I am. You wait till you get a nice house with it

185

inside, then you'll wonder how you managed.'

Maggie tried to hide her feelings, knowing that was what Tony wanted – a nice house.

'Sounds like you'll be glad to get back home,' she said.

'Na. In fact I reckon my house will seem like a morgue after I've been here for a couple of weeks.'

'I know how you feel,' said David. 'It must be nice to come home to a warm friendly house.'

'Where d'you live then, son?' asked Bella, pouring out the tea.

'Greenwich.'

'Oh very nice. Got a house, have you?'

'Yes, but it feels a bit empty at times.'

Maggie stirred her tea. She suddenly felt embarrassed. 'Thank you for bringing me home,' she said softly.

'It was no trouble.'

Bella took the cups into the kitchen.

'Maggie – do you mind if I call you Maggie?'

She laughed. 'Course not, everybody else does.' For some unknown reason she wanted to keep the conversation light-hearted.

'Maggie, could I come round and—'

'You don't normally ask. Have you any more news?'

'No, but I would like to come and have a chat with you one evening, that's if you don't mind.'

'No, course not. Is it about Tony?'

'In a way, yes.' He stood up. 'Well, I think I'd better be off. Got to do some work sometimes.'

'I hope I haven't kept you.'

'No, course not. Bye, Mrs Ross,' he shouted.

Bella poked her head round the door. 'Bye.'

When they'd heard the front door shut Bella asked, 'What was that all about?'

'I don't know. He said he wanted to see me.'

'About Tony?'

'I don't know.'

Bella sat next to Maggie. 'You know what I reckon?'

Maggie shook her head.

Bella straightened herself up. 'I reckon he's setting his cap at you.'

'What?' Maggie laughed. 'Don't talk daft. I'm married to your son, remember. 'Sides, he's a policeman.'

'He is rather nice, though, and very considerate – that is, for a copper. You could do worse. And he's got a house.'

'And he might live with his mother. 'Sides, I ain't looking for anyone else. I'm married.'

'I think we've got to accept that Tony's . . . Well, you know . . .'

'No, I don't know,' said Maggie angrily. 'I'm surprised at what I'm hearing, and surprised at you accepting that Tony could be dead. And now you're trying to get me married off.' Her voice rose and her tears began to flow. 'What did I do to make him run off like this?'

'I dunno, love, and I ain't trying to get you married off. I'm sorry, Maggs, I wouldn't upset you for the world, especially after what you've been through lately. I just want to see you and the kids happy again, but I think we should face up to—'

Maggie jumped up. 'I ain't staying here to listen to you. I won't be happy till Tony comes back. I love him – d'you hear? – and I know he'll be back, I just know he will. You wait and see.' She rushed into her bedroom and slammed the door.

Bella sat back, acknowledging her thoughtlessness, knowing Maggie was down after losing the baby. She walked to the window and looked down on the market. Somehow she had to tell Maggie what Benny had told her, that he thought Tony had been involved with a Mr Windsor and a gambling syndicate. If he owed that man money that could mean trouble for all of them if he came here. Benny said Windsor was a nasty bit of work. They would have to look at those books again. Did the W stand for Windsor, and not Wally as they had first thought? And what kind of trouble had Tony got himself – and Maggie and the kids – into? In some ways it would be safer for her to have that copper hanging around.

Maggie's arm was being gently shaken. 'Mummy, Granny Ross said are you getting up for tea?'

She sat up. 'Sorry, darling. I must have dropped off.'

Laura climbed on the bed and sat beside her. 'Have you been very ill?'

'No, not very.'

'Then why was you in hospital for such a long time?'

'I was a bit ill and very tired.'

'We missed you. I wanted to come to see you in hospital but Granny Ross said the nurses wouldn't let me. I think that's ever so rotten of 'em, and them not having any babies as well. We've got haddock for tea. Are you going to get up?'

'Yes, my darling.' Maggie sat up and hugged her daughter.

'Feeling a bit better?' asked Bella when Maggie walked into the living room.

Maggie nodded. 'I'm sorry for going off like that.'

'Don't worry about it. It was my fault.'

As they sat at the table both Bella and Maggie couldn't find the right words to say. But they both knew Tony was filling their thoughts.

At six o'clock Eve came racing up the stairs. She threw her arms round Maggie's neck.

'It's good to have you back home, I've really missed you, and I'm so sorry about the baby. What d'you think brought it on?'

Maggie shrugged, smiled and said, 'I wish I knew.' She wasn't going to tell anyone about Mr Windsor, or his sidekick Reg Todd. 'Thanks for coming back and taking care of everythink. I dread to think what effect it would have had on the kids to see me like that.'

Eve shrugged. 'That's what friends is for. That was good of that copper to take Bella to the hospital every day, wasn't it?'

'Yes, it was.'

'What's he like then?' asked Eve, peering into the mirror and running her little finger over her bright red lips.

'He ain't a bad bloke for a copper,' said Bella. 'Think he's got a soft spot for our Maggs here.'

'Don't start on that again,' said Maggie, giving Bella a dirty look.

'Oh dear, have I asked the wrong thing? Is he good-looking though?'

'Trust you to ask that,' said Maggie.

'Well, is he?'

'He's not bad at all,' said Bella. 'And he's a widower.'

'Is he now?' said Eve. 'And he's taken a shine to our Maggs then?'

'No he ain't, and she talks a lot of rot sometimes.'

'Sounds like I'll have to meet this bloke.'

Bella tutted and laughed. 'Can't keep yer hands off 'em, can yer? Remember you're a married woman.'

'Did your brother come and see you?' asked Eve, changing the subject.

'No, but he sent a letter.'

'Well, I reckon all this worry about his money could have brought this on,' said Eve.

'What money?' asked Bella quickly.

'Ain't she told you?'

'No she ain't.'

'Eve, it ain't nothink to do with Bella. This is between me and my brother.'

'If it concerns that son of mine, then it's to do with me as well.'

'Tony borrowed some money off him, that's all.'

'How much?'

'A few pounds.'

'How much?' asked Bella forcefully.

'Twenty pounds,' said Maggie.

'What?'

Maggie didn't answer.

'And do you know, that brother of hers had the cheek to take the two pounds Maggs was saving to take the kids to Ramsgate with.' Eve sat back.

'Eve, I told you, it's none of your business.'

'That's settled it. We're going to Ramsgate as soon as you feel up to it,' said Bella. She waved her finger at Maggie. 'And I don't want any arguments about it, it'll be my treat.'

'I can't let you pay for—'

Bella held up her hand. 'Shut it.'

Eve giggled. 'So, do as you're told. When you thinking of going then?'

'It's up to Maggs.'

'I don't know. What about the stall and the stock? I noticed there wasn't that much when we came past.'

'Benny's been keeping his eye on things for you, and I've been keeping yer book up to date. By the way, I didn't tell yer before but old Wally Marsh died.'

Maggie almost said, 'I know,' but quickly recovered. 'He did? When?'

'A week or so before you went in hospital.'

'Was that the sod that come here?' asked Eve.

'Yer,' said Bella. 'I went to see him at the auction room, you know. In fact it was me and the Inspector what took him to the hospital.'

'Well, you ain't got any more worries about him turning up on your doorstep then, have you?' said Eve.

'No,' said Maggie thoughtfully, and she wasn't going to tell them that it wasn't him she was worried about. 'We could go to Ramsgate the week after next if you like.'

'Only if you feel up to it.'

Maggie smiled. 'I'll be all right. Besides, the kids need a break.'

'So do I,' said Bella laughing, 'after all this washing and ironing. I don't know how those two get into such a state.'

Chapter 17

Laura and Jamie looked tanned and happy as they skipped along Kelvin Market holding the sticks of rock they were going to give the stallholders.

'I reckon they'll be a right sticky mess when they get 'em,' said Bella.

Bella had laughed when Laura told them what they wanted to buy everybody. 'I can just see old Mrs Russell, and Mr Goldman trying to get their teeth round that.'

But Maggie was pleased they wanted to share some of the money the traders had given them.

Where was Winnie? She was always the first to greet them. Her stall was there, and she knew they would be home today. 'Where's Winnie?' she called to Ada.

'She didn't come back from the pub. Fink she met a couple of old cronies she used to know.'

'Did she say if she'll be back later?'

'I would fink so,' came the reply. 'Only hope she ain't legless.'

Maggie was concerned. Winnie never left Ada in charge all day, especially on a Saturday, their busiest day. Perhaps she was in the flat with a cup of tea waiting. That would be the sort of thing Winnie would do.

'All right then, Fred?' asked Maggie smiling.

'Yer, gel. You look as if you've all had a good time.'

'Yes, we have. I see Winnie's gone off.'

'Yer.' Fred carried on serving his customers.

'You gonner stay over the weekend then, Bella?' asked Maggie, when they reached her front door.

'If you want me to, love.' Bella put her bag on the floor while Maggie opened up. 'But I don't want to get in the way, and I'll have to go home soon to pay me rent. Don't want 'em chucking me out.'

Maggie sensed this light banter was to hide the anxiety she too was feeling. Although she guessed Winnie would be upstairs and even though Wally was no longer on the scene, she was still very apprehensive at what they could find if Mr Windsor had paid her a visit while they'd been away.

Their few days' holiday had been a huge success, thanks to Bella and the wonderful weather. They could never have had so good a holiday without Bella's money. Maggie had felt relaxed and happy sitting in the warm sunshine watching the children play on the sands, but now, as she returned home, all the old worries and uncertainties began to crowd in on her.

Had Mr Windsor been back? How was Bill managing? The stall was looking half empty. The week after next Jamie would be starting school, which would give her more time to try to find stock.

'You could always move in with Benny if they did chuck you out,' Maggie laughed half-heartedly as they mounted the stairs.

'Don't start on that bloody nonsense again. This weather

and these stairs kills me feet. Won't be sorry to get these shoes off.'

Maggie pushed open the living-room door and stood in the doorway for a moment just looking round. She let out a sigh of relief. It was just as she had left it. 'Yoo-hoo, Win, we're home. Are you there?'

Bella was right behind her. 'I tell yer, gel, I was a bit worried at what you might find in here.'

Maggie turned on her. 'Why? Wally's dead.'

'Oh yer, so he is.' Bella knew she would have to tell Maggie soon that Mr Windsor was out of prison and would come looking for Tony. But would that be worrying her unnecessarily? Did he know where Tony lived?

'Win, are you here? We're home,' called Maggie, walking into the kitchen.

She came back out. 'That's funny, she ain't here.'

'P'raps it's like Ada said, she's had a skinful with some old mates.'

Maggie frowned. 'But that's not like Winnie.'

'Well, don't worry about her now, just put the kettle on. I'm parched.'

That evening when the children were in bed, and after Bill had brought in the day's takings, Bella and Maggie sat waiting for Eve to arrive.

'The stall ain't doing so well, is it, Maggs?'

'No, I'm worried. You don't think Bill's . . .?'

Bella shook her head. 'No, he's an honest enough lad. D'you know what I think the trouble is: lack of the right kinda stock.'

'It's the lack of any kind of stock. Some of that rubbish

has been hanging about for years. I'll have to go to see what Benny's got on Monday.'

'People have changed. They seem to have a few bob these days for silly knick-knacks. Look at what was on sale down at Ramsgate. You'll have to find other places to buy from, try to go a bit up-market.'

'I know, but what? And where will I get the money from to buy that sort of stuff? And will it sell?'

'You could give it a try. I'll have a talk to Benny next week. I'm surprised Winnie didn't come back to see you,' said Bella, changing the subject.

Maggie moved over to the open window, the noise of the market packing away drifting up. 'So am I. I see Fred and Tom are putting her stall away. You don't reckon she's been taken ill, do you?'

'Wouldn't like to say. Na, that lot down there would know soon enough. She got her stall out this morning, didn't she?'

'So Ada said. She didn't come back after going to the pub.'

'And she was all right then?'

'I expect so.'

'D'you think she got Brahms?'

'Dunno. Still, if she did Gus would tell someone, surely?'

'Unless she managed to stagger out on her own.'

Maggie sat down. 'I could pop up to the Dog later, then if they don't know, tomorrow I'll go round her place, that's if she ain't here by then.'

Bella gave a little grin. 'I know I shouldn't say this, but then you know my warped sense of humour, gel. This market'll get a bad name if all the traders keep disappearing.'

'Bella, what a rotten thing to say. Mind you, if it got in the papers with pictures, somebody might recognise Tony.'

Bella didn't answer.

Eve threw her arms round Maggie when she came breezing in. 'I ain't half missed you.'

'Christ, we've only been gorn a week,' said Bella.

Eve looked lovely. She was wearing a small beige straw hat with an upturned brim. Her light floral frock fitted snug over the hips, then flared out.

'You look very nice,' said Maggie.

'Treated meself. D'you like it?' She did a twirl.

'Lovely,' said Bella. 'Only wish I was a few stone lighter.'

'Well, you two look as if you had a nice time. It's been bloody hot up here, I can tell you. Look at your tanned faces. I really envy you. Did you have a paddle? Did the kids enjoy it?'

'Yes they did, and they brought you back a stick of rock.'

'Did they? Can I go and thank 'em?' asked Eve, going to their bedroom door.

'If you like.'

Eve was back almost at once. 'They're fast asleep.'

'I expect they're worn out. It's been a long day for 'em.'

'They look ever so well, and young Jamie's hair has gone really fair. I left Dan in the pub – d'you fancy a drink?'

'I was going to call in to see Gus, but I can't leave the kids for too long.'

'Course you can,' said Bella. 'I'll look after 'em. Go on, go out and enjoy yourself for a half-hour.'

'I wouldn't mind.'

'Right, grab your bag and we'll be off,' said Eve, poised at the door ready.

'You got enough for a drink, Maggs?' asked Bella.

'Yes thanks.' She was glad Bill had taken a few shillings today.

'Well,' said Eve, when they were outside, 'did you really have a good time?'

'Yes we did.'

'I'm glad.' Eve put her arm through Maggie's. 'Now, Mrs Ross, what's the future got lined up for you?'

'I wish I knew, Eve. But one thing's for sure, I've got to try and earn enough money to keep our heads above water, and to pay off Alan.' Maggie wanted to add, 'And Mr Windsor as well,' but she knew that wouldn't be wise – not just yet anyway.

Maggie was greeted like a long-lost soul when she entered the pub. It was the first time she had been in there since she'd lost the baby. Drinks were put in front of her at an alarming rate, but with Eve's help she made sure she didn't offend anyone. She was pleased that neither Tony nor Inspector Matthews was mentioned.

'You're looking really well,' said Beatie, sitting at their table. 'That holiday's done you the world of good.'

'I couldn't have done it without Bella's help.'

'She's a good 'en. The way she looked after those kids of yours while you was in hospital – well, she's a diamond.'

'I know, and I'm gonner miss her when she goes back home.'

Dan put another drink on the table.

'Thanks, Dan,' grinned Maggie. 'But I think I've . . .'

He leant closer. 'It ain't from me, it's from Ding Dong. He's just walked in.'

Maggie looked up and waved to him. The last she'd heard he'd been in the clink. She wanted to run over to him right away, but knew she couldn't. 'Thank him, oh and, Dan, could you ask him if he'll be around on Monday morning?'

'Why's that, gel? You want to put a bet on?' asked Beatie.

'No, I'd like to have a chat with him, that's all.'

'If it's about Tony, well, gel, if you want my advice I'd call it a day. After all, you ain't seen hide or hair of the old bugger for months now, have you? I think Bella's given up about ever seeing him again. It's a shame.'

Gus began yelling for Beatie.

'All right, all right, I'm coming. Can't sit down for a minute before he starts shouting for me.' Beatie stood up.

'Beatie, was Winnie in here lunchtime?'

'Dunno, I was upstairs.' Beatie moved over to the bar.

'What was that about?' asked Eve.

'Winnie didn't put her stall away and I wondered if she'd been in here.'

'So why do you want to see Ding Dong? Is it about Tony?' asked Eve.

Maggie nodded. She giggled – the drinks were going to her head – and when Ivy began playing she sang her heart out, and all thoughts of Winnie went completely.

When Ivy got to a sentimental song Maggie wanted to cry. She missed Tony so much and longed for his arms round her, and to be made love to.

When Ivy changed her tune so Maggie's thoughts changed. How was she going to manage to pay off Tony's debts? And exactly how much did he owe? How was she going to live and keep the children fed, and clothed? The drink was making her feel very sorry for herself. Tears began to trickle down her cheeks. Ivy began belting out 'Pack Up Your Troubles in Your Old Kit Bag'. Maggie wished she had an old kit bag she could just pack all her troubles into and then throw it into the Thames.

She woke with a thumping headache. Gently she lifted her head off the pillow. She could hear the children laughing, and Bella singing. She lay back down again. They didn't need her.

A racket in the living room brought Maggie back to her senses. It was Winnie's voice. What was she doing here on a Sunday? She moved as quickly as her head would allow, grabbed her dressing gown and went into the living room.

'Good morning, miss,' said Bella breezily. She turned to Winnie, who had a swollen, bruised cheek. 'D'you know, me and Eve had to almost put her to bed last night, she was in a right old state when she got home.'

'What happened to you?' asked Maggie, her voice thick with sleep. 'Where was you yesterday?'

'Could I have a quiet word?'

'Course. Come in the bedroom.'

'Don't mind me,' said Bella curtly.

Maggie closed the door and sat on the bed.

'You look bloody awful,' said Winnie.

Maggie smiled. 'I know, and me mouth feels like a sewer. But say, have you seen yourself? How did you get that? I know, you walked into a door.'

Winnie looked in the dressing-table mirror. 'As a matter

of fact I did walk into a door, or to put it another way, the door came and hit me.'

Maggie laughed. 'Oh me head. Don't give me that, Win.'

Winnie sat on the chair. 'I got this because of your old man.'

'What?' Maggie felt the colour drain from her face. 'You've seen Tony?' she whispered.

'No, but I seen those two blokes that was with him that time in the pub and I asked 'em about Tony.'

'You did? What did they look like?' asked Maggie, almost dreading the answer.

'The older one was well dressed in grey, and the other one was bigger and . . . You all right?'

Maggie felt sick. 'Yes, thanks, got a bit of a hangover.'

'Serves yer right, silly cow. As I was saying. I went up the Dog for a quick one yesterday lunchtime as it was so bloody hot, and there as bold as brass was these two blokes sitting there. I said to Gus I thought they were the blokes that was in there with Tony.'

'Gus didn't say anythink last night.'

'Probably didn't think any more about it. Anyway, when I turned round, they'd gone, so I downed me stout and went out to try and see 'em. They was just getting into a car so I banged on the window. Anyway, to cut a long story short, they told me if I didn't know where your old man was, to piss off and mind me own business. Well, I told them in no uncertain words what I thought about them.'

'Tea up,' yelled Bella. 'D'you want it in there?'

Maggie opened the door. 'If you don't mind.' Maggie took the two cups from Bella.

'What's she got to say for herself that's so private?' asked

201

Bella in a hushed voice, nodding her head towards the bedroom.

'I'll tell you all about it later.'

But Bella didn't look too happy as she closed the door.

'So why didn't you go back to your stall?' asked Maggie.

'I was going to, but I wanted to find out what they knew so I banged on the car window again. Well, the young one – he didn't half look wild – shoved open the door and caught me face. I fell over, and as you can see I ain't no lightweight. The old man rushed round, picked me off the ground and shoved me in the car. I tell yer, gel, I was frightened ter death. I thought they was gonner kidnap me. Anyway, they took me to the hospital, then scarpered. In the car the old one was giving this Reg a right telling off, said he was worried somebody might have seen what happened. So anyway, be the time I got out of the hospital I knew it was too late to put the stall away. I wasn't worried as I guessed Fred and Tom would do that for me, and I had to get back to Mum.' She took a gulp of her tea. 'This morning I thought I'd have a stroll round to the lockup just to see what Ada had been up to, then I thought I'd better pop in to see you and let you know what happened, and to find out if you had a nice holiday.'

Maggie sat listening. 'I'm glad you did. Yes, we had a good time. Win, I was getting worried about you.' So Tony has caused someone else pain, she thought.

'Don't worry about me. I'm all right.'

Maggie stood up. 'It ain't all right,' she shouted angrily. 'There's you, Mr Goldman, how many more? Did they tell you why they wanted Tony?'

'No.'

'It's about money. It's all about money.' She threw her arms into the air. 'He owes my brother eighteen pounds. Wally came here for his books, so God only knows what that was all about. Mr Windsor, that's the old boy's name, came here for money, and I've no idea what he owes him.' She sat down again. 'I don't know what I'm gonner do. I'm at my wits' end.' She put her head in her hands and wept.

Winnie put her arm round Maggie's shoulders. 'Go on, love, you have a good cry. Does Bella know about this?'

Maggie shook her head.

The bedroom door flew open. 'What's going on in here? What have you been saying to upset her like this?' yelled Bella.

'Bella, I think you'd best send the kids out, then we'd all better sit down and have a chat.' Winnie was still holding Maggie close.

Bella glanced from one to the other – they looked so sad and dejected. 'They've gone out to play already.'

Winnie helped Maggie to her feet and into the living room. After settling her on the sofa she said to Bella, 'You sit here with her and I'll put the kettle back on.'

They sat drinking tea while Winnie told Bella all what had happened, and then Maggie told her about Mr Windsor coming to the house, but not about Reg pushing her.

When they finished Bella walked to the window. She peered down on the market. It always looked so empty on Sundays. Apart from the trains the only sound that came drifting up was from the Salvation Army band. 'I've got something to tell you now.'

Two heads shot up.

'You know somethink?' asked Winnie.

'Just that Benny told me about this Mr Windsor. Maggs, I didn't say anythink before as I didn't want to worry you. I didn't know he'd been here.'

'Who is he?' asked Maggie.

'He's part of a big betting syndicate, and it seems Tony's mixed up with him, and, according to Benny, if anyone owes him money, he can be a very nasty piece of work. You'll have to go and see that copper of yours,' said Bella. 'You can't go on being threatened like this.'

'Look, you don't 'ave to mention to him about what happened to me, do you?' asked Winnie.

'Why's that?' asked Maggie.

'Well, as I said, it was an accident really.'

Maggie turned to Bella. 'Anyway, what can the Inspector do?'

'I'm sure he'll be able to tell you all about Mr Windsor,' said Bella.

'What if it's somethink I don't want to hear?'

'I think we've got to face up to it, gel, there's a lot we don't want to know about, but . . .' Bella sighed. 'At least we know Mr bloody Windsor ain't done nothink to Tony otherwise he wouldn't be looking for him.'

Maggie hadn't thought of that.

Chapter 18

On Monday morning, although Maggie knew she should be going to see Benny to buy stock, she thought that going to the police station was more important, even though she had promised Winnie not to mention her dealings with infamous Mr Windsor.

'Maggie,' said Inspector Matthews, when he saw her sitting in the waiting area. 'I must say you look very well after your holiday. Did you have a nice time?'

'Yes thank you.'

The young policeman standing behind the counter looked up, full of curiosity.

'Well, Mrs Ross,' said the Inspector, glancing across at him, 'what can I do for you?'

Maggie looked around.

'Come through to my office.'

Sitting in the chair he offered, she was cross with herself. Why did she always feel embarrassed in this man's company?

'I think there is something I should tell you. In fact both me and Bella – Mrs Ross – think you should know.'

David Matthews sat back and played with a pencil.

Maggie fiddled with her handbag. 'You see, there is this Mr Windsor, he keeps asking about Tony, and Saturday—'

The pencil snapping in two made Maggie jump. David Matthews threw the pieces on to his desk. He leant forward. 'Have you seen Mr Windsor?'

Maggie nodded. 'He came to the flat.'

'When?' The question came like a gun shot.

'That evening before I went in the hospital.'

David Matthews jumped up and walked round the desk. 'Why didn't you tell me before? What did he want?'

'Money that Tony owes him.'

'Which you haven't got? Maggie, now tell me the truth, did he . . . did he knock you about?'

'No.'

'Are you sure? He has a reputation, you know. And you're sure he wasn't the cause of you losing the baby?'

'Course.'

He sat on his desk facing her, his face full of concern.

She was aware of his eyes searching her face, but couldn't meet his gaze. She could feel his warmth close to her. 'I think it was just one of those things,' she said softly.

Suddenly he bent down and, taking hold of her shoulders, pulled her to her feet. 'Please, Maggie, you must be careful.'

'Inspector Matthews.' She quickly stood up, and although she wanted to melt into his arms, she pushed him away. She needed someone to hold her and take care of her, but she was married to Tony.

'Please call me David.'

Tony flooded her thoughts, and she moved away. 'That ain't very professional.'

He moved back to his seat behind the desk. 'I'm afraid I don't feel very professional when you're around.' He quickly took a cigarette from the packet that had been thrown amongst the papers that were strewn over his desk and lit it, angry with himself for almost losing his self-control.

Maggie sat down. She didn't know what to say. She had wanted him to make a pass at her, but now ... 'Inspector Matthews,' she said slowly and very deliberately, 'I don't think Mr Windsor could have hurt Tony, otherwise he wouldn't be looking for him.'

David blew the smoke high into the air. 'That's very true, Mrs Ross.'

Maggie felt a barrier had been placed between them, and it had been her doing.

'You do know that Mr Windsor has been in prison?'

'No.' Maggie was taken aback.

'And that he runs a very large betting syndicate.'

'Bella did mention something about that.'

'Well, I believe that your husband has gone to ground because he owes a lot of people a great deal of money.'

Maggie felt her face pale.

'First there was Wally Marsh, and then—'

'Inspector, I know Tony owed money, but I do feel he would have contacted me in some way if he could. You see we love each other very much, and he would never do anything to hurt me and—'

'Maggie,' he ground his cigarette stub into the overfull ashtray, 'how can you sit there and say that when he wasn't around when you lost the baby? And he's supposed to be fond of his mother, but he hasn't got in touch with her either. And what about your lovely kids?' David Matthews lit another cigarette. 'No, I'm sorry, but I think he's gone, left the country. He knew he would be—'

Maggie jumped to her feet. 'No. You're wrong,' she cried. 'He loved me and the children, and he wouldn't go away without me. Not for good,' she added in a whisper.

'Well, what other explanation can you give for his disappearance?'

'I don't know.' She sat down.

'Would you like a cup of tea?'

She shook her head.

'Would you like me to run you home?'

She could only nod. 'I should really be going to see Benny.'

'I could take you there first if you like.'

'I'd better.'

But when they got to Benny's he was out.

The journey back to the market was silent. Maggie sat staring in front of her. She wondered what was going through David Matthews's mind, but couldn't look at him.

She would have been shocked to know that he was thinking of ways to find out the truth about Tony Ross, and with some hope, a body. That at least would settle Maggie's status – widow rather than abandoned wife.

'Did you have a special reason for coming to see me this morning?' he asked.

'Yes. I was worried about Winnie.'

'Winnie on the market?'

'Yes.'

He stopped the car. 'What's happened to her?'

'It seems Mr Windsor was in the Dog on Saturday and, Winnie reckons he was one of the last to see Tony, so she went to have a word with him, and his minder . . .'

'Reg Todd.'

Maggie nodded. 'He accidentally hit Winnie with the car door. They took her to hospital. She's all right, though,' added Maggie quickly.

He started the car again. 'It seems as if I should be having a word with our friend.'

'Who, Winnie?'

'No. Windsor.'

'I don't think that would be such a good idea.'

'Why?'

'I wouldn't want them to come back to me or Winnie.'

'Don't worry, I'll find some way of pulling him in.'

'Thank you for the lift.' Maggie didn't attempt to hang around, she didn't want him to come upstairs.

'I'll be in touch,' he called through the car window.

As she walked up the stairs she queried her own feelings. Why didn't she invite him in? The children and Bella were there. What was she afraid of?

'I'm home,' she called out, pushing the living-room door open.

''Allo, love.'

Maggie was surprised to see Benny sitting in the chair, and in his work clothes.

'Hallo, Benny. I've just been to your place. I didn't see your horse, where is she?'

'Shoved a nosebag on her and left her round the corner. Young Fred down there gets right narked when she starts rummaging among his fruit.'

'I'm not surprised,' said Maggie, glancing in the mirror as she removed her navy straw hat. 'How's business?'

'Not bad. I've brought a few bits over for you.'

'Thanks.'

'You're back quick,' said Bella, smiling. 'Did he bring you home?'

Maggie nodded.

'I was telling Benny here that you're thinking of expanding the business.'

Maggie sat down. 'I don't know how. I've got to find the money first.'

Bella tutted and tossed her head. 'I keep telling her we should be in this thing together.'

'She's right, you know, gel. Seems these days that people have got a few more bob to spend on fripperies, and you're just the gel to sell it.' Benny leant forward. 'D'you know, I reckon with the right sort o' gear you could do very nicely down there.'

Maggie was getting tired of all this advice. 'So what gold mine do you suggest I start looking for to buy all this stuff that's gonner make me a millionaire?'

'You don't have to be so flippant about it, gel. Benny's only trying to help.'

Suddenly it all seemed too much for her. She could feel her patience snap like a broken string. 'Everyone's only trying to help, but what good is it doing? I've got two kids and a shitty business that's just about paying the rent. What am I gonner do?' she cried.

'Pull yourself together for one thing,' said Bella drily.

'I don't want to pull myself together, I want to be left alone, and I don't want to keep having handouts.'

'We're only trying to help,' said Bella haughtily.

'I shouldn't need help. If your son had been a bit more truthful and told me what he'd got himself into I wouldn't be in this state now.'

'I suppose he didn't want to worry you.'

'Worry me? Worry me? So what the bloody hell do you think he's doing to me now?'

'He must have a reason.'

'Like what? Go on, tell me. Am I suddenly gonner get a bundle of pound notes pushed through me letter box with a letter saying, "Sorry, love, but I had a few gambling debts. Here's some money to keep 'em sweet as I don't want you and your friends to worry about being beaten up"?'

'You don't have to talk to Bella like that, love,' said Benny. 'Not after she's paid for you all to have a nice holiday.'

'That's it, ain't it? She pays for this and that, she ain't got a bottomless purse. And I don't like taking money off her.'

'I did my bit towards the holiday 'cos I wanted to.'

'I know, and I'm really grateful. But I still think Tony should show himself. I hate him, d'you hear? I hate him for what he's doing to me and the kids.' Maggie sat in the chair and wept.

Bella went to put her arms round her.

'Go away. Leave me be. I don't want to keep relying on you.'

'I don't mind. After all, we are family.'

'I don't want to be family. I want to be left alone.'

'Oh very nice, I must say.' Bella began collecting the tea

211

things. 'I ain't staying where I ain't wanted.'

'Well, go then. And if that son of yours turns up, tell him to drop dead. That way at least you'll get his insurance.'

Bella stood riveted to the spot.

'Maggie, that's a dreadful thing to say,' said Benny, pushing his trilby back and scratching his forehead.

'That's it. I ain't staying here to listen to this sorta talk.'

'Well, go on then, shove off. Leave me alone.'

Benny looked from one to the other. 'Maggie, I don't think you should say things like—'

'And you can go, an' all. I don't want any more of your condescending handouts.' Maggie walked into her bedroom and slammed the door.

When she heard the front door shut she began to cry. At first it was a gentle cry, then as she got angrier it became a wail and she pummelled the pillow with hate, anger, and frustration.

'Maggs, Maggie? You all right, gel?' Winnie's voice broke into her distress.

She sat up and wiped her eyes.

'What the bloody hell's been going on up here?'

'Why? What d'you mean?'

'There's you looking like you've been crying for hours, and there's Bella storming off down the road, swinging her bag and pushing everybody out of the way, and poor old Benny in tow, trying to keep up. Bella's face looked like thunder. When I asked if everything was all right I just got a mouthful of abuse and told ter mind me own business.' Winnie sat on the bed.

'I told Bella to clear off,' said Maggie.

'Oh, that's very bright, I must say. Why?'

'I don't know really.' She gave a loud sob. 'I just feel I want to be left alone, I suppose.'

'Well, love, you shouldn't upset Bella, of all people. After all, she's been good to—'

Maggie jumped off the bed. 'That's the bloody trouble. She's been good to me, and all I seem to do is take from her.'

'But it's family, gel, and if we can't look after family then where would we be?'

'And I don't need you to tell me that.'

'Oh very nice, I must say. What's got into you?'

Tears filled Maggie's eyes. 'I thought it would have been obvious.'

'Course it is, love. You've probably got a bit down after losing the baby, but you've got to be positive about all this.'

'So what's your suggestion?'

'I'll put the kettle on. By the way, did you go and see your policeman?' she called from the kitchen.

'Yes,' replied Maggie.

'Well, what'd he say?'

'Not a lot really. He might pull that Mr Windsor in.'

'I ain't gonner make a complaint,' said Winnie quickly, coming back. 'Don't want the likes of him coming sniffing around.'

'He said he'd find some excuse.'

They were sitting drinking tea when Winnie said, 'You know, you'll have to make your peace with Bella.'

Maggie held her cup with both hands. 'I know. But I've got to try and find a way of managing on my own.'

'Now how yer gonner do that?'

'I don't know, Win. I really don't know.'

'What about that brother of yours? Can't he help?'

Maggie tossed her head. 'Can't see him being of any use, not with the money I owe him.'

'You mean Tony owes him as well?'

'Me, Tony, what's the odds? Helen will still want it all back.'

Winnie poured her tea in the saucer and began slurping. 'Have you heard from him lately?'

'He wrote to me when I was in hospital, but he ain't been over. Probably didn't think it was worth it till I'd got some money for him.'

'Is it much?'

'Eighteen pounds.'

'Phew, that's a tall order.'

'I know.'

'How many more does Tony owe to?'

'I dunno. And I don't know how I'm gonner pay 'em back.'

'I always liked Tony, but now after all this – well, I reckon he's turned out to be a right cowson. And if you ask me—'

'I don't want any more advice, thank you.'

'And let's hope we don't have a bad winter, 'cos it gets bloody hard down there then.'

Winter was the last thing on Maggie's mind; she was too worried about the present. 'Winnie, what am I gonner do?'

'You've just got to go on. Think of the kids.'

They sat quietly for a while, then Winnie said, 'Look, I'd better go. You all right now, love?'

Maggie nodded. 'For the time being.'

Maggie sat going over and over in her mind ways to salvage the situation, but they all came back to money, and the lack of it to make a start. She looked round the room. If the worst came to the worst, she could always pawn something, but what? This was her home and everything meant so much to her. Besides, did she really want everybody to know how bad things were?

It was Bill knocking on the living-room door that brought Maggie out of her thoughts. She had been thinking about all she'd said to Bella and Winnie. She knew she was wrong, but how could she tell them that part of the reason things were getting on top of her was the fact she needed someone to love her and look after her.

''Allo, Maggs,' said Bill, putting his leather money apron on the table and snatching his cap from off his head.

'Sit down, Bill.'

He sat on the edge of the chair. 'You all right?' he asked.

She gave him a slight smile. 'Just a bit low, that's all.'

He nervously twisted his cap in his hands. 'Maggs, I know things ain't very good down there.' He nodded towards the window. 'We've gotter start doing something soon. What chance is there of you getting more—'

'Benny did bring a few bits in. I haven't sorted them out yet. But I'm gonner see about it tomorrow. I know I should have gone out today, but, well, somethink come up.'

'I saw Bella and Benny rushing down the road. I thought they might have got some news.'

'Bella had to go home.'

'Thought it looked like she had a bee in her bonnet. Everythink all right?'

215

'Yes, she had to pay her rent in case they threw her out.'

'Oh.'

Maggie stood up. 'What sort of things do you get asked for now?'

'Don't get asked for much at all really.'

'Oh come on, Bill, people must say somethink.'

'Well, a lot of punters are doing up their places and some ask for fancy plates and pictures to put on the walls.'

'That's interesting,' said Maggie thoughtfully.

'You ain't thinking of getting that sort o' stuff, are you?'

'Don't know. Why?'

'Don't want too many breakables.'

Maggie laughed. 'And if I decide what to sell, while you're working for me, you'll do as I say.'

He flushed and looked down at his cap. 'Don't yer think Tony's coming back then?'

'I don't know.' She wanted to add that at this moment she didn't care. 'But in the meantime I've got to look after my kids, and with the winter coming, I've got to think of better ways of making a living.'

Bill stood up. 'I best be going.'

Maggie emptied the contents of the apron on to the table.

Bill moved towards the door. 'Maggs, will you be running the stall?'

'Some of the time. Why?'

'Nuffink. Bye.'

When she heard the front door shut Maggie began counting out the money.

'This is ridiculous. This won't keep a sparrow alive,' she said out loud, and began piling up the few coppers and silver. Two and six. Bill hadn't even earned the rent and his wages today. She got her notebook from the sideboard and started a new page. She licked the lead of her pencil. 'Well, girl, this has been quite a day for you. So far you've upset Bella and Benny, and Winnie didn't look that pleased, and now poor Bill's worried about his job.'

Chapter 19

The following morning Maggie went to the auction room where Wally had worked. After studying the catalogue she waited for the auction to begin as she thought it would give her some idea what the dealers were buying.

She sat on the edge of her seat fascinated, carefully watching as item after item was sold, afraid to move in case they thought she was bidding. Bill appeared to be right. Wall plates and pictures were selling very fast, but right out of her price range.

At the end of the auction she wandered around turning over some of the goods that were left. If only she could go upmarket and not have to bother with all this rubbish. She managed to buy a few items, among which was a chipped china butter dish, a small milk jug and sugar bowl, and a glass cake stand. She was very taken with some odd bits of jewellery, and bought a couple of cheap rings, various coloured-bone bangles and round pearl button earrings that ranged in sizes. Twice she picked up a diamanté brooch and some matching earrings and twice she put them down. They were a bit more than she was prepared to spend, but would they sell?

She knew she should save some money for the rent and it was Jamie's fifth birthday next Monday. What could she get him? He would be starting school that day as well. Thank goodness she didn't have to buy him any new clothes, as Bella had already taken care of that before she left. Bella. Guilt filled Maggie. Should she go and make her peace with her? She stepped back.

'Careful, love.' An elderly, portly grey-haired man held her arm to steady her.

'Sorry.' She knew she had trodden on his foot. 'Did I hurt you?'

'No, you're only a light little thing. I see you like pretty things.' He too picked up the jewellery.

'Yes, but will it sell?'

'Depends on your clients. D'you have a shop?'

'No, a stall at the market.' Maggie began to wander to the far end of the room.

'Don't know about that trade. What sort of mark-up do you have?' he asked, trailing behind her.

'I could only put a few pence on them.'

'Do you do the buying?'

'Most of the time.'

'I don't think I've seen you here before.'

'No, I don't usually come to the auction.'

'So, what brings you here today?'

Maggie felt like telling him to mind his own business, but thought better of it. 'Do you work here?' she asked politely, ignoring his question.

He laughed. 'Good heavens no. I just pop in to buy a few bits of furniture, and to see what's selling.'

'So did I. Do you have a shop?'

He nodded. 'Inherited it from Father a few years ago. I wanted to get rid of it, but Mother won't hear of it. But I must admit it is very lucrative.'

Maggie wanted to laugh. He looked well into his fifties, so how old was Mother? Together they wandered back. 'So where's your shop then?' Maggie was drawn to the jewellery again.

'Peckham.'

'That's quite near to—' Maggie didn't know why, but she suddenly stopped. She wasn't going to tell him it wasn't that far from Rotherhithe. 'Is it just furniture you sell?'

'Yes. We like the old stuff that has real character.'

'Oh I see.'

'Could I take you for a coffee or something?'

'No I'm sorry, I have to get back.'

'You have a husband waiting for his dinner, I suppose?'

'Something like that.'

'There is another big auction at the beginning of October, perhaps I'll see you here then.'

'Perhaps.'

'Here, let me give you my card. Who knows, your husband might be interested in buying a nice antique chair or table. We have some really beautiful pieces.' He fished in his wallet and handed Maggie a card.

She laughed. 'I shouldn't think so but thanks all the same. Freeman's Fine Furniture. Sounds very grand.'

'You, my dear, will always be sure of a warm welcome at our shop.'

'Thanks, but I must go. Bye.' Maggie put his card in her handbag. Her thoughts were still on the jewellery. She would dearly love to buy it, but knew she had to be cautious. As she walked to the door she wondered what Tony would have done. 'You have to invest money to make money' was one of his favourite sayings. She suddenly stopped and turned on her heel. She had changed her mind.

There was a heart-fluttering moment as she handed over nearly all her cash for the jewellery. 'What's the odds? Nothing ventured, nothing gained,' she said bravely to herself, walking outside and patting her handbag. Although her purse was empty she was pleased with her purchases. After all, it was very pretty and bound to sell.

When Maggie turned into the market she saw Ding Dong ahead, walking towards the Dog. She quickly caught up with him.

''Allo, gel, everythink all right?' he enquired when she called his name.

'Not too bad.'

'I was just going in for a quick half. D'yer fancy one?'

She nodded. Although drinking at lunchtime was the last thing on Maggie's mind, she did want a word with him, and hopefully they might be alone, as apart from the traders not many people frequented the pub this early in the week.

Inside Maggie moved to a seat away from the bar and Rene, who was listening with rapt attention to a tale one of the breweries' reps was telling her.

''Ere y'are, gel, get that down yer.'

'Thanks, Ding Dong. I was very sorry to hear you've been pulled in again.'

'Yer, me case comes up next week. Bloody nuisance, but there you are. It goes with the job, I suppose.'

'What d'you think you'll get?'

'Just a fine, I reckon.' He bent his head closer. 'Yer see, if I get the right judge I'm all right as he likes a bet on the side.'

'Did Tony have many bets?'

Ding Dong laughed. 'I should say so. Must have lost a packet over the years. You still ain't 'eard nothink then?'

'No.'

'I must say I miss taking his money.'

It was Maggie's turn to look round and then move closer. 'Does he owe you much?'

Ding Dong looked uncomfortable. 'A bit.'

'How much?'

He took a swift noisy drink from his pint and wiped the froth from his lips with the back of his hand. 'Well, it ain't ser much me, yer understand, it's the big boys.'

'How much?' Maggie asked again.

'Dunno orf hand. Must be in the region of about, what, forty smackers all told.'

Maggie took a loud gasp. 'Forty pounds.' She felt sick.

'It's round about that, give or take a few quid.'

'And is some of that Mr Windsor's?'

It was Ding Dong's turn to take a loud breath. This time he moved his chair closer. 'What d'yer know about him?'

'Not a lot. He came to see me.'

Ding Dong went pale. 'He did? When?'

'A while back.'

'What'd he want?'

'Money, like everyone else.'

'Does he know Tony's done a runner?'

Maggie was playing with her glass, she looked up. 'Yes. What makes you so sure Tony's only run off?'

'Well, it stands ter reason. He owes a lot and he's gorn orf to make a few bob so that when he comes back he'll be in the clear.'

Maggie hadn't thought of that. 'But surely he would have told me where he's gone?'

'Dunno about that.' He sat back. 'Yer see, my theory is that what yer don't know, well then yer can't tell anybody, 'specially the likes of Mr Windsor.'

She certainly hadn't thought along those lines before.

'Fancy another?' He picked up his glass.

Maggie shook her head. 'No, thanks. And is some of that money Mr Windsor's?'

'Most of it.'

'What about you?'

'Nuffink really, just a couple of bob.'

'If you tell me how much I'll pay you back.'

'You don't have to do that, gel. I liked your old man. Always gave me a drink, even when he didn't win, so let's call it quits. I'll just get me pint.'

Maggie was thinking over what Ding Dong had said when Beatie came and sat next to her.

'He's had to go off.' She pointed to where Ding Dong had been standing. 'Gus wanted a bet on the two thirty. Well, how're you keeping? Bella got the kids?'

'No, they're out somewhere. They'll be yelling for their dinner soon.'

'Bella gone back home then?'

'Yes.' Maggie wasn't going to tell her why.

'So, what you been up to then?'

'I've been to the auction this morning. Thought I'd have a look round and see what's selling these days.'

224

'You finding it hard then, gel?'

'A bit.'

'So what is selling then?'

'Well I thought I'd try a few new things. Got a bit of jewellery here. Say, what d'you think?' Maggie took it from her bag and laid it on the table.

'Not bad.' Beatie picked up the brooch and turned it over. 'Give it a good clean and I reckon you should sell it OK, just as long as it didn't cost too much.'

'No, only a couple of bob for the lot.'

'Don't care for this cheap imitation stuff meself, I prefer the real thing. I must say.' She looked across at Gus. Satisfied he was busy talking she bent her head closer, 'That's something I do miss your Tony for. As you well know, now and again he'd come in with the odd trinket or two, and at a very reasonable price, and no questions asked.'

Maggie sat open-mouthed.

'Mind you, we never see you done up with yer rings and things. Me, I have ter wear me finery all the time, just in case Gus takes it into his head to sell 'em back to him, or pawn it.'

'Did you get all your rings from Tony?' Maggie asked in a hushed voice.

'Yer, most of 'em, but then you must know that. He said you didn't want 'em, said they was too flash for you.'

Maggie smiled. 'Oh yes, I forgot.' She didn't like to say that she had never seen them before they adorned Beatie's fingers. Were they real? If Tony had given them to her, at least she would have had something to pawn. But where did Tony get them from?

Beatie was still talking but her words weren't registering. 'I must go.' She stood up.

'Maggie, I said have you got your snaps yet?'

'Snaps?'

'Pictures of your holiday. Bella said she took some good ones.'

'Oh yes. No, Bella's still waiting for 'em.'

'Let me see them when you get 'em. Like to see pictures of the sea, as that's the nearest I'll ever get to it.' Beatie laughed. 'Look after yourself, gel.'

Maggie walked out into the sunshine. 'Well,' she said to herself, 'that was a very enlightening half-hour In fact it's been a very enlightening morning all round.'

Bill looked anxious when he saw what Maggie was displaying on a corner of the stall that afternoon. 'Don't know about selling all these fancy bits,' he said.

'Well, we can only give it a try.' Maggie stood back and admired her handiwork. She had carefully cleaned the bits she'd bought, and arranged the items of jewellery on a piece of black cloth she'd managed to get Tom Cooper to part with. 'I think it looks very nice.'

'Yer, 'sall right.'

Maggie smiled. She could see he wasn't impressed. 'Well it makes a change from broken lamps and rusty tools.'

'S'pose so.'

She hoped the punters would be more enthusiastic than Bill.

Chapter 20

Saturday morning Maggie was singing as she got herself ready to go down to the stall. 'Come on, you two, hurry up and finish your breakfast. I've got to go down and give Bill a hand.'

'Why?' asked Jamie.

'I like to chat to people and see what they'd like to buy.'

'Why?' asked Laura.

'I have to do the buying now, and I want to make sure it's right, otherwise we might starve.'

'We won't starve, will we, Mum?' asked Laura, worry puckering her suntanned brow.

Maggie laughed. 'Course not. Now come on.'

'Mummy, we gonner have a tea party on Monday for Jamie's birthday?' asked Laura.

'I think we could have a few children in after school.'

'I'll be all growed up then,' he said, beaming.

'Daft, you don't get grown up just 'cos you're going to school,' said Laura.

'Well, it's more growed up than being at home.'

'Stop it, you two. You'll have to tell me who's coming to this birthday tea.'

'Will Granny Ross come?' asked Jamie.

'I don't know.'

'I hope so. She gives us nice presents.'

'She didn't say goodbye,' said Laura.

'She had to leave in a hurry.'

Laura slid down from the table. 'Don't you like Granny Ross?'

'Of course I do.'

'Did you like Daddy?'

Maggie felt her heart lurch. 'I love your daddy very much.'

'So why does everybody leave us?'

Maggie was at a loss for words. What had she done turning Bella away like that? She had to go to her and make her peace, if only for the children's sake.

'Will Daddy be here for my birthday?' asked Jamie, licking the bowl that had had his porridge in.

'I'm afraid not.'

'Will he be here for my birthday on the twenty-fourth of November?' asked Laura.

'I can't promise.'

'I wish he would come back. I ain't got no one to play football with.'

Maggie stooped down and held him tight. 'I miss Daddy as well.' She blinked back a tear. It wouldn't do to let the children see her crying.

'Why don't you ask Uncle Dan to play with you? Or what about that policeman that comes to see Mum? He ain't got no kids.'

Maggie looked up at Laura. 'How do you know that?'

'I asked him.'

'Do you think he'd take me to the park?' asked Jamie eagerly.

'I don't know, he's a very busy man,' said Maggie, straightening up.

'Well, I'll ask him to come to my party, then I'll ask him to take me to the park.'

Laura gave Jamie a nudge. 'He might get you a new football.'

Jamie's eyes lit up. 'Would he? Mummy, could you ask him if he would?'

'No I won't. You can't go round asking people for presents.'

'Well then, he ain't gonner come to my party if he don't bring me a present.'

'Jamie, I can't tell him that.'

'Oh go on, Mummy. If he ain't got kids of his own he might like to take Jamie out.'

'I don't know.'

'Oh please, Mummy, please.'

Maggie smiled as she tousled Jamie's hair. 'You two have the cheek of the devil.'

'Will you, please?' pleaded Jamie, smoothing down his hair.

'I'll see, but I won't make any promises. Besides, he might be too busy. He has a lot of crimes to solve.'

Maggie was upset that this was going to be the first birthday that Tony wouldn't be around. If he was in hiding would he remember the date? If so, would Jamie get a card from him? Maggie suddenly felt hopeful. Monday could be the day she had been waiting for. 'Now come on, you two, shoo, I've got a lot to do.'

As she did the washing-up Maggie reflected further. What if Jamie did get a card from Tony? That would be the best birthday present ever, just to know he was still alive and thinking of them. Jamie needed a man around and she thought about what he'd said. Should she ask David Matthews to his tea party? Was it wrong? She smiled to herself. Well, it wasn't her idea, and he could only say no. She would go and ask him on Monday morning after the postman had called, and tomorrow she would have to go over to Bella and say sorry.

'Good ter see you down here, Maggs,' said Winnie.

Maggie nodded and grinned. Over these past few months she had enjoyed the few hours she had spent tending the stall. The noise, smell, chatter and bustle had a thrill of its own. She felt she belonged.

'I'm pleased ter see you've got a bit of new stuff,' said Winnie, picking up a ivory-coloured bone bracelet. 'I reckon that'll do all right round here. We ain't had this sorta stuff here before.'

'Well, not many have had money to spend on themselves,' said Maggie, fiddling with her display. 'I hope we take a few bob today. I've got to get something for Jamie's birthday.'

'When's that then?' asked Winnie.

'Monday.'

'Monday? I reckon this lot don't mind chipping in and getting him somethink. Here, Ada, keep yer eye out. I'm just gonner go round and squeeze a few bob out o' these tight-arsed sods. Won't be long.'

'But, Win . . .'

230

'It ain't no good you shouting after her, Maggs. She won't take no notice of yer,' said Bill. 'Once she gits a bee in her bonnet, she's off.'

Maggie laughed. Bill was right, there was no stopping Winnie when she started something.

Half an hour later Winnie returned. 'Here you are, gel. There's a few bob there.' She handed Maggie a paper bag. 'Watch the bottom don't fall out. I even managed to con a couple of bob out of Gus.'

Maggie was surprised at the weight of the bag and almost dropped it. 'Winnie, I can't take all this.'

'It's mostly pennies. 'Sides, ain't fer you, it's for young Jamie. Now go on, take it upstairs and count it out, then tell us what he wants. I reckon old George in the toy shop will knock a bit off of whatever it is.'

Maggie could feel the tears well up in her eyes. These people were so kind. 'I know he wants a football.'

'Reckon there's enough in there to get him half a dozen. No, get him somethink else. What about a scooter?'

Maggie had to wipe away a tear that had spilled over. 'He'd really love one of those. He was hoping that Tony would make him one.'

'Don't like those home-made things. He could end up getting splinters, and those bloody ball-bearing wheels make a bloody racket on these cobbles. No, get him a posh one.'

Maggie hugged Winnie, 'Thanks, I'll pop in later. Mind you, he won't want to go to school and leave it.'

'He's starting school? It don't seem five minutes ago he was born. A lot of water's flown under the bridge since then.'

Maggie could only nod and quickly turned to rearrange the items on display.

'I must say it suits you being down here.'

Maggie looked up to see Alan and Helen standing there. She pushed the paper bag out of sight. 'Hallo, you two. You look well. Where did you go for your holidays after all?'

Helen plumped up the back of her hair, and smiled. 'We went to Devon, to a lovely hotel, and we had lovely weather. You should see my tan.' Her voice was loud enough for Tom Cooper to catch.

'It ain't yer tan I'd be interested in, gel, it'll be yer white bits – that's if of course you ain't been sunning yerself in the nuddy.'

Everybody laughed and Helen went very red.

'So what you two doing round this way?' asked Maggie, dreading the answer. She quickly glanced at the bag of money; she wasn't going to part with any of that.

'We thought we'd pop Jamie's birthday present over, and the little gift we bought the children, just a small souvenir, you understand.' Helen sounded very patronising.

'That's very kind of you. Would you like to come upstairs?'

'A cup of tea would be very welcome,' said Alan. 'Are you sure you can leave the stall?'

'Course. Bill always looks after it. I'm just down here to get people's reactions to the new things I've got.'

Helen took an earring from off the display. 'I must say you seem to have got hold of some very interesting bits and pieces.'

'Do you like those?' asked Alan quickly.

'They're not bad, but not really my taste.'

Helen quickly put it back on the stall, but Maggie could sense by the way she analysed it that she liked it, so that surely was silent praise indeed.

'Won't be long,' said Maggie to Bill. 'Keep your eye on everythink.'

'Sure.' He winked.

As she made her way to her flat she hoped Alan wasn't going to ask for more money.

Helen settled herself on the sofa. 'So, where are the children, out with Mrs Ross?'

'No, she had to go home, they're around playing somewhere.'

'Don't you worry about them mixing with some of those scruffy kids down there?'

'No, they've known them all their lives.'

Helen visibly shuddered. 'Well, I'd be worried sick that they might come home with fleas or impetigo or something.'

Maggie chose to ignore that remark.

'Did you manage to get away, after all?' asked Alan.

'Yes. Bella paid for our holiday.'

'Alan said you were thinking of going to Ramsgate. Was it there you went in the end?'

'Yes, we had a lovely time,' said Maggie, smugly. 'I'll just put the kettle on.'

When she returned to the living room, Helen was busy rummaging through her bag. She brought out a small parcel. 'Here's a car for Jamie's birthday, and I bought them both a little joke cup.' She handed Maggie two tiny china cups that had 'A present from Devon' written on them, and they had holes all round the top; they also had a handle.

233

'You have to try and see if you can drink out of them without spilling any liquid,' she said with a smirk.

Maggie turned them round. She couldn't see Jamie and Laura getting very excited about these; they would have preferred a stick of rock.

'I'll show you how you do it,' said Helen, eagerly taking one from Maggie's hand. 'See, you drink through the hole in the handle. I thought they were very clever and I can just see your two taking them to school and fooling all the other children.'

'Thank you, they are very good.' The kettle's whistling took Maggie into the kitchen.

'How is Doreen?' Maggie asked when she returned with the tea tray.

'Very well. She's with a friend for the day. They have a very large house at Eltham,' said Helen.

It had to be a very large house, thought Maggie.

The conversation lapsed when a urgent banging on the front door sent them hurrying down the stairs.

'It's Jamie,' yelled Fred. 'He's up there, been in a fight, so Laura said.' Fred pointed in the direction of the pub end of the market.

'Oh no.' Maggie hurried up the road with Alan on her heels.

Jamie was sitting on the pavement with blood on his shirt.

'Who did this?' screamed Maggie.

'It was that boy,' said Laura, pointing at four scruffy-looking boys standing on the opposite side of the road. They began laughing and walking away.

'I'm all right, Mummy, honest.' Although Jamie had tears

in his eyes he grinned and wiped his nose with the back of his hand, spreading the blood across his face.

'Come on, I'll take you back home. And as for you lot,' shouted Maggie, 'you'd better keep your hands to your-selves otherwise you'll feel mine. He's a lot younger than you.'

'Yer, and what you gonner do, bring yer fancy copper ter give me a hiding? Look, I'm quaking in me boots,' shouted one of them.

The others started laughing.

'Saucy sods,' said Maggie. 'I've a good mind to go—'

'Leave it, Maggs,' interrupted Alan. 'It's not worth get-ting into a scrape over.'

She glared at Alan. 'What d'you mean? Look, he's hurt.'

'No I ain't.'

'What's going on up here?' said Winnie, puffing up to them with Helen at her side.

'Look at Jamie's nose. Those kids did it,' she pointed to the backs of the boys, 'and Alan here won't go after 'em.'

Alan looked sheepish.

'Well, Maggie, you can't expect Alan to look after your brood as well. That's Tony's job, and he should be here to—'

'Don't start, Helen,' said Alan.

'Well, didn't I say earlier that you shouldn't let your children run about in the street with all this riffraff?'

Winnie tutted and tossed her head at Helen.

Maggie felt it was best to ignore Helen and turned to Jamie. 'What was all this about?'

'They said you was a copper's nark.'

'Me?' Maggie was taken aback. 'Why did they say that?'

235

''Cos you go out with a copper. I told 'em you didn't go out with him, he only comes round 'cos me dad's gone away. Then they all laughed at that so I kicked the one with the cap in the shins, and he punched me on the nose.'

Winnie burst out laughing.

'I don't think it's any laughing matter,' said Maggie angrily.

'Well, he was defending your honour.'

'Come on, let me take you home and get you cleaned up.'

Maggie held Jamie's hand. In many ways she was very proud of him, certainly more than of her brother.

As soon as he was cleaned up Jamie was off out again.

'And don't get into any more arguments,' shouted Maggie behind him. She noticed Helen wince. She wouldn't shout out like that, it wasn't ladylike.

Soon after that the living-room door burst open and Eve came in, laughing.

'Jamie's pleased with himself, told me he's been in a fight, and guess what?' said Eve. 'I've just been invited to a birthday . . . Hello, Alan, and Helen. What are you doing over this way?' There was a hint of sarcasm in Eve's voice.

'We've brought young Jamie's present over.'

'That's nice of you. See you've been away as well.'

'Yes, Devon, a very expensive hotel.'

'Lucky old you. Here, Maggs, I love the new stuff you've got.'

'Do you? Do you think it will sell?'

'I should say so. Bill's sold that diamanté brooch and earrings already.'

'He has?' Maggie was overjoyed. 'I was a bit worried it might be too expensive. I'd spent over my budget, and what with Jamie's birthday coming . . . I wonder who bought them and if they'd like me to look out for more.'

'De-da!' Eve opened her bag with a flurry and produced the earrings and brooch.

'Oh Eve, you shouldn't have bought—'

'I wanted them.' She moved over to the mirror and put the earrings on. 'Well? What d'you think?'

'They look smashing,' said Maggie. 'But I can't let you pay full price. You can have 'em for what I paid for 'em.'

'I will not.'

'I can't take your money.'

'Don't talk daft, you're supposed to be making a living,' said Alan. 'And if Eve's happy paying that price, well then, that's business.'

'But she's also a friend,' said Maggie.

'Maggs, you wasn't exactly charging the earth for 'em,' said Eve, turning her head so when they caught the light they sparkled.

'There's no friendship when it comes to money,' said Helen. 'As your husband knew only too well.'

'Trust you to come out with something like that,' Maggie snapped. 'I ain't got any more money for you, Alan, if that's what you've really come for.'

'We didn't. Helen, I do wish you hadn't said that, especially in front of Eve.'

'Eve knows all about it,' said Maggie, glaring at Helen.

Helen ignored her and, taking a powder compact from her handbag, peered into its mirror and proceeded to powder her nose.

'We only came over to give Jamie his present,' said Alan, looking very uncomfortable. 'If you've finished your tea, dear, then I think we'd better go.'

Helen snapped her compact shut with a loud click. She tutted, stood up, brushed down her frock and silently left the room.

Alan kissed Maggie's cheek. 'Sorry about that.'

'That's all right. Bye, Helen,' Maggie called down the stairs.

There was no reply.

'Bye, Maggie,' said Alan. 'I'll be seeing you some time.'

When they heard the front door shut Maggie angrily banged the table. 'Why does she always have to make me so wild?'

'It's one of her charming ways,' said Eve.

'And why did she have to be here when Jamie got a punch on the nose?'

'Winnie told me what happened. He's very proud of it, you know.'

Maggie smiled. 'I know.'

'What are these?' She picked up one of the cups.

'Helen brought them for the kids. They're a joke – you have to drink out of 'em without spilling any.'

'You can't, that's impossible. It'll fall through all the holes.'

'That's the joke. You drink through the handle.'

'Oh,' said Eve, obviously not very impressed.

'Eve, did you really buy that stuff because you liked it? Or was it just to help me out?'

'I really like it, and I'll tell you something else, I reckon Helen did too.'

'I thought so, but she's probably too stuck-up to buy anything off of me.'

'That's her loss. I was watching her face through the mirror when I put them on, and she almost turned green with envy. If you can get hold of any more stuff like this I'd like to browse through it first before you put it on the stall.'

Maggie's face broke into a smile. 'I never know when to believe you.'

'Well I'll tell you this, there was two of us arguing over them.'

Maggie laughed. 'Oh yer? So how come you won?'

'I ain't telling. But I think you could be on a winner with this stuff.'

'There's only one trouble with all this.'

'What's that?'

'Where do I get the stock from?'

Eve shrugged. 'Where did you get this lot from?'

'The auction, but it's only stuff they get hold of now and again and it could be weeks before they get any more.'

'Well, don't ask me. You're supposed to be the buyer now.'

Maggie sat down. 'Eve, you know those lovely rings Beatie wears? Well, it seems Tony sold her most of 'em.'

'No.' She laughed. ''Ere, you ain't thinking of going in for the real stuff, are you?'

'No, don't talk daft. What I'm saying is that Beatie thought I knew all about it, but I didn't.'

'So, he done a few deals on the side. You always knew that.'

'Yes, but not very expensive stuff.'

'So how do you know they were expensive?'

'Beatie said she only liked the real thing.'

'But we don't know they're real, do we?'

'But Beatie would have. I expect she's had 'em valued.'

'Dunno about that. She couldn't very well take 'em into a proper jeweller's now, could she? They could have been knocked off.'

'But Tony would have known.'

'Exactly. Let's face it, gel, your Tony could spin a right old tale when he wanted to, and he was a bit of a rogue one way and another.'

'Yes I know.' Maggie stood up and went over to the window. She looked down to the market. 'But what did he do with the money?'

'He must have gambled it away,' said Eve softly.

'Eve, this bloke Mr Windsor – he runs a betting syndicate – Tony owes him forty pounds.'

'Bloody hell.'

Maggie turned. 'Eve, I'm so frightened.'

Eve went to her friend and held her close. 'I know.'

'What am I going to do?'

'I wish I knew, Maggs. I only wish I knew.'

Chapter 21

When Eve left, and the children had finished their dinner, Maggie was down on the market again. It was then she found out from Bill how Eve had managed to buy the bits of jewellery. She was telling the truth, there was another woman interested in it, but Eve had offered more money.

'Was that wrong, Maggs?' asked Bill, looking worried.

'No, course not. After all, business is business.' But Maggie wasn't really pleased about it. She felt Eve might have done it out of sympathy, and she didn't want people feeling sorry for her.

A number of the other small pieces of jewellery had gone and that cheered her up, and she hoped that once she found another source to buy from, it could be the turning point in her fortunes.

She stood with the warm comforting sun on her back, trying to work out the best way to display to its advantage any future stock. She enjoyed talking to the women that came and browsed, and managed to get a few ideas of what they would like to see. Some did ask after Tony, but she found their questions difficult to answer. One or two wanted to know if he'd been banged up inside. Prison was a part of life round here. All she said was he had to go away, which got her a few funny looks.

Throughout the afternoon the noise and patter from her fellow traders was interrupted by the Blackshirts once more. Today they seemed louder and more intrusive than usual. Once or twice Maggie looked up, concerned that when the arguing and heckling got to the pushing and shouting stage it was beginning to get out of hand.

She told the children to keep well away from them. 'Stay down this end of the market.'

'You all want ter be bloody well locked up,' shouted Winnie to them. 'Go on, sod off.'

A young man wearing a black shirt came across to Winnie. He was tall and slim, and stood over her menacingly. 'When Hitler's race takes over this country, you, old woman, had better watch out.'

'Don't you talk ter me like that, you saucy sod. I remember what happened in the last lot, and what a bleeding bunch of savages the Germans was.'

'What's up, Win?' asked Tom Cooper, coming and standing next to her. He was as tall as the youth, but a lot broader.

'This young whippersnapper 'ere reckons we're all gonner be put down when the Germans get here.'

There was a catch in Winnie's voice, and Maggie could almost feel the sorrow and anger that was written over her face.

Tom Cooper went up close to the young man and with his finger poked him in the chest. 'Clear orf. Don't come round here causing trouble, 'cos we don't like the likes of you mouthing orf.'

The young man, who Maggie noted had gone white with

temper, clenched his fists. He looked around at all the hostile faces closing in on him, turned and walked away.

Fred moved up to Tom. 'Think they bloody well know it all. I tell yer, mate, if there's another war I reckon we'd flatten 'em.'

'D'yer reckon there will be another set-to then, Fred?' asked Winnie.

'Wouldn't like ter say. Tell yer something, though, it'll be a bit different to the last lot.'

'What, the war to end all wars?' commented Tom Cooper cynically.

'Don't say that,' said Maggie. 'I couldn't bear it.'

'Well, I ain't got no one to lose this time,' said Winnie, walking away.

'My dad fought in the war,' said Bill. 'He got a bit of shrapnel in his leg. Me mum keeps it in a box on the mantelpiece.'

Maggie looked surprised. 'I didn't know that.'

'Never told anyone, only Tony.'

'Is he all right now?'

'No, he died a while back.'

Maggie stood and looked at Bill. Tony had never mentioned anything about him or his family in the years Bill had worked for him. Maggie felt sad that all Bill's mother had left of his father was a bit of shrapnel in a box.

Maggie turned away. Over these past months there had been a lot of things she was finding out about Tony, the main one being that he had never told her very much at all.

★ ★ ★

At the end of the day Maggie went upstairs and left Bill to put the stall away. The squeaking of the stalls and barrows' wheels as they rumbled over the cobblestones mixed with the chatter and noise drifting up through her open window.

Suddenly there was a lot of shouting and yelling and an almighty crash of glass. Maggie hurried to her window to see some of the Blackshirts running away laughing. She leant out and saw Tom, Fred and Bill hurrying from the lockup. They stopped in front of Mr Goldman's window. Glass was strewn over the pavement.

'You two stay here, I'm just going downstairs,' she said to the two anxious children's faces that looked up at her.

'Mummy, Mummy, please don't leave us,' cried Laura, her face full of fear as she threw herself at Maggie's legs.

'It's that man, he's come back again.' Jamie too rushed up to her with tears spilling from his eyes.

Maggie held them both. 'No it ain't that man. I told you, he's dead. It's just some silly young blokes throwing a brick through poor old Mr Goldman's window, and I've just got to make sure he's all right. I won't be long. You look out and see.' Maggie edged them towards the window. 'See, Tom, Fred and Bill's down there.'

'So why must you go?' asked Laura.

'Just in case Mr Goldman's been hurt.'

'Like when that nasty man pushed him?' said Laura.

'Yes, love.'

'Why don't people like Mr Goldman? He's nice,' said Jamie.

'I'm afraid there are some very stupid people out there. Now let me go, and I'll be back in a mo.'

A small crowd had gathered and Mr Goldman stood with his head bent, surveying the damage.

'Mr Goldman, Mr Goldman,' shouted Maggie as she pushed her way through.

He looked up.

'Are you all right?'

He came over to her. 'Yes thank you, dear. As it was Saturday I was out in my back room. Silly young things.'

'Has someone called the police?' she asked.

'Na. It's always the same, you never see a bleeding copper when you want one.' Tom looked very pointedly at Maggie.

'There's not a lot of point,' said Fred, coming over to them. 'We know who they was but we've got to prove it, and they're sure to stick together on their story.'

'I'll tell yer if I got me hands round their throats I'd give 'em Hitler.' Tom Cooper looked very angry.

'Why did they pick on Mr Goldman's window?' asked Maggie.

He took hold of her hand and gently patted it. 'I'm a Jew, my dear, and I'm afraid Hitler and some of his fellow men don't like us.'

'I think that's awful.'

'So does nearly everyone, but he has a very powerful charisma, and some people are beginning to think like he does.'

'Well, with a bit of luck they won't be round this way again,' said Tom Cooper. 'Otherwise they'll have us lot to answer to.'

Gradually the people began to disperse.

'We've got some tarpaulins in the lockup,' said Fred. 'So

Tom, young Bill here and me will nail 'em to your window for now, and we'll get all this glass cleared away.'

'Thank you, that's very kind of you.'

'Are you sure you're all right?' asked Maggie again.

Mr Goldman nodded. 'Yes thank you, my dear. You go on up to the children, they look very uneasy.'

Maggie looked up at the two small faces peering down on them. They did look very worried.

For a while the sound of banging filled the air as the tarpaulin was fixed over the window. Maggie sat thinking about what had been said about Hitler. Please don't let there be another war, she prayed silently. I've got enough to worry about as it is.

On Sunday afternoon Maggie and the children were on the train to Downham. She was very apprehensive. What sort of greeting would they get? But it was for Jamie's sake she had made the effort, and hoped Bella would also let bygones be bygones.

Her fears had been unfounded, for when the front door was opened they were as usual clutched to Bella's ample bosom like a long-lost tribe. She wasn't the kind of person to hold a grudge.

'What a lovely surprise,' she said, taking the children's faces and kissing them all over. 'And who's got a birthday then tomorrow?'

Maggie noted the expression on Jamie's face. He smiled weakly but didn't comment. Maggie guessed he was worried about a present.

As they marched down the passage Bella said over her shoulder, 'I was gonner get Benny to drop a little something off, but now you're here he don't have to bother.'

Jamie squeezed his mother's hand, and she looked down to see a very broad grin spread across his face.

Maggie was surprised to see Benny sitting at the kitchen table. He was very spruce and had even taken his trilby off, showing his sparse grey hair.

'Benny, I was coming over to see you this week.'

''Allo, love.' He stood up and kissed her cheek. 'I must say you're all looking well.'

'Benny come over and did a spot of gardening for me, so I give him a bit of dinner,' said Bella quickly, almost as if making an excuse for his presence.

'She's a grand cook,' said Benny proudly.

'I know,' replied Maggie. 'So, how's business then?'

'Not too bad. Managing to keep me head above water, as they say.'

'Where's your horse?' asked Laura.

'She's back home in her stable. Got her nose in her feed bag, I shouldn't wonder.'

'Why didn't you bring her to see Granny Ross?'

'I don't somehow think Granny Ross would like that.'

'I know bloody well I wouldn't. Christ, could you see me neighbours' faces if they had a horse and cart stuck outside all afternoon?'

'Still, they wouldn't have to go far for manure for their rhubarb,' laughed Benny.

'What do they want manure on their rhubarb for?' asked Jamie.

'To make it grow,' said Benny.

'Then they eat it?' Jamie's blue eyes were wide open with amazement.

'Lovely,' said Benny, grinning. 'I likes a nice bit of the old rhubarb pie.'

'Ehg!' said Laura. 'That's not very nice.'

'It smells,' said Jamie, holding his nose.

'Here y'are, kids, take this lemonade into the garden,' said Bella.

'Bella was telling me you're thinking of getting some new stuff. Any idea what line you're looking for?'

'Can I have a biscuit?' asked Jamie.

'Jamie,' said Maggie sternly, 'what have I told you? You wait to be asked.'

'Yer, I know, but when you grown-ups start talking you forgets all about us.'

'As if we could forget you,' said Bella, pulling him close and kissing him again.

This time Jamie did rub his cheek.

'Go on, off with you.' Maggie gave him a light pat on the bottom.

'So, he'll be five tomorrow?' said Bella.

'Yes, and they're back at school as well.'

'A big day for the boy then?' said Benny.

'Yes, I only wish his father was here to see it.' Maggie had a job to keep the sob from her voice.

'Still heard nothing then?'

'No, Benny, nothing. Bella, I'm giving Jamie a little tea party tomorrow after school, any chance of you getting over?' Maggie wanted to get away from the subject of Tony, which was still very painful to her.

'Don't think I can, love. See how I feel in the morning.'

'Ain't you well?' Maggie was suddenly filled with guilt as well as alarm.

'Just a few twinges. This leg still ain't right.'

'Keep telling her to go back to the quack, but you know what she's like.'

Maggie smiled, pleased Benny was concerned about Bella.

'Maggs, I've been thinking,' said Bella. 'D'you think if Tony's – you know – all right and hiding somewhere, he might send Jamie a birthday card.'

'I've been thinking that as well. I'll be down those stairs like a shot in the morning.' Maggie sat back and wiped her cheek with the back of her hand. 'It would be the best present ever,' she sniffed.

'Yer, well, don't hold out too many hopes, gel,' said Benny, clearing his throat.

'Talking of presents . . .' Bella hurriedly left the kitchen.

Maggie blew her nose. 'There was a set-to at the market last night. Those bloody Blackshirts broke Mr Goldman's window.'

'No! Did you hear that, gel?' said Benny to Bella when she returned holding a parcel. 'Did the police come?'

'No, he didn't want them to.'

'Poor old bugger,' said Bella. 'I dunno what this world's coming to. Is he all right?'

Maggie nodded.

'By the way, there's the photos of our holiday. They're very good, if I say so meself. You staying for a bit of tea?'

'If that's all right.'

'Wouldn't bloody well ask yer if it wasn't.'

'Can I take these and show Win?'

'Course.'

'We mustn't stay too long. Remember school tomorrow.'

Bella sat down. 'Little Jamie starting school. I bet you'll shed a few tomorrow.'

Maggie could only nod. Tears were very close today. She knew that tomorrow her baby would be, as he would say, 'all growed up', and there wasn't another one to fill his place.

Chapter 22

It was very early and Maggie lay in bed listening to the whoops of delight as Jamie rushed into the living room and began opening his presents. He was shouting for Laura and Maggie to come and see what he'd got.

Could this be the day she had been waiting nearly four months for? At last some sign that Tony was still alive? Would he send Jamie a card or present?

Maggie slipped on her dressing gown. It would be a while before the postman came.

Jamie, wearing the Red Indian outfit Bella had given him, was racing round the room on his scooter. Thank goodness it has rubber tyres and not those noisy ball-bearing wheels, thought Maggie as she quickly jumped out of his way. 'After school you must go round and thank all the traders. And you mind the paint work, young man.'

Jamie grinned. 'The truck Auntie Eve give me is just like the one Uncle Dan drives. He said he'd take me out in it one day. Can I go, Mummy?'

'I should think so.'

Between getting breakfast, helping to open presents and getting the children ready for school, Maggie watched and listened for the postman. She worried that Jamie might be sick with all the excitement.

Suddenly the plop of letters falling to the floor raised a yell from Jamie and he rushed from the room.

'Be careful,' she shouted after him. 'Don't fall down the stairs.'

He raced back into the living room, clutching an assortment of envelopes. 'I'll open 'em, then you can read 'em to me.'

'Let me help,' said Laura.

'No,' he said, hiding them behind his back.

'Oh, Mummy, tell him to let me.'

'Now sit at the table, both of you, and we will read them together.' Maggie's hands were trembling as one by one Jamie handed her each birthday card to read. Apart from the usual ones from all the market traders, Eve and Dan, Alan and Bella, there was one from David Matthews.

'You gonner ask him to my party this afternoon?' asked Jamie.

'I'll see.'

'Oh Mummy, you promised.'

'He may be too busy.'

Gradually the collection of envelopes was reduced to a heap of litter, and the cards carefully stacked on the sideboard.

'I'll put them all up properly later,' said Maggie, taking some of the dirty dishes into the kitchen. 'Now come on, get dressed, it's nearly time for school.'

In the kitchen, away from the children's eyes, she stood and let her tears fall. Had Tony forgotten Jamie's birthday?

'Mummy, would you tie my tie for me?'

Maggie turned and through her tears smiled at her son standing there looking very smart in his new white shirt and grey trousers, with his tie hanging round his neck.

'Mummy, what you crying for?'

Maggie bent down and hugged him. 'I'm crying 'cos my baby's all growed up and leaving me.'

'I ain't leaving. I'm only going to school round the corner.'

'If that hospital had let you have that baby it promised you, you wouldn't be left on your own.'

Maggie looked up to see Laura standing in the doorway. She had never mentioned the baby since Maggie had first come home from the hospital.

'Yes, darling, you're right. But we can't always have what we want.'

'I asked God to let Daddy come to my party,' said Jamie. 'D'you think he will?'

Maggie thought her heart would break. 'I don't know.' She wiped her eyes, gave a little laugh and tousled his hair. 'I'm being silly. Now stand still while I try to do a proper knot.' This should be your job, Tony, she thought. She was sure Tony wouldn't let his son's birthday pass without something. Perhaps the next post would bring the long-awaited answer.

Maggie helped Jamie on with his new blazer that Bella had bought, and tucked up the sleeves. 'You'll soon grow into this.'

When they got down into the market most of the traders were standing looking at Mr Goldman's window.

''Allo, love. Fancy those bleeders doing this,' said Winnie to Maggie. 'If I had my way I'd kick all their arses. Do the police know about this?'

'He didn't want any fuss,' said Fred.

'See you in a jiff,' Maggie said to them as she shepherded Laura and Jamie past. She didn't want them to start asking questions and getting upset about the incident again.

Winnie began to walk back to her stall with Maggie, but Jamie hung back. Winnie glanced over her shoulder and, giving him a wink asked, 'So, who's this young man you're walking out with then, Maggs?'

'Don't you go messing me hair up, 'cos Mum's put water on it to keep it down. And don't kiss me.'

Maggie laughed. 'Well, he was my baby till this morning, now he's all growed up.'

Jamie took hold of his mother's hand.

'I won't kiss you then, not today. Happy birthday, son,' Winnie laughed, but Maggie noted her eyes became watery.

Alone with her thoughts, Maggie walked back very slowly from the school.

'All right then, gel?' asked Winnie. 'It must be a great wrench when the last one goes.'

She nodded and said sadly, 'I was hoping there'd be a birthday card from Tony.'

Winnie didn't have an answer.

'I'll get Jamie to bring you down a bit of cake after his party.'

'Blimey, how big's this cake?'

'Not very big, but we've only got about four or five kids coming. I only hope they bring handkerchiefs this time. At Laura's they didn't stop sniffing, and a couple had the longest candles you ever saw.'

'That was in the winter,' said Winnie. 'We all get candles then, especially standing around out here.'

Maggie laughed. 'I'd better start getting ready for 'em.'

While Maggie was busy preparing for the tea party, someone banged on the front door. Maggie froze. Who would come calling at this time of morning? Her heart lifted. Could it be her Tony? There was no key behind the door now. She ran down the stairs and flung open the door.

'It's you.'

'Who were you expecting?' asked David Matthews.

'Well, certainly not you. You'd better come in,' she said before she had time to think about it. She looked up and down the market. Everybody was busy so perhaps she wouldn't get too many remarks.

David removed his trilby and followed her up the stairs. 'I had to come over to see Mr Goldman and his window.'

Maggie pushed open the living-room door. 'But I thought he didn't want the police involved. Have a seat.'

'He didn't.' David sat down. 'The officer on the beat saw the window had been smashed, so he called in and asked him what it was about. When I heard about it I thought I'd come over and have a word, just to make sure it was Blackshirts and not our friends back again.'

Maggie flinched at the thought of Mr Windsor. 'That was a good idea. Thank you for Jamie's birthday card.'

'It's my pleasure. Looks as if he's had plenty.'

'Yes.' She wanted to say, But not from the one person he really wanted one from. 'Would you like a cup of tea?' she said instead.

'If it's not too much trouble.'

'I was coming over to see you later.'

'You were?' He looked concerned.

'Yes. Jamie would like you to come to his birthday tea. I

told him you may be too busy.'

'I'd love to come. As a matter of fact I've got a present for him. Has he got a football?'

'No, but that was high up on his list.'

'I was going to bring it over after school anyway.'

'Well, you'll certainly be his favourite today.'

David's eyes met hers. 'What about you?'

Maggie felt embarrassed and quickly looked away. 'I don't know what you mean.'

'I'm sorry. How did he take going to school?'

'Couldn't wait to leave me. I just about managed to give him a kiss.'

'He's a fine lad.'

'He looked so grown up in his blazer and tie. I only hope I've tied it right.' Maggie's voice had a slight catch in it. 'I'll put the kettle on. There's the photos from our holiday on the sideboard,' she called from the kitchen.

David Matthews came into the kitchen holding the photographs. 'These are good. It looks as if you had a nice time.'

'Yes we did,' said Maggie filling the teapot. 'Would you like a biscuit?'

'No thanks.' He followed her back into the living room.

'I was hoping Tony might have sent him a card but . . .' Once again tears welled up in her eyes.

'Maggie, I honestly think you've got to accept that something has happened to Tony.'

'I'm beginning to feel that way as well. If he was alive I'm sure he would have sent him at least a card.' Maggie fished in her overall pocket for her handkerchief.

David took her hand. 'I don't like to see you so upset.'

His sympathy warmed her and the tears flowed.

'Please don't cry.' He put his arm round her shoulders and held her close.

'I'm sorry,' she sniffed, 'but the thought of Jamie starting school just . . .' She looked up at him and their lips met, gently at first, then with a passion that surprised her. She wanted to be loved.

'I'm sorry,' he said, breaking away. 'I shouldn't have done that.'

Maggie blushed and bent her head self-consciously. 'Well, I didn't exactly stop you, did I?'

'No, but I was in the wrong.'

Maggie moved away. 'I must get on.'

'Of course.'

'You will come back this afternoon?'

'If you're sure.'

'Yes, I'm sure,' she whispered.

Jamie came racing out of school and Maggie couldn't believe her eyes. His shirt was out of his trousers, his socks were down inside his shoes, and his tie skew-whiff. He had a grin from ear to ear on his cheeky face.

'Well, did you like it?'

'It was smashing. The bestest day of me life.'

'Good. What happened to that smart little lad I sent to school then?'

'You should have seen him in the playground, Mummy,' said Laura. 'He was tearing about like a mad thing. I told my friends he wasn't really my brother.'

'Oh Laura, how could you?'

Laura pouted. 'Well, he was mad.'

Maggie laughed. 'Come on, let's get back home and get

you tidied up, young man, before your friends arrive.'

'Did you go and see that policeman?' asked Jamie.

'He had to see Mr Goldman, so he popped in.'

'Is he coming?'

'Yes.'

'Great. Has he got me a present?'

'You'll have to wait and see.'

Jamie skipped and ran all the way home, not stopping to talk to anybody.

An hour later two other boys, and a girl to keep Laura happy, were sitting at the table eating fish-paste sandwiches followed by jelly and ice cream.

Only one little boy had a cold, and when he wasn't sniffing he made full use of his shirtsleeve.

'That policeman ain't come,' said Jamie grudgingly.

'Don't talk with your mouth full,' said Maggie. 'I expect he'll be here later. He is a very busy man.'

Maggie took some of the plates into the kitchen. She leant against the cooker and gently touched her lips. She didn't want to admit to herself how much she had enjoyed his kiss. She only knew it had to be wrong.

The knock on the front door sent Jamie flying down the stairs to answer it.

'Mummy, Mummy, look what the policeman give me.' Jamie thrust a football into her hands.

'It's very nice,' was all she could manage to say.

'I've got Saturday off, so could I take Jamie to the park?'

'Please, Mummy, please.'

'How can I refuse? But only if you're sure.'

David Matthews looked at her and his smile softened. 'Oh I'm sure all right.'

Maggie couldn't take her eyes away from his. She wanted him to kiss her and hold her again, and she knew he was thinking the same.

'What time?' asked Jamie, breaking the spell.

'Whenever it suits you, young man.'

'I'll be up early.'

'Can you stay long?' Maggie asked David.

'I'm off duty.'

'That's good. Now you can see me blow out me candles,' said Jamie.

'I'd better light them first,' said Maggie.

David followed her into the kitchen. 'I could stay all evening, if that's all right with you.'

She knew she should be saying no, but her heart was ruling her head. 'That would be nice.'

The cake with its five candles blazing was duly carried into the living room. The loud off-key rendering of 'Happy Birthday to You' brought a big smile to Jamie's cherubic face. He took a deep breath and quickly blew the candles out.

'Did you make a wish?' asked Maggie.

He nodded.

'Tell me,' said Laura.

'No, 'cos it won't come true if I tell.'

Maggie kissed his cheek. 'That's right. You let it be your secret.'

At last the children left. David was in the kitchen helping Maggie with the washing-up.

'I haven't been to a tea party for years,' he said, placing a plate in the cupboard. 'I'd almost forgotten how to play blind man's buff.'

'We always have a few children in for tea on their birthdays.'

'You are very lucky, they are smashing kids.'

'Thanks.'

'Tony's a lucky bloke.'

'David,' she put the washing-up mop down and faced him, 'if he was alive I'm sure he would have sent Jamie a card. I think I have to really believe he must be . . .' her voice had a sob in it and she couldn't bring herself to say the word, it sounded so final.

It was just as the children were going to bed that Eve and Dan came in, and after the good-night kisses the first question Eve asked was, 'Did he get a card from Tony?'

Maggie shook her head. 'By the way, Eve, Dan, this is Inspector Matthews.'

David stood up. 'Please, call me David.'

'Are you here on official business then, David?' asked Eve.

'No, I was this morning. Had to come over to see about Mr Goldman's window.'

'That was bloody awful,' said Dan. 'Want locking up, the lot of 'em. When's he getting the new glass in then?'

'Tomorrow.'

'That was a bit of luck for you,' said Eve, 'having to come over here for that.'

'Yes, it was, then it seems I'd been invited to Jamie's party.'

'Oh?' said Eve, raising one of her finely pencilled eyebrows quizzically.

'I think Jamie only invited him hoping to get another present,' Maggie said quickly.

'And did he?' asked Eve.

'Yes, David gave him a football.'

'I bet you was the most popular bloke,' said Dan.

'It did go down rather well,' said David.

'And the fact he's taking him to the park to play on Sat'day,' said Maggie.

'Not on duty then?' asked Eve.

'No, not unless somebody murders somebody.'

'Well, let's hope it's a quiet day for you.' Eve sat back on the sofa.

'I think I'd better be off. It's been very nice meeting you all.'

Maggie went down to the front door with David. 'Thank you for Jamie's football.'

'Don't mention it. And I'll see you on Saturday.'

'Yes,' said Maggie. 'That'll be nice.'

Maggie was a little disappointed that he made no attempt to kiss her good night and as she made her way upstairs said under her breath, 'And I really look forward to Saturday.'

'Well,' said Eve, echoing Maggie's thoughts, 'did he kiss you good night?'

Maggie could feel herself blushing and quickly turned away. 'Don't talk daft.'

'Let's face it, he is rather dishy.'

'He don't seem to be a bad bloke – for a copper, that is. That was nice of him to give Jamie a football,' said Dan.

'Is he married?' asked Eve.

'He was. His wife died; she had TB.'

'That was rotten for him. Where does he live?'

'Greenwich way, I think. Eve, you're so bloody nosy.'

'Just keeping a beady eye out for me best friend.'

'Yer, I bet.'

'Greenwich way, eh? Very smart too, and he is rather nice – and you could do worse than keep him hanging around.'

'I don't want him hanging around,' Maggie protested.

'Come on you two, give it a rest,' Dan chipped in. 'Eve, we'd better be off, got a busy day tomorrow.'

'OK.' Eve stood up. 'I'll tell you somethink for nothink: I reckon he fancies you. He's got that look in his eyes.'

Maggie laughed. 'Go on, scram.'

When Maggie closed the front door she stood leaning against it for a while. Eve was right. He was nice, and Maggie knew she could be very happy and relaxed in his company, and feel very safe, which was something she hadn't done for quite a long time.

Chapter 23

Maggie had taken the children to school, and as she returned the noise and hubbub from the glaziers repairing Mr Goldman's window brought back to her Saturday's scene. She hoped it wasn't going to be repeated. What if Mr Goldman had been near that window or, worse still, her children playing there? She shuddered at the thought, and carried on with the tidying up. All the while she was thinking about stock. Most of the rough bits and pieces Tony had bought in the past were still stuck on the stall. The china and odds and ends she'd bought had gone. She had to go and see Benny. Just lately he seemed to be coming up with some real bargains at very reasonable prices that enabled her to put on good mark-ups. She had asked him if he was charging her the right price, but he'd grinned and said he was in this business to make money, not do anybody favours. Maggie's thoughts went to Bella. Did Benny sell her, Maggie, the stuff cheap because he was sweet on Bella, or was Bella paying the difference?

Maggie was about to put their holiday photographs in the sideboard drawer when the card that the old gentleman she'd met at the auction room had given her caught her eye.

Freeman's Fine Furniture. Peckham High Street. She stood studying it for a moment or two. Maybe he would know where she could buy some more jewellery at a reasonable price.

That's what she wanted to sell, and she decided that instead of seeing Benny she would go along and ask this acquaintance. After all, she had to find another supplier soon.

It wasn't a very long bus ride to Peckham and not many shoppers were out and about on a Tuesday morning. She pushed open the door to Freeman's and the bell above rang loud and frantic. She peered into the drab interior. It took a moment or two for her eyes to adjust to the gloom. The musty smell of old furniture mixed with wax polish filled Maggie's nostrils. The showroom was full of large heavy-looking items. She wandered over to a beautiful table and carefully ran her fingers over the wood. It looked very expensive.

'Yes?' An abrupt deep voice made her spin round. An old woman emerged from the shadows at the far end of the room. She had draped round her bent shoulders a bright red silk shawl with a deep fringe that swayed as she moved. She leant heavily on a stick and shuffled towards Maggie.

'Oh, could I speak to . . .' Maggie stopped. She didn't know the man's name. She smiled the broadest smile she could muster. 'I think it must have been your son, Mr Freeman? I met him at the auction room. He told me about your shop.' Maggie felt very nervous and intimidated by this old woman, whose eyes appeared to be very dark brown, almost black, and penetrating. As she got nearer, Maggie could see the skin on her wrinkled and lined face was practically translucent, and her hands liver-spotted.

'My son? What do you want with my son?'

'I would like to ask him about buying stock.'

'Stock? What kind of stock? And pray, where is your shop? We don't want any competition round here, young lady.'

'I don't sell furniture. I have a stall on Kelvin Market. I sell jewellery.'

'Jewellery? We don't sell jewellery. What do you want with my son?'

'I met your son last week at the auction room. I wondered if he knew of anywhere else I could buy from.'

'Get out.'

'I beg your pardon.' Maggie drew herself up to her full five foot three.

'I said get out. We don't want the likes of you dirty old costermongers round here, common market trash, you lot are.'

Maggie was boiling with anger. 'How dare you speak to me like this? I ain't a costermonger. I only came to see your son, not to be insulted by the likes of you.'

'Get out.' The old woman flapped her hand as if shooing a fly away. 'I've met your sort before, coming round here on any pretext to get your hands on my Charles and his money. Little gold-digger.'

Maggie stood with her mouth wide open. 'I ain't after your son. I'm a married woman with a couple of kids.'

'That's what they all say. Now get out, d'you hear? Get out.' She raised her stick menacingly. Maggie flew for her life.

Maggie stood for a while outside the shop, trembling,

trying to gather herself together before she found the strength to move away. Her mind was in a turmoil. What sort of woman was this? And how could they do any business with a woman like that around? And what about that poor man – fancy having a mother like that.

Maggie caught sight of a café on the opposite side of the road. She quickly crossed over, went in and sank into a chair.

'You all right, love?' asked the large woman behind the counter. Her face below her white mobcap was flushed and jovial-looking.

'Yes thank you.'

'Look a bit peaky ter me. What d'yer fancy?'

'A cup of tea, please.' Maggie noted she was the only customer.

Strong tea in a thick cup was duly placed in front of her.

Maggie couldn't believe what had just happened, and felt she had to tell someone. 'I've just been into Freeman's.'

'Was you on your own?'

Maggie nodded.

The woman laughed and, wiping her hands on the front of her white overall, went behind her counter. 'I bet you've just seen old mother Freeman. She's a nutter. Every young pretty girl what walks into that shop she thinks is a potential threat to her.'

'Why?'

'She don't want anybody to take her dear Charlie away from her.'

'I only went in to ask him about stock. I couldn't believe it. I thought she was going to hit me with her stick.'

'Yer, she can be a bit frightening at times.'

'So where does she keep her precious Charlie then?'

'He was probably out delivering furniture. They have a very good business over there – well, ever since Charlie took it over.'

'I can't see how, not with a mother like that.' Maggie sipped her tea then sat back. 'I've certainly had a wasted journey then.'

The woman leant on the counter. 'So what sorta furniture was you looking for?'

'Not furniture. I sell bits and bobs on a stall, and I was thinking of selling jewellery.'

The door opened and another customer walked in, carrying a round wicker basket. Maggie couldn't see what was inside. Her long black tangled hair was twisted and pinned on top of her head. She was wearing a voluminous black frock that reached the ground and she looked very gypsy-like.

'Tea and a bit of dripping toast please, Doris. And I'll have some of that lovely thick jelly from the bottom on it if yer don't mind.' She took a sprig of heather from her basket and walked towards Maggie.

'Here, girl,' Doris shouted over. 'Lil here might be able to help.'

Maggie looked at the woman. She was unkempt and looked as if she hadn't two ha'pennies to rub together, so Maggie couldn't see how she could help her.

Lil came and sat at Maggie's table. 'Buy some lucky white heather, love. And what's she on about?' She inclined her head towards Doris.

'She's just had an encounter with old mother Freeman,' said Doris.

Lil threw her head back and laughed. 'I bet you gave her something to think about. Was you after her Charlie?'

'No I wasn't.' Maggie was getting fed up with this conversation.

'So, gel, what was yer after?'

Maggie was a bit apprehensive about telling this woman what she wanted. But she didn't have much choice in the circumstances, and who knew, she may be able to help her. 'I've got a stall,' she wasn't going to say where, 'and I'm looking for some stock. I'd like to buy jewellery. Only cheap stuff, you understand.'

Lil sat forward. 'Paste, glass, that sorta thing?'

'Yes,' said Maggie, leaning forward eagerly. 'Do you know where I—'

'Dunno. What's it worth ter me?'

'I'm sorry. I don't understand.'

Lil turned to Doris. 'See she ain't been in this business long. Look, love, you don't ever get something for nuffink, even information has ter be paid for.'

Maggie sat back. She suddenly thought about Tony. What would he say in this situation? 'How do I know what you're telling me is good information?'

Lil laughed again. 'Maybe she ain't ser green. Pay fer me cuppa and toast and I'll tell you fer nuffink.'

'Two cups please, Doris.'

When Doris put them and Lil's toast on the table she too sat down with them.

Lil poured the tea into her saucer and began to drink making loud slurping noises.

Maggie sat there staring.

'Couldn't take her anywhere, could you?' said Doris.

268

'Here, watch it, gel,' said Lil, wiping her mouth with the back of her hand. 'Otherwise I'll take me custom elsewhere. Now listen, young lady. If you go along to Percy's Emporium, and tell him Lil sent yer, he'll see yer all right.'

'What's an emporium?' asked Maggie.

'A posh name for a shop that sells a load of old rubbish,' said Doris.

Maggie looked at Lil. 'I don't want to buy a lot of rubbish.'

'Don't listen to her,' said Lil. 'He does a good line in costume jewellery, and if you buy a few bits he'll give you a good discount.'

Maggie was trying hard to suppress her delight. 'So where is this Aladdin's cave then?'

'Over the Elephant, I'll write his address down for yer.' She produced some paper from her basket and much to Maggie's surprise, wrote the address in a well-formed hand. 'And don't ferget to tell him Lil sent yer.'

'No, no I won't. Thank you very much. I'll go over there right away. Doris, give Lil another cuppa.' Maggie put the paper in her handbag and gave Doris money for the tea.

'Let's have a butchers at yer hand, love.'

Maggie looked surprised. 'Why?'

'She tells fortunes,' said Doris.

Maggie reluctantly put out her hand.

Lil took hold of it and after studying her palm, gently ran a long tapering finger along one of the lines. 'Just as I thought. You've had a lot of grief lately. Am I right?'

Maggie nodded.

'Well, gel, I'm afraid there's a few more tears ter come. I can see a lot more grief for you before it starts to get better.

269

But I can tell yer that in the end it will all turn out all right.'

Maggie looked at her hand. 'Can you tell me how long I've got to wait for it?'

'No, sorry.'

Maggie sat forward. 'What else can you see? Can you tell me about—'

Lil waved her hand at Maggie. 'Show's over.' Lil poured her tea into her saucer again.

'Well, I'll be off now,' said Maggie, sorry the reading had come to an end. There was so much she wanted to ask her. 'And thanks once again.'

'Good luck to yer, gel. 'Ere, take this to give yer luck.' She handed Maggie a sprig of heather. 'And take care. And let yer heart rule yer head.'

Maggie left the café in a state of bewilderment. What did the woman mean? And what else was going to happen to her? Was Lil really a gypsy? She put the heather in her bag, wondering whether it would bring her luck. She glanced across the road at Freeman's. What a good thing Charlie had been out.

Maggie couldn't believe Percy's Emporium. It *was* just like an Aladdin's cave. Her eyes grew wider and wider as she slowly wandered around. Beads glinted. Brooches sparkled. Fancy paste animals that had bright green and red eyes twinkled. There were tiny ornaments on stands, lovely shaped glass vases, and beautiful wall plaques. Maggie wanted to run round gathering up everything she saw. She crossed her fingers and prayed the price would be right. She waited till she found an assistant on her own, then asked, 'Excuse me. Where can I find Percy?'

'He's over there. Is there anythink I can get you?'

'No thanks.' Maggie knew the woman's eyes were following her as she went to the far end of the room. 'Excuse me,' she said to a portly balding man bent over a box. 'Are you Percy?'

He shot up and their eyes were level. 'Yes, who wants to know?'

'I'm Maggie Ross, and I've just been talking to Lil.' She gave a little laugh. 'I don't know her other name, and she told me you might sell me some stock for my stall.'

He looked her up and down suspiciously. 'Did she now? That wouldn't be Gypsy Lil, by any chance, would it?' he replied gruffly.

Alarm filled Maggie. What had that old woman sent her to? 'I don't know.'

'She's a bloody old witch.' Maggie turned round to see the woman she had first spoken to standing behind her.

'Be fair, Mabel, she does have an uncanny knack of predicting things,' said Percy, looking up at the woman.

'I don't trust her, and you shouldn't either.'

Maggie was looking from one to the other. All she wanted was to buy some stock, and now it seemed she had got herself involved in a family argument. 'I'm sorry, I must have made a mistake.'

'No you ain't. What was it you wanted?' asked Percy.

'Well, you see I've got a stall and I was looking for jewellery, only cheap paste.'

'Come with me.'

Maggie followed him to the end of a long counter.

'This the sort of stuff?'

She nodded. Earrings, necklaces, brooches and little hair

ornaments. She could have hugged him. 'How much?' she asked, carefully replacing the brooch she was fondling.

'How many?'

Maggie couldn't answer. 'It depends.'

'How much you got to spend?'

She was desperately trying to work out what she could sell them at. 'Couldn't you give me some idea what you will charge me for a few bits?'

'If we make you up a pound's worth, how would that do?' asked Mabel.

'Well yes, I suppose so.' That way Maggie could at least see what she would get for her money.

Percy laid out the objects on a tray. 'These do?'

Maggie was quickly trying to work out what she could sell for. 'I could go to another ten shillings,' she said.

'You don't want to believe everything that Lil tells you, yer know,' said Mabel.

'Oh, why's that?'

'Reckons she can tell the future, she's just a fraud.'

Maggie gave a silly little laugh. 'I don't listen to all that nonsense.'

'She kept telling us we was gonner have this great disaster. Well, as you can see we're still here. But she put the bloody fear of death up poor old Percy here. I reckon it was just a ploy to get him out – her son's always took a great interest in this place.'

Maggie didn't comment, but she listened carefully while Percy bagged up her goods. Why was Mabel telling her all this? Percy was such a quiet man and Maggie could see who was in charge of the business.

'I hope we can do business again, young lady,' said Percy.

'So do I.' Maggie smiled. She felt happier than she'd felt for a long while.

She sat on the bus and, smiling, patted her handbag, pleased with its contents. She thought about what Lil had told her. Even if there was going to be more grief, at least there was light at the end of the tunnel. So perhaps Tony was going to come back after all. She desperately hoped so. Then her life would be complete.

Chapter 24

As the week progressed Maggie became more and more thrilled as her purchases appeared to bring a lot of interest from punters and stallholders alike, and she was selling well.

Saturday saw her smiling and brimming with confidence when people came and chatted, and bought.

'Reckon you wanner charge a bit more for this stuff,' said Winnie, sauntering over as the lunchtime lull approached. She picked up a brooch.

'Not yet. I'll wait till people get used to seeing it.' Maggie took hold of Winnie's arm and gently ushered her away from the stall. 'Look at Bill's miserable face. He ain't all that pleased about it.'

'That's his hard luck.'

'But what if he wants to leave, how would I manage without him?'

'Offer him more money.'

'I can't. I ain't exactly making a fortune.'

'Well, get more stuff and put a penny or two on the price. You'll soon cover his wages.'

'I can't afford to buy more, not just yet.'

'Look, Maggs, it ain't for me to tell you how to run your business, but see how today goes, then look what you've got left, and if you really think it's gonner work, why don't you take out a loan?'

Maggie looked shocked. 'What? Me borrow money? You of all people should know what happened to Tony over that.'

'Yes but that was for gambling, not stocking the stall.'

'I don't know.'

'Well, think it over. You don't want an opportunity like this to pass you by. It's you that's got to feed you and the kids now. Remember there's always eyes and ears round here looking for something new to flog, and if they see you doing well, well, before you know it everybody will be selling this stuff.'

'They wouldn't, would they?'

'Give 'em half a chance. Some of 'em would sell their grandmother for a bob or two if they thought they'd get away with it. By the way, a word of advice, gel. Don't let on to anyone who your supplier is.'

When Winnie walked back to her stall Maggie was stunned. She stood and thought about what she'd said. Would someone else get hold of stock like hers? What if they got it cheaper? Where did Percy get it from? All these questions were going through her mind. And what about a loan? She looked at the stall. It really did look rather pathetic. She needed more stock from Benny as well as Percy to make it look special, and borrowing money was something she would have to think really hard about if she wanted the stall both to look right and to pay. And, after all, Christmas was coming.

All morning business had been brisk, and Maggie knew

she would have to go and see Percy on Monday.

'Hallo, Maggie,' said her brother, coming up and giving her cheek a kiss as she stood behind the stall.

'Alan. Helen, what are you doing over here?' Maggie offered her cheek to Helen for the obligatory kiss. 'Two Saturdays in a row.'

'We'd thought we'd just pop over and see how you're doing. This looks nice,' Alan picked up a diamanté hair slide.

'You should have seen what we've sold,' said Bill. 'Can't say it's my line, but Maggie 'ere seems to think it's OK.'

'Been doing well then, have you?' Helen asked him.

'I should say so.'

Helen picked a pair of large pearl earrings off the black cloth. 'It's not the sort of thing I'd wear, but I expect they would sell well over this way. People round here like things that are cheap and cheerful.'

Maggie gave Helen a sarcastic smile. 'Would you like a cup of tea?' she asked.

'Why not?' said Alan.

'We can't stay too long. Remember we have to pick Doreen up.'

'Just a quick one,' said Alan.

Maggie felt like telling them not to bother, but she guessed they had another reason for this visit.

As soon as they were in the flat Maggie asked, 'Have you come over for some more of your money?'

Helen gave Alan a sneering look.

'No, course not,' said Alan quickly, looking very embarrassed.

Maggie could see by Helen's expression she was behind this.

'So things are going well down there? Who's looking after the children while you're on the stall?' asked Helen.

'Well, they're at school all week, and on Saturday they usually play round here.' She went into the kitchen.

'I didn't see them,' said Alan, following her.

'No, they're out.'

'Who with? Eve?'

'No. Inspector Matthews.'

'What, the policeman who's supposed to be looking for Tony?' enquired Helen, walking into the kitchen.

'Yes.' Maggie began filling the kettle.

'What they doing with him?' asked Alan.

'David bought Jamie a football for his birthday and as today is his day off he took them both over to the park.'

'David, eh. And you let him?' said Alan.

'Course, why shouldn't I?'

'Sounds to me like he's trying to get his feet under the table.'

'No, Helen, he isn't. He's a very nice man.'

'Is he married?' It was Alan's turn for the questioning.

'He's a widower.'

'That's convenient,' said Helen, looking at her nails.

'What d'you mean?'

'And what does Bella have to say about this cosy arrangement?'

'Helen, sometimes I . . .' Maggie wanted to give her a piece of her mind but decided against it. 'She likes him.'

'You wanner watch it, Maggs. If Tony comes back and finds this nice little setup – well, I dread to think what would happen,' said Alan.

Maggie slammed the kettle on the gas stove and turned

on him. 'If Tony does come back, first of all he's got a lot to answer for, and second, if he can't be bothered to send his only son a birthday card, then if you ask me he ain't worth worrying about.' Tears sprang to Maggie's eyes.

'My, my, we are touchy.'

'Helen,' said Alan, and looking sheepish put his arm round Maggie's shoulder. 'I don't want to upset you, Maggie, but I do worry about you.'

She shrugged him away. 'What did you really come over here for, money?'

'No, I told you, to see how you are.'

She dabbed at her eyes. 'As soon as I can I'll pay back a bit more of what Tony owes.'

'That's not what I'm after.'

'I must go down to Bill,' she said, breaking away from Alan and heading for the door.

'What about our cup of tea?' asked Helen.

'You'll have to have it next time.' Maggie didn't want to talk to them.

After that episode Maggie went over to Winnie. 'Who do I see about getting a loan?'

'They upset you?' Winnie inclined her head in the direction Alan and Helen had taken.

Maggie shuffled her feet.

'What'd he want? His money?'

'He didn't say as much, but that was the real reason. It's her, you know.'

'Is that what you want the loan for? Look, Maggs, you can tell me to shut up if you like, but to borrow money to pay Alan back – well, if you ask me it's a bit daft. Think of the interest.'

'Have you quite finished? I want the money to buy stock, lots of it, then if I make enough I can pay off Alan and everybody else.'

'It's gonner take you a bloody long time.'

'Then they'll just have to be patient, won't they?'

At two o'clock, just before closing time, Winnie took Maggie to the Dog and Duck to meet the loan club man, Mr Shore. She wanted to borrow five pounds. At first he was reluctant to lend so much, but after he'd explained the interest and charges and she was still keen to borrow, he agreed.

'Maggs, that's a lot of money,' said Winnie as they walked back to the stalls. 'You sure you're doing the right thing?'

'No, I'm not. But I've got to get some money from somewhere.'

'Yer, but you've got to pay a bloody lot back.'

'Well, it was your idea.'

'I know, but five pounds – what about the interest? Two bob in the pound, and the longer you have it the more you pay.'

'I know. I know. So I'll have to try and pay it back quick then, won't I?' Maggie tried to appear nonchalant about it, but deep down she felt sick. What was she thinking of?

Monday morning saw her over at Percy's again.

'Well, this is a surprise. Didn't think we'd see you so soon again,' said Mabel.

'Hopefully I'll be over every week.'

'So what yer buying this time?'

'About the same, but more of it.'

Mabel opened her watery blue eyes wide. 'How much yer got?'

Maggie held her breath. 'Four pounds.' She decided to keep a pound back in case she didn't make next week's rent. Then she needed money for Benny's bits. But last week's profit would take care of that.

'Four pounds?' repeated Mabel. 'Looks like you're on to a winner over your way.'

Maggie crossed her fingers. 'I hope so.'

The following two weeks saw Maggie becoming more and more self-assured, and once again she had been to see Percy. This time, as her profit was going up, she spent five pounds, but still kept a pound back for emergencies.

Another part of her life was happier too. 'Looks like he's becoming a regular visitor,' said Winnie as she and Maggie stood watching Jamie and Laura skipping down the road holding David Matthews's hand.

'It's only the second time this has happened, and it's nice of him to take them out, and they do like him.'

'What about you, gel?'

Maggie blushed. 'He is very nice.'

'But still a copper.'

Maggie turned to fiddle with her display. 'Don't start making something out of nothing.'

'How's Bella doing these days? Don't suppose we'll be seeing much of her once the weather turns.'

'I'm going to try and get over tomorrow. The stall and the buying seems to be taking a lot of my time.'

Winnie looked about her and moved closer. 'Paid off any of that loan yet?'

Maggie smiled. 'Hopefully I'll be able to pay off a pound this week.'

Winnie grinned. 'That's good. 'Ere, you ain't told anybody else, have you?'

'No, not even Eve, although she did want to know where I got the money from to buy this amount of stock. I told her Bella lent me a few bob.'

'Well, it certainly looks good.'

'Mummy, Mummy,' shouted Jamie as they ran towards her. 'Look, Uncle David bought us a great big ice cream.'

Maggie noted all eyes were on her. 'That was very kind of you, but you shouldn't have.'

'It was my treat.'

'Mummy,' said Laura, grinning and moving closer to her, 'Uncle David was telling us about his house. He's got a big garden and a tree he said he could put a rope over and make us a swing, but he said we'd have to ask you first if we could go.'

Maggie looked at David.

He shrugged his shoulders. 'I'm sorry, I should have said something before telling them. I can understand if you don't approve.'

Maggie was so embarrassed she wanted to die. She turned her back on the stallholders. 'We'll talk about it later. Bill, watch the stall while I see to the kids. Bye, David,' she said softly.

David came up close. 'Could I see you tomorrow?'

'No, I'm taking them to see Bella.'

'I could take you all in the car.'

'Oh please, Mummy, let's go in Uncle David's car.' Jamie's shrill voice stunned everybody into silence.

Maggie could feel eyes boring into her back.

'Oh go on, Mummy, please,' pleaded Laura.

Maggie wished herself anywhere but there with everyone listening.

David moved very close to her. She could feel his breath on her cheek.

'Look, I'm sorry about this,' he whispered. 'I'll call round tomorrow, you can let me know then.' His words were for her ears only.

As David walked away Jamie said, 'You're mean. Why couldn't we go in his car?'

'Come on, Jamie, upstairs,' said Maggie crossly. Why did he have to say that in front of everybody? She didn't dare look at the traders. She knew all the remarks would come when it was time to put the stalls away. And she was right.

'I know it ain't none of me business, gel,' said Tom Cooper, 'but I don't think you should make an 'abit of letting that copper hang about.'

'I can't stop him,' said Maggie, making sure all the small pieces of jewellery were carefully boxed.

'Well, you could tell him you don't want him ter see the kids,' said Mrs Russell.

Maggie felt she had to stand up for herself. 'He ain't doing any harm. 'Sides, the kids like him and being taken to the park.'

A train rattled past, making conversation impossible.

'But when Tony does walk his arse back here he'll certainly have somethink to say about it.'

Maggie went and stood by Mrs Russell's flowers. 'Do you honestly think he's coming back?'

'We all like to think he is.'

'In the meantime I'm grateful for someone to take Jamie for a game in the park as his father don't seemed to be very bothered.'

'Maggie, stop that.' Mrs Russell smacked Maggie's hand. She was absent-mindedly pulling the petals off a daisy. 'That ain't gonner give yer the bleeding answer to yer prayers.'

Maggie smiled. 'Well, according to that daisy he don't love me anyway.'

'Who you talking about?' asked Mrs Russell.

'Tony, of course.'

Mrs Russell tutted and shook her head. 'I don't believe that fer one minute.'

'Just remember what I said,' said Tom Cooper. 'Send that copper packing.'

Maggie felt like telling him to shove off and mind his own business, but she knew she depended on these people to stand by her if she ever needed them. She smiled. 'I'll tell him,' adding silently under her breath, 'but will he listen?' And did she want him to?

Chapter 25

Maggie had just finished washing up the dinner things when Jamie rushed down the stairs to answer the knock. Maggie knew it was David.

She was wiping her hands on the bottom of her apron when he walked into the living room clutching his trilby. 'I'm sorry about yesterday. Did you get much stick from the others?'

'A bit.'

'I've got the car outside. Please, let me take you over to see Mrs Ross.'

She looked down at the two pair of eyes studying her and smiled. 'How can I refuse?'

'Goody, goody,' shouted Jamie. 'Can I take me football?'

'Jamie, behave.'

'Our gran's got ever such a big garden, but she ain't got no trees in it.'

David laughed.

'Right, into the kitchen you two and let me wipe your faces.'

'Oh Mummy, do we have to?' asked Laura.

'Yes.'

'Well, don't you be too rough,' said Jamie.

'We won't be long,' said Maggie, smiling at David.

It didn't take long for them to get ready and soon they were seated in David's car heading towards Downham, past green fields and tall trees.

'You have a bit of a journey to Greenwich every day.'

'It's not too bad. Going home in the winter to an empty house is the worse part of it. I would move nearer to Rother-hithe, but I like to do a bit of gardening, it helps relax me.'

'Is your garden bigger than our gran's?'

'I don't know, Jamie, I've never seen your gran's.'

'This a smashing car. What's it called?' asked Jamie.

'A Morris.'

'My daddy said he was gonner get a car, but he never did,' said Laura.

'Daddy said a lot of things,' said Jamie, 'But he never keeps promises. He didn't even send me a birthday card.'

'Well, I reckon he's dead like that man told us,' said Laura matter-of-factly.

Maggie looked at David.

'Why don't you have a game of I-spy?' said David.

'That's a good idea,' said Laura. 'I'll start.'

'Why is it always you? Mummy, let me start.'

'To save all arguments I'll start,' said Maggie, pleased David had moved the conversation away from Tony. The rest of the journey was full of laughter when Jamie and Laura weren't sure if the objects began with C or S.

''Allo, love,' said Bella, opening the door and kissing all three of them. 'It's good to see you.

''Ere, ain't that that copper's car?' she asked, coming out of the doorway.

'Yes.'

'Oh no, not more bloody trouble?'

'No, he just brought us over here.'

'Did he now? Go on into the garden, kids.'

'I've got my football what Uncle David gave me for me birthday.'

'Uncle David, eh?' Bella raised her eyebrows. 'Well, he coming in or not?' she asked.

'He wasn't sure.'

Bella walked down the path. 'Come on in,' she beckoned to him, then turned and walked back to her front door. 'Silly sod, what was he gonner do, sit there till yer come out?'

Maggie smiled. 'Probably. He's used to sitting in a car waiting for people. I half expected to see Benny here,' said Maggie when they went into the kitchen.

'He does come over most Sundays – been helping me with the garden.'

'Oh I see,' said Maggie.

'Don't say it like that. There ain't nothink wrong with him giving me a hand, and me giving him a bit of dinner in return, is there?'

'No, course not.'

When they were seated at the table Maggie opened her handbag. 'I've got a little present for you.'

'Me? Why? It ain't me birthday.'

'I know.' Maggie leant forward excitedly. 'You see, I've found this new place, Percy's Emporium, to buy from.'

'That's a bloody posh name. What's he sell, and what's his prices like?'

'Very good.' Maggie handed her a small brooch that had the word 'Mother' written in gold-coloured wire.

'This is lovely,' said Bella, admiring it. 'What'd it cost?'

'I ain't telling you, but don't worry, it ain't gold.'

'You must let me pay.'

'No, I told you it's a present. Besides, you spend enough on us, so let me treat you for a change.'

'So, has this Percy got some good gear?'

'I should say so, it's like a treasure trove.' Maggie went into great detail about how she met Doris, Mabel and Percy, and of course Mrs Freeman brought hoots of laughter. She also told them about Lil, and that she was a fortune-teller who had read her hand.

'Don't hold with that sorta thing,' said Bella. 'Could be very unhealthy. I hope you didn't take any notice of what she told yer?'

'She did tell me I was to expect more grief, but it will all turn out all right in the end.'

'Did she say how long?'

'No.'

'Well then, anybody could tell you that. Have you heard of this Lil?' she asked David.

'Can't say I have, so she hasn't got a record – well, not round our way anyway.'

Maggie laughed. 'Still it's given us something to talk about.' Deep down she was concerned with what Lil had told her, and she wasn't sure how she could cope with more grief.

All too soon it was time for them to leave.

As they moved up the passage Bella took hold of David's arm and held him back. 'I'm glad you brought Maggs over,' she said quietly. 'She could do with a bit of looking after.'

'Thank you for the tea. If she wants me to, I can nearly

always manage to alter my shifts and bring her over.'

Maggie noted the pain on Bella's face when Jamie took hold of David's hand.

Maggie held her close and whispered, 'Don't worry, we will always be around.'

The singsong they had all the way home was very off key, and conversation was impossible. But Maggie could see David was really enjoying himself.

'Would you like to come up for a cup of tea?' she asked when they arrived at her door.

'That would be very nice, but only if you're sure it's not too much trouble.'

'Let me get these two to bed first, then we can sit and have a chat. Thanks for taking us over there.'

'My pleasure.'

'And David, there's something I want to ask you,' she said, before turning to attend to the children.

He sat on tenterhooks waiting for Maggie to see to the children. Restlessly he lit a cigarette and wandered over to the window. What did she want to ask him? There were so many things he wanted to ask her. He had so much to offer her. He knew he was falling in love with her, but he also knew he had to be very careful not to show his feelings. He didn't want to frighten her away. If only there was some concrete news of Tony Ross.

'There, that's them down for the night.' Maggie closed the door. 'You can sit here while I put the kettle on.' She went to go into the kitchen.

David stubbed out his cigarette and was right behind her.

'It's all right, I can . . .' her voice trailed off as he came close to her.

'I'll give you a hand,' he croaked.

'You don't have . . .' Maggie felt silly, she knew she was sounding pathetic. 'David, please, don't.'

He knew it was wrong as he took her in his arms and kissed her warm inviting lips, softly at first, then full of passion. Maggie didn't resist.

He buried his head in her neck and whispered, 'I promised myself I wouldn't do this. But I can't help it. You are so lovely and look so vulnerable. I want to take you away and protect you and love you.'

Maggie gently pushed him away. 'This is so wrong.'

'Why?'

'I love Tony.'

'Do you? Deep down, do you after all that he's putting you through?'

'But what if he's dead?'

'But what if he's not?'

Maggie couldn't answer his question. 'I'll make the tea.'

They stood in silence watching the blue flame dance round the kettle. Neither knew what to say. Maggie made the tea and took the tray into the living room.

David sat on the sofa, while Maggie sat at the table.

'I'm sorry, Maggie.'

'It's all right.' She began stirring the tea in the pot vigorously.

'What was it you wanted to ask me?'

'It was about Mr Windsor. I've not heard anythink more from him.'

David came and sat at the table, touching her hand tenderly. 'No, he won't be bothering you any more.'

'Why?'

'I told him Tony was missing, presumed dead, so there was no use trying to collect his money as you didn't know anything about it, and if he did, he'd have me to answer to.'

Maggie pulled her hand away. 'Do you think Tony's dead?'

'What else can we think? It's what, almost five months – you would have heard something by now. He didn't send Jamie a birthday card, and from what you've told me about him I don't think he would have let that pass.'

Maggie looked down. 'You could be right, but how can I be sure?'

'If he changed his name when he left there won't be any records.'

Maggie's tears began to fall. 'What if he's wandering about not knowing who he is?'

'We've gone through that theory before. He must have had some form of identification on him – even his railway ticket would have told them where he came from.'

'I suppose you're right. Have I got to spend the rest of my life wondering if I am a widow or not?'

'I'm afraid that would be a possibility.'

Maggie looked up at him. Tears streaked her face. 'What am I gonner do?'

'Maggie, come and live with me.'

'What? I can't.'

'Why not?'

'I've still got to wait for Tony.'

'Maggie, I'm very fond of you.'

'Please, David, don't.'

'The children like me.'

'I know.'

291

'I'm off next Sunday, let me take you to my house. Please.'

'I don't know.'

'The children will love it.'

Maggie stood up. 'How could I just go off and live with you? What would the traders say, and what about Bella? She would be horrified. And what about the stall? Tony's dad, Jim, took years to get to that spot – I just can't throw it all away. And what about my brother? And what if Tony comes back?' she said softly.

'All these questions.'

Maggie bit her lip. 'But they have been my life.'

'But that part could end and you can start again.'

'I don't know.'

'Is that all that's stopping you from coming with me?'

'No. Yes. I don't know.'

'All I can say is that I mean it.'

'I wish this mystery could be cleared up.'

'So do I.' He stood up and took his hat from the chair. 'Maggie, don't let other people rule your life. You deserve to be happy.'

'You going? What about your tea?'

'I'm sorry. But I can't trust myself to stay here with you. I might say or do something I'll regret for ever. I'll collect you about eleven. Don't worry about dinner, I'll do something for us. I'll see myself out.'

He went. Maggie stared at the door. She didn't want him to go. But what *did* she want? She poured out her tea. Suddenly everything was going so well for her. She had found a good supplier and the stall was doing fine. She was even thinking of sending her brother two pounds next week, and she didn't have to worry about Mr Windsor, David had seen to him. She should be happy, but now he had given her another problem to solve. Part of her wanted to go with him, but she also knew she loved Tony, and had to be here for him, and that feeling would never go away.

Maggie hadn't seen Eve all week, and on Saturday night when she came round and the children were in bed Maggie said, 'David took us to Bella's last Sunday in his car.'

'Did he now? What did Bella have to say about that?'

Maggie laughed. 'I took her a brooch to soften her up.'

'You crafty cow.'

'No, it wasn't for that reason. She likes him. She reckons he's not a bad bloke for a copper.' Eve joined in with the last few words.

Maggie sat forward. 'Eve, he wants to take us to his house tomorrow.'

'What, over Greenwich?'

Maggie nodded.

'You going?'

'I don't know.'

'What do the kids say about it?'

'I haven't told them.'

'What you gonner do?'

'Half of me wants to, but . . .'

'Look, Maggs, I know it ain't none of my business.'

Maggie laughed.

'What's so funny?'

'Everybody says that, then they proceed to tell me what to do.'

'Oh well, please yourself, I was only gonner give you my opinion, but if you—'

'Sorry, Eve. Come on, don't get huffy. What was you gonner say?'

'I was gonner say that it wouldn't be a bad idea to go over. What you afraid of? Has he been coming on a bit strong?'

It was Maggie's turn to get rattled. 'No he ain't. And I ain't afraid of nothink.'

'Well, I think you are, and if you want my opinion I reckon you're falling for him.'

Maggie stood up. 'Don't talk daft.'

'So in that case why won't you go over there?'

'I didn't say I wasn't going, it's just that—'

'And the kids will be with you.' Eve laughed. 'That should stop any hanky-panky.'

Maggie laughed with her, but she knew her friend could see through her.

Chapter 26

The following Sunday evening after Maggie had put the children to bed, she plonked herself on the sofa next to David. 'I feel exhausted. Thank you for a really lovely day.'

David smiled. 'It should be me thanking you. Mind you, they certainly keep you on the go.'

'And you.' Maggie laughed. 'I'm surprised you could keep up with them, playing football, pushing them on the swing you made them, and doing our dinner.'

'I'm not that old. But honestly, I can't ever remember enjoying myself so much. They are a great pair.'

Maggie leant back. 'Yes they are.'

'I'm so glad you decided to come.'

'So am I.'

Maggie had been very impressed when David had arrived on the stroke of eleven. Jamie and Laura, who were all spruced up ready, were having a job to sit still and curb their excitement.

'Didn't have any choice, did I? I really would have been the wicked witch if I'd said no.'

He put his arm round her. 'You could never be wicked.'

Maggie moved away. 'Please, David, no.'

He held up his hands. 'Sorry.'

'You have a lovely house,' said Maggie. She knew she had to change the subject, even though she wanted David to hold her and kiss her, but if she allowed that where would it stop?

David lit a cigarette, fidgeting awkwardly. 'It felt good hearing all that laughter and noise today.'

'There was certainly plenty of noise.' Maggie tried to stifle a yawn. 'I'm sorry.'

'I think I should go. I have a busy day tomorrow.'

'So do I.'

'You over to see your Percy?'

She smiled and nodded. 'Don't you let Mabel hear you call him my Percy.'

'Everything still going well?'

'Yet it is.' She sat forward excitedly. 'I can't believe how well it's going.'

'They'll soon have to change the name down there to Maggie's Market.'

She laughed. 'D'you know, I've even managed to start . . .' She stopped. She had been going to say, 'paying Alan back, and the loan,' but she hadn't told David Tony owed money to her brother, or where she'd got the money from to buy the jewellery. 'Saving for Laura's birthday.'

'When's that?'

'Five weeks' time, November the twenty-fourth.'

'How old will she be?'

'Seven,' Maggie said wistfully. 'I don't know where the years have gone. It's on a Sunday so you must make sure you get that day off.'

'If you really want me to.'

'Laura certainly will, and so do I,' she said softly.

David resisted his desire to pull her into his arms and instead walked to the door. 'When can I see you again?'

Maggie shrugged.

'I'll pop in some time, and thank you again for a lovely day.' He lightly kissed her cheek.

Maggie closed the front door behind him.

Yes it had been a lovely day, she mused. David had a nice house, though not big like Alan's, and the children loved the garden. She softly sang to herself, letting her mind wander as she folded the children's clothes. She thought about the wedding picture of David and his wife that had stood on his sideboard. She looked a lovely woman, and he was so handsome smiling down at her, they must have been very happy. He said that now, because of her death, he threw himself into his work. When Maggie went upstairs to his bathroom she felt she wanted to go into his bedroom, not just to be nosy, but to see if he'd kept it as she imagined his wife would have done.

'So, what difference would it make to you?' she said out loud to herself.

The weeks sped past and Maggie couldn't believe how well the stall was doing. Although Benny was still providing her with some of the things Tony always sold it was the jewellery that was her first love. Every Monday she was over to see Percy, and every week she bought more and more with her profit as new customers came. Her business had really taken off.

'Your stuff's certainly bringing in new punters,' said Tom Cooper.

'It's good to see new faces,' said Winnie. 'Everybody seems to be benefiting. The word's definitely getting around.'

Maggie felt very proud and confident. She was even managing to pay back Mr Shore, the loan club man.

'I'm surprised you borrowed money off him,' said Gus one Monday when she went in the Dog to see Mr Shore.

'He's the only one I know who'll lend it to me.'

'Yer, at a price.'

'Well, I'm able to pay him back.'

'I hope so, love. I certainly hope so.'

Twice Maggie had been able to send Alan a two-pound postal order. She hoped this would keep him away. She didn't want him and Helen to keep coming over for they had the knack of upsetting her.

David was becoming a regular visitor most Sundays. That way, she told him, she wouldn't get so much hassle from the other stallholders as if he visited while they were around. Sometimes they went to Bella's, other times Maggie did the dinner and they went to the park, and on other Sundays they went to David's house. Although Maggie wanted him, and she knew he felt the same, they kept their distance. She didn't ask him to the pub when she went with Dan and Eve on a Saturday night as she didn't want Gus and the others to know she was seeing him socially.

'I dunno why,' said Eve one Monday evening when they were sorting over Maggie's latest buys. 'At least it keeps all them undesirables away from you.'

'I know, but I think they would resent me going out with him.'

'Why?'

''Cos I'm still married to Tony.'

'Yer, but Bella accepts him.'

'Only 'cos he's good to the kids.'

'Maggie, do you love him?' she asked.

'No, course not,' she answered abruptly.

'OK. Don't bite me head off. I only asked.'

'Sorry. Eve, I could get very fond of him, I s'pose, but only if . . .'

'It must be bloody hard, all this not knowing, and not having any of you know what. You don't, do you?'

'No I don't.' She couldn't tell Eve that she longed to be held and made love to. When would that happen again, if ever? 'It's Laura I'm worried about. I'm hoping Tony will send her a birthday card.'

'Do you still think he's alive?'

Maggie put the ring she was trying to display on some cardboard to one side. 'I don't know. I would like to think he is, but then again, if he was, and not telling me . . .' She blinked hard to stem a tear. 'We'll just have to wait and see if he remembers, won't we?'

'I hope he does. She's at a funny age.'

'I know.'

Maggie wasn't surprised to see Alan on the Saturday before Laura's birthday.

'Business seems to be brisk,' said Alan as he stood watching the customers come and go.

Maggie smiled. 'I'm doing very nicely, thank you.'

He took her to one side and, keeping his voice low, said, 'You know you didn't have to send me that money. You knew I'd be over some time and you could give it to me then.'

'I just wanted you and Helen to know that I intend paying you back every penny Tony borrowed.'

'But I don't want you to go short.'

'Thanks, Alan, but don't worry about me. I'm doing all right. Yes, love, a shilling a pair.'

'They're only a tanner in Woolworth's.'

'They may look like those, but I can assure you the backs won't fall off of these after one wear.'

The woman turned the earrings over, and put them on. She peered in the hand mirror Maggie kept on the stall. 'I must admit they do look better. All right, I'll have 'em.'

Maggie put the earrings in a small paper bag.

When the woman was out of earshot Bill said to Alan, 'She's got the gift of the gab, just like her old man.'

'What do you think of all this?' Alan asked Bill.

'Not a lot. Would rather be selling stuff like what Tony got – tools and the like. This lot's too sissy for me.'

Maggie laughed. 'As long as I'm paying your wages, you'll sell what I say.'

'She's getting bossy as well,' added Bill.

'I've got Laura's birthday present here.'

'Leave it here, I'll take it up later.'

'Her card's inside.'

'Thanks, Alan.'

'I suppose I'd better go.'

Maggie didn't offer him a cup of tea. She didn't want to leave the stall as she knew she made a better job of selling than Bill did. Also, she didn't want Alan hanging around any longer than necessary, then reporting to Helen on how well she was doing. She held her face close to her brother's for the obligatory peck on the cheek, then carried on serving.

That evening Maggie was busy making a jelly, cooking fairy cakes and generally preparing for Laura's birthday tea.

'I didn't get any cards today,' said Laura, coming into the kitchen.

'I expect you'll get them tomorrow. After all, your birthday isn't till tomorrow.'

'There ain't no post then.'

'I expect people will find a way.'

'What about them on the market? They ain't gonner leave it till Monday, are they?'

'Don't know. You'll just have to wait and see.' Maggie smiled. Laura's cards and presents were hidden away, but she wouldn't get the doll's pram they'd bought for her until Eve brought it round from her flat.

'Well, they better not forget me.'

'You don't even know if they've bought you anything,' said Maggie, pouring the cake mixture into the tin.

Laura's face was filled with alarm. 'I told 'em it was me birthday. They ain't forgot, have they?'

'Not telling.'

'But they always buy us somethink. Can I lick the bowl?'

'Shh, don't let Jamie hear, otherwise he'll want it.'

'Well, he can't, 'cos it's my birthday. Mummy, do you think Daddy will remember my birthday?'

Maggie was taken aback. The children rarely mentioned Tony these days – it was almost as if he had never existed – though sometimes Maggie would go to his wardrobe and hug his suits, just to remember his smell. 'I don't know, love.'

'I've said a prayer every night to tell God to remind him. Do you think he will?'

For a few moments Maggie couldn't answer, for she knew there would be a catch in her voice. She blinked quickly to stem the tears, then bending down she held her daughter close. 'I can't answer you. I only wish I could.'

Laura giggled. 'You've got all flour on your face.'

'Go on, cheeky, start getting ready for bed.' Maggie tried to sound cheerful, but she shared Laura's thoughts: would Tony remember? Or must she now accept that he was dead?

It was raining on Sunday but that didn't dampen Laura's spirits. And the afternoon had her jumping with joy when her school friends arrived. David had collected Bella and Benny, and Eve and Dan brought the pram round.

'Felt a right fool walking along pushing this,' said Dan.

'You didn't push, I did,' said Eve.

'I still felt a fool.'

Laughter and noise filled the flat. Even Mr Goldman came up to join in.

There was paper and cards everywhere.

When Bella and Maggie were alone in the kitchen Bella said, 'You've pushed the boat out on this one, ain't yer?'

'Well, now I'm earning a few bob what's the odds?'

'What about your brother?'

'I've been paying him back as well.'

Bella smiled. 'I'm pleased about that. That's a lovely doll,' she inclined her head towards the living room, 'that he bought Laura.'

'David's very good to them. What d'you think of the

clothes? I've been busy, ain't I?'

'They're very nice. Mind you, I dunno where you get the time to make 'em.'

'When the kids are in bed.'

'Do you see much of him?'

'Most Sundays, but you know that.'

'Yer, it's just that I wondered if he came here in the week.'

'No, he doesn't. That was good of Benny to give her that necklace.'

'He's not a bad bloke.'

'Well then, why don't you marry him?'

Bella didn't want to answer that question. 'I'm really pleased to see things are getting better for you. You've worked bloody hard.'

'I've got to thank that Lil for telling me about Percy. I couldn't do it without him.'

'You getting stuff at a good price from him?'

Maggie nodded. 'The more I buy the bigger the discount, and I think he likes me, as I always seem to get more for me money.'

'In some ways it's a good thing you lost that baby.'

Maggie stood and stared at Bella. 'How can you say that?'

'Well, you couldn't run the stall and look after a baby as well, now could you? Something would have had to go by the board.'

'I would have tried to manage somehow.'

'I know that, but all that traipsing round looking for stuff to sell before you found out about that Percy – that could have been hard.'

Maggie felt like telling her to shut up, she didn't want reminding of her lost baby, but she knew it was better to keep quiet.

'I'm pleased you managed to keep the stall going. Those licences are bloody hard to get hold of, 'specially up that end. Wouldn't like to see it lost, not after all the years we've had it. And a word of advice: remember you've got Christmas coming up, so you wanner get plenty of stock in for that.'

Maggie was pleased Bella was off on a different tack. 'Don't worry, I intend to.' And she wasn't going to tell anyone, not even Winnie, that she was going to take out a bigger loan to buy Christmas stock.

'I must tell you this. That Mrs Saunders – you know, who runs the haberdashery stall? – came up and give me the once-over. D'you know, she told me not to sell ribbons and the like otherwise she'd have my guts for garters.'

'What did you say?'

'Not a lot, just told her I only use ribbons to hang some of the bone bracelets on,' Maggie laughed. 'But guess what? Winnie told her that my guts wouldn't look very nice hanging on her stall and she couldn't see many girls wearing 'em. She didn't half get wild, and waddled off down the road muttering to herself.'

Bella also laughed. 'Winnie's a nice woman.'

'Yes she is.'

'I don't think her and that Mrs Saunders hit it off when Jim was there.'

'D'you know why?'

'I think one of her kids pinched a pair of shoes. Mind you, that's going back years.'

'But Winnie would never let that rest.'

As Maggie wiped the dishes her thoughts suddenly went to Lil. She must have got her prediction wrong, because in many ways this was a good time. She was happy and making money. But she also knew the grief would never really be over all the while Tony was away.

Chapter 27

Maggie sighed. It was dull and miserable outside, the kind of Monday morning when nobody wanted to leave their bed. Winter was well and truly on its way.

The postman dropping the letters through made her jump up, grab her dressing gown and rush downstairs. She was ever hopeful that there would be a birthday card for Laura from Tony.

Again she was disappointed, and hoped Laura wouldn't be upset before going to school. She would tell her the postman hadn't been yet.

She got dressed. This morning she was going to Percy's as usual, then at lunchtime she intended to see about getting a big loan. Maggie was pleased she'd managed to pay back four of the five pounds she'd first borrowed, and hoped Mr Shore would see his way to lending her the ten pounds she had in mind. 'Ten pounds,' she whispered. 'That's a lot of money, and a lot of interest to pay back.' But Percy had told her to get the stock in well before Christmas as he soon sold out of all the good gear. She smiled confidently to herself and, after putting the kettle on, set about preparing the children's breakfast.

Maggie shuddered when she opened the front door, she wasn't looking forward to being out and about in this weather.

'Did you have a nice birthday, young lady?' asked Winnie when she caught sight of Maggie trying to hurry the children along.

'Yes thank you, and thank you for my lovely doll's pram. Uncle David bought me a pretty doll with a real china head and brown eyes that open and close. When I get back from school I'll show you.'

'I'd like that.'

Maggie tightened Jamie's scarf. 'Laura can bring you all down a bit of cake after school. Now come on, kids, otherwise you'll be late. I'll have a word later on,' she said to Winnie over her shoulder.

On her way home from Percy, Maggie reflected as usual on her good luck at finding him. He too was talking about Christmas and the new lines he was getting next week. It was all going to be very exciting.

She took her purchases upstairs before going along to the Dog and Duck.

'Hallo, Rene. Thought Monday was your day off?'

''Allo, Maggs. Don't often see you in here at lunchtime,' said Rene. 'Gus has got the accountant in, so I've had to come in. Did you wanner see Gus?'

'No, I'm looking for Mr Shore. Has he been in yet?'

She leant over the bar, revealing more of her bosom, and bent her head closer. 'He's in the bog. Here, you ain't borrowing money off that shark, are yer?' So far Rene hadn't been in when Maggie had met Mr Shore to pay back any of the money.

Maggie couldn't deny it. 'Why do you say that?'

'Well, if yer don't pay up, it could be . . .' She stopped and looked up as the dapper Mr Shore came over to Maggie.

'Hallo, my dear. Come to give me some more of my money?' he grinned. 'Good customer, this one is,' he said to Rene.

He got out his book when he and Maggie were seated. 'Only a pound to go, plus interest. So, how much you paying me this time?'

Maggie looked round nervously. 'I would like to borrow some more.'

He licked his pencil. 'Don't normally let you have more till this lot's been paid up.'

Maggie sat back dejected. 'I can let you have it in a week or so.'

'How much more did you want?'

She cleared her throat. 'Ten pounds,' she said softly.

His head shot up. 'How much?'

She went to speak but he put up his hands to silence her. 'That's a lot of money, young lady, and a lot of interest.'

'What do I owe you now?'

He quickly added up the figures. 'As you've had it over a relatively short time I'll only charge you a pound interest.'

'But I thought you only charged two bob in the pound, and I only had five pounds.'

'Ah yes, I do, but then there's a charge for the loan, the loan book I gave you and administration charges, and if it went over three months there's another charge.'

Maggie sat back. What was she getting herself into? She was beginning to see how easy it must have been for Tony to get into deep water.

DEE WILLIAMS

'So, do you still want ten pounds?'

She nodded. 'Will that be two pounds' interest?'

'Only if you pay it back within three months.'

There wasn't any way out; she needed more stock for Christmas. 'Yes, please.'

Mr Shore smiled and took out his wallet.

'Still paying off that money?' said Winnie when Maggie came back from the Dog and Duck.

'Getting there,' said Maggie breezily.

'It looks as though it was worth it.'

'Winnie, have you ever borrowed money off of him?'

'Na, never had cause to, but a lot I know have. I think he's as fair as any of 'em. Why?'

'Just wondered, that's all.'

'Laura was pleased with the pram then?'

'I should say so. It was really nice of 'em all.'

'So the tea party went all right?'

'Yes, Bella and Benny came over.'

'And did Uncle David then?'

'Yes, he did as a matter of fact.'

'Just remember to keep yer feet on the ground, gel. Don't get carried away. You never know what's round the corner.'

'Well, I don't think it will be Tony. He never even sent her a card.'

'The cowson.'

Maggie had been dreading Laura coming home from school. Would she ask about a card or had she forgotten?

'What you looking for?' asked Maggie that afternoon as Laura sifted through the papers on the sideboard.

'I thought there might be a card from Daddy,' she said quietly.

310

'There better not be,' said Jamie. ''Cos he didn't send me one. He don't love us any more.'

'I'm sure he does. It's just that he didn't have me to remind him,' said Maggie, fighting for the right words to say.

'Well I reckon that man was right,' said Jamie, 'and he's dead.'

That statement shook Maggie, it was so forthright. For the first time it occurred to her that Wally might have been telling the truth.

'I think we must accept that something has happened to Daddy.'

'See,' said Jamie. 'Told you so.'

'Now come on, sit up at the table. You can finish off the jelly and cake.'

'Great,' said Jamie, scrambling on the chair.

That night, when Maggie went to tuck them up, Laura was softly crying.

'Laura love, what's wrong?'

'Was Jamie right when he said Daddy don't love us any more?' she sobbed.

Maggie held her close. 'I can't answer your questions truthfully, Laura, because I really don't know.'

Laura's sobs racked her tiny body. 'Has he gone away 'cos we've been naughty?'

'No, my darling.' Laura seemed so small and vulnerable. At that moment Maggie hated Tony viciously. How dare he make his children so unhappy? She kissed her wet cheek. 'Now settle down. You don't want to go to school with red puffy eyes, do you?'

Laura shook her head. 'Mummy, I didn't wish for Daddy

to come back when I blew out my candles.'

'Oh,' said Maggie. She couldn't think of any comforting words.

'You see, Jamie did, and it didn't come true.'

Maggie thought her heart was going to break. She choked back a sob. 'Do you want to tell me what you wished for?'

'No, just in case telling won't make it come true.'

Maggie smiled and kissed her. 'Remember we've got Christmas to look forward to next,' she said, trying to make it sound lighthearted.

Laura gave her a weak smile. 'Good night, Mummy. You'll never leave us, will you?'

'Never.'

'Promise?'

'I promise.'

The rest of the week saw the traders battling with the rain and cold. On Friday when Maggie went down to see Bill he looked very miserable.

'What's wrong with you?' asked Maggie.

'I'm cold and fed up.'

'Why? You know what being on a stall's like, you've done it for years.' But Maggie too was worried about the weather.

'To tell the truth, Maggs, I miss Tony.'

Maggie began to feel angry. 'So do I, but walking around with a long face ain't gonner bring him back, and it don't encourage people to hang around and look over the goods.'

Bill shuffled to his feet. 'No, I know. It's just that I dunno what to say when these women put on the stuff, then peer in the mirror and ask me what I fink, as if it matters.'

'Course it matters. They like a bloke's opinion.' She smiled. 'Anyway, how's your mum?'

'She's not too bad. Her sister from Essex is coming on Sunday.' He brightened up. 'I like my uncle, he's a smashing bloke. He was in the air force during the war. Mum says him and me dad were the best of mates. Don't see him very often. I think they want me mum to go there for Christmas. I hope so – it'll be a nice change from just the two of us sitting looking at the fire.'

'Don't you go out with the lads?'

'Sometimes, but at Christmas they usually stay in with their families, 'Sides that, I wouldn't leave me mum, not on her own.'

Maggie smiled. 'Let's hope we have a good Christmas, then I might give you an extra Christmas box.'

At least the thought of that brought a smile to Bill's face.

The following Monday Maggie was full of excitement about going over to see Percy. She hadn't told anybody she had borrowed ten pounds. The children were having their breakfast when there was a banging on the front door.

'I'm coming, I'm coming,' Maggie said, hurrying down to open it. 'Winnie. What you doing here? What's wrong?'

'Just letting yer know, gel, that Bill ain't turned up. Your stall's still in the lockup.'

'What?' Squabbling from upstairs made Maggie look round. 'I'll get these two off first, then I'll be along to sort it out. I wonder if he's all right?'

'D'you want Fred and Tom to get it out for you?'

'No, no thanks. I've got to go and see Percy so the stall

will have to stay put for today. This afternoon I'll go round and see if Bill's all right.'

'Please yerself. See you later.'

Maggie closed the door. As she ran up the stairs to stem the argument, she said to herself, 'That's all I need at the moment – Bill being ill.' She admonished herself for being selfish. It could be that his mother had been unwell.

On the way home from Percy's Maggie sat on the bus and smiled to herself. Her bags were loaded, she had spent every penny she owned. 'Alan will have to wait till after Christmas for some more of his money. So will Mr Shore.' She felt so happy and confident that for now she ceased to worry about her debts.

Later that afternoon she went to Bill's mother's house for the first time. It was in the middle of a dirty and run-down row of terraces in a miserable area. The houses looked like Bella's had done before it was pulled down. Skinny scruffy kids with runny noses, who, even though it was cold and damp, didn't have any shoes on, were running about or pushing babies in prams that held two and three children. Maggie shuddered and knocked on the door.

No one answered. Perhaps Bill was at the hospital. She began to get agitated and banged again, this time much harder.

The next door opened. 'Ain't nobody in then, love?' asked a thin seemingly old woman.

'Don't look like it.'

'Fought young Billy might be there. His mum, Jenny's, gorn off.'

'She in hospital?'

'Na, love. She's gorn ter stay with her sister out Essex

way for a few days. They took her yesterday in the car. Nice car he's got. Mind you, it's a good fing too, if yer asks me. Wouldn't be surprised if she didn't stay there fer good. She ain't been all that well lately – it's her chest yer know – and this damp don't help none. Her sister and her old man – lovely couple they are, and good to her – they've been wanting her ter go up there fer years, but it was young Billy what kept her here.'

'So where's Billy now?'

'Dunno. He went with 'em, but I fought he was coming back. P'raps he changed his mind.'

Panic filled Maggie. What if he had gone to live in Essex? What would she do without him?

Maggie thanked the woman and left. As she walked home her mind was churning over and over, and she was full of fear at the prospect of managing the stall alone. She wasn't strong like Winnie and one or two of the other women who took their stalls out day after day. She couldn't rely on Tom and Fred for favours as after a week or two they'd get fed up. And what about the children? She would have to get them to school and still feed them, then there was the washing and . . . Perhaps I'm worrying unnecessarily, Maggie thought. I've got plenty of stock, thank goodness, and if I run out . . . well, I'll just have to wait and see.

Maggie told Winnie about what had happened.

'Don't worry about it, gel. We'll make sure you don't lose out if he's gorn off. But I can't see him letting you down like that, not at this time o' year.'

But the following morning there was no sign of Bill again. Fred helped Maggie to get set up, and between them

Winnie, Fred, Tom and Mrs Russell kept an eye on it till Maggie came back from taking the children to school.

At the end of the day they all helped her put it away.

All week it was the same, and Maggie was cross there hadn't been any news from Bill.

On Saturday morning when Eve came round and heard the story, she stayed to help out.

'I ain't half enjoying myself,' she said, after serving a customer. 'Mind you, I wish I'd put thicker drawers on. There's a bloody draft blowing up me knicker leg.'

Tom Cooper laughed. 'I've got some lovely red flannel on me stall, gel. Come over and I'll get yer measured up.'

'You wanner watch him, gel,' said Mrs Russell. 'He'll be asking yer to take yours off for a pattern.'

'Now that's what I call a good idea,' said Tom.

Despite the cold, all morning there was plenty of laughter and easy-going banter. Maggie too was enjoying herself, and she was selling well.

Towards the afternoon Eve said she had to go and get Dan's tea ready. 'I'll be round later.'

Trade had died down and the hurricane lamps that hung from the stalls had been lit. Despite the cold a warm glow hung over the market and the lovely smell of roasting chestnuts filled the air. Since the incident with Mr Goldman's window the Blackshirts had moved to another corner, a street away from the market and their shouts no longer disturbed the traders.

Maggie stamped her cold feet and banged her hands together to try to bring some life back into them. She joined in with the carols coming from the Salvation Army band. Three weeks to Christmas, and if trade stayed like this, and

Bill came back, it would be great. She felt warm and happy inside. She was showing everybody she could manage.

''Allo there, me old Maggs.'

Maggie turned and saw Bill staggering towards her. 'Not so much of the old. Bill, you all right?'

He giggled. 'I fink I'm a bit pissed.'

'Oh very nice,' said Winnie. 'And where yer been all week?'

He held on to the stall. 'Bin out with me mates. I have got mates, yer know.'

'I expect you have,' said Maggie. 'Win, can we borrow your chair? Now sit down here, Bill, and tell me why you've not been here.'

'Well, it's like this. I do miss Tony, yer know, Maggs?'

'Yes, Bill, we all do, but getting drunk's not gonner help him or me. I need you here, so where have you been?'

'Did I tell yer me auntie came ter see me mum?'

Maggie nodded. The state he was in there was no point in trying to hurry him.

'Well. Me auntie and me uncle Ron came ter see me mum and we all went to Romford – that's in Essex, yer know. Me uncle's got a car. I like me uncle, yer know. We had a smashing day, and when it was time ter go, me mum said she didn't want to go back home. Me auntie's always on to her to go and live with 'em.'

'What's he doing here?' said Tom, catching sight of Bill. 'You should be 'ere helping Maggie, not piss-arsing about. And what's he doing sitting down? He should be on his feet.'

'He's having a job to stand,' said Winnie. 'Been sniffing the barmaid's apron, if you ask me.'

'He's drunk?' asked Tom.

'Yer,' said Winnie.

'What's going on over here?' asked Fred. 'I see, so he's turned up then. Where's he bin?'

'That's what we're trying to find out,' said Winnie.

'Don't mind them,' said Maggie, beginning to get a little impatient. 'Where have you been all week, and why have you got drunk?'

Bill laughed. 'Stayed with me auntie for a few days, then I went up the West End wiv some of me mates. Met some lovely ladies.'

'Oh my Gawd,' said Winnie. 'I hope he ain't caught nothink.'

'I remember when I went up west and my—'

'OK, Fred,' said Winnie. 'We'll hear all about that another time. Carry on, son.'

Bill laughed. 'I've had a smashing time. Well, I had to find out what . . . well, you know, what it was like first, didn't I? D'yer know what some ladies—'

'They ain't ladies, son,' said Tom.

Bill had a huge grin on his face. 'Well, I fink they're ladies, and after that I went and joined the army.'

Everybody was stunned into silence.

'Ain't yer gonner congratulate me? There's gonner be another war, yer know, so I fought I'd get in first, and then I'll be a sergeant.'

'Bill,' said Maggie quietly, 'what does your mother have to say about this?'

'I ain't told her yet.'

'But after your father—'

'Yer, I reckon she'll be a bit upset.' He laughed again. 'If

I get a bit of shrapnel in me, she'll have a pair then to put on her mantelpiece, won't she?'

Maggie threw her arms round his shoulders. 'Bill. Oh Bill, you stupid young boy. Your mother is gonner be heartbroken when she knows.'

'Yer, but she's got Auntie Milly. 'Sides, she's better off up there. D'yer know, they've got a lav inside. 'Sides, it's better than round here with the fog.'

'I think you'd better come upstairs with me and have a lay down.'

'Yer, I do feel a bit tired.'

'Not surprised,' said Tom, grinning. 'He's probably worn himself out with all that unaccustomed exercise.'

'Keep an eye on me stall, Winnie, while I take him upstairs,' said Maggie.

Tom helped Maggie get Bill on his feet. 'Put your arm round me shoulder.' Bill was almost a head taller than her.

'Can you manage him?' asked Tom.

'Just as long as he puts one foot in front of the other.' Maggie thought they must have looked a funny pair, staggering along together.

'When you going in the army, son?' called Winnie after them.

'Monday,' came back the answer.

Maggie almost dropped him. 'Monday! But how am I gonner manage?'

Bill didn't answer, his eyes were closed and he still had a silly grin on his face.

'I bet you're dreaming about your lovely ladies,' she said to him.

He just nodded.

As they steadily mounted the stairs Maggie's worries crowded in. What if there was going to be another war? Would Tony come back to them then? And what about Bill's mother? She didn't need another casualty in her life.

Chapter 28

Jamie and Laura thought it very funny to see Bill sound asleep on the sofa. His loud snoring was sending them into fits of giggles.

'What's he doing here?' asked Eve when she arrived later that evening.

Maggie went through the whole story.

'So, how you gonner manage the stall on your own now he's going?'

'I don't know, especially as this should be our busiest time of the year.'

'Well, I'd throw him out, letting you down like this.'

'I wouldn't do that, Eve. He's not had it easy.'

'So what does he reckon the army will do for him then? That ain't no bed of roses.'

'He's young, so let's hope he makes a go of it.'

Eve's face softened. 'I enjoyed being down there today, so I'll give you a hand on Sat'days. How many till Christmas?'

'Thanks. Three. Christmas Day is on a Wednesday this year. I'll be glad of an extra pair of hands. I'll pay you.'

'I hope so, even if it's only a pair of earrings.'

'I think I'll be able to manage a bit more than that.' Maggie looked down at Bill. 'It's his mother I feel sorry for. I don't suppose he'll be here for Christmas.'

'I still reckon he's a silly sod. Fancy joining up.'

'What if he's right and there is another war?'

'Like Dan says, we'll worry about that if and when it happens. He said he can't see Baldwin leading us into another one.'

'God, I hope not.'

'Have you talked about Christmas with David yet?'

Maggie shook her head.

'Will you spend it with him?'

'Dunno. I'll have to see Bella sometime over the holiday.'

'How will you get stock and run the stall?'

'I must have known something as I've already bought a lot. It's only Benny I've got to see, but he always keeps a few good bits for me.'

'Is that it, all what's on the stall?'

'No, I've kept some back.'

'That's a bit daft.'

'Not really. If you don't let the punters see it all at once, they think there's only one or two left so they'll buy them, not knowing I've got another half-dozen up here.'

'You crafty cow. No, honestly though, I'm glad you're making a go of it. If Tony ever did come back you'd find it hard to take second place down there now, wouldn't you?'

'Yes I would. But perhaps I could have a bit of his stall and still sell jewellery.'

Eve smiled. 'One thing's for sure, he'd certainly see a different Maggie.'

'Have I changed that much?'

'Only for the better, and stronger. Now what's gonner happen with him?' Eve pointed to Bill, still sprawled out and snoring.

'He'll have to stay here for the night. Then perhaps David will take him home in the morning.'

When Maggie walked into the living room the following morning Bill was sitting holding his head.

She laughed. 'Believe me, I know exactly how you feel.'

'You do?' he croaked. 'Can't ever imagine you getting drunk.'

'I've had me moments. Fancy a cuppa?'

'Please. Me mouth feels like a bit o' sandpaper.'

Maggie handed him a cup of tea and sat beside him. 'Bill, do you remember why you got drunk?'

He slowly nodded. ''Cos I'd joined the army.'

'What made you do that?'

'Me uncle was telling me what a good time him and me dad had.'

'But your dad died because of the war.'

'I know. Me uncle was in the air force, but I still thought I'd go in the same regiment as me dad. I want to go, Maggs, I really do. I'm sorry if I've let you down.'

She patted his hand. 'Well, let's all hope there's not another war, and you'll soon be a sergeant.'

'I hope I ain't been a nuisance.'

'Course not. So, what you gonner do now?'

'Well, I've got to go home and get packed.' He laughed. 'That ain't gonner take long. Then I'll get a few of me mum's bits together and leave the rent next door, then Uncle Ron's coming over to sort everythink out.'

'Ain't you gonner say goodbye to your mum?'

He shook his head. 'I'm gonner write her a letter. Then when I've finished me training I'll be able to go and see her.'

'You've got this all worked out. She's gonner miss you though, and she'll be very upset.'

'I know, but I've been thinking about this for a long while, ever since those Blackshirts broke Mr Goldman's window. That really got to me and I felt I wanted to do somethink about it, but I didn't want to leave me mum on her own. But now I don't have to worry about her.'

Maggie kissed his cheek, causing him to blush. 'You're a smashing bloke, and I hope you come and see us in your uniform. Now, what about a bit of breakfast?'

'Thanks, Maggie, I'd like that. And Maggie, I only wish your story could have a happy ending.'

Maggie swallowed hard. 'So do I Bill. So do I.'

That afternoon, when David took her and the children to Downham, Maggie told Bella and Benny all about Bill.

'It made me look at him in a different light,' she said. 'I never knew he was such a warm sensitive lad.'

'I s'pose we all try to hide our lights under bushels, so the saying goes,' said Bella. 'But fancy him going and joining the army.'

'It's his poor mother I feel sorry for,' said Maggie.

'What d'you think, Dave, d'you reckon we'll have another war?' asked Benny.

'Wouldn't like to say. Things don't look good over in Europe, and now Mussolini's walked into Abyssinia that could spell trouble.'

'Now let's stop all this war talk,' said Bella. 'More to the point, how are you gonner manage without Bill?'

Maggie shrugged. 'I don't know.'

'Well, I reckon he could have waited till at least after Christmas.'

'So do I, but there you go, he didn't, so I'll just have to manage. Eve's gonner help out on Saturdays, so that's useful, and if I can afford someone else who I can trust, then I'll take them on.'

'That's the trouble – trying to find someone you can trust,' said Bella. 'What about stock?'

'Got most of me Christmas stuff in.'

Bella looked shocked. 'You 'ave? Where d'you get the money from?'

'Saved it,' lied Maggie, 'and if Benny could bring me over some of his little treasures, then everythink will be great.'

'Oh, that's all right then,' said Bella.

'Don't get a lot this time a year,' said Benny.

'I'd come and give you a hand, but I can't stand about, not in this cold, not now. Getting too old.'

'Bella, you'll never be too old. 'Sides, I wouldn't expect you to. And talking about Christmas, you coming over to me for the day?'

'Don't you think you'll have enough to do without feeding me? 'Sides, how would I get over there? Ain't no trains running Christmas day.'

Maggie gave David a glance. 'We'll talk about that nearer the time.'

'In fact me and Benny was discussing it just before you come in. He said he'd like to spend it with me, so p'raps you could all come over to me.'

'We'll see,' said Maggie. She didn't want to make plans that might not include David.

All the way home Maggie was deep in thought, wondering what would happen in the next three weeks. Would she hear from Tony?

'Penny for them,' said David.

'They ain't worth a penny.'

'You've been very quiet since we left Bella's.' He took a quick look over his shoulder at the two children nestling under the tartan blanket. 'I think they're asleep. Maggie, are you worried about another war starting?' he said in a very low voice.

'In some ways, but at the moment my biggest worry is getting the stall out and selling the stock. I don't know how I'm gonner manage on me own.' Worry was keeping her voice low.

He patted her hand. 'We could easily solve that one.'

'How?'

'You could come and live with me. Give up the stall. I could look after you.'

'David, don't start on that again. You know I would never do that.'

Giggling came from the back seat.

'I'd like to go and live at Uncle David's,' said Jamie.

'Please, Mummy please, let's go and live in his lovely house,' shouted Laura.

'Sorry,' said David, 'I thought they were asleep.'

'Oh go on, Mummy, please,' piped up Jamie. 'We could play in his garden and—'

'I said no. Now all shut up.'

The journey was finished in silence.

When they arrived at Maggie's door David asked, 'Do you still want me to come up?'

'Course. If you put the kettle on I'll get these two to bed.'

'Mummy, why can't we go and live in Uncle David's nice house?' whined Laura.

'Because I say so.'

'We could have a bedroom each and I wouldn't have to sleep in the same room as him.'

Jamie jumped up and down on his bed making the springs ping. 'Go on, Mummy, please. That'll be great. I could hang all me planes up and leave me toys all—'

'Jamie, shut up and stop that. We are not going so don't let me hear any more of it.'

'Well, I think you're mean,' said Laura.

'And we wouldn't have to go down to our rotten lavatory. I hate all those rotten spiders.'

'Jamie, get to bed.'

'Daddy always said he was gonner get us a nice house. Now we could have one you won't go.'

'Daddy said a lot of things but he's not here now.'

'I bet you told him to go away. It's your fault and I hate you.' Laura's face was red with anger.

Maggie stood dumbfounded. She loved her children so much and she knew they loved her, but how long had this been building up? She tried to cuddle Laura but she hid under the bedclothes. 'Come on now, Laura, you don't mean that.'

'Yes I do,' came the muffled reply. 'Go away.'

Jamie slid under his bedclothes. 'And I hate you as well, so don't kiss me good night.'

Tears ran down Maggie's face. Anger built up inside her

and she stormed out of their bedroom, slamming the door behind her.

David jumped to his feet and she entered the room. 'Maggie, is everything—'

Her face was like thunder. 'No it ain't.'

He went to hold her but she pushed him away.

'What's wrong?'

'You've just turned my kids against me.'

'I don't understand.'

'Get out!' she screamed.

'I beg your pardon.'

'I said get out. I don't ever want to see you again.'

'I'm sorry. What have I done?'

'You know I won't live with you. You know I won't leave this place. But no, you have to keep on. You and your fancy talk have turned my children against me.'

David gave a little nervous laugh. 'I'm sure they don't mean it.'

'You didn't see the hate in their eyes all because I won't walk away from everything Tony worked for. Now please leave.' She picked up his trilby and handed it to him.

'But, Maggie, I—'

'I don't want to hear. Now go.'

'Well, if you're sure.'

'Oh believe me, I'm sure.' She held open the door.

They hadn't noticed the living-room door being quietly opened. Jamie and Laura ran and held on to David's legs.

'Please, take us with you. We don't want to live here,' said Laura.

'We don't like going outside in the dark to the lav,' said Jamie.

David looked bewildered. 'I'm sorry,' was all he could think of to say.

'You two, get back to bed at once.' Although she was close to tears Maggie's voice was strong.

'You're rotten,' said Laura, turning away from her.

'Come on now, do as your mother tells you.'

'Will you come and take us to your house again?' asked Laura, releasing her grip on David's leg.

David looked at Maggie, who moved away from him.

'Not if Mummy doesn't want to. Now go on back to bed.'

'Will you come and tuck us in?' asked Jamie.

'I'd better not. I must go now.' He picked up his hat and left.

Laura and Jamie ran into their bedroom. Maggie could hear them crying. She too sat and cried. What had she done? Why didn't she want to go and live with David? She knew she was falling in love with him, and he could make them all happy. But she also knew she could never leave the flat in case Tony ever came back. Was this how she was going to spend the rest of her life, waiting?

When Maggie opened her swollen puffy eyes the following morning all that had happened yesterday filled her mind. How could her children hate her? Why did David have to say that in front of them? He knew they often pretended to be asleep if they thought they would hear something to their advantage.

It was quiet outside, the street sounds muffled. She got up and drew back the curtains. She couldn't see out for the thick fog. She sat back on the bed. 'Oh no,' she moaned aloud. 'This is all I need. Nobody will come out in this weather.' She wandered into the kitchen, still talking to herself: 'I must get the children up. I'll buy them a comic or some little treat, anything to show them I love them a lot.'

She pushed open the bedroom door and went to shake Laura. 'Come on, love, time to—' The bed was empty. She rushed over to Jamie's bed and threw back the clothes. His bed too, was empty.

Her screams were heard by Mr Goldman, who began banging on her front door with his fists. 'Maggie, what's happened? Open this door. Maggie!'

When the door was opened, Maggie stood there ashenfaced.

'My dear, whatever's happened?'

'It's Laura and Jamie . . .'

'Oh my God.' He tried to push past her, but she did not move. 'What happened to them?'

'They've gone, Mr Goldman. They've gone. They've run away.'

'Gone? What? What d'you mean, they've gone? Gone where? And who took them?'

'Nobody. They've just gone.' Suddenly the enormity of this hit Maggie and she began screaming again.

'Maggie, please, calm down.' He took hold of her shoulders. 'Please, Maggie, calm down. They can't have got far, not in this weather. Now go up and get your coat. You'll catch your death of cold standing here in your nightclothes. Have they taken anything with them?' Mr Goldman began coughing. 'This fog gets down your throat. They can't be that far away.' He took hold of Maggie's arm. 'Now do as I say.'

Maggie turned and dreamlike went upstairs. 'This is all

David Matthews's fault,' she yelled, suddenly coming out of her trance and rushing into the children's bedroom. They had taken their hats, coats, scarves and gloves, and their wellingtons.

She grabbed her coat and flew down the stairs.

'Where do you think they would have made for?' asked Mr Goldman.

'Greenwich.'

'What? That's miles away. Why would they go all the way to Greenwich?'

'That's where David Matthews lives, and they want to live in his house.'

'I see. Look, why don't you go into the Dog and wake the landlord. He'll help you.'

Maggie began crying. 'Why should all this happen to me? What have I done to deserve such misery?'

Mr Goldman had a job to put his arm round Maggie's heaving shoulders as he was shorter than her. 'There, there, my dear, they can't have got far.' He suddenly straightened up. 'Have you looked in the lavatory?'

She shook her head. 'They wouldn't go in there, not in the dark, they're too frightened. Besides, they've got a bucket under their bed.'

'Well, I think perhaps we'd better start there, just in case. Let's do that first.'

When they pulled open the rickety wooden door, from two deathly white faces two pairs of wide open eyes were staring at them. They were huddled together like babes in the wood. With their teeth chattering loudly they managed slight smiles. Maggie threw herself at them and held them tight.

331

Mr Goldman gently patted their heads. 'Now come, the pair of you. You've given your mother quite a nasty shock. I think we should all go back in the warm, don't you?'

Two heads nodded vigorously.

Maggie laughed and cried together. They were safe.

Chapter 29

Once upstairs Mr Goldman went into the kitchen to put the kettle on while Maggie lit the fire. She sat rubbing the children's cold hands and feet.

'Why on earth did you do a thing like that?' she asked.

Laura looked at Jamie. 'We didn't think you'd care if we ran away.'

Maggie held them close. 'You silly girl, of course I care. I love you both so very much.'

'We was going to see Uncle David, but it was too foggy, so we decided to stay in the lav. We couldn't get back indoors 'cos we'd shut the front door, but we knew you'd find us,' said Laura.

'It was ever so cold in there,' said Jamie, getting closer.

Maggie put her arm round them both. 'Now promise me you will never ever do anything like that again. I would die if I lost you two as well.'

'Do you want me to stay and make the tea?' asked Mr Goldman, coming back into the room.

'Only if you want to,' said Maggie.

'If it's all the same to you I'll get downstairs. I do have a lot of orders to finish before Christmas.'

Maggie stood up. 'Of course. Thank you for being here.'

He took her hand. 'That's what life is all about, my dear. Besides, there are times when you've been there to help me. Now go on back and give them plenty of love.'

'I will, and thank you.' Maggie kissed his cheek.

'Now you two, it's hot porridge and toast for you.'

'What about school? Will we be late?' asked Jamie.

'No, but after your little adventure I think it best that you stay home.'

'All right then,' said Laura. 'But only for today.'

Maggie was pleased they both liked school so much.

'Mummy, why won't you let us go and live with Uncle David?' asked Laura.

'You could marry him,' said Jamie. 'Then it would be like in our storybook and we could all live happy ever after.'

Maggie sat between them. 'Now I want you both to listen very carefully to what I've got to say. First of all I love you both very much, and the reason I won't go and live with David is because if your daddy came back and the flat was empty, he wouldn't know where to find us, would he?'

They both shook their heads.

Jamie looked puzzled. 'But we don't know where Daddy is, do we?'

'No, Jamie, we don't, but until I'm certain that he won't be back I shall live here for ever.'

Laura picked at her fingers. 'Mr Goldman would tell him if we moved away.'

'Yes, I know that, but I still want to wait and see.'

'Don't know why,' said Jamie. 'It'll be more fun with Uncle David.'

'D'you think Daddy will ever come back?' asked Laura.

'I don't know. Now how about that breakfast?'

As Maggie stood in the kitchen stirring the porridge she thought over what she'd told them. Did she really believe in her heart that Tony would return, or was she just looking for an excuse not to go and live with David?

The thick, yellow swirling fog persisted for two days. It was a real peasouper and clung to everything. Very few people ventured out and even the trains stopped running.

Maggie felt she was trapped inside her home. She looked at the shoe boxes filled with the jewellery. Ten pounds' worth. Panic filled her. If she couldn't sell it before Christmas, what would she do about the money she owed? She put the boxes away again. There were a few more selling days to go, so she could only hope the weather improved. She knew Benny would be over when he could and that she could pay him later. But that would mean more debt.

It was Thursday before the stall came out and Maggie was pleased that although she only took half a crown, it was just enough to pay the week's rent for the stall. After that, things just ticked over.

Saturday morning saw Eve muffled up to the eyebrows.

Winnie laughed at all the scarves she had wrapped round her neck.

'Well, I ain't standing here freezing me whatsits off.'

Tom Cooper gave Eve a wave. He liked her because she was always ready for a dirty joke and good laugh. 'You ain't got any whatsits,' he shouted over to her.

'No, I know. They got froze off last week. So, Maggs, how's things?'

'Not too bad.' Deep down Maggie was worried. Although

trade was steady there were only two more Saturdays after this one to Christmas. Would this lot be cleared by then?

'Seeing David tomorrow?' asked Eve.

'Don't think so.'

'He working?'

'Something like that.' He sometimes had to work on a Sunday so that didn't come as any surprise to Eve. But Maggie didn't know whether or not he would come round.

At the end of the day, when the stall was locked away and Eve had left, Maggie sat and counted out the takings. Thirty bob. By the time she had bought food, coal and paid the rent there would be nothing left to pay off the loan or Alan, and Christmas was getting closer. She chewed the end of her pencil. Had she been overzealous and bought too much stock? What if she couldn't sell it? Would Percy take it back? How would she pay Mr Shore, and if it went over three months what interest would she end up paying?

Maggie felt her stomach churn. So much for trying to be the big businesswoman. It was all going wrong.

All day Sunday, between her chores, Maggie kept looking out of the window hoping David would turn up, but by the evening she knew her hopes had been in vain. Had he gone for ever as well?

Monday was the start of another wet and windy week. Maggie could have cried with the cold that, despite the many layers of clothes, ate its way into her bones, and the lack of customers didn't help to lift her spirits. Those that did come up to her stall had their heads bent and gave her a quick cursory glance, all eager to get back home. Maggie felt her face was frozen into the smile she tried hard to maintain. She spent a lot of time jumping up and down in an effort to bring life back into her feet. She had never realised it could be so cold and soul-destroying just standing around waiting for people to spend a few pence.

Even Winnie, who always looked on the bright side, was getting downcast. By Wednesday Maggie wanted the comfort of David around and she tried to think of an excuse to go to the police station to see him.

Thankfully, on Saturday the weather improved a little. At least the rain had stopped, and Maggie felt more optimistic as she displayed her stock.

'I hate this time o' year,' said Winnie.

'Don't you like Christmas then?' asked Maggie.

'Na, not really. Me and Mum just sit and listen to the wireless. Where's Eve?'

'Dunno, she's late.' Maggie looked at the shops. The shopkeepers had begun to decorate their windows. 'You going to put up any bits to make the stall festive like?' she asked Winnie.

'Might put a bit of holly round the shoes,' she laughed. 'Got ter be careful none falls inside otherwise I could lose a customer.'

'I thought I'd drape a bit of greenery round and some sparkly paper, might help the sales.'

'Not doing so well then, girl?'

'Not bad, but we've got to get into the spirit.' All the while Maggie was keeping her eye out for Eve. But it was Dan who came up to her.

'Eve's got a filthy cold. I told her to stay in bed, but she was worried about you on your own so I said I'd come round and give you a hand.'

'Thanks, Dan. Poor Eve. Will she be all right?'

'Yer, I'll give her a good dose of whisky when I get back. Now d'you wanner go up and see to the kids?'

'If you don't mind. Win here will give you a hand if you get rushed off your feet.'

Winnie laughed. 'Chance would be a fine thing, love.'

Upstairs Maggie gave the children their dinner, banked up the fire and once again made her way down to the market.

'That bloke round the corner's selling the same sorta stuff as this, but a lot cheaper,' said a woman, picking up a bone bracelet.

'What?' yelled Maggie. 'There ain't any other stalls round there.'

'Na, he ain't got a stall, it's a suitcase.'

'Oh no,' cried Maggie. 'That's all I need. You stay here, Dan, while I go round and give him a piece of me mind.'

Maggie rushed round the corner in time to see the old man hurrying along the road carrying his suitcase.

'All right then, missis?' said the policeman who had been watching him.

'Why don't you arrest him?' yelled Maggie. She felt like jumping up and down with temper.

'We won't worry too much about the likes of them, only if they're causing an obstruction. We just tell 'em to move on.'

'But he's taking my trade.'

'Oh yes, you've got a stall round the corner.'

'Yes I have, so what you gonner do about it?'

'Nothing. Come on now, live and let live. After all, he was a soldier and was wounded, so he told me.'

'Didn't look very wounded to me.' She glared defiantly at him, hands on hips.

A few people had stopped to listen when they heard Maggie's raised voice.

'Now come on, missis.' The policeman took hold of her arm.

'Leave me be.' She tried to shrug him off but he was holding on to her very tightly.

'Yer, leave her alone,' shouted a man in the small crowd that was now gathering.

'What she done then?' asked another.

Maggie had tears of temper and frustration running down her face.

The policeman was getting embarrassed. 'Now come on, missis, move on otherwise I'll have to take you in.'

'Well, go on then, arrest me,' she said defiantly.

'She's got two kids at home. Leave her be,' yelled a woman. 'What's she done anyway?'

'I'm only trying to look after my rights.'

'Oh, she's one of them,' said a young man in the crowd.

'I have to pay rent. That bloke doesn't.'

'Maggie! Maggie! What the bloody hell's going on?' Winnie's voice could be heard above the din.

Maggie turned to see her waddling towards her.

'OK, officer, I'll take her.' She grabbed Maggie's arm. 'What the bloody hell d'yer think you're doing?'

'I wanted that copper to arrest that bloke that was selling without a licence.'

'Yer, and you very nearly got yourself arrested. Silly cow. Good job that Mrs Black came and told us, otherwise you might have been carted off.'

'Don't care if I was. It ain't fair,' said Maggie, slumping along like a spoilt child. 'I have to pay rent, he don't.'

Maggie turned and gave the policeman a filthy look and shouted, 'He should be locked up.'

'There's a lot of things not fair in this world, and you being locked up in prison ain't gonner feed your kids. Now get back to your stall,' said Winnie.

'What if he comes back again?'

'Who, the copper?'

'No, that bloke with the suitcase.'

'There's not a thing you can do about it.'

'We'll see about that.'

'Now you listen to me. Don't you dare do anythink daft like that again, d'you hear?'

Maggie nodded.

'Think of those kids.'

Maggie certainly gave the traders something to chew over for the rest of the day.

Dan found it very funny. 'That would have been a turn-up for the book, you in clink.'

'It ain't funny, Dan,' said Winnie. 'She was very stupid and I was worried.'

'Eve will be sorry she missed that. She would have given him a run for his money. I ain't half enjoyed meself today.'

Maggie smiled. Dan had been trying to be as helpful as Eve but he was clumsy. His large fat fingers broke the backs off two pairs of earrings when he rushed to serve a good-looking well-built young girl. They stood laughing and giggling like a couple of kids as he tried to put the earrings on her.

'Good job Eve ain't here,' said Winnie. 'She'd give him what for.'

'It's all good harmless fun,' said Maggie. But she wasn't

so pleased when he got a gold-coloured chain necklace so twisted in a girl's hair that Maggie had to break it and put it to one side.

The afternoon wore on. The lamps were lit, and the Salvation Army began playing carols, but as darkness fell so did Maggie's optimism, and she couldn't get into the festive mood. That man with the suitcase was bothering her. Would he be back next Saturday?

It was getting late and nobody was making any attempt to move away.

'Why ain't we packing up?' asked Dan, looking anxiously at his watch.

'Always try to hang on a bit later these last couple of Sat'days,' said Winnie. 'And you can't go till the others move off.'

Maggie looked at Dan. 'If you want to get back to Eve I understand.'

'I can't leave you.'

'Well, I can't move, not till they do. I thought being up this end was an asset, but it can also be a nuisance.'

When it got to nine o'clock Maggie was beginning to panic. 'I'll have to go up and see to the kids. They ain't had any tea yet. And I expect the fire's out as well.'

'Look, pack all your stuff up and we'll see about putting your stall away later on,' said Winnie.

'Thanks.'

'I best be off,' said Dan. 'You had a good day then?'

'Not too bad.'

'It's been bloody cold though, ain't it?'

Maggie nodded. 'Give me love to Eve. Hope she's better soon.'

'So do I. Bye.' He waved to them and made his way home.

'He's a nice bloke,' said Winnie. 'That Eve's lucky to finish up with someone reliable like him.'

'Yes, she is,' said Maggie, thinking about the small amount of money nestling in her stallholder's apron pocket.

She raced up the stairs to find the children huddled together on the sofa.

'We're ever so cold,' said Laura.

'And hungry,' added Jamie.

'I'm sorry.' She poked the fire, making flames dance. 'I'll get your tea right away.' She threw her money bag on the sideboard.

Later that evening she got out her notebook and counted out her money. It was disastrous, and with Christmas so near she wondered how she'd manage. What could she do to shift the stock?

On Sunday Maggie hoped that David would visit them, but once more she was disappointed. Was he as fond of her as he had said? She'd hoped he'd come back, for the children's sakes. Everything was beginning to make Maggie really miserable and she couldn't see any way out.

The following week, again the wind and rain dampened everybody's spirits, despite the cheerful holly and Christmas trees hanging round Fred's stall and fairy lights twinkling in the shop windows. Rows of chickens and turkeys were hanging outside the butcher's. Maggie looked in the toy shop. What could she buy Jamie and Laura for Christmas? Should she blow everything she earned on them, or should she try and pay back some of the money?

Overnight it became very cold, freezing the streets and pavements and making them very treacherous, so once again few people ventured out. Maggie's fortunes were looking bleaker by the day.

On Wednesday afternoon Maggie was very surprised to see Benny coming towards her.

''Allo, gel,' he said. 'Got a few bits for you.' His eyes had lost their sparkle and Maggie noted they were red and bloodshot, and he didn't have his work clothes on.

'Hallo, Benny. You look very smart. Don't often see you round this way in the week, or out in this weather. You should be at home in the warm with your feet up. Everything all right?'

He nodded.

''Allo, Benny,' said Winnie, coming over. ''Ere, where you off to all tarted up? You ain't gotter see a policeman, have you?' She laughed and turned to Maggie. 'That's the only time we see 'em dressed up is when they've got to appear in front of the beak.'

'No, I ain't gotter see a policeman. It's just that it's too cold to be out sitting on a cart. 'Sides—' He stopped to blow his nose.

Winnie's attention was drawn to her stall. 'Just coming, love.'

'I don't know how Bella managed to run her stall in this cold,' said Maggie, banging her hands together.

'You been ter see Bella lately?'

Alarm filled Maggie. 'No, not for a couple of weeks. Why?'

Benny shuffled his feet. He looked uncomfortable.

Maggie suddenly realised he looked very sad. 'Benny? What's happened?'

He swallowed hard. 'It's Nellie.'

'Nellie?' repeated Maggie. 'What, your horse?'

'Yer. Thought Bella might have told yer.'

'No. What's happened to Nellie?'

'Knacker's yard.'

Maggie felt upset. 'Knacker's yard. She ain't . . .?'

He nodded.

Maggie touched his arm. 'Benny, I'm really sorry. She was a lovely old thing. What happened?'

'She fell and broke her leg. So I had to have her put down.'

'That's awful. What you gonner do?'

'Dunno. She's had a good run, been part of me life fer years. Better than a wife – at least she never answered back.' He gave her a slight smile.

Maggie patted his hand. 'But she couldn't keep you warm in bed though, could she?'

'No, love, you're right there.'

'What are you gonner do?'

'Dunno. Ain't done nothink without Nellie.'

'Will you be over Bella's on Sunday?'

'Should think so. Don't know what to do now, though. Feel like a ship out o' water. Can't walk the streets on me own, can I?' He looked so sad.

'I'll try and get over this Sunday, but this weather hasn't been so good.'

'You selling well?'

'Mustn't grumble.' How could she tell him things weren't that good? 'I've got to see Bella to find out about what we're all doing for Christmas.'

'Will Dave bring you over?'

It was Maggie's turn to look uncomfortable. 'I don't know.'

'Everythink all right with you two?'

'Yes, of course.'

'Bella's a fine woman, you know.'

Maggie nodded. If only she was as strong in character as her.

When Benny left she felt really down.

'Poor old Benny,' said Winnie when Maggie told her. 'He's had the horse fer years.'

'I know.' Maggie began putting her stock into boxes. She couldn't help selfishly thinking how Benny's misfortune would affect her. When things did get better and she had some cash for more stock, Benny would no longer be able to supply her.

'Hello, Maggie.'

A familiar voice brought a smile and a blush to her face.

'David.' She quickly looked round.

'What the bloody hell does he want?' said Tom Cooper. 'Not more trouble.'

Winnie came over to Maggie and David. 'Ain't seen you round here for a while. I hope it ain't bad news.'

'No, not at all, just making sure everyone's all right.'

Winnie inclined her head towards Maggie. 'Have you told him you nearly got arrested on Sat'day?'

'No I ain't, and I didn't.'

'Arrested?' David was taken aback. 'What for?'

'I just had a few words with a policeman, that's all.'

Winnie laughed. 'Thought you might be here to run her in.'

David looked from one to the other. 'No, I was just passing, that's all. Are you sure everything's all right?'

Maggie knew everybody was taking an interest. 'It is now.' She would have loved to throw her arms round his neck and kiss him long and passionately.

He moved closer, and bent his head towards her. Maggie held her breath.

'I'm sorry I haven't been around but . . .' He looked up at the faces. 'Look, can we talk?'

'I've got to put my stall away, then we'll go upstairs.'

'Let me give you a hand.'

To Maggie suddenly it was Christmas. The fairy lights in the shop windows were burning brighter and even the trees and holly on Fred's stall seemed to be greener.

'First time I've seen a copper working,' said Tom Cooper when David began pushing the stall.

'Can see he ain't used to it,' said Winnie.

'Quick, get out his way otherwise yer might get run over. 'Ere, mate, is it an offensive to be run over by a market stall?' said Tom, jumping out of his way.

Everybody was in good humour and stood back laughing as David battled with the two wheels, trying to keep them straight over the cobbles.

Maggie laughed. She realised it had been a while since she had laughed, and it felt good.

When they reached her front door Maggie saw that David looked serious.

'Anythink wrong?' she asked.

'I wasn't sure what kind of welcome I'd get.'

She smiled. 'It's the good-will-towards-men time of year. Besides, I've got over my tantrums now.' She pushed open the door. 'I had a bit of trouble with another bloke selling, and I did have a problem with them two.' She nodded towards the stairs.

'Not through me, I hope.'

'Well, yes, it was in a way. You see they were coming to see you.'

'See me? When? How?'

'I'll tell you later.'

Chapter 30

'Uncle David,' yelled the children when Maggie pushed open the door and he walked in.

Then Laura looked guilty and slumped into the chair, trying to make herself as small as possible.

'It's all right,' said Maggie, guessing she felt a little apprehensive about seeing David again. 'I'll make the tea.' Maggie stood in the kitchen, happier than she'd been for days. He had come back to them. The loud chatter from the living room told her the children were over their fear of never seeing David again, and their laughter was a joy to hear.

David was told about how they only got as far as the lav in their attempt to run away. He in turn told them never to do that again, otherwise Father Christmas wouldn't visit them if he didn't know where they lived. They hung on to his every word.

Jamie giggled. 'It was ever so cold, and ever so dark and creepy in there.'

'I was worried about the spiders,' said Laura.

'You told me there wasn't none,' said Jamie.

'I only told you that so you wouldn't cry.'

'I didn't cry. Well, not very much.'

Maggie kissed the top of his head. 'Anyway, you won't be doing that again in a hurry.'

Maggie went on to tell David about Nellie. 'Poor old Benny, he was so upset.'

'He's had that horse for as long as I can remember,' said David. 'I like Benny, he's a real character. A bit bent at times, but not a real villain. I wonder how he's going to get about now? Can't see him buying another horse, not at his time of life.'

'I'm going over to see Bella on Sunday and she'll tell me all the news.'

'You must let me take you.'

Maggie looked at the two faces grinning at her. How could she refuse? 'OK.'

Soon it was time for the children to go to bed. Maggie would have liked to have sent them off as soon as she walked in – she wanted David to herself.

'Well, that's them down,' she said, closing the door. 'Mind you, I don't know about sleeping. They're very pleased to see you, you know.'

'What about you?'

She smiled. 'Me too.'

'I'm sorry about my big mouth. I shouldn't have kept on to you, but I hate to see you unhappy and worried.'

'I'm all right.'

'Are you? Now what's this about you almost being arrested?'

Maggie laughed and told him all that had happened. 'I was very angry. He was taking my customers away, and I can well do without that.'

'And I can well do without you being run in. Seriously, though, how are things?'

'Not bad, I suppose.' She wasn't going to tell him the truth. 'David, why are you here? And in the week as well.'

He lit a cigarette. 'I couldn't get to see you last Sunday as I had to go up north. The weather's really bad up there.'

Maggie sat up. Something in the way he was speaking told her that this wasn't strictly a social call. 'David, have you had any news?' She was dreading the answer.

He tapped the end of his cigarette into the ashtray.

She wanted to scream at him to get on with it, but she could sense it was something he wanted to say very carefully, and she suspected it was something she didn't want to hear.

The door opened and Laura asked, 'Mummy, will Benny be at Granny's on Sunday?'

Maggie jumped up. She wanted to push her out of the room. 'I expect so, why?'

'Now Benny ain't got Nellie, me and Jamie's gonner do him a drawing of a horse.'

She smiled. 'That's very nice of you. Now, back to bed. Remember it's school tomorrow.'

The door closed, and Maggie sat down again. 'David, is it about Tony?'

'It was.'

'Was!' she cried out. 'What d'you mean, was?'

'I had to go up north. Yorkshire to be exact. You see they had a bloke in custody, and they wanted him to be identified. It was in association with a murder and nobody knew anything about him, just that he came from London.'

'Murder?' Maggie felt her head swimming.

351

'It was a nasty business. He'd killed his wife.'

'His wife?' repeated Maggie.

'He said she was his wife. He was a cockney, and said his name was Bill Bailey. Well, they knew that was a joke to start with, and wondered if he had a wife and another life somewhere else. They went through the files of missing men, dark-haired, early thirties, looking for anything that showed he had other connections and one of the names they came up with was Tony's. As it was my case, I had to go.'

Maggie felt the colour drain from her face. 'And was . . .?'

'No. After all we have his photo on file, remember, so I could tell them it definitely wasn't Tony.'

'Did you see the man?'

'Yes, I spoke to him.'

'Did you know him?'

'No. Are you all right?'

She nodded. 'Will this nightmare ever go away?'

'Not till he walks back into your life, or they find . . .'

'David, why did you come over here to tell me all this, getting my hopes up and then—'

'I had to see you again. I was looking for an excuse.'

'Did you need one?'

'I wasn't sure.'

Maggie stood up and looked out of the window. She wanted to kiss him and tell him he was more than welcome in her home, but she couldn't speak. At this moment she didn't know what she wanted most, Tony dead, or alive.

'Well, am I?'

She nodded.

'Do you still want me to take you to Bella's on Sunday?'

'If you don't mind.'

'It'll be my pleasure.'

She smiled. 'I was hoping you'd say that.'

When David left it was with just a kiss on the cheek. Maggie knew that he too felt under strain.

As David drove home he knew that Tony would always come between them, and it would take time to get back on the understanding they had before he'd put his foot in it. How he wished it had been Tony up there; then he would have been out of Maggie's life for good.

It was the last Saturday before Christmas. Eve was better and was as usual enjoying herself, laughing and joking with everyone but Maggie was on edge. Was that bloke round the corner? She wanted to go and see, but she was aware that everybody thought she'd been making a big thing about it, though they didn't know the financial trouble she was in.

Maggie wasn't that surprised to see Alan. She was pleased he was alone, and as usual she felt guilty about his money.

'Helen OK?' she asked.

'Yes, very busy getting ready for Christmas. We're having a few friends over on Boxing Day. Any chance of you getting over, Maggs?'

'I don't think so.'

'Got plenty of mistletoe?' asked Eve.

'I think Helen's getting it today, so I mustn't hang about. Got to give her a hand, you know.'

'Alan,' Maggie moved away from Eve, 'I ain't got any more money to give you just yet, what with Christmas and everything.' She kept her voice very low.

'I didn't come over for that. So how's things? You managing without Bill, then? Selling plenty?'

'Not too bad.' Maggie had written and told him about Bill going in the army.

'There's a little gift for you and the children.' He handed her a paper carrier bag.

'Thanks. Yours is upstairs. I'll just pop up and get it. I won't invite you up as I don't like leaving Eve on her own for too long.'

'I understand, I'll wait here for you.'

Maggie hurried away. She hated this bland conversation. Tony and the money he'd borrowed had caused this rift between them.

Alan left and the afternoon dragged on. Maggie was worried. It wasn't the sort of day she'd been hoping for. Twice she managed to go round the corner to see if the man with the suitcase was taking her trade, but she never saw him. She knew the takings would be down, and that night when she counted out the money fear gripped her. Only two more trading days to Christmas.

Maggie sat back and looked at the pile of silver and coppers. What should she do – send Alan another pound or pay back some to Mr Shore? 'No, bugger it,' she said out loud. 'After I've put the rents and coal money away I'll spend it. We're gonner have a good Christmas. Monday I'll get a tree, get the fairy lights and the decorations out, then I'll go to the toy shop. I'll even get me and Laura a new frock. Everybody will have a great Christmas. After all I don't owe any to Mr Windsor, and the rest will have to wait.'

On Sunday Maggie was very quiet as David drove her to

Bella's. She wanted Bella to come to them, but knew it would be a big chore, and at the moment half of her didn't want Christmas at all.

'So are you coming to me?' asked Maggie, trying hard not to make the invitation sound too half-hearted.

'No, love. Me and Benny 'ere reckon you should come over here. It'll give you a break. 'Sides, when have you got time to do the shopping?'

'I can always pop to the shops, they ain't that far away. But how would I get over? We'd have to come late on Christmas Eve.'

'We can't do that!' yelled Laura frantically. 'Father Christmas might not find us.'

Maggie smiled. 'I'm sure he will, he's very clever.'

David gave a slight cough. 'Look, I'm not doing anything that morning so I could bring you over.'

Bella laughed. 'Where you spending the day, then?'

'I shall be on—'

'Look, if you're not on duty why don't you spend it with us?' she interrupted.

Maggie couldn't believe it. This was all that she had wanted to happen.

'I'd like that. I am normally on duty over Christmas, as I don't have anyone to share it with, but I can always make other arrangements.'

'Right, that's settled then,' said Bella. 'I'll expect to see you about one. That'll give me a chance to get it all ready.'

'What are you doing, Benny?' asked Maggie.

'Well, as he ain't got Nellie to worry about he's coming over here the night before,' said Bella. 'And don't look like that. We're going up the pub, and he's staying in the spare room.'

Maggie felt like laughing out loud. 'Well, let's hope you don't get too drunk to do the dinner.'

'I'm so glad I'm going to see you over Christmas,' said Maggie, after they arrived home and the children were in bed.

'I'm pleased as well.' He walked to the door. 'I won't stay, got a lot of paperwork. I'll see you on Christmas morning.'

He was keeping his distance, thought Maggie as she closed the door behind him. She was in a turmoil. Although she'd kept him at arm's length that's not what she really wanted. Had he changed his mind about her living with him?

Maggie's thoughts turned to Christmas Eve. She should have asked him to come over as Eve and Dan were taking her to the pub. But what if she had a few too many drinks? She knew she would throw caution to the wind and beg him to stay. But what if Tony came back?

David's thoughts were also on Christmas Eve. If only things were different. If only Maggie would let go. But he knew she never would.

It was late on Christmas Eve when the stall was finally put away. All afternoon, despite the carols coming loud and joyful from the Salvation Army and the drunks singing bawdy songs, Maggie felt cold, tired and irritable. She had so much to do she wasn't sure she really wanted to go out tonight.

Everybody else had been full of the Christmas spirit. All

day people had been waiting at Fred's stall and he had been working flat out. Mrs Russell had sold almost all her flowers, but Winnie, Tom and Maggie had had very few customers.

'Food's what's on their minds today,' said Winnie, banging her hands round herself to keep her circulation going.

When the punters finally began to drift away Fred took Winnie's arm and Tom grabbed hold of Mrs Russell and they danced and sang as bottles were passed round. Fred said it was to keep out the cold. Maggie tried to join in, but her heart wasn't in it. She still had most of the stock left even though she had been selling it off cheap. There was no way she could pay Alan, or any of the loan. The little money she had left after paying the rent and coal went on presents. 'Sod it,' she said to herself as she climbed the stairs. 'I'll let 1936 look after itself.'

The lights on the tree sparkled and two eager little faces looked at her when she walked in, making her forget her own misery.

'After tea it's a bath.' The thought of dragging the tin bath up the stairs and filling it made Maggie feel more dismayed. Her thoughts went to David's bathroom. If she moved in with him she wouldn't have to do this.

'I've left me list on the table,' said Jamie, squeezing the flannel over Laura and making her squeal. 'Should we leave something for Father Christmas to eat?'

Maggie smiled. She had to be cheerful for their sakes. After all, Christmas was for children. 'I think we could leave him a biscuit and a drink.'

'What about his reindeer?' asked Laura with a worried expression.

'I hope he's going to leave them outside. Now come on, jump out.'

She rubbed them dry. Their faces were glowing with delight. Maggie held them close. They smelt so clean and fresh and she loved them dearly. 'Now bedtime.'

For once there were no arguments. Maggie finished emptying the tin bath and struggled down into the yard with it.

As she draped the damp towels around the fire guard she reflected on past Christmas Eves. They had been so different. Bathed and fed, the children were in bed and out of the way by the time Tony came home, usually a little worse for drink. They would then go to the Dog and by closing time Tony could just about walk home. Then, after playing Father Christmas, they would make love. Remembering, Maggie let a tear run down her cheek. She desperately wanted to be loved. To have someone to hold her, caress her, and to make her feel a whole woman again. She so desperately wanted to be looked after. Please, Tony, she begged silently, after all this time, let me know what's happened – let me get on with my life.

The scene at the Dog and Duck was a familiar one for Christmas Eve. Gus was wearing his red Father Christmas hat and Beatie had tinsel draped all over her, and everyone was happy and singing. It seemed to Maggie that she was the only one who was miserable and felt out of place, though she did her best not to show it.

After a few drinks she too relaxed and was soon up dancing with the rest of them.

'Want us to come up with you?' asked Eve, when they reached Maggie's front door.

'No thanks. I'm going straight to bed after I've done me Father Christmas bit.'

'Maggie.' Eve held her tight. 'We all know how hard it is for you and what you're going through, more so this time of year. I only wish there was something I could do.'

'So do I, Eve.' She choked back a tear. 'And thanks for all your help.'

'That's what mates are for,' said Dan, hugging Maggie in turn.

'We'll see you on Boxing night, that's if you fancy coming out for a drink.'

'Thanks. I'll see.'

'Then we've got New Year's Eve. Christ, we've had some great New Year's Eves in the past, ain't we, girl?'

'Trust you to open your big mouth,' said Eve, giving Dan a push.

'Why? What did I say?'

'Good night, Maggs,' said Eve, pulling Dan's arm. 'You've got as much tact as my arse,' she said, dragging him down the road.

Maggie laughed as she watched them go. She could hear Eve going on at Dan till they turned the corner. If Dan was in a loving mood he'd better play his cards right before he got home.

Before she closed the door Maggie looked up at the sky. It was black and full of stars. The air was cold and crisp – definitely a night made for love.

She sighed. 'Well come on, Mother Christmas, let's get this job over.' She stopped at the bottom of the stairs, thinking. Dan was right, they had had some good New Year's Eves, but that was all passed. Let's hope they could go into the next one with a bit more hope.

She tingled with the thought of what that could bring.

Maggie. Get hold of it tight. We all know how hard it is
for you and what you're going through, more so this time of
year. I only wish there was something I could do to help.'

'Start it, Dot. She choked back a sob. 'And thanks for all
your help.'

'That's what mums are for,' said Dot, hugging Maggie as
hard.

'We'll see you on Boxing night, that's if you fancy
coming out for a drink.'

'Thanks, I'll see.'

'There we go for New Year's Eve. Cheer up, we've had some
good New Years, even in the past and I say, girl.'

'That you keep in your big mouth,' said Maggie, giving Dot
a push.

'Why? What did I say?'

'Good night, Maggie,' said Dot, rubbing Dot's arm.
'You've got as much sad in you,' she said she said, trudging
him down the road.

Maggie laughed as she watched them go. She could hear
Eve going on at Dot till they turned the corner. If Dan was
in a loving mood he'd better play his cards right before he
got home.

Before she closed the door Maggie looked up at the sky.
It was black and full of stars. The air was cold and that
definitely a night made for lovers.

She sighed. 'Well come on Maggie, Christmas, let's get
this job over.' She whipped at the bottom of the stairs,
pausing. But was right, they had had some good New
Years. Perhaps next year it passed, 'Let's hope they could
go into the next one with a bit more hope.

She sighed with the thought of what that could bring.

366

Chapter 31

'Thank you, Bella, that was delicious,' said David, pushing his chair back from the table. 'I don't ever remember having a Christmas dinner like that before.' He stopped. He looked sad. 'Well, not for many years anyway. And that pudding.'

'Thank you, son. Made it meself, always have done.'

Maggie wanted to hold him close. She would know how to look after him.

'And me and Jamie found a thru'penny bit in it as well,' said Laura.

Bella gave Maggie a wink; that had been arranged. Bella's face was glowing with drink as well as praise. She was wearing her bright green crêpe paper hat that came from a cracker, at a jaunty angle. She was still grinning at David. 'So, how about you doing the washing up then? Better than singing for yer supper.'

They all laughed.

'See, you don't catch me saying too much,' said Benny, pushing the red paper hat he was wearing back from his eyes.

'And you can give him an 'and,' said Bella.

'No, I'll do it.' Maggie began clearing the table.

'Me and Benny will just have a quiet sit-down with the kids,' said Bella, following the children who had rushed off into the front room to play with their new toys.

'It won't be very quiet in there,' said Maggie, filling the washing-up bowl with hot water and throwing in a handful of soda from the stone jar on the windowsill. 'I'm so glad you could stay. Tea towel's in that drawer.'

'So am I, it's been really great.'

Maggie was conscious of him standing close to her. She could feel his warmth. If only she could let her real feelings take over. She turned and her paper hat fell to the floor. They both bent together to retrieve it. Their eyes and hands met. Maggie thought she would die of anticipation.

'Mummy, Mummy,' said Laura, rushing into the kitchen, giggling. 'Granny and Benny's fast asleep and they ain't half snoring.'

'Well don't wake them.' She turned to the sink and carried on with the washing-up.

It was in the evening after the tea things had been put away and they were all sitting round the fire having a quiet drink that Bella suddenly announced, 'By the way, Maggs, I've got to tell yer, me and Benny's getting married at Easter.'

Maggie almost dropped her glass. Her mouth fell open but no sound came out. Suddenly tears were rolling down her cheeks.

'What you crying for, love?' said Benny, taking her hand. 'Don't you like me?'

'Oh Benny, I love you, and I'm so pleased for the pair of you.' She threw her arms round his neck, then jumped up to hug Bella.

'Congratulations,' said David.

Maggie was drying her eyes.

'What you crying for, Mummy?' said Laura.

'It's just that I like to see people happy.'

'Well, I think you're soppy,' said Jamie.

'Can I be your bridesmaid?' asked Laura.

'It won't be that kind of wedding,' said Bella.

Laura returned to the puzzle she was doing. 'I would have liked to be a bridesmaid.'

'Why are you waiting till Easter?' asked Maggie.

'The weather's a bit better then, that's all, and it'll give Benny time to clear out all his rubbish from over that stable.'

'It ain't all rubbish.'

'Well, you ain't bringing it here.'

Maggie smiled. Theirs was certainly going to be a very interesting marriage.

'If you want a hand, remember I've always got the car,' said David.

'That's real kind of you, son,' said Benny. 'I might well want a hand.'

'When did all these plans start?' asked Maggie.

'A couple of days ago. He's like a fish out o' water without that bloody horse, and he was round here most of the time, so I said we might just as well be married and stop the neighbours talking. That way I'll get a few bob out o' him as well for his bed and board.'

Benny laughed. 'Don't you believe her. She's got a very soft spot for me.'

'Yer,' said Bella. 'The only soft spot I've got's in me bleeding head.'

The laughter and toasts to Benny and Bella followed, but Maggie felt ill at ease. Nobody had mentioned Tony. It was just as though he didn't exist any more.

It was when they were leaving that Bella took Maggie to one side.

'I know who you're thinking about and I only wish he was here, love,' she said tenderly. 'And I wish you was happy as well. I can see it in your eyes you're not, and there ain't a thing I can do about it.'

Maggie held her close. 'I'm all right. Just as long as you're happy and certain you're doing the right thing.'

'I am, Maggs. Been fond of the old goat for years, but don't tell him that. It was that horse that stood in the way.'

Maggie kissed her. 'Thanks for a lovely Christmas.'

'You take care. Me and Benny will be over to make sure you're all right.'

As David drove them home Maggie sat back and reflected on the day. In her eyes it had been almost perfect.

'Would you like a cup of tea?' she asked, after David had carried a tired little Jamie up to bed.

'Yes, please. He's heavy when he's asleep.'

'It's been a long exciting day for them.'

'And as for Benny and Bella . . .' he said, settling himself on the sofa.

'Yes, that was a surprise. I wonder what Tony will make of it – a new dad.' Maggie hurried to the kitchen when the kettle boiled.

David was right behind her. 'Maggie, I'm not going to pull my punches. I love you and I want you to come and live with me.' She went to speak but he held up his hand to stop her. 'I'm not going to say any more. I don't think you'll ever be free from Tony, and a home waits for you if ever you want it. I want to make love to you now, right this minute, but I won't. Now I'll have my tea and go.' He went back into the living room.

Maggie's eyes were wide open. What could she say? Was this going to be the end of their friendship?

'David,' she said, following him with the tray of tea things. 'What if I was free?'

'That would put a different light on things, wouldn't it? But you're not.'

His attitude frightened her. It was almost an ultimatum.

'Give me time.'

'Of course.'

'You will still come and see us, won't you?'

He smiled. 'Of course.'

She wanted to throw her arms round him and take him to her bedroom. But this wasn't the way she'd been brought up. If I was Eve things would have certainly been different by now, she thought to herself.

That evening the pub was quiet till Maggie told everyone about Bella and Benny. They all decided it was the best thing that could have happened to them, and despite the absence of the newly engaged pair an impromptu party was held in their honour.

Maggie didn't take the stall out on Friday, the day after Boxing Day, and she shouldn't have bothered on Saturday as business was bad and she certainly didn't need the steady drizzle to dampen her spirits. The only light relief all day was telling everyone about Bella and Benny. Winnie decided to have a collection and get them a present.

'They'll be tickled pink,' said Maggie as she was handed the bag of money.

'What yer gonner get 'em, love?' asked Winnie.

'Don't know. I'll have a think about it. I'll let you know before I get it, though.'

The stalls were put away early and Maggie knew her takings were a disaster again. She counted out the money Winnie had given her. Two pounds. That would pay her rents and the coalman for the next two weeks. She put the money in the drawer, feeling both tempted and guilty. Would the traders find out if she kept it?

That night she tossed and turned. She lay in bed thinking about the money for the present. What had she got herself into? Why did she think she was cleverer than Tony? Was she just like him? He hadn't stolen, but he had run away from his responsibilities. To her, her children's welfare was the most important thing in her life, and if it meant stealing to keep them warm and fed she was prepared to do that. Besides, she thought, turning over, I don't think the traders would really mind if they knew the reason.

She desperately needed the money. She looked round the flat. That mirror would have to go. Monday, she'd go to the pawn shop.

After a fitful night Maggie woke to the sound of rain beating on the window. Thank goodness it was Sunday. She turned over and went back to sleep.

David sat in his dining room watching the rain drip from the bare trees. Everything in the garden looked dejected and lifeless. This is how he felt without Maggie. He wanted to go and see her but what excuse did he have? How could he make her see she was wasting her life? But what if Tony Ross came back? Would she still want Tony? David felt guilty at almost brushing him aside, but what else could he do? 'If I'd stayed I would have made love to you, and that could have been the end of our friendship. I love you, Maggie Ross,' he said to himself, 'and those lovely kids, and I know we could be happy.' Bella had made up her mind to get on with her life, but Maggie hadn't the same freedom. Where the hell was Tony Ross?

David decided to go to work. He couldn't stay here feeling sorry for himself. At the station there was always something to do, and someone to talk to.

'Anything interesting happened over the holiday?' he asked the young officer at the desk, when he arrived.

'No, sir. Not on our patch, only the usual drunks. There's been a big fire over the Elephant. A warehouse went up, suspected arson. Seems an old boy got killed.'

David stood still, then slowly walked back to the desk. 'Do you happen to know the victim's name?'

'A Mr Collins, Mr Percy Collins. Does it ring any bells, sir?'

'No, not for me, but I know someone it will affect.' He turned and left the station.

'David,' said Maggie. 'I didn't expect to see you here today.'

'I've just come from the station. Children, would you mind going to your bedroom? I've got to talk to Mummy.'

Maggie fell back on to the sofa. 'Oh no.'

Laura and Jamie for once did as they were told without any questions.

'No, Maggie, listen. It's not Tony, it's Percy.'

367

'Percy. What, the Percy I buy from?'

'Yes.'

'What's happened to him?'

'I'm afraid he's dead.'

Maggie felt the colour drain from her face. 'Oh no! He was such a nice old man. How did it happen?'

'His warehouse burnt down and he was trapped inside. They think it might have been deliberate.'

'Who would do a thing like that?'

'I don't know. I haven't been over there yet, but I will.'

'Poor Mabel, is she all right?'

'There wasn't any other name mentioned.'

Maggie suddenly put her hand to her mouth. 'Lil. Lil, she said they would have a tragedy, and she said I . . .' Maggie's tears fell. 'She told me I would have a lot more grief in my life,' she cried, burying her head in David's shoulder.

He put his arm round her and gently held her close. He wanted to kiss away her distress. Her sobs hurt him.

When she pulled back he handed her his large white handkerchief.

She blew her nose. 'Thank you. I'll wash it.'

'Don't worry about it.'

'Can you find out more about how it happened for me?'

'Yes, I'll go over tomorrow and ask around.'

'I'd like to go to Percy's funeral.'

'I could always take you.'

'Thank you. David, what more grief could I have?'

'I don't know, and I don't think you should take too much notice of what an old woman told you.'

She gave him a weak smile. 'Well, time will tell.'

'What will you do about stock?'

'I don't know. At the moment I've got more than enough to keep me going, it's the selling that's the problem.'

'Are you having money problems?'

'No, course not. Would you like a cup of tea?'

'Thought you'd never ask.'

When Maggie opened the door Laura and Jamie came in.

'What have you been up to?' asked David.

'Been doing drawing,' said Laura, looking round.

'What did you want Mummy for?' asked Jamie.

'I had to tell her something.'

'Why does my mummy always cry when you come here?' asked Laura.

'She doesn't always cry.'

'A lot of times she does,' said Jamie.

Laura sat next to him. 'D'you know, I think she loves you and don't want our daddy to come back.'

Jamie wriggled in beside David. 'And we think she wants to live at your house.'

David smiled. 'Whatever your mummy decides is OK by me.'

"I don't know. At the moment I've got more than enough to keep me going. It's the selling that's the problem."

"Are you having money problems?"

"No, of course not. Would you like a cup of tea?"

"Thought you'd never ask."

When Maggie opened the door Laura arose and came in.

"What have you been up to?" asked David.

"Been doing drawings," said Laura, looking round.

"What did you want Mummy for?" asked Laura.

"I had to tell her something."

"Why does my mummy always cry when you come here?" asked Laura.

"She doesn't always cry."

"A lot of times she does," said Laura.

Laura sat next to him. "D'you know, I think she loves you and don't want our daddy to come back."

Frank weighed in beside David. "And we don't like she wants to live at your house."

David smiled. "Whatever your mummy decides is OK by me."

Chapter 32

The alarm broke into Maggie's troubled sleep early on Saturday morning. She buried her head in the pillow and groaned. She didn't have to get out of bed to know it was another dark dismal day with the rain beating down like stair rods. Nobody would venture out today unless they were mad or really had to, and then it would only be a quick shop for their essentials. It was to be yet another awful barren day. Nobody would come out in this weather to buy a pair of lousy earrings.

She turned over and gazed at the ceiling. Worry was making her feel ill. In the two weeks since the New Year she had only managed to take the stall out once. Already 1936 had started terribly and seemed to be going from bad to worse. Since Christmas Maggie hadn't even taken enough to pay the rent on the stall or the flat. Coal and food were her first priority.

She cast her eyes round the bedroom. She had taken so many of her trinkets to the pawn shop, careful not to remove anything that would be noticed by Bella or Eve. She had told them she'd got a good buyer for her large mirror, and they accepted that. She looked at her hand. There was

371

always her engagement ring. But that would feel as if she had severed her finger. She studied the five-diamond ring. If it came to it, that too would have to go.

She worried about the mounting interest on the money she owed Mr Shore. Maggie wanted to cry, she felt so guilty about keeping the traders' money for Bella's present, but what could she do? The children had to be kept warm and fed. She wanted to tell someone about the mess she'd got herself into, but who?

She gave another moan and turned over. The fact that Percy's Emporium had burnt down and she wouldn't be able to buy more stock when she finally managed to shift the large amount she already had was another problem she could foresee. She got cross with herself. That was selfish and wicked. Percy was dead. Poor Mabel had to start a new life, knowing Percy's death was brought about by himself, getting drunk and knocking the paraffin stove over. 'Well at least Mabel *knows* he's dead,' she said out loud. Was Lil right? Was this the grief she had told Maggie to expect?

In some ways she could understand Tony running away. This was how he must have felt when everything was closing in on him.

To think she was so happy up until a few weeks before Christmas. She had been selling well, and even managed to pay Alan back a few more pounds. Only one to go, then she took out the big loan. How long would that take to pay back at this rate?

Maggie dragged herself from her bed, made a pot of tea and took it into the living room. She sat at the table absentmindedly stirring the leaves round and round in the pot, and as always when she was alone, thoughts of David filled her mind.

She was really very fond of him, and knew she could love him if she could let go of her hopes about Tony. But was it hope now or just the final confirmation that Tony was dead that was stopping her from loving David? She knew that at the back of her mind she still lived in the hope that Tony had lost his memory and would return one day. All those years of happiness just couldn't be swept away.

Maggie toyed with the spoon. David wanted to offer her so much. He had a lovely house and the children adored him, and he had a steady job, and could give her the security she longed for. And, as Eve would say, on top of all that he was good-looking. She sighed. How could she just go and live with him? What if Tony did come back? But somehow she knew he wouldn't, not now.

A letter plopped on the front doormat. She went down to retrieve it, feeling sorry for the postman trudging about in this rain.

The envelope felt damp and the ink on the postmark was smudged. She didn't recognise the handwriting and as she climbed the stairs, began to open it.

When she reached the top she pulled out the letter. It was just one page. A photograph and another envelope fell to the floor. Picking them up she glanced at the envelope. It bore Tony's handwriting and was addressed to Mrs M. Ross. Her heart began beating fast and tears filled her eyes. She looked at the photo. Tony was laughing and had his arm round a woman a lot younger than he. Tears of joy streamed down Maggie's face. She was laughing and crying at the same time. She felt dizzy and sick with excitement. He was alive. At long last he'd written to her. But who was this woman? She staggered into the living room and sat at the table. Her hands were trembling as she read the single sheet of paper.

The address was Cardiff, Wales, and dated 8 January 1936. What was he doing in Cardiff? They didn't even know anybody in Wales.

Dear Mrs Ross,

I'm afraid I don't know your Christian name as Peter never told us about you or any of your family. I assume you must be a relation of some sorts. I found this letter in his drawer and it had a note attached asking this to be posted in the event of anything happening to him.

Well, I'm sorry to say our dear Peter had a terrible accident. It was just before Christmas. The sea was running very high. Everybody said he was silly to take the boat out, but then if you knew Peter you would know what a headstrong devil he was.

His body was washed up two days later. My daughter is still devastated. You see, they were hoping to be married at Easter.

Maggie gave a little cry. 'Oh no.' She read and read that paragraph, trying to make the words sink in. He was going to get married. Putting the letter on the table she picked up the photograph. On the back was written 'Peter and Thelma, November 1935.' Through her tears Maggie looked at Tony with his arm round this pretty young woman. They were laughing and looked so happy. This was taken in November, the month of Laura's birthday. Maggie sat as if in a trance. She couldn't believe what she had just read. Her tears continued to fall.

'You did lose your memory. I was right all along, and now you're dead. My darling, my darling,' she whispered. 'And we never said goodbye. You were going to marry this girl at Easter not knowing you still had us.'

Suddenly it hit Maggie that he'd written her a letter. Even as she wanted to shout and scream, throw herself into the street, to cry and cry, it somehow struck her as bizarre that he might have been married at the same time as his mother. Maggie knew she had to control herself and try to remain quiet for the sake of the children, who thankfully were still in bed.

'How could you do this to us? Why did you leave us? Now you're dead. Or somebody calling himself Peter is dead,' she said softly, gently running her fingers over his smiling face. Although stunned, she knew she had to finish the letter before reading Tony's explanation.

If you know of any member of his family, perhaps you would be kind enough to pass on this sad news. I couldn't let you know about his funeral before as we hadn't been through his things till after he was buried, it was then we found this letter. Incidentally he is in our local cemetery and we are having a monument put on his grave. It the short time we have known Peter, we all loved him very much.

I thought you might like this photo of Peter and my daughter. They were so happy.

If you are ever down this way, please come and have a chat and a cup of tea.

Yours very sincerely,
Mrs Eileen Walker.

They didn't know he had a wife and family, so what did they think was his surname?

As much as she wanted to read Tony's letter, Maggie couldn't bring herself to open it. It had her name and address on the envelope, in his hand. She turned it over and over. If only David or Eve, or even Winnie was here, they could read it to her. But she wasn't sure she wanted everybody to know.

Slowly Maggie began to prise the envelope open. She was afraid of its contents.

The first few pages were written in pencil, and very scrawly and all over the place, which was unusual for Tony as he took great pride in his handwriting. There was no address, but the date was Friday, 17 May 1935. Maggie gasped and put her hand to her mouth. That date was etched in her mind, the day he disappeared.

My darling Maggie,

I must write all this down while it's still fresh in my mind. You see at this moment I fear for my life.

I expect by now you are wondering where I've gone. Well, it is a very long story, and I hope that in the end you understand and forgive me.

Forgive my handwriting as I am sitting on a train writing this. Fortunately I managed to win a few bob on the horses to pay my fare. This train is going to Cardiff, always fancied spending a holiday in Wales.

My darling, I haven't always been straight with you. But I have always loved you, and since we got married I've never fooled around with anybody else, you've got to believe that. You and the kids mean everything to me, and I hope that by the time the new baby's here all my problems will be just a bad dream and you'll never read this letter, well not till years later when in our old age we sit and have a good laugh over it.

Today I had the misfortune to bump into a bloke who'd just come out of prison. As you know I've always liked a little bet and unfortunately I owed Mr Windsor a few bob.

Maggie was in shock. He had known all about them and he hadn't cared.

Well, to cut a long story short, Mr Windsor is a real villain and he threatened to, would you believe it, kill me. It was then that I decided to make a run for it and got on the first train that come along.

I know he won't hurt you or the kids, that's not his style, besides, he don't know where I live.

As soon as I've made enough money to pay him off I'll be back, large as life and twice as handsome. Just remember I love you and the kids very much.

All my love, Tony. xxxx

'Don't you believe it,' sobbed Maggie. 'How could you, Tony? It was through him I lost our baby.'

There was another page that was written in ink. It didn't have a date on it.

My dear Maggie,

I have decided to write to you because by now you should have our new baby. One day I will post this and then you'll understand why I did what I did. You are always in my thoughts, and when I'm on my knees in church I pray you are all well and I only wish I was with you.

I still haven't made quite enough to pay back Mr Windsor, so it's best I stay low.

It might sound a bit morbid but I'm leaving a note to ask Eileen, that's my very kind landlady, to post this if anything happens to me. The reason being that I've changed my name and bought a small fishing boat, and the sea can be a very lively lady. You know me. I had to do something on my own, couldn't work for a boss. Imagine me fishing. It's a great life, and young Jamie would love it, away from all that smoke and fog.

I expect you're managing all right, they're a good bunch on the market, and Mum will always see you all right, she's got a few bob stashed away.

I hope in the near future we shall all be together again. If not in this world, then it will be in the next. I love you.

Tony. xxxx

Maggie was stunned. So many thoughts were milling about in her head: what will Bella say when she reads it? How dare he just walk away and leave all his responsibilities, and how dare he write this letter when he was with that girl? Would he have ever come back to us? 'Why, Tony, why?' she cried out, first in anger, then in self-pity. She picked up the photograph. 'I've been a good wife. We could have sorted out your problems if only you'd told me and not run away. I've got problems but I've got to stay here and face them.' She threw the photo to the floor. 'You bloody two-timing bastard. So how do you think we—' Maggie stopped when she saw the living-room door open.

'Why are you shouting, Mummy?' asked Laura.

'Hallo, love. I'm angry with the weather,' Maggie smiled, quickly gathering up the photo and letters and stuffing them into her overall pocket.

Laura came and sat at the table. 'Why are you crying?'

'Somebody I know has died.'

'Who?'

'You don't know them.'

'Who's the picture of?'

'Nobody you know. I'll get you some porridge. Is Jamie awake?'

'No.'

Maggie went into the kitchen. She looked at the photo again. She wasn't really telling Laura lies. The man in the photo wasn't anybody she knew. This was a man who called himself Peter something, not the daddy they had known and loved.

Maggie stood slowly stirring the porridge. When Bella reads this she'll swear he'd gone off his head, she thought.

Maggie could hear Jamie and Laura squabbling. Suddenly she had to get out. She needed to talk to someone. Eve was the closest.

'Sit up and behave yourselves,' she said, walking into the living room carrying two bowls of steaming porridge. 'Now listen to me very carefully.'

Laura's head shot up. Her face full of expectation. 'Is it Daddy that's dead?'

379

'Why did you ask that?' Maggie sat at the table, unable to stop the tears.

'Well,' said Laura, her eyes blinking quickly, 'I heard you shouting about a two-timing bastard.'

Jamie looked up and loudly took in his breath. 'You mustn't say that,' he said, shocked.

'That's what Mummy said, and that's what Tom Cooper says about Daddy, so I thought . . .' her voice trailed off.

'Yes, you are right, it is Daddy,' Maggie said softly.

'But you said it wasn't someone we knew.'

'Yes, I know I did. You see I didn't know what to say.'

Jamie's eyes grew wide. 'Where is Daddy?'

'He had to go away, and he's had an accident.'

Laura began to cry. 'Was he run over?'

'No, he drowned.'

'Daddy can't swim,' said Jamie, his voice breaking as he tried to control his tears.

'Will we be going to his funeral?' asked Laura, wiping her eyes.

'No, I'm afraid not.'

'Why not?' asked Jamie.

'Daddy has been buried already.'

'My friend went to her granny's funeral,' said Laura. 'She said everybody was crying, but she didn't 'cos she didn't like her granny, but she said the cakes they had after were ever so nice.'

Maggie wanted to smile. With Tony being away for so long he had become almost a stranger to them. 'I've got to go round to see Auntie Eve this morning, so for an extra special treat I'm going to take you to the Saturday morning pictures.'

'Wow.' Jamie jumped up in the air. 'Really, Mum?'

'Course. Now finish your breakfast.'

'We'll get ever so wet,' said Laura, sounding grown up and practical.

'We can dry out round Eve's.'

Jamie was stuffing porridge in his mouth. 'My mate goes every Sat'day, and he says the Lone Ranger's really brave.'

'Jamie, don't talk with your mouth full.' Maggie was thankful their tears had quickly disappeared.

Later, when they stepped outside the door, the wind and rain took their breath away.

''Allo, Maggs. Bloody awful day, ain't it? Only had a couple of punters so far. You was wise not to get your stall out. I'm 'aving a right job keeping everything tied down.' Fred stamped his feet to keep warm. Rivulets of rain dripped off his trilby when he moved his head.

'It might brighten up later,' said Maggie, fighting to get her umbrella up.

'Won't be a lot of point staying if it don't clear up,' he called after her, but his last words were lost in the wind and rain as Maggie quickly moved on.

'Christ, what you doing round here, and in this weather as well? You're soaked.'

'I had to talk to someone.'

'Well, it must be very important to drag you out on a morning like this. Where's the kids?' asked Eve.

'I took 'em to Saturday morning pictures. I've got their wet things here.'

'Leave 'em in the hall and come through. I'll make you a

cuppa, you look like you need one.'

'Is Dan around?'

'He's in bed, why?'

'I'd like him to be here.'

'Why?' Eve's face turned ashen. 'Christ, you've heard from Tony.'

Maggie nodded.

'Dan, Dan, quick get up.' Eve rushed from the room, shouting all way to their bedroom. 'Yes, it is important. Now get up.' She was back almost at once.

Maggie was sitting on the sofa. 'You'd better read this.' She handed her Mrs Walker's letter.

Eve sat next to her and began reading. She let out a gasp. 'I don't believe it,' she said softly.

'Hallo, Maggs,' said Dan, walking into the living room. His hair was tousled and he began tucking his shirt into his trousers, his braces dangling round his knees. 'So what's all this about?'

Eve handed him the letter and Maggie passed Tony's letter to her.

Once again Eve was stunned into silence.

'Who's this Peter then?' asked Dan.

Maggie gave him the photograph. 'Read the back.'

'The two-timing sod.' Dan stood up. 'When did you get this?'

'This morning. Why?'

'Well, I reckon we ought to go to this 'ere Mrs whatser-name and tell 'er we want his real name to be put on his gravestone.'

'Dan, sit down and read this.' Eve passed the first sheet of Tony's letter to him.

Dan flicked the corner of the page. 'Fancy the silly sod running off like that. If we'd known we could have all rallied round.'

'I don't think so,' said Maggie. 'Not with the amount he owed.'

'True,' said Dan. 'But not to let you know. Not to even . . .'

'Wait till you read this page, Dan,' said Eve, handing it to him. 'I reckon he's gone round the twist, all this church and praying stuff.'

'Christ, he couldn't pay his debts but he could buy a bloody boat,' shouted Dan.

'He probably borrowed it,' said Maggie. 'It's the bit from her mother saying her daughter was going to marry him what upset me the most. What did he reckon he was going to do with me, send Mr Windsor round to finish me off?' She began to cry.

Eve put her arm round her. 'Come on, Maggs. Don't let that sod get you down. You've done all right without him so far.'

'No I ain't. I ain't took enough this week to pay the rent.'

'I'm sure your landlord will understand,' said Dan, looking uncomfortable.

'I don't even know what name he's been buried under,' sniffed Maggie.

'Does it matter?' asked Eve.

'What if in years to come the kids want to know, what can I tell them?'

'You could always write to that woman,' said Dan.

'Yer, and tell her daughter her so-called boyfriend was about to commit bigamy,' said Eve caustically.

Maggie began to cry again. 'What's Bella gonner say?'

'I don't know. I expect she'll be as stunned as we are. Dan, put the kettle on again, there's a love.'

'Would you like something a bit stronger than tea, Maggs?'

She shook her head. 'I've got to pick the kids up from the pictures soon.'

'Dan'll do that for you. When you gonner see Bella?'

'I'll go in the morning. I don't think I can cope with going today.'

'If you like I'll go with you,' said Eve.

'No thanks, I'll be all right.'

Eve stood up and took a cigarette from the packet on the mantelpiece. She offered Maggie one. She shook her head. 'Maggie,' said Eve blowing the smoke in the air, 'will this make any difference between you and Dave?'

'I don't know. Why?'

'Well, you're a free woman now. When are you seeing him again?'

'Tonight. He's coming over for a bit of tea, and he's going to help Jamie with that plane they're making.'

'Would you move in with him?'

'No, course not.'

'There's nothing to stop you marrying him now.'

Maggie didn't answer.

Eve sat next to her. 'Do you love him?'

'I don't know. I think I could.'

'Look, give it time. He's a smashing bloke and thinks the world of you, and the kids, and they like him.'

'I know, but I don't want him to think that—'

'What, that you're just looking for a meal ticket and a

good home?' Eve stood up and pointed her finger at Maggie. 'Now just you listen to me. Tony was all right, but he left you in a bloody mess. If he really loved you he would have been here when you lost that baby, and besides that, he reckoned that Mr Windsor wouldn't hurt you, but he did, didn't he?'

Maggie's head shot up. 'How do you . . .? I never told—'

'I ain't that daft, and when you started calling out about men I guess somebody had been to see you, and then there was the bruises on your arm.'

'Does anybody else know?'

'No. Thought it best to keep it to meself. Then there was that bloke Wally scaring the living daylights out of the kids. I couldn't see Dave ever letting you down like that.'

'Shut up, shut up,' shouted Maggie, putting her hands over her ears. 'I don't want to hear any more.'

'What's going on in here?' asked Dan, walking in with a tray of cups and saucers.

'I was just telling her a few home truths.'

'Oh.' Dan walked over to the sideboard and took a bottle of whisky out. He poured some into each of the cups.

Maggie was crying. 'What am I going to do?'

'Drink this tea, for starters. Then me and Eve will take you and the kids home, then you can start thinking about yourself and your future for a change.'

Maggie gave them a watery smile. 'I suppose you're right.' But the thought that was going through her mind was that now she was free, would David Matthews still want her and her debts?

Chapter 33

On the way home, Eve and Dan stopped at the eel shop and bought pie and mash for dinner. While Maggie was putting it on the plates Jamie was racing round the flat with his coat inside out and buttoned at the neck.

'Jamie take that coat off and sit at the table.' Maggie was on edge and beginning to lose her temper.

'It's me cape. I'm the Lone Ranger.'

'I don't care. Now be quiet and sit still.'

'Come on, son, do as your mother tells you,' said Dan softly, taking his coat.

'Auntie Eve, did Mummy tell you our daddy's dead?' asked Laura as she poured the parsley liquor over her mash.

'Yes, she did.'

'Well, at least we know now why we didn't get any birthday or Christmas presents from him. Has he been dead a long while?' She sounded very grown up and confident.

Maggie looked at Eve. What could she tell them? It was Dan that gave her the answer.

'I think he must have been, but Mummy only found out today.'

Laura smiled. 'Oh, so that's why we went to the pictures, and not to his funeral.'

'Something like that,' said Eve.

Maggie was relieved she had quite happily accepted that explanation.

As the afternoon wore on Eve and Dan were reluctant to go.

'I don't like leaving you on your own,' said Eve.

'I'm not on my own, not with these two tearing about.'

'Look, we'll come round this evening. What time will Dave be here?'

'About seven, I expect. He's not on duty tonight.'

'I like Dave,' said Dan. 'Even if he is a copper.'

Maggie smiled. She wasn't going to answer that. 'I'd like to see David on my own for a while, so if you can make it about eight, that'll give him time to walk out if he wants to.'

'Why should he walk out?' asked Dan.

'I'm not unobtainable now, am I?'

'He won't do that.'

'How can we be sure?'

Dan smiled. 'I know he won't.'

Eve stood up. 'We'll see you later.'

They exchanged goodbye kisses, and Maggie was left with her thoughts.

Maggie looked anxiously at the clock. He was late. The rain was still beating down. Had he had to go out on a case? Was he all right? It was times like this when she worried about him that she knew she was very fond of him.

'I hope Uncle David hurries up. I want him to show me how to do this bit.' Jamie was looking at all the odd-shaped pieces of wood strewn over the table that somehow were miraculously going to be turned into an airplane.

At last there was a banging on the knocker.

'It's Uncle David,' shouted Jamie, racing from the room.

Maggie could hear him excitedly telling David about their going to the pictures.

'Hello, Maggie,' he said, walking in and putting his hat on the sideboard. 'I'm sorry I'm late. Had to see to some paperwork.'

'That's all right.'

'You didn't take the stall out today, not in this weather, did you?'

'No, didn't see the point.'

'Our Daddy's dead,' said Laura.

David's head shot up. 'What? How d'you know?'

Maggie handed him the letters. 'Read this one first.'

He took the letters, and sat on the sofa. As he began to read Maggie noted the change of expression on his face. He didn't make any comments. She handed him the photograph.

'Come into the kitchen while I put the kettle on.'

David followed her. He closed the door. 'How could he do this to you?' he exploded. His voice was full of anger but carefully modified. 'And to think he was going to get married while he still had you. He wants bloody horsewhipping.'

'Shh, please don't.'

He held her close and whispered, 'Oh Maggie, what can I say? All that you've been through, and now this.' He buried his head in her neck and kissed it.

Tears began to fill her eyes. 'I thought he loved me.'

'He probably did in his own way, but I think you've got to face up to it, Tony Ross did what Tony Ross wanted to.'

The door was pushed open and they quickly jumped apart.

Jamie was standing there with a piece of balsawood in his hand. 'Could you show me where this bit goes?'

Maggie turned to the sink. She didn't want Jamie to see she was on the verge of tears again.

'Course,' said David. 'Come on.'

Maggie and David didn't have time to talk alone again for almost as soon as the children had gone to bed Eve and Dan arrived.

They spent most of the evening discussing the situation.

'When you going to see Bella?' asked Eve.

'Tomorrow,' volunteered David. 'I'm taking them over in the car.'

'Wonder what she'll make of it?' said Dan.

'What about all this money he owes?' asked Eve.

Maggie felt her stomach churn. What about all the money *she* owed? If she couldn't get the stall out soon the interest would mount up on her loan. She still hadn't told anyone about it. 'I'm gonner try and pay off me brother, though it'll take a while, but I'm afraid Mr Windsor really will have to sing for his. There's no way I can pay all that back.' Maggie stopped. She knew there was also the money for Bella's present. Because of the bad weather and the stalls not being taken out, Winnie hadn't asked her what she was getting them.

'Don't worry about him. I suggested Windsor wrote off the debt when Tony disappeared and he came bothering you. He knows I'm on the scene now so he won't threaten you again.'

Maggie smiled at David.

It was nine o'clock when Dan suggested they went to the Dog.

'I'd rather not, not tonight,' said Maggie.

'I'll stay here as well,' said Eve.

'Come on, Dave old man, surely you could do with a drink?'

He looked at Maggie. 'Would you mind?'

'Course not.'

'You'd better take a key,' said Maggie.

Eve looked at her surreptitiously.

'Well, I don't want to keep rushing up and down the stairs,' she said defensively.

The front door was closed quietly.

'Well,' said Eve almost at once, 'you gonner marry him?'

'Give us a chance. Besides, he ain't asked me.'

'But would you?'

'I don't know.'

Eve lit a cigarette. 'If you ask me you'd be a bloody fool not to. Do you love him?'

'Not like I loved Tony.'

'Well, he was your first.'

'And the father of my children. I'll make us a cuppa.'

Eve sat back on the sofa when Maggie left the room. How could she make Maggie see that David would be the best thing that ever happened to her? What if she blackened Tony's name even more? But Eve knew that would be pushing their friendship to the limits and that was something Maggie could do without at the moment.

Eve nervously tapped her cigarette into the ashtray. She wandered over to the window. She could say they had an affair after they were married and that would be the last straw in Tony's character assassination. It would be a lie of course but with her reputation before she married Dan, Maggie would believe that. She loved Maggie and wanted her to be happy with David. Even though Eve had wanted Tony all those years ago, after he got married he did remain true to Maggie, until now. Her saying anything now would cost her their friendship. And what about Dan? She loved him very much. Tears filled Eve's eyes. And losing him and Maggie was something she wasn't prepared to do.

'You all right?' asked Maggie, sitting at the table.

Eve dabbed at her eyes, nodded and joined her. 'Maggie, I want you to be happy.'

'Give me time, Eve. Give me time.' She sighed. 'Eve. I've done something, and I've got to tell someone or I'll go mad.'

Eve looked up surprised. 'Look, if you're gonner tell me you and Dave have . . . well, it ain't nobody's business but yours.' She smiled. 'Not that—'

'No. It ain't that. And by the way we haven't. It's just that I've . . . I've got myself into a lot of debt.'

'What? How?'

'Before Christmas I borrowed ten pounds from a Mr Shore, he's a moneylender, and I can't pay it back and all the time the interest is building up and . . .' The words came bubbling out faster and faster.

Eve sat back. 'Oh Maggs. What can I say? Ten pounds. Christ, that's more than what Dan earns in a month. We all thought you was doing so well down there. What with the nice frocks you bought Laura and yourself for Christmas, and the money you spent on—'

'I know, I know, I was a bloody fool. But I needed stock and how was I to know the weather was going to be that bad?' She banged the table. 'Eve, what am I gonner do?'

'I don't know, Maggs, I really don't know. What about your brother, have you paid him back yet?'

Maggie shook her head and tears ran down her cheeks. 'Not all of it. There's something else.'

Eve face went white. 'What else?' she whispered.

'Winnie got up a collection for Bella and Benny and I spent it on the rents and coal and food . . .' The words were lost in sobs.

'Oh my God.' Eve stood up and took another cigarette from her handbag. 'I would have thought you of all people would have learnt your lesson from Tony and the money he owed. Just how did you think this would all end?'

'I don't know. I've been pawning as many things as I dare. Oh Eve, my life's in such a mess.'

'I must admit you have been a bit of a silly cow.'

Maggie burst into tears. She was glad of the relief of telling someone, but she also needed sympathy and wasn't getting it.

'Does Dave know?'

Maggie shook her head. 'No, only you.'

Eve began pacing the floor. 'I just don't know what to say.'

'Eve, what am I going to do?'

'I dunno.'

'I can't even think of marrying David, not with all these

debts. He might think I'm only marrying him for security.'

'Not if he loves you, he won't.'

'I can even understand Tony running away. That's what I want to do right this minute.'

'Oh yes, and where would you go? Wales?'

Maggie's tears flowed. 'Don't be funny.'

'Funny is the last thing I feel,' said Eve, sitting down again. She looked up at the clock. 'They'll be back soon. Do you want us to stay?'

Maggie nodded.

'Well, you'd better do something about your face. You look a mess.'

'Eve, what would you do?'

'Look, you've got to make up your mind if you're gonner tell Dave or not. I can't see any way out of it; this ain't gonner go away.'

'No, I know.'

'Well then, what's it to be? Do you want us to stay and be here with you, or . . .?'

'I think perhaps I'd better be on me own. Tomorrow I'll go and see Bella and tell her everythink.'

'You'll have to do that anyway. Let's hope she ain't gotta bad heart, otherwise you might—'

'Shut up, Eve.'

'Pardon me, sorry I spoke.'

'I'm sorry, it's just that I'm so on edge. I just don't know what to do for the best.'

'If you want my advice, for what it's worth, I'd come clean, tell 'em all. That way once the tittle-tattle dies down they'll have nothing to hang on to and you can bury Tony in your mind for ever.' Eve crushed her cigarette into the ashtray. 'Now, have you got anythink stronger than tea in this house?'

'There's a bottle of whisky in the sideboard.'

'That'll do.'

The whisky didn't give Maggie any Dutch courage, and when David and Dan came back she suddenly lost her nerve.

'Don't bother making yourself comfortable,' said Eve, putting on her hat. 'We're gonner go.'

'I wanted one of Maggs's cheese sandwiches.'

'I said we're going.'

'What's upset her?' said Dan. He grinned. 'See you've been at the whisky. S'pose you're all randy and can't wait ter get me home, then?'

'Shut up, you silly sod. Maggie wants to be left on her own.'

Dan patted David on the back. 'This could be your lucky night, mate.'

'Shut up,' shouted Maggie.

Dan sat back down and looked astonished.

'What's wrong?' asked David.

'Sit down, Eve.'

'But, Maggs—'

'I might as well get it over and done with.'

David looked worried. 'What is it?'

They all sat very quiet while Maggie told them the whole story.

When she'd finished she went into the kitchen, leaving them stunned. Eventually Eve followed her.

'I think you'd better make Dan his cheese sandwich,' said Maggie.

'Yer, yer. OK.'

All the while Maggie busied herself making tea she listened for the living-room door to shut. Then she'd know she had lost David for ever. But all she could hear was the clinking of glass, the whisky being poured out.

'Well,' said Dan, when they went back into the living room, 'we reckon we could have an answer to some of your problems.'

Maggie looked at David.

'I don't know much about market stalls.'

Maggie giggled, partly because of the whisky and partly in relief. 'I couldn't see you selling jewellery.'

'Not selling the goods, but selling the licence.'

Maggie sat up straight. 'I couldn't do that. It ain't mine to sell.'

'It ain't Tony's now, is it?' said Dan, munching on his sandwich.

'No, I know, but what would Bella say?'

'That's something we could find out tomorrow.'

'How much d'you reckon it's worth? I could ask at work,' asked Eve.

'Dunno, but some of the traders would know,' said Dan. 'And hopefully it could be enough to pay off that loan shark.'

'And as for the money for Bella's present, well, I'm sure she would rather have you spend it on the children, don't you?' said David.

Maggie very slowly nodded. 'I expect so, but it was still stealing.'

'And as for your brother, he'll have to wait. Besides, he shouldn't have been such a silly sod lending it to Tony in the first place,' said Dan.

'You two got this sorted quick,' said Eve.

'Yer, well, when you get a couple of intelligent blokes together it's surprising what you can come up with.'

'That's all very well,' said Maggie, 'but what if Bella won't sell the stall, and what am I going to live on after that?'

'You'll have to get yourself a job,' said Eve. 'That way you'll be sure of money coming in every week.'

'But what about the kids?'

'Look, Maggs, take one thing at a time. Dave here's taking you to see Bella tomorrow so you can get that sorted.'

Maggie sat quietly thinking it over. Was this a light at the end of a long dark tunnel? Eight months of uncertainty. Now Tony was dead she didn't feel anything. Maybe her love for him had died months ago.

'Look, Maggs, we'll be off.'

'All right, Eve.'

'I'm off as well. I'm giving them a lift,' said David.

'You don't have to go, do you?'

'I think it best. I'll be over tomorrow.'

They said their good nights and Maggie was alone. David had been very distant. Why didn't he want to stay? Was it all over between them? She loved him and wanted him, but she wasn't sure whether he wanted her now.

She would have to wait till tomorrow to find out that.

Poor Bella. Maggie was dreading telling her that, after all this time, the hope and wondering was finally over. Her son was dead. Bella was strong and she was going to start a new life with Benny, so Maggie hoped this wouldn't upset her too much. But then there was the business of selling the stall – how would Bella react to that?

Chapter 34

Maggie was silent on the way to Bella's. It was a journey she had been in fear of making ever since Tony went away.

The noise from the back of the car told her the children weren't interested in grown-ups' worries.

'Hallo, you lot,' said Bella on opening the door, then crushing them one by one to her ample bosom. 'Thought you might be over. Benny, go and light the fire in the front room, there's a love. It's all laid up ready.'

Benny kissed Maggie's cheek as he passed them. 'Good ter see you. Bring yer bits in here, kids. This fire don't take long to get going.'

Bella was beaming. 'Never thought the day would come when I'd be lighting two fires in one house. Christ, I remember when we could just about afford the coal for one. What's up? You two look like you've lorst a tanner and found an 'apenny.'

Maggie gave her a slight smile.

'Right, that's them sorted,' said Benny. 'I'll just wash me hands.'

'I'll go and stay with the children for the time being,' said David.

399

'Why? What's happened?' Bella's eyes were darting from one to the other as David left the room.

'Bella, I've had a letter.'

Bella sat at the table. 'From Tony?'

Maggie nodded. She put her hand on Bella's. 'I'm afraid he's dead.'

'But you said . . . a letter? But how?'

'You'd better read them,' said Maggie.

Tears filled Bella's eyes as one by one she read the letters and passed them to Benny.

'How dare he do this to you?' Bella's reaction wasn't what Maggie had expected. 'The bastard. Gitting married indeed. If I'd have known about this I'd have been down there and chopped off his bleeding cobblers.'

'What did he tell all these lies for?' asked Benny. 'And how could he say he was gonner marry this girl?' He was studying the photograph.

'I know he was me son, but to do that to you and those lovely kids. I'll never forgive him, you know. Never. Good job my Jim ain't here. He'd give him a right pasting.' Bella quickly left the room.

Maggie went to stand up.

'Leave her be, love,' said Benny. 'Let her have five minutes on her own.'

Maggie nodded. 'I might as well get every bit of bad news over at once.'

'What bad news?'

'I'll wait for Bella to come back, if you don't mind.'

'No, course not. I'll put the kettle on.' Benny looked worried.

A few minutes later Bella came back into the kitchen.

'Sorry about that.' She was still wiping her bloodshot eyes.

'Bella, I might as well upset you a bit more, and if you want to chuck me out – well, I understand.'

Bella opened her eyes wide. 'You gonner get married? Well, I can't say I blame yer, he's a nice bloke.'

Maggie looked embarrassed. 'No, I ain't getting married. It's . . . I'm finding this very hard.'

Benny and Bella were hanging on her every word.

'Bella, I've got myself into a lot of trouble.'

Bella jumped up. 'Christ. You're not having a baby?'

'No, no, I'm not. I ain't done nothink to . . . no. I'm in a lot of debt.'

'What d'you mean? I know you've been trying to pay off Tony's debts, but that don't mean to say you should have got yourself—'

'No. Bella, listen.' Maggie went into all the details of what she owed, and the money for the present.

'I see what yer mean,' said Bella finally.

'But you only did it for the kids,' said Benny.

'And my own ego as well. You see, I thought I was as clever as Tony.' She hung her head and nervously played with her fingers. 'But I wasn't. Dan and David have come up with a scheme to help me out, but it will need your approval.' Maggie hesitated. 'I could sell the pitch.'

Maggie waited for a reaction, but when Bella didn't reply, she stood up and gathered up her handbag.

'Where're you going?'

'Well, you don't want me around, so I'll be off. Don't worry, I'll never stop the children from seeing you any time you want. And one day I'll write to the women in

Wales and find out what name Tony used so if you or the children ever want to visit his grave, you'll know which it is . . .' Maggie's last few words were lost in her sobs. She turned to go.

'Sit down.' It was an order from Bella that startled even Benny.

'Right. How do you feel about him?' Bella inclined her head towards the front room.

'I like him, but I don't know about . . .' Maggie dabbed at her eyes. 'And I don't want him to think I'm only looking for somewhere to . . .'

'He don't think that. 'Sides, you don't have to be in a hurry to do anythink. Go and get him.'

Maggie did as she was told.

'Right, young man.'

Maggie was suddenly terrified. Oh no. Was Bella going to tell David to marry her?

'Maggie here's told us the whole story. And I reckon what you and Dan suggested is a damn good idea. She shouldn't be out in all weathers, and leaving those kids on their own anyway. As for the money she owes that loan shark, well I reckon the pitch is worth that much, and the money for the present, well we can forget that.'

'But what can I tell the other traders?'

'Tell 'em you bought us a pair of sheets. Then even if any of 'em do ever come over here, which I doubt, they'll never see them. But as for your brother, that was my son's debt so I'm gonner pay it off.'

Maggie went to speak but Bella put up her hand to silence her.

'So, that's all your immediate problems out of the way.'

'How you gonner manage?' asked Benny.

'I don't know. It's not as though Tony took out any insurance.'

'Well you couldn't get it anyway,' said David. 'Not without a death certificate.'

'That means I can't get his penny-a-week one out?' said Bella.

''Fraid not,' said David.

'The sod. All right, don't look at me like that. I know he was me son but I can't believe he would do a thing like this.' Tears filled Bella's big brown eyes again.

Benny put his arm round her. 'Come on, love. Remember we've got our wedding to look forward to.'

Bella's head shot up. 'How can you think of that at this time? I've lorst me son.'

Maggie and David looked at each other and shifted in their seats.

'Look,' said Maggie, 'we'll go, leave you on your own to get over the shock.'

'No, stop and have a bit of tea first.'

'Only if you're sure.'

Tea was a very strained affair. Maggie was pleased Bella managed to keep her feelings under control in front of the children, but she still looked very tearful.

'I shouldn't have jumped down Benny's throat like that, but I couldn't help meself.'

'He understands,' said Maggie, as they did the washing-up.

'Yer. I'll take him for a drink later, that'll cheer him up.'

'The wedding still on?'

'I should say so. Every time I think that Tony might have been getting married at the same time . . .' She sniffed and fished her handkerchief out from her apron pocket. 'I don't know what he was thinking of.'

'Unless they had money?'

'S'pose that could have been the reason. He was a bastard.'

Maggie put her arm round Bella's shoulders. 'We've all got to try and put it behind us. You've got a new life to be getting on with, and I know Benny will make you happy.'

'I know, but what about you? Have you got anythink to look forward to?'

'I don't know. But I do have the children.'

'That's the one good thing that came from Tony.' Bella smiled and dabbed at her eyes.

'Come on, let's go in the front room. It'll soon be time for us to go.'

'Do you want me to come in?' asked David when they arrived at Maggie's door.

She looked at him. She had to know how he felt about her. 'Only if you want to.'

He smiled and closed the door behind him. 'I'd like to very much,' he whispered.

Maggie felt her heart leap. This was what she wanted to hear. She ushered the children into their bedroom.

'Uncle David, will you read us a story?' asked Laura, poking her head round the door.

He looked at Maggie.

She shrugged her shoulders. 'That's up to you.'

He grinned and took her hand. 'Please, and I would like the job for life.'

'Back to bed, Laura.' When the door was closed Maggie turned to David. 'I don't want you to think—'

He pulled her close and kissed her. 'Maggie, I've loved you for such a long while and it would make me so happy, now that you're free, if you would marry me.'

She threw her arms round his neck and held him tight. 'I too have loved you, but been afraid of my feelings.'

'Hurry up,' shouted Jamie, from the bedroom.

'Well, have I got this job for life?'

'Only till they grow up, or we have one of our own.'

'I'd like that very much.' David walked into the children's bedroom with his arm round Maggie's slim waist. 'Me and Mummy have got something to tell you.'

They began giggling.

'How would you like it if me and David got married?'

Jamie jumped up. 'Great. Would we go and live at your house?'

Maggie nodded.

'Will you get married when Granny and Benny does?'

Maggie looked at David.

'I suppose if Benny and Bella wouldn't mind we could have a double wedding.'

Maggie giggled. 'That'll be different.'

'So, Mummy, could I be your bridesmaid?'

'I should think so.'

It was Laura's turn to giggle. 'See, I told you that if you didn't tell anyone your wish when you blew out your candles it would come true.'

Maggie looked puzzled. 'What did you wish for then?'

'That you and Uncle David would get married and that we would all live happily ever after.'

Tears filled Maggie's eyes. She suddenly thought of Lil. At last her grieving was over. The happy time was here, and with David she knew it would go on for ever.

A selection of bestsellers from Headline

LIVERPOOL LAMPLIGHT	Lyn Andrews	£5.99 ☐
A MERSEY DUET	Anne Baker	£5.99 ☐
THE SATURDAY GIRL	Tessa Barclay	£5.99 ☐
DOWN MILLDYKE WAY	Harry Bowling	£5.99 ☐
PORTHELLIS	Gloria Cook	£5.99 ☐
A TIME FOR US	Josephine Cox	£5.99 ☐
YESTERDAY'S FRIENDS	Pamela Evans	£5.99 ☐
RETURN TO MOONDANCE	Anne Goring	£5.99 ☐
SWEET ROSIE O'GRADY	Joan Jonker	£5.99 ☐
THE SILENT WAR	Victor Pemberton	£5.99 ☐
KITTY RAINBOW	Wendy Robertson	£5.99 ☐
ELLIE OF ELMLEIGH SQUARE	Dee Williams	£5.99 ☐

All Headline books are available at your local bookshop or newsagent, or can be ordered direct from the publisher. Just tick the titles you want and fill in the form below. Prices and availability subject to change without notice.

Headline Book Publishing, Cash Sales Department, Bookpoint, 39 Milton Park, Abingdon, OXON, OX14 4TD, UK. If you have a credit card you may order by telephone – 01235 400400.

Please enclose a cheque or postal order made payable to Bookpoint Ltd to the value of the cover price and allow the following for postage and packing:

UK & BFPO: £1.00 for the first book, 50p for the second book and 30p for each additional book ordered up to a maximum charge of £3.00.
OVERSEAS & EIRE: £2.00 for the first book, £1.00 for the second book and 50p for each additional book.

Name ....

Address ....

....

....

If you would prefer to pay by credit card, please complete:
Please debit my Visa/Access/Diner's Card/American Express (delete as applicable) card no:

Signature .... Expiry Date ....